CAN'T ....UND IT

"You know, I couldn't tell you which is worse." Rabbit stared down at his wet gloves. The leather was stiffening in the cold. "Dead bodies used as food, or dead bodies walking around."

In the past he would have had trouble believing what she was saying, but what with the things he'd seen in the Hills, well, he was beginning to take a few things on faith.

"I need to know what's going on out there in Ingleside," she said. "I need to head over there."

Rabbit stared at her. Was she saying ...

"I'm going tonight."

Shit. "To the boneyard? Tonight? At night?"

She nodded. "Ling and Gart said that's when the strange things have been happening."

"Wait. I decided. Dead people walking around is worse."

She let out a short, hard laugh. "Agreed."

Rabbit lowered his head. "You're right, I suppose. Best way is to go take a looksee." He glanced her way. "Don't suppose you'd be willin' to wait until Boone and Hank get back." He had a pretty good idea what her answer would be, but it was worth a shot.

"I can handle it." She opened her canteen. "Or should I say, *we* can handle it." She raised her brows at him as she tipped the canteen.

Yep. That's what he thought she'd say.

He stared back at her, straight-faced. "If you're waitin' on a reaction from me, I haven't decided the best way to display my opposition to that plan."

For Beaker
Keep Writing Your Buns Off!
We Love You

Can't Ride Around It

Cover Art by C.S. Kunkle
Cover Design by B Biddles & Ann Charles
Editing by Eilis Flynn
Formatting by B Biddles

Library of Congress: 2019919304
E-book ISBN- 978-1-940364-74-2
Print ISBN-: 978-1-940364-75-9

DEADWOOD UNDERTAKER

Can't Ride Around It

Book 3

Ann Charles
Sam Lucky

illustrations by
C. S. Kunkle

Dear Reader,

A question we are often asked is: "How did you two end up together?" After all, Ann grew up in Ohio and South Dakota, bouncing between her divorced parents; and Sam hailed from eastern Washington. Geographically, many, *many* cornfields, big rivers, wide-open plains, and a handful of rather large "hills" more commonly known as the Rocky Mountains separated us. Yet here we are, writing supernatural western stories together while raising two wonderful kids ...

The History of Ann and Sam
by Ann Charles

Once upon a time, I went for a job interview at a company near Seattle that made maps of the local landscape for engineering and other purposes. When I walked in the office's front door, there was an IT guy sitting at the front desk working on the receptionist's computer. I gave him my name and said I was there for the receptionist position. Six months of working together later, that "guy" and I had become friends who periodically went to lunch. He introduced me to dim sum (yum!) and convinced me to give Indian food a try (chicken tikka masala—double yum!!), mentioning that maybe someday he would make me dinner (he enjoyed cooking and had worked at a restaurant or two in the past). Three years later, I was a divorcée and this guy's days of good-timing bachelorhood were numbered. Cats and kids and more cats followed, along with a lot of amazing home-cooked dinners as well as travels full of wild adventures both on and off the page.

The History of Sam and Ann
by Sam Lucky

The last yellow-gold sunbeam of the day broke the horizon and silhouetted a lonely figure standing in the middle of the road.

A long-legged shadow stretched from his feet far down the gritty, dusty street. A wide-brimmed black hat atop the tall man's head brushed the bottoms of the clouds, or at least that's how he felt, bolstered by the glow bursting from the saloon. The radiance beckoned, overwhelming his resistance. The arrow-straight course his life had followed was about to take a wild turn, and there wasn't a damn thing he could do but hold on tight.

He squinted at the batwing doors of the saloon and struck a match on the thigh of his canvas pants to light his hand-rolled cigarette. Then he remembered he had quit the habit.

Damn. Haven't yet made her acquaintance and that lassie already has me forgettin' myself.

Put plainly, he was here to see a girl.

You see, a calico, newly arrived to the borough he called home, was in that drinkery and while his intentions were pure, he wasn't sure if there was a meetin' of lips or a flat hand across his jaw awaitin' his arrival.

But he was bound and determined, either way.

He smoothed down his leather vest and adjusted his hat and with his best swagger headed toward the radiance inside. Full of fire and vitality he climbed the steps. I'll rope this filly, he thought.

As he reached the porch wearing a mile-wide smile, the toe of his boot caught the top step and held tight against his desperate and fleeting attempt to pull it free. Stumbling forward, arms swinging in great windmills against his momentum, he crashed into the batwing doors, slamming them into the walls with a BANG!

The piano stopped.

The silence was deadly.

He was the focus of every eye.

It didn't matter. From the radiance that almost closed his eyes, she emerged, smiling, and beckoned him to her. He grinned, lopsided, and … he can't remember anything after that.

Acknowledgments

Rabbit, Boone and Clementine would like to thank the following folks for their help making CAN'T RIDE AROUND IT (Deadwood Undertaker Book 3) sparkle and glitter:

Our children, Beaker and Chicken Noodle. We've been fortunate to be able to spend so much time at home with you these last six months. It's been like the Arizona mountains version of *Little House on the Prairie*, only with even fewer visitors.

Our kickass First Draft team: Margo Taylor, Mary Ida Kunkle, Kristy McCaffrey, Marcia Britton, Paul Franklin, Diane Garland, Michelle Davis, Vicki Huskey, Lucinda Nelson, Bob Dickerson, Stephanie Kunkle, and Wendy Gildersleeve. You all moved at the speed of light this time, returning feedback and edits lickety-split!

Our eagle-eyed editor, Eilis Flynn, for having our backs.

Diane Garland, the goddess of WorldKeeper, for making it easier for us to keep track of so many details, including all of those foreign swearwords.

Our Beta Team for searching our story haystacks for those last few erroneous needles.

C.S. Kunkle for using your big ol' imagination and making the story come to life even more.

Our readers—Your love for the characters spurs us to keep hitting the keys time and again.

Author Jacquie Rogers for agreeing to drop everything, read our book, and give us the perfect cover quote.

And Hank. Your time is coming.

Also by Ann Charles

Deadwood Undertaker Series
(written with Sam Lucky)
Life at the Coffin Joint (Book 1)
A Long Way from Ordinary (Book 2)
Can't Ride Around It (Book 3)
The Backside of Hades (Book 4 Spring 2021)

Deadwood Mystery Series (Book #)

Nearly Departed in Deadwood (1)
Optical Delusions in Deadwood (2)
Dead Case in Deadwood (3)
Better Off Dead in Deadwood (4)
An Ex to Grind in Deadwood (5)
Meanwhile, Back in Deadwood (6)

Wild Fright in Deadwood (7)
Rattling the Heat in Deadwood (8))
Gone Haunting in Deadwood (9)
Don't Let It Snow in Deadwood (10)
Devil Days in Deadwood (11)

Deadwood Shorts: Seeing Trouble (Book 1.5)
Deadwood Shorts: Boot Points (Book 4.5)
Deadwood Shorts: Cold Flame (Book 6.5)
Deadwood Shorts: Tequila & Time (Book 8.5)
Deadwood Shorts: Fatal Traditions (Book 10.5)

Jackrabbit Junction Mystery Series

Dance of the Winnebagos (Book 1)
Jackrabbit Junction Jitters (Book 2)
The Great Jackalope Stampede (Book 3)
The Rowdy Coyote Rumble (Book 4)
In Cahoots with the Prickly Pear Posse (Book 5)

Jackrabbit Junction Short: The Wild Turkey Tango (Book 4.5)

Dig Site Mystery Series
Look What the Wind Blew In (Book 1)
Make No Bones About It (Book 2)

AC Silly Circus Mystery Series
Feral-LY Funny Freakshow (Novella 1)
A Bunch of Monkey Malarkey (Novella 2)

Goldwash Mystery Series (a future series)
The Old Man's Back in Town (Short Story)

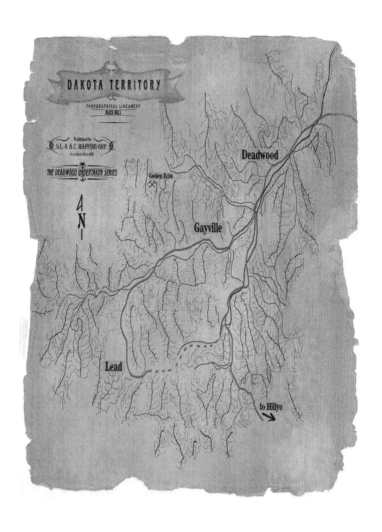

"*The best way to cheer yourself up is to try to cheer somebody else up.*"

~Mark Twain

One

Winter 1876
Deadwood, Dakota Territory

Jack "Rabbit" Fields was not a complicated man by any means. That was his estimation, anyway. His reputation was shoot 'em or buy 'em a drink. He liked it that way.

He knew a good thing when he saw it, whether it was a healthy horse, a solid business venture, a sure bet, or a pretty sage hen. When it came to locking horns with any curly wolves he ran into along the trail, he tended to shoot first and ask questions later—a notion that had saved his hide more times than he could count.

Rabbit grabbed a handful of snow from the top of a wagon wheel and began to shape it into a ball. Nope, not complicated one bit, unlike his partner in the livery business, Boone McCreery. Being complicated was in Boone's nature, along with his proclivity toward over-cogitation.

Since they were kids, Boone had been the one who had to think a thing beyond its duration. Take the time they were twelve and Boone was contemplating the purchase of a pig for their uncle at the autumn hog auction in Agua Fria. While prime hog after hog went to the highest bidder, Boone sat and pondered, too busy considering an undersized ear or turned-in hoof to put in a bid. He'd ended up with the runt of the sale by overindulging his thoughts.

Their uncle Mort, who'd adopted them when they were wagon-train orphans no bigger than overgrown possums, couldn't decide whether to laugh or bang his head against the barn door most days when it came to Boone's over-thinking habit. Early on, the tendency to ponder to no end had earned Boone the nickname "Molasses," which Rabbit was fond of using to stoke the fire in Boone when needed.

Boone would have Rabbit believe that thinking things out was the wise man's way. That it was smarter to take the time to contemplate every damned little thing.

"Somebody's got to watch out for you," he'd say.

But Rabbit's pistol watched out for both of them plenty over the years, and more than ever since they'd arrived in Deadwood, where the streets were filled with some of the best and worst humanity had to offer.

"Jack Rabbit!" Hank Varney called from the street near the front of Keller's Livery. The same livery Boone and Rabbit had bought and registered on paper just two days prior. They were going to need to change the name now that Keller was heading back east to rejoin his family.

Hank was a fast friend to Rabbit, and he hadn't given Boone time to consider the pros and cons of a friendship. Nope, that wasn't Hank's way. If he had a biscuit, he'd give a friend half in a heartbeat and put an arrow in the ass of anyone who tried to take the other half.

"Hiyo, Hank!" Rabbit waved. "Come back and help us push this buggy outta here."

Rabbit and Boone had gone to work immediately selling off the derelict wagons and buggies and tack overcrowding the livery's storage lot even though Boone had resisted the idea at first. Mr. Molasses had struggled to get past the idea that the owners might come back. He'd always had a soft heart for a sad story. Then again, a short time ago Uncle Mort's freight wagon had been one of the many abandoned pieces of equipment in this very storage lot that had been sold before he and Boone could recoup it.

Rabbit could understand Boone's hesitation, but the lot needed to be cleared. More equipment and rigs were arriving every day, practically every hour, and they had the biggest livery in town. As a compromise, they'd decided to start by selling the older stock first. Unfortunately that meant moving most of the damned wagons and buggies out of the way to reach those that had been pushed to the back of the lot, wedged up against the crumbly rock forming one side of Deadwood Gulch.

"Rabbit, push the neck yoke back and forth," Boone called from the back of the buggy. "This wheel is frozen in the mud. We need to break it loose."

"Wait for Hank. He can help push." Rabbit closed one eye and squinted into the bright cloudless morning sky. The day was colder than a bucket of snowman snot, especially with the dang wind.

Rabbit scooped up another glove full of snow and packed it into the ball he'd started. He gauged the distance and height and then lobbed the snowball at the blanket of snow that had accumulated on the roof of the buggy they were attempting to break free. A small avalanche slid down the backside, landing with a satisfying *swish-ploosh!* Right about where Boone was standing.

"Son of a rat catcher. Rabbit!" Boone popped out from behind the buggy, his hat drooping down over one ear and onto his shoulder, weighed down by a healthy pile of snow.

Rabbit burst into laughter. "Commence to shiverin', icy britches."

Boone leaned forward and gingerly tipped his black hat, dumping the load of snow on the ground. "Went down my neck, you scrawny chicken rancher." He took off his hat, shook it, and flopped it back on his head.

Rabbit held his stomach. "Hoo hoo! Your pretty green eyes were big as wagon wheels. You needed a bath anyway. A shave, too, ya scruffy sheepherder."

"You sound like Hank." Boone glared at Rabbit while he wiped at the slushy snow running down his back. "That's gonna end up on your list of regrets before we're done."

Rabbit kept chuckling. Payback or not, seeing Boone wearing a bonnet of snow over his dark hair and rosy cheeks was worth it.

"Movin' wagons I see." Hank joined them, slapping Rabbit on the back. Tall and lanky, and tough as nails, Hank reminded Rabbit of an old ironwood tree down in the desert. Not that Hank was that much older than Rabbit, maybe a decade or so was all. This morning, the older man's whiskers had a layer of frost on them.

"Watch that rascal." Boone shook the front of his coat, still trying to get the snow out. "He'll douse ya."

"Ho there, Boonedog! Didn't see you back there."

"Glad you're here, Hank. Now you can help us give this buggy a push."

Hank eyed the wheel that was buried up to the spokes in frozen mud. "Looks like the wheel there is done for 'til spring."

Boone scowled. "You're probably right."

"What say we cook some coffee?" Rabbit suggested, thinking about the hot, fiery forge inside the livery. "Thaw the innards."

Twenty minutes later they were melted a little around the edges and sitting at the table in the livery loft, warming their hands on steaming tins of coffee.

"You been busy at The Pyre lately, Hank?" Rabbit asked.

The Pyre was one of two undertaker establishments in town. It was a typical house of the dead except for one key thing—it was run by a woman.

And not just any woman.

Clementine Johanssen had come to town six or so months previous and gone into the business of burying the town's dead, which was a thriving trade in a booming gold town as rough and rowdy as Deadwood. Taller than most *hombres* and tough as rawhide, she could knock a man sky-westward and crooked eastward in a flash. Hell, Rabbit had seen her do nearly that more than once.

In addition to burying the dead, Clementine also was an ace at killing troublemakers of the otherworldly sort, and made a mighty fine fourth *compadre* in their posse. Trained to fight from a young girl up, she came into their newfound friendship with a healthy dose of gumption. Not to mention a cabinet full of deadly weapons that made Rabbit swoon.

Clementine had been visiting them in the livery every day for over a week, teaching them all she could about the weapons they would use and the creatures they would face if they continued to associate with her and Hank. Rabbit had never chopped and stabbed so many straw men in all his born days. Of course he hadn't. What sane soul would? Boone would probably agree. They were both sore every night from head to toe after exercising muscles they hadn't even known they had.

With Clementine coming around so much, Rabbit and Boone hadn't seen the need to visit her at The Pyre. Hell, Rabbit's preference was to avoid that place anyway, if possible. He wasn't exactly squeamish around a dead body, but that place felt like an eerie stage stop on a one-way trip to a long sleep.

"Miss Clem and me ain't busy so much these days," Hank said, answering Rabbit's question. "New undertaker in town is doin' drop-dead business."

Boone laughed. "That's a good one, Hank. People dying to get into his place, are they?"

"Hoo hoo, Boonedog." Hank shook his finger at Boone.

"Miss Clem appears happy about the situation," Hank told them, taking a moment to sip from his cup. "She's been practicing with her weapons a lot. She works with you boys pert near ever' day, but by herself, too. Occurs to me the letter from that Rogue character had some persuasion on her. She even swings that big sword, *Ulfberht*, around now." Hank's gaze lifted to the ceiling, a smile rounding his whiskered cheeks. "Like watchin' a fancy dancer spin and jump."

Rabbit smiled along with Hank, thinking of the times he'd watched Clementine swing her blades. She moved like greased lightning when she fought. It was a fine sight to see.

Across the table, Boone was scowling at the wall and tugging on his ear, something he'd been doing more often lately, especially when Clementine was around. The last time Rabbit had seen Boone so preoccupied with his damned ear was when he fell for that dark-eyed, sweet-talking *señorita* down in Las Cruces. Unfortunately, it turned out she was married, and to more than one *hombre* at that. Since that fiasco, Boone hadn't paid much attention to the ladies. Mr. Molasses always took his time picking out a woman, the same as he did hogs way back when, often losing out to other stallions in the meantime.

Rabbit cleared his throat.

Boone blinked and looked at Rabbit. "Uh, anyway, I think that Rogue is trouble. Wish I'd seen her there in that saloon in Galena. Don't know what I'd have done. Be good to know what she looks like, though."

The Rogue Executioner was another deadly female in town in the same killing profession as Clementine. However, where Clementine, like Boone, considered her steps deliberately when it came to spilling blood, the Rogue wasted no time weighing options. She quickly slayed anyone or any *thing* she considered worthy of execution. She'd kept Clementine's two exam tables busy in previous months with bodies bearing their enemies' insignia in the form of a tattoo or brand.

"I think that Rogue is a real fireball." Rabbit winked at Boone. "I'd like to sit with her a spell. All that action, but nobody knows who she is. She must be a hoot to watch fight. Must have a real interestin' story or two in her."

"Sit with her a spell." Boone smirked. "She might just pin your ears back, if you're not careful."

"Oh! Jack Rabbit. Miss Clem gave me this." Hank fished in his pocket and pulled out a linen bag.

"What? Another blade?"

"Nosiree. Don't feel like one of them blades you been playin' with."

"Playin'? Take a look at this." In one fluid movement he stood, jerked a shiny slender throwing knife from his belt, and flung it across the room. *Thwap!* It stuck into a board he'd hung on a stack of hay at the other end of the loft.

Hank opened his mouth so wide it took up half his face. His round eyes took up the other half. He nodded his head exaggeratedly and slapped his knee. "I'll be a hellbent horny toad!"

"I know!" Rabbit pulled another knife and held it up. "When

she gave me these things, I thought she was pullin' on my rooster tail, but I gotta tell ya, I like 'em. Quick as a sidewinder on hot sand and before you know it, I'll be able to shave those whiskers from your chin from across the loft."

Hank rubbed his whiskered chin. "Better'n a six-shooter?"

"Quieter, anyway."

Hank nodded. "Well, here." He handed Rabbit the bag.

"Wonder what Miss Clementine thinks I need." He opened the bag and pulled out a silver and turquoise bear pendant on a leather lanyard. "Hey now! Uncle Mort's bear."

"Miss Clem says you forgot it when you departed on your Santa Fe gallivant after your uncle's funeral."

"I surely did. Distracted, I guess." Rabbit strung the loop of leather over his head and rubbed the silver bear. He couldn't help but smile. "Feels like a little piece of Uncle Mort is here now."

His head began to spin, but only a little, like what tended to happen when he slammed a whiskey on an empty stomach or sipped a little too much McCuddle's Original Magical Tonic. But he hadn't had either for better than a day.

That was odd. He rubbed his temple, waiting for the feeling to pass. Instead, the back of his neck prickled, same as it did now and then when he was a kid playing near the old horse graveyard in the ravine behind Uncle Mort's woodshed. He felt the air shift behind him. The tingling in his neck spread south, down his spine, making his legs itch to skedaddle.

He looked at Boone and Hank, wondering if they were feeling something far from ordinary, too. They sat at the table, sipping coffee as if they were having tea with the queen of England. Hank broke out a deck of cards and began to overhand shuffle.

Rabbit's stomach weighed heavy. There was something behind him now, he knew it without even turning.

Sheeat! Someone is lookin' at me.

He craned his neck, peeking over his shoulder.

What he saw made him spin back around. "Nope."

"What 'nope,' Jack Rabbit?" Hank looked up, still shuffling the cards.

Rabbit shook his head. "Fuck that."

Yet he couldn't help but glance behind him again. The sight was same as before. He scowled and focused on Boone and Hank.

"You two see that?" He jabbed his thumb over his shoulder.

"The bed? Stairs? What?" Hank asked.

Rabbit frowned. "Boone? What do you see?"

Boone shot Rabbit a wide grin, his eyes sparkling. "I see a real handsome man. Kinda *loco*, though."

"Ain't exactly helpful, are ya? Hank, anything else?"

Hank looked up from the cards he was dealing and tilted his head to see around Rabbit. "Don't see nothin', Jack Rabbit. Just the bed over there." He went back to flipping the cards into three piles.

"Jack, turn around." The gravelly voice that spoke sounded far away, yet right in Rabbit's ear. A very familiar voice. "Let me look at you."

Rabbit froze, his heart thumped in his chest like it was trying to break free and race back to New Mexico.

"Jonathan Virginia Fields." The voice grew louder. "Turn around this minute!"

Rabbit gulped. Only one person had ever used his full name since his mother had died back on that wagon trip west. Rabbit did as ordered, moving slowly, his gaze aimed down at the straw-covered floor. His legs felt like heavy piles of meat with the bones removed.

"Look at me!"

Rabbit let his gaze lift to the bed, in front of which a pair of boots stood with legs attached. His gaze eased up and up, until he locked eyes with his uncle, who'd been dead for way too long to be standing in the loft right now.

Two

"A in't real," Rabbit said, trying to convince himself.

"What ain't real, Jack Rabbit?" Hank asked.

"What does that mean?" Uncle Mort snorted. "And you know how I feel about you using the word 'ain't,' boy."

"Isn't," Rabbit corrected himself out of habit.

"What isn't real?" Uncle Mort scanned the room. "Where are we? Looks like a hayloft."

"In the loft of a livery," Rabbit told him.

"I see." Uncle Mort stepped toward Rabbit, his feet drifting a little way with each step as if he were on ice. He was pale, like he'd been whitewashed.

Rabbit took a step back, cringing. *What the hell!*

"Since when are you afraid of your uncle, boy?"

"Uh, since … you … Well, since you died. I went to your funeral." Rabbit's voice cracked on that last word. Was he dreaming this? He glanced around the loft and ran into Boone's frown.

"Rabbit, what are you doing?" Boone fanned the cards in his hand, not even glancing in Uncle Mort's direction. "Get over here. Hank dealt you in."

Rabbit shook his head. It was a trick. Somehow. Boone was fooling with him. Payback for that snowball earlier. Yeah, that was it. He looked behind him again. Nope, that wasn't it. What couldn't possibly be his uncle stood watching him.

Uncle Mort was dressed in the long, threadbare, light blue nightgown he always wore to bed back home on the ranch, along with his favorite old boots. As Rabbit stared, his uncle's form undulated slightly, as if pushed this way and that by the gentle gusts that coursed through the loft. He could even see the bed and wall here and there through his body.

"Sheeat." Blood rushed and roared in Rabbit's ears. The room began to tilt, enough to make him reach out with both hands to steady himself. "I must've broke my brain."

"Rabbit." The sound of Boone's voice calmed Rabbit a bit, making the room level out. "Who are you talking to?"

"Uh, Uncle Mort," Rabbit said over his shoulder.

Boone chuckled. "Tell him to join us. We need a fourth hand."

Uncle Mort scowled down at his body and then up at Rabbit. "Do I remember something happening in a … ?" He attempted to put his hand on his chest, but it passed through. "Well, I'll be." He passed his hand through his chest again. Then through his leg. Then he put the tip of his finger on his nose and it sank up to his wrist.

"Jehoshaphat, Uncle Mort!"

"Look at that." His uncle sawed the side of his hand through his silver beard and neck and then flopped his head to the side.

"Uncle Mort! Don't do that!"

Uncle Mort laughed with the same deep belly laugh Rabbit had heard a thousand times growing up. "That would scare the trousers off of Carlos."

Rabbit wondered how Uncle Mort would feel if he found out Rabbit and Boone had sold the ranch in Santa Fe to Carlos, his uncle's good friend and ranch foreman.

A chair scraped across the floor behind Rabbit. A moment later Boone was at his side. "Right here, is he?"

Rabbit could tell by the sarcasm in Boone's voice he wasn't along for this ride.

"Yep." Rabbit pointed at Uncle Mort. "Right there. You can't see him?" Then he said to Uncle Mort, "Seems I'm more higgledy-piggledy about this than you."

"I'm not higgledy-piggledy'd," Boone said.

"Not talkin' to you," Rabbit shot back.

"No sense in theatrics." Uncle Mort continued passing his hand through various parts of his body.

"You know," Rabbit crossed his arms, "you died a while back."

Uncle Mort paused for a second and then nodded. "Yep. That seems right." He shook his head. "Or maybe not. Hard to tell."

"Torn to … uh …" Rabbit corrected his course out of consideration for the dead. "Killed by a *Bahkauv*."

"That what that thing was? Hmm. Can't recollect the particulars too well."

That was probably a good thing. The *Bahkauv* hadn't taken any mercy. Rabbit scratched his head, still having trouble believing his eyes. Sure sounded like Uncle Mort.

"I saw you outside and inside that mine," he told his uncle. "Only you was dead at the time."

"I knew you boys would be upset if you didn't find me, so I gave you a nudge my way."

If that was a nudge, what was this? "And then I saw you again at The Pyre after we paid our respects at the boneyard."

"I tried to explain things that time, but you wouldn't answer."

He hadn't been able to hear Uncle Mort that time for some reason. What was different now besides being in the haylo …

"Ohh!" Rabbit grasped the bear pendant hanging from his neck. "The pendant!" He gaped at Boone. "It's gotta be."

"What is going sideways in that head of yours?" Boone put his hand on Rabbit's shoulder, his forehead lined. He stared into Rabbit's eyes. "You been nipping at that bottle of McCuddle's?"

"Here, hold this." Rabbit slipped the pendant from around his neck and shoved it into Boone's hand. "See anything?" He waved in the direction of Uncle Mort.

"He can't see me," Uncle Mort said, sounding sad about the fact.

"Like what?" Boone asked. "Dancing girls in lacy dresses?" He smiled like a fool, as if he really was watching dancing ladies.

"No, do you see Uncle Mort?"

Boone sobered. "Enough, Rabbit. I miss him too, but this isn't helping anyone."

"Just me then." Rabbit's brain ached trying to reconcile the situation. Some McCuddle's might help right about now.

"What are you two goin' on about over there?" Hank held up his hand of cards. "Think I got ya both beat already."

"Uncle Mort is standing right here." Rabbit pointed at his uncle again.

"You don't say." Hank's chair scraped back. He joined the two of them. "Right here?" He pointed in the wrong direction.

"No." Rabbit took Hank's hand and placed it within touching distance of Uncle Mort's shoulder. "Here."

"Well, imagine that. Pleased to meet you, Uncle Mort." Hank stuck his hand out for a shake, right through Uncle Mort's shoulder. "Suppose to me yer just Mort. My name's Hank."

"My pleasure." Uncle Mort stuck his hand through Hank's arm.

"Said he's pleased to meet you, too, Hank." Rabbit found the whole situation becoming, oddly enough, not that odd at all.

Boone crossed his arms. "Okay you two. The jig is up."

"Who is *he* talking to?" Uncle Mort's brow furrowed.

"So, Boone and Hank can't see you or hear you?" Rabbit asked his uncle. "Only me."

"That appears to be the case." His uncle was still trying to catch Hank's outstretched hand.

"Why not? Why just me?" Rabbit grabbed the necklace from

Boone's hand and slipped it back around his neck.

"That's ironical, isn't it?" Uncle Mort gave up on Hank's hand. "The one boy who wouldn't listen to me is the only one that can hear me now? Maybe it *does* have something to do with that bear pendant I got from Chief Seiva."

"The old Navajo who lived near the ranch?"

"That's him. He liked Isadora's prickly pear jelly on his biscuits." Uncle Mort made a show of squeezing his head flat between his palms. "She made the best jelly."

Rabbit's thoughts got stuck on Isadora's sweet-yet-tart prickly pear jelly for a moment but then came back around. "But how?"

"Remember the ceremony when you turned fourteen? When Chief Seiva gave me that pendant? He gave you one as well."

Rabbit tried to think back, but the time around that ceremony had always been at best a fuzzy memory of dancing, singing, and drinking. That concoction the old Navajo had made them drink had tasted horrible, but boy did it get Rabbit roostered. "I lost mine, I think."

"You did. But I didn't. Do you remember the rite he performed over us?"

Again, that was a fuzzy few days. "Uh, hmm." Rabbit shook his head.

"Well, maybe that was it. Or not."

"Is he talking to you right now?" Hank squinted in the wrong direction, apparently trying to see Mort.

"Yep."

"No, he's not." Boone returned to the table and picked up his cards. "He's hallucinating." He shook his finger at Rabbit. "No more McCuddle's for you."

Hank tipped his head to the side. "Never talkin' to the departed before. Wearin' clothes, is he?"

Uncle Mort scoffed. "It would be ill-considered to wander this earth with my clothes mislocated, although I wouldn't exactly call my old nightwear appropriate for traveling."

"He's wearin' the nighttime gown he wore in the winter back home." Rabbit stuck his hand out and gingerly touched his uncle with his fingertips. When his fingers sunk into Uncle Mort's wispy shoulder, he yanked his hand back and stared at his fingers. They felt cold, like he'd stuck them in a snow bank.

Uncle Mort scowled at Rabbit's fingers. "It's disconcerting, this talk about my decease-edness."

"Sorry, Uncle Mort."

Hank rubbed his whiskers. "Miss Clem put him in a nice shirt and trousers before the funeral, didn't she?"

"Yep, but now it looks like he's ready for bed. Except he's still wearing his boots."

Uncle Mort's eyes widened. "A woman clothed me?"

"She's like an Amazon. You'd like her." Rabbit grinned. "Booney, it'd be nice if you'd demonstrate your cordial nature and maybe say 'Hi' to your ol' uncle."

Boone rested his forehead on the table and sighed loud and long.

"Stuck in that outfit is he?" Hank put an index finger to the side of his nose.

Rabbit chuckled a little at the idea.

Uncle Mort looked himself up and down. "Let's hope not. No way for a man to be seen, in his evening attire, drafts blowing about." He felt around close to the top of his head.

"No nightcap, Uncle Mort." Rabbit moved over to the table, pulling out a chair for his uncle before sitting next to Boone. "Booney don't believe you're here, Uncle Mort."

Uncle Mort float-walked toward them. "He'll come around. It strains the sensibilities, I would think."

"It's strainin' my noggin, that much is sure," Rabbit said. "How about you, Hank?"

Hank returned to his chair and cards. "Workin' around Miss Clem exposes me to some things, but this? I never. What's it like? Ask him for me."

Rabbit picked up the cards Hank had dealt earlier. "He can hear you, I think."

"I can hear him," Uncle Mort confirmed. "Ask him what's *what* like."

"He wants to know what's *what* like."

"Oh, for chrissake!" Boone raised his head, shaking his fists at the roof.

"Well, the afterlife," Hank said. "Bein' a wispy sort."

"I'm a wispy?" Uncle Mort chuckled. "I suppose that sums it accurately. Hmmm. Tell Hank that sometimes it's dark and sometimes it's light."

Rabbit relayed his uncle's message to Hank, who thought on it for a minute and then asked, "Why are ya back here?"

"That's a good question," Rabbit said, lowering the lousy hand he'd been dealt. "Why are you? Is it because I took your pendant?"

"The pendant is why I'm here. Well, not *why* I'm here. I'm able to be here and talk to you because of that. Possibly. Or maybe not." He shook his head. "I wanted to come back because I made a promise to your momma just before she died."

Rabbit frowned. "What promise?" And why hadn't Uncle Mort ever mentioned a promise when he was alive?

The livery door downstairs slammed shut. "Hank?" Clementine's voice rang out.

Fenrir, her horse, whinnied "hello" from a stall below.

"Up in the loft," Hank hollered back. "You should probably come see this."

She took the steep stairs two at a time and joined them at the table. Her dark auburn hair was plaited, as usual, her cheeks pink from the cold. She unwound her scarf and let it hang around her neck. She looked from Hank to Rabbit to Boone, holding on the latter a moment longer before returning to Hank. "See what?"

"This is the woman who dressed you," Rabbit told his uncle.

"Jumpin' Jehoshaphat, she's a tall girl!"

Rabbit laughed at his uncle's gape-mouthed expression. "You should see her fight, Uncle Mort. She can whip her weight in wildcats. The first time we met her, she lifted a grown man off the floor and then broke both of his arms and his nose."

"She fights?" Uncle Mort asked, still gawking at Clementine.

"And kills. It's what she does."

Clementine's gaze narrowed. "Has he been drinking McCuddle's tonic again?" she asked the others.

"Rabbit thinks he sees Uncle Morton," Boone said flatly.

"The pendant made him start seein' ghosts," Hank explained.

She focused on Rabbit, her forehead wrinkled. "You can see your uncle Morton? Here? Right now?"

He nodded to all of her questions.

"Can you converse with him?"

He nodded again.

She rubbed her hands together. "Well, isn't this a wonderful surprise."

"I'm not so sure yet," Rabbit muttered.

"You believe him?" Boone asked.

"Of course. In my line of work you realize there is always at least some truth behind myths and legends. The *Bahkauv* is a perfect example. A creature thought to be a myth, but we all know better, don't we?" She patted Rabbit's shoulder. "Turns out we may have a shaman on our hands."

"A what?" Rabbit asked.

"I'm going to need some of that dingdang tonic if this keeps up," Boone said.

Uncle Mort smiled. "So, this is the woman who dressed me?"

"What did ya need me for, Miss Clem?" Hank asked.

"How many bodies were in the shed out back of The Pyre?"

"Stacked like cordwood. Prob'ly eight or ten anyway."

"Huh." She bit her lower lip. "Then we have a problem."

"How's that, Miss Clem?"

"The shed is empty."

Three

The next day ...

Clementine flexed her left hand, spreading wide the long blades on the Eagle Claw she wore. The sharpened metal blades gleamed in the late morning sunlight shining through the front window of The Pyre.

"It is the still and silent sea that drowns a man," she said aloud in the quiet parlor, repeating the old Viking warning her grandfather had used many times during her years of training.

What would her afi say about the trouble brewing here in the Black Hills?

She dipped a rag in a small jar of oil Hank had procured from somewhere in Deadwood's Chinatown.

"Afi would probably remind me that it is only a fool who lies awake all night, brooding over her problems only to be exhausted come morning with her troubles the same as the night before."

And he would be right.

Yet, she continued to brood in the morning light.

As she rubbed oil into the finger hinges of the claw, a bead of sweat rolled down her back under the layers of her silk chemise, thick shirt, and wool vest. The Pyre was warm. Warmer than she usually kept it given her clients' tendency toward increasingly malodorous emissions when the temperature was anything approaching comfortably warm. But due to the lack of *bone bags*, as Hank occasionally called the deceased, occupying her two tables, Clementine had stoked the stoves in the parlor, the exam room, and even in her bedroom at the back of the building.

Deadwood's new undertaker had hung his shingle and quickly began nabbing most of her business in just a few days' time. She imagined him down the street in his little shack, rubbing his bony fingers together and cackling with glee.

She set down the rag, reaching for the steaming cup full of herbal tea she'd brewed on the hot stove. "As if you wanted to be an undertaker." She took a sip of tea. "Ever."

She exchanged the cup for the rag again.

Lowering her voice, she imitated Hank's cheerful tone and said, "He makes a pretty pine box for folks to rest eternal."

A furniture maker, Hank had called him. She dipped the rag in oil. Months of experience had taught her there certainly wasn't much money to be made caring for the newly dead. It made sense that the woodworking skills necessary to build a fine coffin could be used in the construction of furniture as well.

Of course the flourishing town of Deadwood certainly welcomed anyone willing to ply their trade along the muddy, slushy streets, from merchants to craftsmen, sponsors to financiers. Dealers in human vices and corruption found profitable business here, judging by the profusion of opium and cocaine dens, brothels, and gambling establishments lining the length of the main street … on both sides.

Ironically, the only residents *not* making their fortunes in the booming town of Deadwood were the unlucky fellows who forsook everything to stake and work claims that lacked the one thing they sought—gold. Or at least silver. And the poor doves populating the brothels and gambling houses.

She wiggled her fingers, working the claw hinges. They moved so smoothly it would be easy to forget she was even wearing a weapon.

She hadn't met the new undertaker yet, but Hank spoke kindly of him, and she respected Hank's opinion. It was just as well, now, another undertaker being here to take over most of the work. It was time for Clementine to focus on the killing side of death, the job for which she'd been contracted.

Desperate, greedy, or power-hungry souls were being recruited into the ranks of at least two factions from what she could grasp. Lifeless bodies with a brand or tattoo of a *caper-sus* symbol, the melding of a goat and swine displaying allegiance, had passed through The Pyre too many times since her arrival last summer. Unfortunately, Clementine had yet to figure out to whom they'd pledged their loyalty.

And now bodies were disappearing.

Experience had taught her that there were few reasons to steal dead humans, and none of them were good.

She suspected one of two things: Either the bodies were being fed to bestial *others* now roaming the Hills, or someone was building an army with the dead.

An army of *Draug*. She grimaced, memories of carnage and ruin she'd faced so long ago lurking in her mind.

She slowly bent each finger hinge in her claw.

But who was responsible? Could it be the one who contracted her, Masterson? The few times they'd talked, he had been guarded in what information he chose to convey. Had Masterson placed her in town as an undertaker to simplify the acquisition of bodies used to create *Draug*?

After weighing that thought, she shook her head. Clementine couldn't think of a reason for Masterson to amass a *Draug* army; or for that matter, to release the bloodthirsty beasts she'd recently encountered roaming the Hills. But she needed to talk with him again soon to determine what exactly his motivations were. *And* who his foes might be.

She contemplated the saloon in Galena … and Augustine.

Lieutenant. That's what the Rogue had called Augustine, which made sense. With unbounded recklessness and bravado, he'd not yet developed the wisdom or experience to rise further. But who would allow such carelessness in their ranks?

In any case, there was no taking back what happened in Galena. Clementine had exposed her identity during the fight with Augustine, and whoever worked his puppet strings was no doubt aware that she, a Slayer, was here now.

Her stomach growled. She tugged off her claw and set it on the desk, exchanging it for the half biscuit left over from yesterday's breakfast that she'd been warming on the top of the stove. She should have gone down to the Grand Central Hotel this morning to eat, but she didn't feel like putting up with the prying stares and lewd comments that invariably came at the sight of a woman wearing pants.

She frowned toward her exam room as she broke a crumbly piece off the biscuit. The lack of bodies passing through her establishment would hamper her ability to track *others* and their doings in Deadwood, the *caper-sus* symbol, and any happenings resulting in odd deaths in the area. But with Boone, Jack, and Hank ambling up and down the streets and patronizing businesses, she was still receiving reports on a regular basis.

Clementine nibbled on the warm, slightly salty biscuit while listening to the muffled clamor of the street seeping through the door and window. The murmur of voices discussing the important events of the day came in waves, rising, fading, then reaching a crescendo, and then fading again in an almost mesmerizing rhythm. Glass crashed on the walkway down the street. Horses whinnied and snorted. Footfalls plodded this way or that, stomping mud and snow from boots, followed by doors creaking open and then thumping shut.

In spite of the humanity surrounding her, she felt hollow inside. Hank visited every day, busying himself with chores and storytelling. She met with Boone and Jack most afternoons, teaching them new fighting techniques, along with how to use their new weapons. But the evenings were quiet. Monotonous. Depressing. Lonely.

Stuffing the last bit of biscuit in her mouth, she covered her face with her hands as she swallowed. What was the matter with her? Since when was being alone a problem? She was a killer. She was born and bred to travel the world alone. But ever since …

She peeked through her fingers at the swirl of blankets beside the stove. A well-gnawed bone protruded from the folds. "On top of it all, I miss Tinker."

The three-legged pup hadn't been to The Pyre for a number of days. If Tinker wasn't at the livery with the horses and Fred the Mule, she was with Boone and Jack, keeping the Santa Fe Sidewinders company while they worked on the foundation of what Jack was calling, "The Sidewinder Hotel."

Clementine sighed. "Great Odin's beard! I'm envious of a dog. How pathetic is that?" She reached for the bone. Maybe she should take it to the livery …

The door flew open and slammed against the wall. *Bang!*

Hank stomped some of the snow from his boots on the plank walkway before tromping inside. He flung the door shut and shed his coat. "Hoo hoo, Miss Clem, you got the fires stoked, feels like."

She smiled, sitting back in her chair. "That I do, Hank. What's this I hear about you being elected the new mayor of Deadwood?" she jested, having fun with him.

Hank stopped short, wide-eyed. Then his face loosened into a big grin. "Miss Clem, yer funnin' me."

When she laughed, he lifted his chin and cleared his throat, hooking his thumbs under his armpits. "Fine citizens of Deadwood. I come on this canundrus day to oritate on the fineries that plague our fine town."

Canundrus? Oritate? She laughed at his choice of words.

He strode to the stove, turned toward Clementine, and

pointed at the ceiling. "I'm arrived presently to promise that I'll do my damnedest ..." He shrank a little, and his winter-bitten cheeks turned a darker shade of pink. "Sorry for that language, Miss Clem." He returned to his speech, finger still in the air. "Dangnabinest ... dangedest ... my darned best to clean this here town up and run it proper. Swearengen's gotta go 'cause he took all my gold dust and coin. And Deadpan Tom—him, too, for almost killin' me with that packrat and nettle stew. Gotta go."

Clementine clapped. "Don't forget Angus Monty."

"Yep. Monty for sure. Outta my town!"

"What else will you do, Mayor Varney?"

"Bone for ever' dog in town," he declared. "Two for Tinkerdoo."

"You already take extra good care of Tinker."

"Sure 'nough. She deserves it. She's made herself to home at the livery. Herds the stock out of the stalls for cleanin', then back in when we're done."

Clementine's heart panged. Her furry companion for the last number of weeks had moved on. "I'm glad she's doing well."

Hank lowered his finger. "Oh. Almost forgot. You wanted me to talk to Ling and Gart 'bout them bodies missin' out back."

She had. "Did you?"

"I did better'n that! They're comin' directly."

"Really?" Clementine would've been content to have Hank speak with the two characters. "Coming here? Inside The Pyre?"

"Yes, ma'am."

She tried not to frown.

Hank took a step toward her. "Now don't you fret, Miss Clem. I'll corral the rascals. And they ain't dipped in opium or whiskey like you wondered."

She tilted her head slightly. Was he sure about that? Having been party to plenty of exchanges with various opium-altered jackasses in the past, she found the idea of conversing with the two chuckleheads tedious if they were drug-addled. Although watching Hank laugh at the two of them was amusing.

"But," Hank continued, "better if you ask your questions, I figure. I might drift from the course if'n I'm the one talkin'."

Maybe so, but Hank was a sponge when it came to reading a situation. And he soaked up every bit of intent in a conversation.

Hank watched her, his brow furrowed. "Could be I tainted these two in your mind with the little bits I told. I should tell you their whole story sometime. The parts I know, anyhow. They been through the fires of hell, these two, and they's comin' out the other side."

"I'd be interested to hear about their history." Especially how a man with blond hair and a strong English accent ended up with the name *Ling*. She'd also like to know how Hank met them, since it seemed the three had been acquainted prior to Deadwood. She glanced at the door. "Didn't you say they'd be here directly?"

"Should be here b'now. Let me check on them boys." He grabbed his coat and headed back out into the cold, leaving the door ajar.

The sound of raised voices had Clementine peering after Hank. Out front, in the middle of the street, two men faced off nose to nose. One stood about average height with clumps of shaggy dark hair squished down over his ears by a wool cap. The other was at least a foot shorter with thick, shoulder-length blond hair being tousled by the breeze.

Ling and Gart. In the flesh.

She tipped sideways for a better view around Hank, who was hurrying toward the animated duo. With arms flailing, they appeared to be arguing about something up and then down the street, oblivious to the crowd of horses and freight wagons attempting to maneuver around them. High or not, the two gravediggers seemed to have as much brains as fish had feathers.

Clementine strode out the doorway after Hank. She stood under the awning on the mud-and-slush-messed boardwalk, hands on her hips, watching as Hank grabbed Gart by his collar and tugged him away from Ling.

What in Valhalla had these two braying donkeys so upset?

"I'll sock that pelican beak!" Gart yelled above the clamor of the street. He raised a fist toward Ling, but Hank had dragged him away enough to make the threat hollow.

Ling shook a finger at Gart. "Make fun of my nose one more time and I'll wallop you so hard, you'll have to catch the stage back to Deadwood!"

Even with his back turned to her, Clementine could hear Hank's shout of laughter. "That's a good'n, Ling."

She grinned as well, but Gart's colorful description of the protuberance on Ling's face was accurate.

"Besides, you don't see good," Ling continued. "Everything is fuzzy for you. Maybe glasses would help." He squinted at Gart, rubbing his eyes with his fists in exaggeration.

Hank dragged Gart out of the street, holding him steady next to the hitching post in front of The Pyre. "I see enough!" Gart hollered. "Enough to know you don't have the sense to—"

"Quiet everyone!" Ling interrupted, cupping his ear with his hand. "Everyone listen. Melon Head is speaking."

"Call me a melon head?" Gart pumped his fist in the air, trying to get to Ling, but Hank held firm.

Ling rubbed an imaginary melon while sneering at Gart. "Round. Smooth. Like a melon."

"Maybe I don't see so good," Gart shot back. "But you don't smell so good. Like a barn with too many cows in it."

Ling's chin jutted. "You stink like the back end of a polecat."

Hank wrapped his arms around Gart right before he lunged at Ling. "Stop it now, you rascals! Simmer down!"

Hel's kingdom! Clementine leaned toward the street. "Ling! Gart!" she barked over the racket.

Gart gave up fighting the air and stilled in Hank's grip.

Ling turned to face her, standing up straight and still.

"You two buzzards get inside. Now!" She thumbed toward The Pyre, her tone leaving no room for argument.

Gart aimed a scowl at Ling. "Now you did it. The madam is mad as a hornet."

"You two sure is a pair." Hank released Gart but kept a hand on his shoulder, steering him in Clementine's direction. "I done told you, Gart. She's not *the madam*. She's *Miss Johanssen* to you." He looked toward the other blunderbuss. "Ling, get in there. Don't keep her waitin'."

Ling grabbed his pickaxe from where he had dropped it in the snow and headed toward the door, drawing up beside Gart. "That hurt," he said, rubbing his shoulder.

Apparently, Clementine had missed some of the action.

Gart opened his arms wide. "Aw. I'm regretful. Let me kiss it for ya."

Ling's gaze narrowed. "Your lack of character leads me to believe you are being disingenuous."

"Yer disin-jinus." Gart scowled back.

Ling shook his head. "Let me spell it for you."

"The both of you, inside!" Hank hollered.

Clementine raised one eyebrow. It was a rare occasion to hear Hank bellow like a horse trader.

Both men scurried inside with Hank stomping behind them like an angry bull. Clementine followed and closed the door behind her, leaning back against it. Her crew stood lined up in front of her with Hank wedged between the two brawlers to curtail the fisticuffs that would inevitably ensue otherwise. The gravediggers' coats were threadbare, their scarves and gloves moth-holed.

Arms folded, she considered Ling and Gart. Slightly gaunt, hollow-cheeked, scruffy. It was probable neither had eaten a full meal in weeks. She needed to pay these men more, especially during the cold months.

Gart suddenly snatched the wool hat from his head and

bowed. Sure enough, between fuzzy puffs of dark hair his head was smooth and round like a melon on top. But he wasn't completely unpleasant to behold. Nor was Ling. Though, neither of them would win a girl on appearances alone. Especially with those patchy beards. It reminded her of mange. Face mange. She tried not to grimace. Did they use dull Bowie knives to shave?

Ling's eyes were focused on her and watching intently. Gart's? Maybe not quite so much. Maybe Hank should help him find some spectacles.

"When was the last time either of you drank your pay?" she asked, staring at each in turn, searching for the telltale signs of a lies.

They looked at each other and then back at Clementine.

"Five weeks," they said almost in unison.

Ling reached around Hank and patted Gart on the shoulder.

Hank smiled proudly at each of them.

"And opium?" she pressed.

"Three months." Ling answered first.

"And four days," added Gart. "Ling still gets the headaches, but hasn't touched drink nor pipe." He grinned wide and nodded at his pal.

Ling nodded back, an unspoken bond evident in the exchange. "Gart chased away the dragon," he told Clementine. "I don't recommend it. Thought I was going to die. Still wish I had. I don't know which is worse, the noises in my head or driving out the dragon."

"The dragon," Gart confirmed.

Ling frowned. "You don't hear the noises."

"The dragon," Gart repeated. "We'll not be allowin' the dragon any quarter."

Clementine continued to study them. So, they'd been clear of liquor for over a month, and opium even longer. And yet Ling was still hearing noises. She couldn't help but wonder if …

Hank cocked his head. "You been hearing noises since when,

Ling?"

"Since the accident on the railroad," Gart answered instead. "I got better acquainted with Ling not long after you moved on to work with the survey crew."

"Oh. Gotcha." Hank rubbed his bristly chin. "You told me somethin' about that. Bad accident, if'n I'm not dis-rememberin'."

"It was a real bell-ringer," Gart added. "Stuff is still rattling around up in there."

"Am I here?" Ling asked.

"See what I mean." Gart reached behind Hank and put his hand on Ling's shoulder. "You're at The Pyre, Ling. That there is Missus Johanssen. Hank is right here with us, too. You remember ol' Hank, don't ya?"

"Shut up, you nincompoop." Ling slapped Gart's hand from his shoulder. "I meant quit answering for me. I reckon Miss Johanssen doesn't want to hear every detail about me no how."

"Fine, Mr. Surly." Gart twisted his wool hat in his hands. "But I can't always tell. You yell out sometimes. *And* your memory is about as good as a gopher's since that clunk on yer noggin. That's what you said."

Ling held up his pickaxe in Gart's face. "I may 'disremember' things from time to time, but I always recall what a mule's ass you are."

"Hey now." Hank batted Ling's pickaxe aside. "Fred the Mule might take exception to that."

Clementine wanted to know more about the noises in Ling's head and about the accident on the railroad, but she could see that the pair was on the verge of tangling again.

She stepped over to her desk and grabbed a few coins from her drawer. "Hank, will you go fetch some food for these two? They look peckish. And grab a couple of biscuits for you and me, too." Her rumbling stomach was demanding more than a few day-old crumbs to eat.

"Happy to, Miss Clem." He pocketed the money she handed him. "I'll head on down to Grand Central." He squinted at Gart and Ling. "Now don't you two rascals act up in front of Miss Clem while I'm gone."

Ling and Gart both attempted a bumbling salute.

As the door closed behind Hank, Clementine nudged her Eagle Claw aside and sat on the edge of the desk, one leg dangling. "Did Hank tell you why I wanted to talk to you both?"

Ling shook his head.

"No, Madam Jo—" Gart cringed. "Uh, Missus Johanssen."

She eyed both gravediggers until they started to fidget. "I want to know what's going on with the bodies we've been storing in the shed."

Four

W hich bodies, ma'am?" Ling was the first to speak up.
Clementine gave him a cockeyed look. What did he mean
which bodies? They only kept one kind of body in the shed out
behind The Pyre. "The dead ones, Ling."

The two men frowned at each other for a second, and then
shook their heads in tandem at Clementine.

"Sorry, ma'am." Ling dropped his gaze, focusing on his old
boots. "Ground is so frozen. And Gart is a slow digger."

Gart objected with a scoff, followed by an elbow aimed at his
partner's side. "Ling uses the wrong end of the shovel
sometimes. It's been real slow diggin', Missus Johanssen."

Rubbing his ribs where Gart had landed the blow, Ling
added, "Burning pots of coal oil helps soften up the dirt but—"

"But Ling still digs slower than grass grows," Gart finished
with a final nod on the subject.

"I understand," Clementine said, trying not to grin.

It was obvious that Ling and Gart had been together so long
they finished each other's sentences, which reminded her a bit of
Boone and Jack, only these two diggers were far more ridiculous
than witty. They would undoubtedly bring down the house with
their act at the Langrishe Theatre up the street if they managed
not to burn the place to the ground first.

"But digging speed does not address our current problem," she explained.

Gart's brow furrowed. "Ma'am?"

"The bodies in—" she started.

"Chickens!" Ling blurted out angrily and shook his pickaxe in the air.

Gart, without taking his eyes from Clementine, grabbed the handle of the pickaxe and forced it down to Ling's side. Brows raised, he waited for her to continue.

She hesitated, her gaze shifting to Ling. "Are you all right?"

Ling turned to Gart. "Did I do it again?"

Nodding, Gart added, "Chickens."

Ling scratched the back of his neck, his face lining. "Damned chickens."

"He does that now and then, Missus Johanssen. Yells out a word. Sometimes two. I write 'em down. Maybe we can string them together some day. Try to figure what they mean." Gart shot a reassuring smile at Clementine. "Don't worry none 'bout him. He's missin' a few buttons off his shirt some days, but he's a good digger. Slow, but good 'nough to do the job."

"I can answer for myself, bonehead," Ling grumbled. "I'm still here."

Gart pointed at Ling's head. "Up there you weren't here when we were."

"That doesn't even make sense." Ling snorted. "I swear, there ain't nothin' under your hat most days, not even hair."

Clementine shook her head. She'd have better luck escaping a maelstrom with frail sailcloth than landing a straight answer from these two. "Gentlemen!"

"Yes, ma'am," they said in unison, returning their attention to her.

She crossed her arms. "The bodies from the shed?"

"The bodies we buried?" Gart scratched at a puff of hair over his right ear.

"No. Where are the bodies that Hank and I had stacked in the shed out back?"

"We take 'em fast as we can," Gart said. "Hard diggin' though. Gets the hands raw sometimes."

Ling tugged off his gloves with his teeth and held up his blistered, knurled hands. "That's so."

Clementine winced at the scabs and seeping wounds. "I'll make you a poultice for that."

"Thank you, ma'am," Gart replied for Ling while looking at his own equally roughened hands. "A poultice?"

"It's a salve you can rub on your hands at night. It'll help heal them."

"Okay, Missus Johanssen." Gart lowered his hands. "Anyway, we been noticin' the last couple three weeks some oddities. Been meanin' to tell Hank about 'em, but keep forgettin'."

Finally! She leaned toward them. "Like what?"

"Well, for one, we noticed a grave, freshly dug by yours truly." Gart thumbed his own chest.

"What about it?" she pressed.

"Been dug again."

"Dug again," Clementine repeated, considering the words.

"Dug and refilled. See, Ling and me, we pack a grave a certain way. Coffin will collapse one day, lessen' it's made of metal."

"Sure as *Jóhonaa'éí* carries the sun on his back," chimed Ling.

Clementine spared Ling a glance. Who was carrying the sun? Never mind. She motioned for Gart to continue.

"Yep. You gotta pile the dirt up about the same amount you think is gonna fill that coffin. Plus, the body will …" Gart cringed before continuing. "If you beg pardon, ma'am, the body will waste some. Little more dirt for that. Any good gravedigger knows that. Piles up dirt in the middle, head to toe. But what most don't put measure to is the ends." He paused, watching Clementine, a cringe still tightening half his face.

"Go on." She had an idea what he meant.

"Yep. The ends. The down yonders." Gart pointed at his feet. "And the ol' nut." He rubbed his smooth head.

"Melon," Ling added and caught a glare from his partner for returning to the earlier insult.

"See," Gart continued, "humans is sorta round in the middle and narrows down the legs toward the feet. Some deceased have little heads. More dirt for them. Some of 'em have big heads. You follow my meanin'?" He didn't wait for her nod. "Do it right, and when the box collapses, the ground ends up nice and even. When Ling and me finish, there's a ridge down the middle and a hill at each end. Some people, you need less dirt in the middle and more dirt on the ends." He put his arms around his stomach and then ballooned them out. "Suffered from an overindulgent life, Ling says."

Clementine coughed out a small laugh. "I understand. So …" she trailed off, trying to lead Gart back to the missing bodies.

"I don't know about that," Gart said, rubbing his smooth melon, "but it's plain simple to me, they spent too much time in the company of vittles when they was alive."

"It means the same thing." Ling rolled his eyes.

"Stop rollin' yer eyeballs," Gart snapped. "Anyways, the grave … graves is more acc'rat. They's a few of 'em now. There be graves out there Ling and me didn't dig. My meanin' is, we dug 'em, but they been re-dug. If you get what I'm sayin'."

In spite of his muddled explanation, she grasped the situation. She sighed, shaking her head slightly. Nothing good would come of digging up the dead. The question now was …

"Chickens!" Ling broke the silence.

Gart took the raised pickaxe from him. "Chickens again," he told Ling and then aimed a wrinkled brow at Clementine. "Comes in spells."

Three months without opium, huh? She wondered if Ling's condition was a result of the injury to his head, lingering effects of the opium, or a combination of both. He seemed thickheaded, but there was still a sparkle in his eyes, unlike so many addicts she'd met.

She'd had plenty of opportunities to try the drug herself. From fiends loitering outside opium dens offering to share a pipe to some of the girls in the cathouses and saloons she visited who often had a supply of laudanum to share, the opportunities to escape reality were abundant.

Years back, she'd tried a sip of laudanum, wanting to see what appealed to so many. The nausea and intense paranoia that followed assured her steadfast avoidance of the offensive tincture ever since. She didn't begrudge the girls an escape with the mind-altering drug, though. Hell, they were afforded practically no diversions from the hard lives they endured.

"You mentioned oddities," she said to Gart, returning to their reason for standing here. "What else have you seen?"

"Well, Ling and me been seein' things around Ingleside."

"Around the cemetery? Like what?"

"Daytime ain't so bad," Gart said. "But at night, we got to seein' things. Hearin' things. They was moving through the trees along the edges of the diggin's. Got to spookin' us, so's we only work in the daylight now."

"That slowed us down," Ling added. "Only working during the day."

Clementine doubted these two were easily spooked given their trade. Who was roaming about the cemetery at night? Or rather *what*?

Gart chewed on the side of his lower lip as he watched her, worry lining his brow.

"I wouldn't expect the two of you to work at night," she assured them both. Especially as cold as it was after the sun set. Clementine motioned to the leather chairs by the stove. "How about you two have a seat while we wait for Hank to return."

Gart put his hand on Ling's shoulder and tried to guide him to one of the chairs.

Ling slapped his hand away. "My mental faculties are more than adequate enough for me to sit in a chair."

Gart sat in the other chair and smiled at Ling. "He gets a little wobbly sometimes."

Ling glared back at Gart. "I can hear you."

"His discourtesy is gainin' ground, too. Got me frettin' enough to make my hair fall out." He snorted at his own joke.

Clementine didn't miss the tenderness in Gart's actions. He cared deeply for Ling. That much was obvious. Their quarreling was not that of disgruntled colleagues, more like born from a familiarity. A friendship forged through many years. Or many trials. Again, she was reminded of Jack and Boone … and of what she had missed out on due to her trade.

She shook off the tendrils of melancholy that came with pining for what couldn't be. She was a killer. For the sake of her life and others, she needed to stay focused on that fact.

"How long have you known each other?" she asked.

Gart looked toward the ceiling. "Let's see. Must be six, almost seven years."

She smiled. "Like a married couple, you two."

Gart slapped his thigh. "Haw! You said it, Missus Johannsen. Just like. He be gnawin' at me day and night, all the time. Like a woman that's been made a wife." He sat up straight, his eyes wide. "No disrespect. Not my meanin' to say 'like a woman.' That slipped out, Missus Johannsen. Meant to say like a … a … dove at …"

Clementine chuckled. "I get your meaning. When you know someone long enough, you almost know what they'll say before they speak."

"That was my meanin', ma'am." Gart relaxed into the chair.

Hank rammed through the door and kicked it shut, toting a burlap sack. "Fatback and biscuits. You two hungry?"

Both diggers nodded eagerly.

Hank shuffled over to the desk and started unloading paper-wrapped pork and biscuits from the burlap sack. "Got enough for all of us, Miss Clem, like you said."

The meaty aroma of fried pork and steamy warm biscuits made her stomach growl loud enough for Hank to hear.

"Sounds like a badger in there." Hank pulled a biscuit apart, folded a hunk of pork between the two halves, and jammed them together. "Here you go, Miss Clem. Fatback and a biscuit." He served up sandwiches to the gravediggers before making one for himself. "That'll get you feelin' right." Hank looked at Clementine, waiting for her to take a bite first.

Good ol' Hank. Always the gentleman.

She bit off a hunk of warm biscuit and smoky, crispy meat that was big enough to fill every little nook and cranny in her mouth. She chewed away, studying Ling as they ate. He joked with Hank and Gart, ate two biscuits, and drank two cups of coffee before he was finished. No "chicken" demon haunted him during the meal.

Gart's spirits seemed lifted now, as well. Food could do that for a person. Fed the mind as well as the body. It did for Clementine, anyway.

Or maybe it was Hank. He brought out the sun for her most days. So did Jack and Boone. Although Boone roused more than just her spirits lately, damn it, and she needed to put a stop to that soon. Somehow.

She tucked away those thoughts for later.

After talking with the diggers, she was reasonably confident that the men didn't know where the bodies in the shed had gone. It was a safe assumption that the dead didn't get up and walk out on their own. Or maybe it wasn't. She'd seen things that tended to keep her mind open when it came to things like that.

Memories of the *Draug* she and her afi had battled in Kremplestadt when she was young began to swirl in her head. Those poor souls … She shifted, tucking those bloody memories away, too.

The dead had been raised back then. Was that what was happening here? In the graveyard? She shuddered at the thought.

She looked up at Hank. He'd been watching her with narrowed eyes. "I'm fine, Hank," she told him and took another bite of her sandwich.

"The boys are itchin' to get back to work at the livery," he said, indicating toward Gart and Ling. "The Sidewinders been payin' them to muck stalls and clean up since these boys ain't been burying many bodies lately."

"The Sidewinders hired them?"

"Yup. They been helpin' build the new hotel, too. Gart's a right fine carpenter. Ling helps with that and the plannin' and such."

Clementine nodded, finishing her biscuit. Of course Boone and Jack would offer these two jobs. That was the kind of men they were.

"We surely thank you for the food and the conversatin'." Gart pulled on his wool cap.

"Thank you, Miss Johannsen," Ling said, rising. "We'll be moving along now. Mr. McCreery told us to hurry right back, as quick as we could." He bowed slightly and took up his pickaxe. "You comin' down to the livery, Hank?"

"He lives at the livery." Gart scoffed. "Why wouldn't he be coming to the livery?"

"I was asking is all." Ling shoved Gart out the door.

"I'll be there directly," Hank told their backsides. He closed the door on the bickering men and turned to Clementine. "Will you be needin' anything more from me, Miss Clem? There's lots of work down to the livery with the hotel building and all, and Boone and me is headin' to Queen City afore long."

She wanted Hank to sit with her in the parlor like they used to, drinking tea and talking about mules and people. To tell her stories of his past and whatever else their "conversating" happened upon. But she shook her head. "I don't suppose so."

She'd be alone again as soon as Hank went out that door, but that wasn't his problem.

"Well, then," Hank said, turning to leave.

She looked at the chairs where Gart and Ling had been sitting. "Hank?" she said as he opened the door.

He looked back to her. "Yes, Miss Clem?"

Cold air swirled in from the street. "How long have you known Gart?"

He scratched his short beard. "Let's see. Met him on the railroad in what? Was '66, I think. He was a hammer man. Still wet behind the ears, though. Could fix anythin' in the camp with a hammer and an anvil. I was drivin' spikes then. We had us some fun, but it was backbreakin' work. For ever'body. Saw six men die. Just keeled right over onto the dirt. Heard about more. Overworked. Bosses always pushin' to put more track down. It was a while later, I went on ahead with the survey crew. Didn't see Gart much again 'til here in Deadwood. Dumb luck. After the railroad, Gart told me him and Ling legged it from job to job. Heard about the gold runnin' in streams in these hills and got to reasonin' they could strike it here."

"So, Gart met Ling *after* you left with the survey crew?"

He closed the door. "Yes, ma'am."

The way he said *ma'am* reminded her of the gravediggers. "He told you about what happened to Ling?"

"He did." Hank sank into a chair by the stove.

Clementine grabbed the burlap bag and joined him in the other chair. She handed him one of Aunt Lou's biscuits and then settled in for a Hank tale, smiling as she nibbled on almost warm bread.

"I was moved on by then, like I said," he explained around a mouthful of baked dough. "Survey crew stays miles ahead of the crew layin' rail. As Gart tells it, he had him a night off and was wanderin' from one bar to the next. See, a tent town moved along with the crew. A handful of mercantiles, saloons, that sorta thing. A few doves and bad whiskey and beer is all it amounted to mostly. The whole of 'em would pack up ever' few days and move out ahead of the rail crew a little way to set up camp again. Anyway, Gart was probably gamblin' and drinkin' his pay away." Hank swallowed before adding, "Gart didn't say that, I added it."

He paused and squinted at the stove. "Don't know if'n that was Reno. Mighta been Reno. Course, wasn't called 'Reno' yet. Not much more of a town than what we got here." He pointed toward the street outside the front window. His brow furrowed even deeper. "Wonder if'n that was Reno."

"That's where he met Ling?" Clementine prodded him to continue. He could figure out if it was Reno or not on the way to Queen City with Boone.

"Yep. Said he got himself into a bad part of the town. Camp. Whatever it was. Down around the opium dens the Chinese set up. Ever'time a town got goin', Chinese started up with the opium dens. Prob'ly to try and forget the bad pay and near-slavery circumstances they was subjected to."

"Have you ever taken opium, Hank?"

"No siree! I seen what the shit …" He winced. "Pardon my language, Miss Clem, but I seen what it does to a man. Women, too. Never touched it. Never will."

Hank's lack of debilitating vices was one of the reasons she'd been interested in working with him out of the gate. That and the fact that the first time they'd met, he'd brought her a bottle of mead. Fermented honey was a golden treasure her ancestors had long used to celebrate prosperous raids and battles. Her instinct told her to hold onto him, so she'd hired him on the spot and still kept him by her side as much as possible.

"Anyway, as Gart tells it, he was so drunk, he tripped over a pile of clothes outside one of them devil pits. Only the clothes had a Ling in 'em. Poor soul appeared close to not breathin', so Gart dragged him back to his tent. Hoo! Musta been a chore seein's he was so drunk. Got Ling there, though. Got him back to somethin' close to livin'. After a day or so, Ling was up and talkin', but couldn't remember much of nothin', I guess."

"So, Ling had the accident after that?" He'd not mentioned a head wound in his tale so far.

"No. Before he met Gart. His head was hurtin' somethin' awful after the accident. Opium kept it manageable, I guess."

"How was he hurt?"

"I never known. Gart knows. Ling knows. I don't. Neither of 'em talks about that part."

"Where did the name 'Ling' come from?"

"Don't know that one neither. I think Gart put it together somehow. You gotta ask him that."

Clementine leaned forward, resting her elbows on her knees. "When did Ling start to hear things?"

"Never asked that. Funny thing, after Ling's accident, he can sing like a mockingbird. Says he doesn't think he could sing a lick before. I heard him sing a couple times. His voice is sweet as honeycomb on a slice of bread. He gets to singin' and Gart gets to whistlin' and they put on a right purty show." He pulled a pipe and a bag of tobacco from his pocket and began stuffing his pipe.

Clementine watched him for a moment while she ate the last of her biscuit. "That's new."

Hank looked up at her. "What's that? Oh, the pipe?" He held it up. "Got this from Moley Brackus. Said this's got curative powers." He shook the tobacco bag. "Don't know about that, but it smells good. He had a bottle of curative for Jack Rabbit, too."

"Well, that's all that scoundrel needs." Her smile took the sting out of her words. Jack had a rowdy history with strange curative concoctions according to Boone, who'd told her several stories about Jack's adventures with tonics. She'd witnessed a few herself since they'd arrived in Deadwood.

"Hoo! Rascal. He sure is a sheepskin full of trouble."

"Yes, Jack is," she said, chuckling.

And so was Boone. She sobered. In more ways than one.

She brushed crumbs off her lap and pushed to her feet. "I want you to double Ling's and Gart's pay, Hank. And I'll want to talk with them again. Especially Ling. I think we need to find out where he's going in his head."

Hank stood and slapped his hat on his head. "Sure thing, Miss Clem." He headed for the door. "I better get hoppin' before Boonedog comes sniffin' for me."

After Hank left, she picked up her Eagle Claw again. She slipped it on her hand. The hinges and blades moved without a sound.

Tonight, while Deadwood partied in the saloons and opium dens, she would pay a visit to Ingleside Cemetery. Those *re-dug* graves Gart was talking about needed to be investigated. The question was, which weapons should she take along with her?

Five

Boone rubbed his shoulder as he stood outside in the snow, squinting in the bright sunshine. It ached occasionally ever since he'd been lambasted by that "white grizzly" beast in the woods outside Deadwood on Rabbit's and his first trip to the Black Hills. Especially in cold weather.

"Good thing it doesn't get too cold in the Hills," he muttered, pulling the collar of his sheepskin coat tighter around his neck. The sun's rays didn't seem to be adding any heat to the frigid breeze gusting through the gulch.

That day when the white grizzly had sent him flying into the rocky wall, Boone hadn't known how lucky he and Rabbit were to get away with just one sore shoulder between them. Thanks to Clementine, he knew now. That long-toothed bastard could have been the end of a pair of Sidewinders from Santa Fe.

Damn it, Rabbit. Now I'm *calling us Sidewinders.*

Boone walked around the side of the livery, looking over the scattering of wagons and carts. *Their* livery. Horse, mule and wagon, and all manner of equipment not useful toward the specific task of pulling color from the hills had been abandoned next to their new acquisition.

And in front of the livery.

And in the alleys between buildings around it.

And in the middle of the street.

He'd had little idea the wagon and tack trade would be so lucrative when they'd bought the place from Keller.

Gold seekers from every part of the country—every part of the world—continued to flock to the Black Hills. There were Chinese tradesmen and merchants escaping famine-ravaged and bankrupt China; down-on-their-luck farmers from back east looking for a new start after the war between the states had left their families devastated and homes destroyed; soldiers looking for a meal or a paycheck or maybe some adventure after being abandoned by the government for which they'd fought; and of course, scoundrels willing to take advantage of their brothers and sisters.

Boone could understand the reasoning of most—the desire to improve one's means. To make a better life. Except for that last group—the scoundrels. Those he couldn't abide. Never had. And neither had Rabbit.

But while Boone was able to temper his distaste for villains, most of the time, anyway, Rabbit always wrestled to pacify his sense of justice. He felt a responsibility to those who found themselves oppressed by the inequities in the world. That was the very reason Pinkertons from New Mexico were doubtlessly on his trail. It was also why he and Rabbit would need to stay away from San Francisco for a while. A long while.

Hell, half the men in Deadwood already called Rabbit *amigo*, and the other half was afraid they'd cross his path. And that other half was probably right. Rabbit would oblige, Boone knew. He'd learned long ago it was best to keep Rabbit busy. Occupied. Like he was at this very moment with loading freight for Boone's trip this afternoon.

Rabbit and he had been bucking wagons and tack all morning, trying to keep the wave of equipment and teams abandoned in front of the livery in order. They'd spent most of their available cash buying saddles and wagons and teams from coinless would-be miners. Fortunately, Hank had found buyers for much of it in Queen City, a small town at the edge of the Black Hills. A delivery of goods there meant refilling the coffers with cash.

Boone watched Rabbit nestle a yoke into a freight wagon stacked so high with tack he figured it would plumb tip over if he gave it a shove.

He did. It didn't even wiggle.

"Doubletree and neck yoke are sound?" Boone pushed on the brake block with his boot heel.

"And the singles and rings. I checked the wagon, Booney. You're good to skin."

Boone rubbed his shoulder again. "Think we packed it too high?"

Rabbit grinned. "Well, listen here. If you don't figure on bein' able to handle this rig down to Queen City, I'll take her for ya."

"I can handle it, broomtail. Only wondering if we should load

a third and hire a skinner."

"Nawp. Sun's too far gone anyway. Put us a day behind loadin' another." Rabbit pulled two bundles of rope from the wagon toeboard and dropped them on the ground.

"Where's Hank?" Boone scanned the sea of hats and animals occupying the street. "It's about time we set sail."

Rabbit squinted. "You a privateer now? Cause I'm partial to pirates, so we may have words if you chase Jolly Rogers."

"Ha! They didn't really fly those flags."

"Did." Rabbit grabbed one rope from the ground and found the end. "Hank took Ling and Gart over to The Pyre earlier to see Clementine. The two gravediggers are back already, though, so I sent them in that old Weber freighter to pick up some lumber and a keg of nails."

"Good. We need to get that lumber for the floor joists stacked out back."

"Gart said Hank would probably be back directly."

Boone grimaced at the sun. It had started downhill already. Twilight was too close for his comfort. With all the reports lately of highwaymen waylaying anything leaving Deadwood, he was reluctant to get caught on the road at night.

Rabbit grabbed the rope from the ground beside the wagon and flung it over the top of the load. He shielded his eyes and looked skyward, too. "Weather's good. No clouds. It'll get cold on you, but no blizzards to slow you down. You'll be there in no time. Maybe take Ling and Gart with you."

Boone didn't take much pleasure from bossing an overloaded wagon through snow-covered trails on short, northern winter days, but Rabbit was right—it wasn't a long trip. And he'd have Hank skinning the other wagon they'd loaded earlier in the day. He grabbed hold of a wheel and shook it. Solid. He and Rabbit knew how to load cargo. That was certain.

Rabbit moved around to the other side of the wagon and cinched the rope tight.

"Yeah," Boone said. "Maybe I will take Ling and Gart. Be nice to take Nickel, too." His horse brought a sense of security and friendship, but Boone couldn't justify risking him merely to make himself feel better. If they had problems, he and Hank could abandon the loads and bring the teams back.

Rabbit watched him for a moment with narrowed eyes. "Nickel will be fine here. Dime and ol' Fred will keep him company."

"All right, mind reader."

"Wasn't me, although a toad could see you frettin' from his lily pad. It was Uncle Mort who figured you out. He can read you like one of them fat books you're always carrying around."

"Toads don't sit on lily pads." Boone shoved his hands in his pockets and scrutinized the area around Rabbit, looking for some sign of his uncle, but knew he wouldn't see anything. "Ol' boy is here, is he?"

Rabbit had strapped on the belief that their dead uncle was hanging around like it was an old, comfortable boot. If Morton truly was ambulating beyond the grave, it didn't help Boone's skepticism that his uncle wouldn't or couldn't show himself to Boone. And how was it Hank and Clementine were so quick to hop on that ghost-believing train with Rabbit? They couldn't see Uncle Morton, or even hear him. They just accepted the notion because Rabbit said it was so.

Chuckling under his breath, Boone shook his head at the lot of them. The whole thing stuck in his craw. Train full of *locos*.

Still, Boone wondered if he was missing something. Could that amulet of Uncle Morton's really trigger some kind of spiritual connection … "Bah!" Now he was starting to go *loco*, too.

"Yep. Stands around thinkin'." Rabbit smirked. "Sometimes his contemplatin' leaks out his mouth. Just like always, Uncle Mort." Rabbit glanced at Boone while finishing cinching down the rope at the front of the loaded wagon. He threw another rope over the back. "Because two ropes is enough," he said, apparently still talking to their uncle's ghost. "This load don't need no rope around the back." He stopped as he rounded the tail of the wagon. "Look in there. Me'n Boone loaded it proper." He threw up his hand. "*Argh!* Fine, *Boone and I* loaded it proper. Is that better?"

Boone meandered over behind the wagon next to Rabbit and studied the stacks of tack. "Uncle Morton is right. It could use one more rope. Right around here and through the handle on that box of bridles—"

"Dadgummit! Not you too, Booney!" Rabbit circled around to the other side of the wagon and pulled the rope through a cargo ring and flung it back over the top. "Got an annoying old coot wearin' my ear out on one side," he grumbled and then looked at Boone with a grin. "And my dead uncle on the other."

Boone laughed. "Whatever you say, curly wolf. Have you seen our new blacksmith yet?"

"Nope."

"Hank said they'd arrive today."

"Yep." Rabbit circled around and laced the rope through another cargo ring and cinched it tight. He pulled on each of the ropes. "All set." He looked Boone in the eyes. "That load is squared away, Booney. Might be a little over but don't worry. It's good."

Boone nodded. Anyone else and he'd have checked the ropes himself.

"There's Hank." Rabbit reached down and scooped up a big handful of snow, packing it into a tight ball.

Boone spotted Hank in the street, heading toward the livery. "Must be done at Cle …" he stalled when Rabbit cocked his arm and let loose.

A second later Boone heard Hank's voice over the din in the street.

"Tarnation!" Hank looked at the remnants of a snowball on

the sleeve of his jacket, and then his eyes locked onto Rabbit. "Jack Rabbit!" He disappeared behind a group of wagons across the lot.

After a moment, his head popped up one wagon closer, and he hurled an oversized ball of snow at Rabbit. It whizzed past Boone's ear and exploded against the lapels of Rabbit's sheepskin coat. Snow and ice crystals peppered his neck and beard.

Rabbit's eyes grew wide and a grin spread across his face. "Now you've done it, scallywag!"

"Hoo hoo! Right in the ol' breadbasket!" Hank taunted.

"Ohhh ho ho, that's cold! Went down my shirt you horn toad." Rabbit shook the snow and ice from his jacket and lobbed another shot. It nailed Hank in the collarbone.

Hank wiped snow from his neck. "Hoo! That does it, you varmint." He disappeared again. When his head popped up, he was two wagons away. Another snowball came flying their way.

Rabbit ducked and the snowball smashed against the side of the wagon next to Boone, spraying him with a few bits of ice.

Backing away from the fray, Boone leaned on a nearby buckboard to watch the battle.

Hank disappeared again and popped up right around the corner from Rabbit, holding another snowball, arm cocked.

Rabbit held up his hands. "Parley!"

Hank dropped his arm, still holding the snowball. "Huh?"

"You got snow down my shirt, you landlubber!" Rabbit rushed him and slammed into his ribs. They both tumbled and flopped into the snow.

Hank grunted as Rabbit came out on top. "That was a dirty trick, you lanky muleskinner." He burst into laughter and struggled to throw the troublemaker off his chest.

"Hello!" A voice called out from behind Boone.

He turned to find a thick-shouldered man in a dark wool coat and a short, skinny lad in baggy trousers standing at the front door of the livery. Boone left the dueling pair rolling in the dirty snow, Hank with an arm wrapped around Rabbit's head.

"Hello there," Boone said when he reached the strangers. "Boone McCreery." He extended his hand. The man pulled off his glove and shook it. His calloused grip was almost too tight.

"You're the man I was looking for. I'm John Beaman."

Ah. The blacksmith.

Beaman's brown eyes were well creased at the corners, his smile almost as wide as he was. "This here is my daughter, Amelia," he added.

What had appeared to be a thin lad at a distance was indeed a female upon up-close inspection, and not as young as Boone had first thought. The dark-haired girl cracked a shy smile and waved at Boone. Amelia's eyes were the same color as her father's, but her features were far more delicate.

"Hank Varney said you were the man to talk to about some blacksmith work," Beaman said.

"I am. Let's go inside." Boone held the door for them, glancing over at the two dunderheads still wrestling in the snow in the livery lot. He debated on hollering for Rabbit, but followed the Beamans into the livery and shut the door behind him instead. Hank and Rabbit would run out of steam soon enough.

As Boone led Beaman and his daughter toward the forge in the back of the livery, Tink raced out from the shadows and crashed into Boone's legs. He scrubbed her neck and jowls as she jumped and circled and jumped again. "This is Tink," he told them. "She takes care of rats. Keeps us company." He knelt and combed the fur on her back with his gloved fingers. "And she pesters the horses. Isn't that right, girl. Can't leave the animals alone, can you? Trouble is what you are."

"Looks like she ran into the trouble," Beaman said. "Lost her leg."

"Yep." That was a story Boone wasn't likely to tell them any time soon. "But she's a scrapper. We thought she'd need that fourth leg. Turns out she's faster on three."

Tink yipped at him and then sniffed at the new guests, one at a time. She finished her inspection and trotted over to the stalls and began digging in the straw.

"I guess you two pass muster. The smithy is over here."

Boone led them back to the forge, holding his arms wide. "Here we are. Should have everything you need. Keller sold us his tools along with the livery."

Beaman scanned the smithy. A smile spread over his face. "Good light from those windows. Good chimney for the forge. Kept the straw back with these batter boards. Looks like Keller was a proper blacksmith. Shouldn't need anything to get started."

"There's a little cabin attached to the back of the livery there." Boone pointed at a door in the corner. "Keller lived in it. Nice place. You and Amelia can stay there."

Beaman's mouth went slack. "You have a room for us?"

"Two rooms, actually. There's a kitchen with a stove. Beds. Should be comfortable for you two."

Beaman grinned at Amelia and then took Boone's hand, shaking it again, vigorously. "Well, I'm bowled, Mr. McCreery. That's unexpected. Didn't know what we were gonna do, what with all the places in town filled up. Can't afford the room we're in down to the Atlas Inn for more than a couple nights."

"Call me Boone, please," he said when Beaman let go of his hand. "You can move in directly. Tonight, if you're inclined."

"I don't know how to thank you, Mr. ... Boone."

"We're happy to have your help, Mr. Beaman. As you can see, you have plenty of work waiting for you. Both of you." He tipped his head toward Amelia. "You're our new hostler, right? Hank will help you with the animals."

"I'm partial, of course," Beaman said, "but I'm confident you'll find my girl is the best you can get."

"Dad." Amelia's cheeks darkened.

"Knows how to groom, feed, mend, and train every beast you

can think of and some you can't."

Boone could think of a few sharp-toothed critters that might surprise the two of them.

"Dad. Stop it." Amelia dipped her chin toward the floor, but her eyes stayed locked on Boone.

He smiled at her. "I'm sure you'll do just fi—"

The livery door banged open.

Boone heard the *thumpthump-thump, thumpthump-thump* of Tink tearing over to the open door.

"You was this close to hittin' her with that snowball, Jack Rabbit." Hank's booming voice filled the livery.

"Ha! Yeah. You see that little calico makin' eyes at me?" Rabbit followed Hank inside and slammed the door behind him.

"She thought you was funny lookin', prob'ly." Hank howled at his own joke. "Heyo, Tinkerdoo! How are ya, girl? Don't knock me down now!"

The two men ambled toward the forge, both still dusted with snow.

"Nah, she thought *you* were funny lookin'." Rabbit swatted Hank on the shoulder. "She could see I was a piece of prime beef cut from a prize angus. She wanted to plate me up and—"

"Rabbit!" Boone stopped him before he put both feet in his big mouth. "This is Mr. Beaman and his daughter, Amelia."

Hank's eyes widened. "Rails!" He hustled over to Beaman and wrapped his arms around the big blacksmith, briskly patting his back. "You made it!" He gripped each of Beaman's shoulders and held him at arm's length. "I ain't seen you in … a long time."

"Closing out two years, I think." Beaman's extra-wide grin was back. "Sure was glad to hear from you. Your letter about the blacksmith job couldn't have come at a better time."

Boone glanced at Rabbit, whose cheeks were red from the horseplay in the snow with Hank. But Boone knew they'd be red right now anyway after his bawdy comment about the "little calico" in front of strangers, let alone a lady.

Rabbit shook Beaman's hand when Hank finally let the big blacksmith go. "Howdy. Name's Jack Fields. Friends call me Rabbit." He nodded awkwardly at Amelia. "Miss."

"John Beaman." The blacksmith pointed at his daughter. "And my girl, Amelia. We're looking forward to working for you, Mr. Fields, and your partner." Turning back to his old friend, he shook his head. "You sure are a sight, Hank."

"Safe travel from Nevada?" Hank patted Beaman's shoulder. "The usual."

Hank pursed his lips and nodded. "That's for another time then." He put his hands on his hips. "And look at li'l Amelia!"

Amelia rushed forward and hugged Hank, barely coming up to his chin. "I surely missed you, Big H."

Big H? Boone and Rabbit exchanged raised brows.

"Not so li'l as you used to be, are ya? Two years and you grew up." Hank stepped back and grinned. "Yep. Almost a full-sized heifer now."

Amelia laughed. "I'm not a cow, Big H." She cast a glance at Rabbit, who was brushing snow off the front of his coat.

Hank turned back to her father. "I'd take the two of you to get some dinner, but me an' Boone here gotta drive a couple freighters to Queen City. Fact, we gotta get skinnin', Boonedog."

Beaman clapped his large hands together. "Sounds like you boys are saddled with obligations, so we'll be on our way. Amelia and I are paid up for one more night at the Atlas. We'll gather our belongings and take up residence behind the livery tomorrow, if that suits you gentlemen."

"Then that's settled," Boone said.

Amelia was still shooting glances at him and Rabbit from under her eyelashes, keeping her gaze mostly averted.

Boone shook Beaman's hand once more. "Glad to have you here." He nodded toward his daughter. "You, too, Miss Beaman."

"We sure are glad to be here." Beaman shook Rabbit's hand

again and then squeezed Hank's shoulder. "I'll see you back here tomorrow then, Hank?"

"Surely will. Maybe then you can meet Miss Clem … I mean, Miss Johanssen. You are gonna like her."

They surely would, because Clementine was too damned likable. Boone rubbed the back of his neck. Last night's hours of tossing and turning had been spurred by more than just nerves about a trip to Queen City. That long-legged wildcat had him too preoccupied these days—and nights.

"I'll walk you two over to the Atlas," Hank continued, "and make sure yer all set up."

What?! Boone frowned at the livery's upper windows. Judging by the angle of the sun's rays coming through, they needed to hit the trail *now.* But Hank was already headed toward the door with Beaman and Amelia.

"Hank," Boone called. "We gotta get skinnin', remember?"

Hank gave Boone a backward wave. "I'll deliver these two and be back directly, Boonedog."

Boone cursed as the livery door closed. He looked to Rabbit. "You checked those lanterns on the wagons, right?"

"You're square, Booney." Rabbit grabbed him by the coat sleeve and tugged him toward the loft. "Hey, how about you come up and take a look at the pictures I drew for that fireplace idea of yours. I think it's gonna work, and you were right."

"About what?" he asked, following on Rabbit's boot heels. About Rabbit being *loco* when it came to Uncle Morton's ghost? About Hank dallying too long and putting them at greater risk of hitting trouble during the run to Queen City? Or about Boone being a fool for harboring feelings of dilection about an ass-kicking killer?

"It should take about only three-quarters of the bricks of doing it the old way." Rabbit started up the loft steps.

"Great." Boone paused at the bottom of the stairs. "At least something is working in my favor."

Six

Rabbit flicked one of his throwing knives into the air and watched it flip end over end before catching it and flinging it across the loft at the burlap sack stuffed with straw.

Thump! It hit the sack of grain next to his target and fell to the floor.

"Goldurnit," he muttered.

"You can't hit the broadside of a barn." Boone sat at the table, sipping at a cold cup of coffee with a smirk firmly planted on his face. "Maybe run up and stab that surly sack of straw."

"Comments from circus clowns are not appreciated."

Rabbit skinned the silver and ivory-handled knife Clementine had taken from Augustine's man in Galena and balanced it on the backs of his fingers and then popped it into the air. He snatched it on the way down by its black blade and flicked it at the burlap sack.

Thump! It fell to the floor too.

"Lotsa style, but the substance ..." Boone shook his head.

Rabbit knew Boone was anxious about the haul. He was tempted to ride along, but somebody needed to stay behind and watch the livery. Initially, Hank had offered to stay back, but neither Rabbit nor Boone knew who the contact was in Queen City. Hank had set up the deal. He needed to be there to close it.

Hell, Boone would be okay. It was just a short run. Queen City in a couple hours. Unload. Spend the night in a hotel drinking and listening to Hank's stories. Home in the morning.

"He'll be fine," his uncle said in his ear.

"What?" Rabbit looked around. No one was there.

"It has occurred to me now that my perspective has been shuffled—that you worry as much about Boone as he worries about you. It's just easier to see him worrying. He wears it. You gobble it down and keep it in your belly, but I can feel it on you now."

"Dagnabbit, Uncle Mort."

"It comes out other ways with you." His uncle floated into sight next to the sack of straw. "You get quiet. Or you jabber."

Rabbit gritted his teeth. "You put any thought to what I said before? Maybe give me a little warning instead of sneakin' up on me every time. You're gonna give me a condition." He pulled another knife from his belt sheath and began tapping it on his leg. "And I don't jabber."

"And you get surly." Uncle Mort tried to pick up one of the knives Rabbit had thrown, but his hand went right through it. "You can't keep that worry inside, boy. You gotta work it through, like Boone does."

"Don't you go telling me ..." Rabbit paused to bobble his head. "I need to be more like Boone."

"Well," his uncle started, giving up on the knife.

" 'Boone's givin' you a lead to follow,' you used to say," Rabbit continued with a growl. "Thought I was done with all that when you died, but here you are tell—"

Rabbit abruptly closed his flap and looked over to see Boone watching him with a mixture of amusement and concern on his face.

"I'm thinking you need a drink, *hombre*." Boone nodded slowly.

"No." Dammit! Why couldn't Boone see their uncle, too?

Then he'd stop thinking Rabbit was one barrel short of a load.

"Haven't been at that McCuddle's?" Boone asked.

"Don't start with me, Booney." He threw the knife at the sack. *Thump*.

"How about this—you ask Uncle Morton why it took me two days to run down that calf that was lost in the north arroyo on the ranch. I never told you, but he knows why."

"Ask him about that calf," Rabbit mocked in a nasally voice. "I don't need to ask him. He can hear you."

"I don't sound like that." Boone was grinning now.

"Boy, do I hate it when you get smug."

Boone gave him a *Who? Me?* look.

"Yes, you." He pointed at Boone. "Well? Tell me about that calf." Rabbit waited, listening to his uncle. "Really? Uncle Mort, that has to be one of the silliest things I ever heard." He paused again, letting his uncle finish. "Jehoshaphat, my brains are going to squeeze out my ears." He turned to Boone.

"Your brains already did leak out your ears. It's just bacon fat and arrogance in there now. What'd Uncle Morton say?"

"That he swore he'd never tell another soul, and he's gonna stick to his promise."

"That much is true. He did swear. But I still think you have one lone rock rattling around in that tin can on your shoulders."

"I thought it was filled with bacon fat." Rabbit watched Uncle Mort swipe his hand through the handle of the coffee pot sitting on the table a few times. "You know you're still in your nightgown. Why don't you put some pants on?"

"I miss coffee." Uncle Mort's shoulders slumped.

A flurry of yipping barks erupted from below in the livery.

"Tink caught a rat," Rabbit said, starting the guessing game, which was something he and Boone had done since they were kids.

Boone shook his head. "I think it's Hank."

"Nope. Bark is wrong. It's a rat. Or a customer."

"Hank," Boone insisted.

"Nope."

"Hilsen!" a familiar voice called out a Norwegian greeting. "Are you boys in here?"

"Clementine," Boone said and knocked on the table like his fist was a gavel. "I knew it."

"You said Hank." Rabbit hadn't even heard the door open.

"I'm pretty sure I said Clementine." Boone cupped his hand to his mouth and hollered, "Up here!"

Rabbit never got tired of watching Clementine bound up the steep stairs into the loft, skipping every other step with her long, strong legs. Even though they were covered in canvas pants, those legs were a sight. Hell, he didn't usually see the shape of a lady's leg above the ankle most days. Long skirts were overly efficient at hiding anything north of the toes.

Tinker bounded up the steps behind her.

"Hello, gentlemen," Clementine said as she crested the last step. She pulled off her thick wool hat and shook out her hair.

She looked at the throwing knives on the floor in front of the target sack and then at Rabbit, her gray eyes sparkling.

He swore under his breath. Of course she had to see those. "I was trying something new. Like a twist this way and then flip. It's quicker if …" He trailed off, demonstrating with his hand.

He hustled over and picked up the knives and slipped them into the sheaths he'd tooled from a worn pair of leather chaps that a miner had left behind in the livery. He'd strapped the sheaths to his belt, carrying five knives in all—two on each side surrounding his guns and another sheathed horizontally along the back of his belt.

He was proud of that last one. That particular sheath had taken him longer than the others, but he could now carry one knife completely hidden under his shirttails or coat, and an underhand throw would have it in the air flying at a target at least as quickly as the other knives.

Clementine eyed him for another moment, and then she turned to Boone. "I thought you were heading to Queen City today."

Boone scowled toward the window. "If Hank doesn't get back here pronto, I'm not going anywhere."

"He's a nervous Nelly," Rabbit told her and drew a knife. He began flipping it end over end, catching it by the blade. He knew he shouldn't poke Boone right now, but he was just too much fun to tease.

Truth be told, Uncle Mort was right—Rabbit was a little apprehensive himself. Too many dangerous men and beasts in these parts. Rabbit had made sure the wagons and teams would give Boone no trouble, but he couldn't control what happened on the trail any more than his *compadre* could.

Boone sat back and crossed his arms. "If it comes down to you saving me, you big strappin' man, I've got a concern or two judging by the way you throw those blades."

"You shouldn't poke the badger," Uncle Mort said to Rabbit. "He might bite. You know Boone's frettin' this trip. It's his way." Uncle Mort walked through Clementine and hovered next to Boone.

"Don't do that." Rabbit shuddered. "I'm not accustomed enough yet." He wished his uncle would act a little more like the living. It was unnerving when he float-walked through a floor. Or a wall. Or through people.

Uncle Mort sank down through the floor.

"Don't do what?" Clementine arched one brow at him.

"He thinks he's talking to Uncle Morton." Boone craned his neck right then left. "Don't see him though, so … Matter of fact, I don't think anyone has seen or heard from Uncle Morton for quite a while. Excepting, of course, Mr. Phenomenal here."

"All right, where's Hank, dammit?" Rabbit was eager to turn the conversation away from his uncle. "It's time for you to mosey, Booney. Gettin' late."

"Almost too late, darn it." Boone pulled out the chair next to him and offered it to Clementine. "What brings you to our humble livery, Miss Johanssen?"

She dropped into the chair, reaching for the coffee pot and Boone's empty cup. "There is a serious lack of diversion at The Pyre currently." She poured some coffee into the cup. "So, I thought I might lend a hand with the hotel foundation."

Boone sat forward, resting his elbows on the table. His gaze followed the coffee cup all of the way up to her lips, seeming to get stuck there. "Rabbit could probably use your help while Hank and I are gone," he said, watching her take a sip as if he'd never seen a woman drink before. "The foundation is about done, but we need to get the floor joists away from the street before they get misappropriated."

Leaning on the back of the chair across from Boone, Rabbit asked her, "Can you lift floor joists?"

She set the coffee cup down. "I can probably help some." She raised her arms like a strongman at the circus, growling and baring her teeth as she flexed.

Rabbit reached out and squeezed her upper arm through her thick coat, grinning at Boone. "Would ya look at that. Pleasin' to the eyes and serviceable, too."

Boone laughed, picking up the shared coffee cup. "I'd hire her on the spot, no questions asked." He toasted Clementine before taking a swallow.

Her cheeks darkened and she lowered her arms.

"As if she'd give ya a choice, Booney." Clementine Johanssen was probably the most capable woman Rabbit had ever met.

And Boone still seemed overly fixated on her face at the moment.

The livery door banged open. Another flurry of yips echoed through the building. "Boonedog!" Hank hollered above Tink's racket. "Let's skin them wagons. Time's a-wastin'!"

"I've been waiting for *you*, Hank," Boone called out, "not the other way round!" He set the coffee cup down and stood, grabbing his lucky hat off the back of the chair next to him. "I'm off finally. You two don't break yourselves." He jammed his hat on his head, sparing Clementine a glance before focusing on Rabbit. "We'll be back tomorrow, so leave the real heavy stuff until then."

"Okay, pa," Rabbit said as Boone picked up the haversack full of fatback, biscuits, and jerky.

"Forceful, isn't he?" Clementine leaned back in her chair, watching Boone with a small smile on her lips.

"Yeah, but he's got a sensitive nature about him." Rabbit stepped in front of Boone, hitting him with a hard stare. "Listen, the ten-gauge and a box of shells are under the seat in your rig. Hank's got my Sharps under his seat."

"Good."

Rabbit brushed off Boone's shoulders and tugged on the lapels of his coat, same as Uncle Mort used to do to both of them before they'd head off on a freight run. "Drop that load and hightail if you find trouble."

Boone nodded once. "We'll be okay. I'll see you both tomorrow." After one last wave in Clementine's direction, he headed down the steps.

"Like I said before," Uncle Mort said, popping back up through the floor. "He'll be fine."

Rabbit cursed. "Won't you just use the stairs like everybody else?"

"I don't need to." Uncle Mort pretended to sit in the chair Boone had vacated, but ended up floating a few inches above it. "And for your information, boy, I'm coming to enjoy my freedom from earthly encumbrances." He eyed Clementine, one bushy eyebrow lifting. "Ya know, I do believe this looker could entice a man to plow through a field of stumps."

"Uncle Mort," Rabbit warned as his uncle reached toward her hair.

He wiggled his eyebrows at Rabbit. "Let's put 'er to work!"

Several hours later as the sun was slipping behind the ridge, Rabbit lowered his tired backside onto the end of a wagon. "Let's take a break."

They'd moved and stacked lumber throughout the afternoon, dealing with livery customers in between. Clementine had kept up with him every step of the way. In fact, if he was honest with himself, he was puffing a little harder than she was.

She sat down beside him. "I've been thinking, Jack."

"Why don't you call me *Rabbit*?"

"Because that's Boone's name for you. Besides, I like 'Jack' better. Now listen, Ling and Gart told me something today that's got me preoccupied."

The two gravediggers had ended up riding along with Hank and Boone to Queen City, which made Rabbit not quite as restless about the run.

"What's that?" he asked and then listened with rapt attention as Clementine told him about the goings-on in the cemetery. When she finished, he sat back with a frown. "So you think they might be making these *Draug* beasties?" The notion of dead folks walking around had him shivering for more reasons than the evening chill setting in.

"That's one strong possibility."

"Or using them as food?"

"Or both."

"That's vile!"

"Yep." Clementine blew out a breath. "Since the bodies were taken from The Pyre, I have to suspect Masterson, as well."

"Your boss? Have you talked to Miss Hildegard about it? I guess she's a madam, not a miss." He corrected himself.

Hildegard was Clementine's confidante. She was also the owner of The Dove, a high-class brothel and bathhouse that Rabbit wouldn't mind warming up in later tonight if he weren't the one in charge of watching the livery. Hildegard's place was the best-smelling establishment in Deadwood, what with the mouth-watering aromas of roast beef and bread cooked up by the crazy Russians in the kitchen and the sweet scent of flowers everywhere else. Not to mention Hildegard had some of the prettiest "doves" Rabbit had ever seen. Nice girls, too, with fine teeth.

"Not yet." Clementine sniffed a couple of times, dabbing her nose with a handkerchief. "There's something I want to check on first."

"You know, I couldn't tell you which is worse." Rabbit stared down at his wet gloves. The leather was stiffening in the cold. "Dead bodies used as food, or dead bodies walking around."

In the past he would have had trouble believing what she was saying, but what with the things he'd seen in the Hills, well, he was beginning to take a few things on faith.

"I need to know what's going on out there in Ingleside," she said. "I need to head over there."

Rabbit stared at her. Was she saying …

"I'm going tonight."

Shit. "To the boneyard? Tonight? At night?"

She nodded. "Ling and Gart said that's when the strange things have been happening."

"Wait. I decided. Dead people walking around is worse."

She let out a short, hard laugh. "Agreed."

Rabbit lowered his head. "You're right, I suppose. Best way is to go take a looksee." He glanced her way. "Don't suppose you'd be willin' to wait until Boone and Hank get back." He had a pretty good idea what her answer would be, but it was worth a shot.

"I can handle it." She opened her canteen. "Or should I say, *we* can handle it." She raised her brows at him as she tipped the canteen.

Yep. That's what he thought she'd say.

He stared back at her, straight-faced. "If you're waitin' on a reaction from me, I haven't decided the best way to display my opposition to that plan."

Boneyards gave him the shivers and conniptions. That was thanks to Boone. When they were six, he'd dared Rabbit to sit on a grave marker until the moon disappeared, and if he did, Boone would give him a bag full of cinnamon rock candy. He was unaware that Boone had roped up a burlap man stuffed with straw high in the tree above the marker. Never in his life had Rabbit heard so many bears and cougars growling, big bad beasts snuffling, and giant, razor-clawed paws scraping through the dirt around him. In retrospect, he was sure most or all of what he'd heard was Boone's work, too.

By the time midnight had rolled around, Rabbit was ready to jump out of his skin at the sound of a cricket. What he didn't know was that just before the moon disappeared below the horizon, Boone had snuck up behind the tree and let that straw man down slowly until it dangled right behind Rabbit. When Rabbit stretched his arms high and wide, his hand bumped the straw man, sending it into a slow spin. He looked around in time to see the straw man's face turning toward him. A shock of adrenaline blasted through him, and every hair on his body stuck straight up. First, Rabbit peed his pants. Second, he ran like the wind. The next thing he remembered after that was being in the house, lying on the floor panting while Boone laughed and laughed. To this day, Boone still swore Rabbit ran faster than a prairie fire with a tail wind all the way home. Ever since then, Rabbit did his damnedest to steer clear of cemeteries and …

"Jack?" Clementine waved her hand in front of his face.

"Huh? Oh. Yeah. Uh, you think it's probably humans? Pokin' around out there?"

She shrugged. "Let's go find out. What do you say? You in?"

Nope! "Yep." Hell, he couldn't very well let her go alone.

"Great!" She hopped down off the wagon. "If we're going to do this tonight, I need to go prepare."

Prepare for what? Or who? Just the notion of meeting up with another beast from beyond shot a surge of energy and excitement through him, making his spine tingle. The run-in with the *Bahkauv* and the *Höhlendrache* had bolstered his confidence in his skills. But back to a cemetery ... He rubbed his hands on his legs. With Clementine by his side, he could handle this. Probably.

"I'll meet you behind Bloom's Furnishings," she said.

"Why there?"

"It's quieter down at that end of the street at night and closer to Ingleside." She started to walk away but then came back. "Guns won't be needed."

"Guns are always needed."

"Trust your knives, Jack." She headed toward The Pyre. "Oh, and bring a shovel," she added over her shoulder.

A shovel? He frowned after her. Did she mean as a weapon? Or were they going to be digging up bodies tonight?

"Sheeat," he muttered and slid off the wagon. Inside the livery, he headed for the forge to warm up. He should have gone with Boone and left Gart and Ling to watch the livery, dangnabbit.

Over the next hour, Rabbit cleaned and oiled his weapons and stocked his belt with cartridges, talking to Tink the whole time. She was good company, not nearly as condescending as Uncle Mort or nitpicky as Boone. He tried not to think about Boone and Hank too much, or fret about all the troubling things that could happen to them on the trail. Sometimes his imagination wasn't his friend, especially after coming to Deadwood.

By the time he'd finished prepping and grabbed a bite of day-old bread in the loft along with some cold coffee, it was time to meet Clementine. He double-checked his new pocket watch. "Almost nine o'clock, Tink. Time to go. Miss Clementine's waitin'."

He holstered his freshly oiled Colt and sawed-off shotgun, but then paused. Clementine had said not to bring his guns.

But it was a cemetery.

He gripped the butt of his revolver. "She asked me to go to a boneyard, Tink. You heard her. At night. Might be there're beasties there wantin' to kill us."

He paced to the end of the loft and back. "You didn't see the claws and teeth on that *Höhlendrache*, or the *Bahkauv*, Tink." Oh, hell. Maybe she had. He knelt beside her and ran his hand down her back and over her stump of a leg. "Then again, I don't know what got hold of you and did that."

She yipped and licked his hand. "Poor girl. Don't worry, you're staying home tonight. No big bad monsters for you."

He stood. If he didn't have his guns and they ran across …

"No. They're comin' with me, Tink. Never been good at taking orders, anyway."

He headed down the stairs, grabbed a shovel, and opened the livery door. As he began to close the door behind him, Tink slipped through. She sniffed the ground and then stood next to Rabbit.

"Tink. You gotta stay home tonight. I don't want you getting hurt again." He picked her up and set her inside. She pushed her nose through the crack in the door when he tried to close it again.

"Tink. Stop it." He pushed her nose back in and closed the door. "Silly pooch."

He took a moment to pull on his gloves, and by the time he turned to head up the street Tink raced around the corner of the livery. She skidded to a stop at his feet, panting.

"Dammit, Tink. Got ya a secret Tinker door in there someplace?"

He picked her up again and shut her inside. This time, he listened at the door. He heard the scratch of claws running off through dirt and opened the door enough to peek inside. As he watched, she disappeared into the darkness at the back of the livery. He closed the door and waited.

A couple of breaths later, Tink rounded the corner of the livery at a flat-out run, slipping and sliding on the snow and ice. She skidded to a stop at his feet, panting.

Rabbit chuckled. "Hey, I got an idea, Tink. How about you come along, too?"

Tink sniffed at a clump of dirty snow and then sat next to his boot, waiting for him to lead the way.

He glanced around. The street in front of the livery still bustled, even at this time of night. The saloon across the way was bright with lanterns and alive with shouts and laughter. "I bet they can't fit one more pair of boots in that place."

Tink yipped and circled twice.

"Off we go, girl. Let's see if we can find us some trouble." Rabbit headed up the street toward Bloom's with Tink next to him, bouncing and sniffing, yipping and barking at anything she found worthy of some attention.

Seven

Clementine shivered. It was damned cold. Again. Or still. Hank's opinion earlier was that it felt a little warmer, but she didn't think so. And now that the sun had vacated the sky and the stars were glittering like icy diamonds, it felt as cold as ever standing in the shadows of Bloom's Furnishings. She had bundled up in her wool coat, gloves, and fur-lined trapper's hat with the flaps fully extended over her ears.

She'd plaited her hair to keep it out of the way just in case. It might need trimming soon. Or not. She'd read once about fighters in the Orient who attached sharp blades to the ends of their braids and used them as whips against their enemies. Now that would be a weapon for which few would be prepared. It might not be lethal, but the element of surprise was crucial in battle.

She chuckled at the idea of whipping her head around in a fight. How peculiar would that look? Hell, she'd probably end up cutting herself with her own blade.

Tonight, instead of blades, she'd chosen to carry her Escrima sticks, which were made of oak. They were slightly shorter than her arms and as thick as a big man's thumb with steel caps on each end. She'd contemplated bringing her mace, but it was heavy and would slow her down in a fight. The Escrima were less lethal but precise and quick, and she was in the mood for precision, not bashing. She wasn't particularly concerned about how lethal she might be with one weapon or another anyway.

Still, the idea of a hair-borne weapon was intriguing. Perhaps it was because the need for combat was growing stronger by the day. The sparring she'd been doing with the Sidewinders almost daily for the last couple of weeks had been stoking the fire to fight—for real. Straw-stuffed sacks and targets painted on wood satisfied the lust only so far.

Her afi had warned her long ago that the will to conquer a foe was in every inch of her being. Blood lust, he'd called it, repeating so many times: *It will serve you in battle, but you must learn to control it, or it will consume you. Strength in serenity.*

"Strength in serenity," she would repeat during her training, day after day. Year after year.

Even after all that, Clementine wasn't sure she had control of her "wild blood." Not always, anyway. Afi had known her temper was her strength … and her weakness. Even before she'd grown into a woman, he'd known. The old hoot.

The Sidewinders seemed to struggle with the same temper problem. One of them did, certainly, and he was running a little late tonight.

Truth be told, they had both surprised her with their abilities. Boone was becoming something of a challenge with the wooden sword shaped like the scimitar that she'd given him. As she had predicted, a sword was the weapon that most suited him. It required a steady, strong hand and head to wield efficiently. Boone had those traits in excess. His swordplay was progressing even more quickly than she had anticipated.

Add to it that he was a cunning and calculating adversary. "Unflappable," Hank called him. Boone also seemed to have a natural ability and quickness using long-bladed weapons in general, and in hand-to-hand duels he bested Jack in almost every contest.

Oddly, losing to Boone didn't seem to bother Jack. Clementine suspected that he was accustomed to getting the stuffing knocked out of him by Boone during horseplay. Jack probably saw Boone as his older brother, and it was the natural order of things to receive a good drubbing from your older brother on occasion.

That was not to say that Jack Fields was anyone's prey. He could deliver a throwing knife almost as quickly as Clementine, if not quite as precisely. Not yet, anyway. But accuracy would come.

Jack was cunning and unshakable, like Boone, but his temper tended to overpower his judgment. That could eventually be a problem if he weren't able to control it. Addressing the issue had been a challenge for her and Boone both. Jack's blood seemed to have a natural tendency to boil. Then again, his temper might play to their favor, if handled correctly. Time would …

The sound of boots crunching in the snow in front of Bloom's interrupted Clementine's thoughts. A tall lean figure appeared from around the corner of the building. She would've been concerned, but this tall lean figure was expected and running late.

"Hello, Jack." The flurry of activity at his feet made her do a double-take.

A scampering, writhing three-legged mass of dog shot toward her. Tinker rammed her legs and knocked her back a step.

"Heyo, Miss Clementine. You can stop thinkin' about me. I'm here. And Tinkerdoo, too. She wanted to heel along, and I didn't see no harm in it."

How did he know she was thinking about … Wait, this was Jack. She chuckled. Of course he'd say that. She knelt on one knee and scrubbed the sides of Tinker's face with her gloved hands. "Hello, furball."

Tinker yipped and circled her, wiggling her butt against Clementine so hard she had to steady herself.

"I suppose bringing her is okay." It might cause some trouble, but Clementine wasn't sure how. Nevertheless, she was happy to see the little girl. That much she *was* sure about.

"Tinkerdoo can help us scout," Jack said.

She stood, smiling down at the dog. "Isn't that what Hank calls her? Tinkerdoo?"

"Yeah, but it sticks in my mind now, dammit. Call her that half the time without thinking about it."

Clementine laughed, glancing at Jack in the moonlight. He looked good. Healthy. Earlier today, she'd given him a more thorough inspection in the sunlight. She'd noticed that the eye Augustine had tried to close permanently during their street fight a short time ago was healed, and the bruising was practically gone. She was tempted to give credit to her amma's healing poultice that they'd used on Jack's injuries, but honestly she wasn't sure if it was the poultice, Jack's quick healing ability, or that damned McCuddle's tonic.

Bah. The first two things she could accept.

"Do you think Tinker can keep quiet when we need her to?" she asked Jack. "At least for a little while when we get there?"

"Dunno. She might get spooked." He grinned crookedly. "I probably will."

Clementine might too, depending on what they came across. She had a feeling there were creatures roaming these hills now that she hadn't seen before, let alone fought. "Did you bring along you-know-who?"

Jack shook his head. "I don't have no control over Uncle Mort. He just shows up. Kinda frustratin', actually. Grouses about being tired and then just goes away. Then shows back up whenever he feels like it. Picks the worst times, too."

She chuckled. "Catches you in the privy, does he?" She'd known Jack long enough to know how to make him blush.

"Miss Clementine! Come on now." She could see his grimace in the feeble light and chuckled some more. "Uncle Mort ain't too good at timin' things right is all I'm sayin'. I did bring the pendant, so he may show. Why do you want the scallywag along, anyway?"

"He may be able to help us."

Jack harrumphed. "Whatever you say."

"You brought the shovel, good. And your knives."

"The Boss and Judge, too." He patted the sawed-off shotgun on his left hip and the nickel-plated Colt on his right. He held the shovel up and shook it. "I got a disagreeable notion about why I'm carrying this. Wanted you to know that before we maybe die."

She waved him off. "I told you, you don't need those guns." Clementine meant it in the broader sense. The things she tended to meet and kill, and by association so would Jack, generally didn't react favorably to flying lead pellets. Sharpened steel aimed at their necks was a different matter.

He raised his chin. "I like my guns."

Odin's eye! Convincing Jack to forgo his guns would be one of the harder-fought battles in training him.

"Fine. But if they get in your way ..." she trailed off.

"They won't."

They would see soon enough. "We should go."

"Tink!" Jack whisper-yelled. She had wandered toward the back of the building sniffing everything she could reach. At Jack's voice she came galloping to his side, panting.

By the time they reached the Ingleside graveyard, Clementine had reiterated to Jack everything Gart had told her about the re-dug graves and strange things the diggers had seen around the cemetery at night.

They stopped in a stand of evergreens a short distance from the cemetery and surveyed the graves in the moonlight. The few standing grave markers cast shadows over the ground covering the eternally resting residents.

Timber was sparse in the cemetery itself. The gently sloping hillside probably had been cleared to provide heat or lumber for mine sluices not long ago. Many of the trees had been removed from the areas surrounding the cemetery as well, but enough stands remained that their dark shadows ringed the collection of burial plots in a sinister black veil.

The back of Clementine's neck prickled. "There's something out there in those trees," she whispered.

"Those boys are right to be nervous out here." Jack squatted near a pickle barrel–sized stump.

"Where's Tinker?"

"She's on the prowl already." He continued to study the shadowy tree line in the distance. "Any manner of beastie could be in those shadows."

Judging by his actions, Jack had spent enough time in her presence to carry a respectable dose of caution. Perhaps he was remembering their battle with the *Bahkauv*. Or the *Höhlendrache*. She hoped so. He needed to be ready for anything.

Where was that darn dog? "Can you get Tinker back?"

"She'll be all right. She's wary."

"I hope so." Clementine hunkered down beside him, watching for movement amongst the grave markers.

After a few seconds, Jack whispered, "Where've you been?"

"What?" she asked, looking in his direction. Was Tinker back?

He was turned away from her, still squatting. "Be nice if you tell me. Fade away like we wasn't talkin' the minute before." He paused, and then grunted. "It's rude, that's why."

"Jack."

He glanced over his shoulder at her. "He said he wants to visit his body."

It took Clementine a couple of blinks to catch on to the situation at hand. "Oh. Your uncle is here. Good."

"Why's that 'good'?"

"I'd hoped that you being in proximity to your uncle's actual body would draw him to you."

Jack faced her. "Beggin' your pardon, Miss Clementine, but why are you so goldurn staked on Uncle Mort being here?"

Before she could answer, he looked the other way again. "If she could hear you, you old corn dodger." He shook his head. "Talk like that." He glanced back at Clementine. "Well, I ain't disagreein'. But there's a way to say it. Not like you did. What's wrong with you?" He snorted. "You know, you're different since you died." He paused again, and then added, "Be a gentleman is all I'm saying."

What in *Hel's* name was Morton saying? "Jack."

Jack focused on her again. "Miss Clementine, he's different now."

"No matter. Can you ask him to have a look around? See if there is anybody else here? Maybe someone we can't see, but he can?"

"Hear that? Make yourself useful. Go on and check around." He stared toward the cemetery, whisper-yelling, "And look for Tink while you're at it!"

She waited for Jack to settle down some, listening to the wind blowing through the pines, doing its own whispering. There was something out there in the shadows, she could still feel it in her bones, and she was pretty sure it wasn't Morton. But the only movement she could see was the trees undulating in the stiff breezes. The cold air smelled fresh, the breeze carrying whiffs of wood smoke from chimneys and campfires.

A grunt of frustration came from Jack. She glanced his way. "It sounds like your relationship with your uncle has changed now that he's passed on."

"Miss Clementine, I swear, it's like I'm raising a youngster. Always complaining. Always naggin' at me. 'I'm hungry,' he says. Codger can't eat no how. 'I'm tired,' he says. Now somebody tell me, how the hell does a ghosty get tired? What do I know about being a ghosty, I guess." He scanned the cemetery. "You see him? I lost him." Before she could get a word out, he continued,

"No, I guess you wouldn't see him anyway. Probably off to take a nap or something. Unreliable. That's what he is. You think that's the way ghosties are, Miss Clementine? Unreliable?"

She bit back a grin. "Apparently some are."

"He gets me worked up." Jack made a snowball and then smashed it between his palms.

"You don't say."

"Now I got a little worry brewing about Tink, too." He was starting to sound exasperated. Having his uncle around wasn't necessarily a good thing, it seemed. Distracting more than helpful. Sort of like the darn dog.

"She'll be okay." Clementine searched the scene for Tinker with no luck.

"He's back," Jack whispered a minute later. "You have a look-see all around?" he asked his uncle. "That was fast. Did you float or walk? What? Never mind. I don't want a story about it." He waited, listening, squinting toward the shadows on the far side of the cemetery. "How many?"

She huffed, aggravated with this conversation by proxy. "What did he say?"

Jack held his finger up. "Hold on."

"Gottverdammt!" she cursed under her breath, eliciting a quick frown from Jack, and probably his wispy uncle as well. She should've come alone. Then she wouldn't have Tinker to worry about, or a saloon-mouthed uncle and his high-strung keeper. But Jack needed the experience, and truth be told, she enjoyed the company.

She contemplated commanding Jack to stay put while she scouted, but she knew he wouldn't obey. Instead, she silently counted to ten and then nudged him. "Well?"

"Okay, okay, okay. Don't get all riled." Jack leaned closer. "Uncle Morton says there are five men in the shadows over there with shovels and ropes."

"All right. Now we have something. Is there anyone or

anything else besides the men?"

"He said there is something else out there, but he doesn't know what it is. A *presence*, he says, that makes him feel peculiar, like he's going to wet his pants." He looked over his shoulder. "You're still wearing your nightgown, though."

"Jack. Concentrate." A presence, huh? Clementine nodded. That was probably why her senses were doing handsprings.

"Maybe that's how a ghost feels when they're scared," Jack whispered. "What presence do you think he means?"

She shrugged. "I would take a guess that he has come across his first *other*, but I'm not sure."

"Oh, sugar!" He reached for his sawed-off.

She grabbed his arm. "Hold on, Mr. Fire-In-His-Pants. We need to see what they're going to do next. Besides, you think you're good for five?" Clementine knew he was, but they needed some sort of plan first.

"Sheeat, where are you going?" Jack stared toward the cemetery.

"He's leaving?"

"He's going to visit his body." He scoffed. "Like I said. Most reliable *man* I ever knew. But as a ghost? Undependable is what he is."

"Look." She pointed to the left of the graves. "There. They're coming out of the shadows." Clementine squinted at the five dark figures making their way toward a mound of dirt near the center of the cemetery. Four carried shovels. The last had a bundle over his shoulder.

Riveted, she watched as the five reached the dark mound and began digging. The man with the bundle on his shoulder dropped it and began slowly circling the others, periodically scanning the surrounding trees. When he looked their way, he paused his unhurried amble and stared directly at them. Or seemed to, at least.

"Ah, shit." Jack's hand dropped to his pistol.

"Don't move," Clementine whispered, still gripping his arm. "He can't see us."

"You sure?"

"Mostly."

A stronger gust rustled the trees around them, making the limbs shiver hard enough to drop some clumps of snow. The guard in the cemetery began to circle again, shifting his attention to the next grouping of trees.

"If they are raising *Draug* here at the graves," she told Jack, "I'd wager they leash them like dogs and herd them back to wherever they're holding them. We may be able to find where that is, but we'll need to let them dig up a body and then follow."

From her right, Clementine heard the *schuff-schuff-schuff* of something pushing its way through the shin-deep snow. "Jack," she let go of his arm. "To your right."

She pulled the fighting sticks from her belt. The *schuff* sound came closer, accompanied by a snuffling and an occasional snort.

Verdammt! She squinted, searching the shadows. "Tinker. Here girl," she called quietly.

"You hear Tink?"

"Yes. Tinker. Tinker."

"Tink. Get over here." Jack peered into the darkness alongside Clementine.

Further back in the trees in the slivers of moonlight, she saw the small, three-legged dog trying hard to run and jump toward them through the snow. Suddenly a large, quick-moving shadow rushed up behind Tinker. Clementine shot to her feet, but she was already too late. The dark figure swung a leg around and delivered a smashing blow to Tinker's ribs. The dog yipped and flew into the darkness, landing out of sight.

"You fuckin' bastard!" Jack was up, pistol drawn in lightning speed. He lit a round at the figure now racing toward them. *Click-boom!*

Clang! Clementine saw a faint flash of spark in the shadows.

Her body pulsed with energy, her senses shooting out surges of warning.

Click-boom! Jack shot again.

Clang!

She recognized their attacker as he charged closer. "Jack! Step aside!" she shouted in between the gunshots.

Click-boom!

Clang! More sparks flashed with each shot.

"It's Augustine," she told him. "He's deflecting your bullets with his sword."

Jack sidestepped but caught his foot on a half-buried snag. He fell, his shoulder sinking into the snow.

Clementine snapped the Escrima into position, one to the side of her head, the other at arm's length in front of her, pointing at the sky. She took a step toward their attacker.

Augustine stopped abruptly several trees away. "Greetings. Mine eyes, if not mistaken, gaze upon familiar faces. What luck befalls me that I should see you delivered to me in such an unsavory place?" He leered at Jack. "How met, my good sir? In the street. And in Galena, too. I must say, you demonstrate an outstanding resilience."

Clementine waited, muscles tense, ready to spring on her opponent.

"But I find that I am also somewhat disappointed. You have—the two of you—caused me much grief of late. In Deadwood. In Galena. It is because of you," he pointed his sword at Jack and then Clementine. "And you as well, that I find myself in this wretched place." He waved his open hand toward the cemetery.

Clementine rolled her eyes at Augustine's *poor-me* whingeing. He should try being the local undertaker on a hot summer day with two bloated, smallpox-covered cadavers on his tables and a third wrapped in canvas waiting out back. She couldn't say which was worse—the overwhelming stench or the incessant flies and their larval offspring.

"My master has demanded penance for my failures. Temporary failures, I assure you, but I regrettably must stand watch, in this dismal place, nothing more than a lowly shepherd herding ungulates with a staff." He scowled toward the five grave robbers who were still busily digging in spite of the commotion Jack's pistol had caused. "These vile hills, inhabited by filthy chattel, and I, Augustine, am subjected to the worst of it. It is truly intolerable." His sword was now pointing directly at Jack. "For this, I blame you."

"Happy to help out a cocksucker such as yourself," Jack scoffed, back on his feet. "Let me know what else I can do to make your day shittier."

Augustine ignored Jack's taunts. "I will turn the course of my master's wrath by dispatching the two of you, posthaste. But I note the absence of the third—that gallant knight. No matter. I will tend to him soon enough."

This *other* certainly enjoyed the sound of his own voice. Clementine pointed an Escrima at her chest. "Your business is with me, Augustine."

"You're the one getting dispatched tonight, you stinkin' buzzard." Jack had his pistol ready to do more talking.

Clementine took another step toward Augustine. "Jack, mind the grave robbers." She kept her focus on her opponent. "That is what they are doing, isn't it? Robbing graves?"

"Such a distasteful term. I am merely collecting that which belongs to us." He took a small step to the side and crouched slightly, sword raised.

"So, it is *Draug* then." Or maybe some other type of necromancer's pet? "I suppose you are responsible for taking the bodies from The Pyre as well."

"I fail to understand why you believe it to be your concern." Augustine let out a loud, warbling whistle.

Seconds later, the *crack* of a distant shot rang out, followed by shouts.

Jack turned, pistol aimed, as another *crack* sounded.

Clementine stepped between Augustine and Jack.

Crack! A bullet hit a nearby tree this time, sending pieces of bark flying. They were coming closer now.

Jack launched himself toward the digging crew, disappearing from her periphery. A moment later she heard the *Boom!* of Jack's pistol. "That's one!" he hollered. "Rotten grave-robbin' sonsabitches!"

She glanced to her left. Out of the corner of her eye, she saw a shadowy figure crumple to the ground. The rest continued to advance.

When she looked back at her opponent, she found that Augustine had shifted his position. She steadied her breath, trying to focus on the task at hand—where to swing first, what to anticipate in return.

"Try to leave one alive, Jack!" she called out. They needed answers. She wanted them from Augustine, but if she ended up killing him, then one of his men would have to do.

Click-boom! "Droppin' like the men you're diggin'!"

Clementine spared a longer look at Jack and the approaching men. "One alive!"

As she spun back toward Augustine, the tip of his blade sliced up her cheek. Adrenaline surged through her body from the sting of steel, a fierce rush of strength and speed that always accompanied her pain.

Crack! Another shot rang out from the cemetery crew.

Where was Jack?

Augustine continued the stroke upward into the air. He pulled the sword in a tight circle, directing it at the center of her chest, and then lunged. Clementine twisted right and flicked her wrist. The Escrima clanged against the sword, deflecting the blade into the meat of her pectoral muscle. Augustine drove the steel in until it hit bone and stuck.

She roared, feeling like she had been struck by lightning.

Boom! She heard Jack's pistol sound off and then, "Fuckers!"

She growled through gritted teeth. *"Du Schweinehund!"* Clementine jerked her shoulder back and growled again at the bolt of pain that shot up her neck and down through her chest. The tip of the sword was stuck soundly in her left scapula near her shoulder.

Crack! Crack!

Augustine leered at her, holding the sword with both hands. "I dare say the damsel fares not so well as she had hoped."

"Dadgummit it!" Jack hollered. "Where's the Boss?"

Crack! They were closer now but just two were left.

"Your knives!" Clementine called out, and then she snapped a kick at Augustine. The toe of her boot bashed squarely into his groin.

The bastard heaved forward. He let out a deep groan, landing on his knees, pulling the sword and Clementine with him.

She cursed as white-hot pain burned in her shoulder.

Augustine released the hilt finally and fell to his hands, coughing.

With the sword still extending straight out from her shoulder, Clementine glared at the quivering pile of Augustine. She struggled to her feet and found Jack standing a short distance away, staring wide-eyed and open-mouthed at the sword.

He hurried over to her. "Brace yourself!"

He grabbed the pommel of the sword with both hands. Another bolt of agony shot through her shoulder and up her neck, making her drop one of the Escrima in the snow.

She gritted her teeth and planted her feet firmly. "Do it!"

He tugged, hard and quick—but not hard enough. The sword was stuck fast. The pain made her eyes roll back, momentarily blinding her. Growling, she lurched back with all her weight. At once, the sword jerked loose of the bone, sending Jack and her both stumbling backward.

As Jack fell into the snow, he heaved the handle of the sword toward Clementine. Augustine lunged, catching it by the blade with his gloved hand. At the same time, Clementine reached for the pommel. She gripped and pulled. Augustine snarled at her as blood began dripping from his glove, but he held tightly. With a hard twist and yank on the blade, he wrestled the pommel from Clementine's grasp with surprising strength.

Behind him, Jack stood with a knife in his hand.

"The gravediggers!" she ordered Jack. "I'll handle him."

She snatched her Escrima from the snow and lifted both in front of her as she had before. Her shoulder throbbed. Nausea churned in her stomach. She winced but held firm. She'd be damned if she'd let this rotten bastard see her pain.

Augustine took a step toward her, sword in hand.

Meanwhile, Jack pulled a knife from his waist sheath and cocked his arm back, but a Tinker-sized blur raced in the direction of the grave robbers before he let loose.

Tinker! Relief washed over Clementine at the sight of her.

Jack pushed through the snow after the dog. His arm snapped forward and the knife disappeared.

A flurry of barks erupted from the shadows under the trees. A moment later, she heard a furious shriek and then gurgling. Jack must have skewered that one in the throat.

"One more!" Jack yelled. "Get him, Tink. He's hightailin' it!"

"*Excusez moi, mademoiselle.*" Augustine pointed his sword at Clementine. "Shall we?"

"We definitely shall." She breathed through her pain, calling out, "Leave one alive, Jack!" There was one grave robber left and knowing Jack as she did, well …

Augustine began to circle slowly. She danced with him.

He lunged, thrusting his sword at her heart.

Clang! She deflected the thrust with a quick flick of an Escrima.

He continued to circle.

"Name the one who holds your leash," she ordered.

"Your skin will hang as a trophy in his halls."

Her temper flared. She'd had enough of the bastard's games. It was her turn. She sprang straight at the tip of his blade. At the last second, with inches to spare, she knocked it aside and followed with a downward swooping blow to his blade arm with the second Escrima. He squealed in pain as bone yielded to oak.

"That's for this!" she pointed at the slit in her cheek that still stung.

"Chicken shit! Come back here!" Jack's voice came from across the cemetery. He must be chasing the last one down. "Drop him, Tink!"

Augustine had shifted his sword to his left hand. His right arm hung limp with an odd angle in the forearm where she'd snapped the bone.

"Your master?"

He spat at her.

"What are you doing with the bodies?"

A smirk was his answer. "Blood will run through every glen and fill every hollow. He will command his horde, lay waste to man, woman, and child. We will release his pets and they will feast on the remains. Death will smother these hills, and those left alive will bow in his mighty presence."

"That's far more dramatic than I expected. Were you in the theater?" She watched him closely, waiting for him to thrust again. "Tell me, who is this mighty *he*?"

Augustine spat at her again.

Her shoulder hurt. And her cheek stung. It had been years since she had been stabbed in battle. Enough of this game! "Who is your master?"

A snowball slammed into the side of Augustine's head and exploded, raining snow and ice all around him.

"Hey, flannel mouth!" Clementine saw Jack out of the corner of her eye, bounding through the snow toward them. She noticed the knife in his hand a split second before it was in the air.

Thwap! It sank into Augustine's chest.

He dropped his sword and closed his hands on the hilt of the knife.

"Dammit, Jack! Right in his heart!"

Augustine plucked the knife from his chest and gurgled something unintelligible. Blood bubbles spilled from the corners of his mouth.

"Shit." Clementine knew it was finished now. He had nothing left to tell her. Or rather, nothing he *could* tell her.

He dropped to his knees, clutching his chest, and gurgled again. "He will come …" he sputtered, "… for you." Crimson bubbles ballooned from his nose and gaping mouth, and then popped, leaving drops of blood that trailed down his neck.

"He will what?" Clementine stood over him, holding her aching shoulder.

Jack slid to a stop beside her, followed closely by Tinker. Both were panting.

Tinker whined with each breath and licked at her ribs.

Jack jabbed his thumb behind him. "One asshole …" He took deep breath. "… still alive. Got a knife in him, though. I think Tink's got some bruised rib—"

"What the hell were you thinking?" she chastised. "I told you one alive. There are things we need to find out."

"This one's still breathing. Never would have thought one blade would drop the curtain on him."

"All I knew is you got hurt. And this smooth-talkin' bastard took a boot to my eye." He sucked in a breath and flexed the hand Augustine had previously skewered with his sword. "Lost my temper." He stepped closer and leaned down, face to face with Augustine. "Didn't ya, fucker? Stomped my head. Then you went and kicked my dog."

Clementine wasn't too happy about any of Augustine's

actions either, but dammit.

"Now how ya feeling?" Jack continued to taunt the dying swordsman. "What'd you say to me? Oh yeah, tell me how fares *your* goddamned spirit now?"

"Jack."

"Fucker." He kicked snow at the gasping man.

She tucked away her Escrima sticks and picked up the throwing knife that had been buried in Augustine's chest moments before. Circling around behind him, she jammed the knife up behind Augustine's ear, piercing his brain. He keeled sideways, twitching, his eyes fluttering.

"Why'd you do that?" Jack asked. "He was still breathin'. We could've asked him some more questions."

"If *you* kill him, that's a problem. If I kill him—well, watch."

Rabbit stared at her.

"Watch *him*." Clementine pointed at the dead lieutenant.

They stood and watched as Augustine's body relaxed into the snow.

Rabbit looked at Clementine and then Augustine and then back again. "What am I watching?"

"Just wait. You might want to back up."

Augustine's body began to shudder, from head to foot. Tinker growled and retreated toward the cemetery.

Jack backed up a few steps. So did Clementine.

Augustine's face began to glow red and orange in small, smudgy spots. Quickly, the spots grew bigger and bigger, and began to connect into larger splotches.

"Jehoshaphat! Looks like he's burning up from the inside!" Jack took a couple more steps back. Clementine did, too.

Augustine's entire face now glowed red and orange. His wool greatcoat began to smoke.

"Here it comes," Clementine told him.

A bright red-orange explosion flared where Augustine lay. His coat burst into flames.

They shielded their faces, blocking the heat.

Foom! Augustine's entire body burst into a flaring ball of light and smoke, rocking the trees around them with a rush of superheated air. By the time the light dimmed enough to look again, he was gone. All that was left was his clothing, burning bright orange, casting light on the surrounding trees.

Clementine frowned at the fire, contemplating what had just happened. Jack was uncharacteristically speechless, allowing her a moment to put one and one together. They both stood and watched the fire in silence.

"I didn't know he was one of those," she said finally.

"Ho-ly smoke!" Jack turned to her. "What the hell just happened? You knew he'd do that?"

"Well, not *that* exactly."

"No shit. What does that mean? Not exactly?"

"We'll talk about it later." Clementine looked toward the cemetery. "Right now we need to get to that gravedigger you left alive. If Odin is smiling down upon us tonight, we might be able to find out something about the *Draug* situation yet."

Eight

Morning, Mr. Beaman!" Boone called from the seat of the freighter as he drove by his new blacksmith standing in front of the livery door. He continued past, reined his team in a tight arc, and backed the wagon up along the wall of the livery. He hopped down into slushy mud and shook hands with his new blacksmith.

Hank, who had followed him up the hill from Queen City, pulled up in front of the newly laid hotel foundation with his load of lumber. "Whoa up, you beasts!"

"Hello to you, Mr. McCreery. I don't see many skinners handle a rig so smooth."

"I've had some practice. What's really a trial is a six-team of oxen. They tend toward ill temper and hard-headedness."

"Sounds like my daughter." Beaman laughed, deep and hardy. It made Boone want to laugh along with him. He pointed his thumb at the open door of the livery. "She's in acquainting herself with the current residents. That Morgan in there is quite a specimen."

Boone nodded and smiled. So was the undertaker who owned her.

"Hiyo, Rails!" Hank lumbered up next to Beaman and gave him a one-armed sideways hug. "Need help movin' your belongin's?"

"Hiyo, Hank. All moved in. Earlier this morning." Beaman grinned and squeezed him back.

"Amelia here too, then?"

"Inside."

"Are the rooms out back suitable?" Boone began unhitching the team.

"Amelia'll want to do that, Mr. McCreery." Beaman crossed his massive forearms. "More than suitable. Thank you again."

Boone re-clipped the trace and turned to Beaman. He was tempted to remind him that a first-name basis was fine but then thought better of it. The smithy would decide what was comfortable.

"Glad to help," Boone said. "Have you seen Rabbit this morning?"

"No sir, but I've been hearing snoring all morning from up in the loft. Stoked up the fire to warm the place, but I've been holding off on the hammer since I get the impression he's in need of some sleep."

Boone looked up at the loft door and shook his head. Must be near mid-day and he was still in bed.

"There's a coal delivery coming later today," he told Beaman. "I know you're low for the forge. Hank, why don't you take Mr. Beaman and Amelia to breakfast. Or dinner. Afterward, if Amelia is ready to start up, she can unhitch and feed the teams." He pointed at the two wagons he and Hank had just driven in.

"She's raring to go, Mr. McCreery."

"All right, then. I need to talk to Rabbit. I'll send Amelia out." Boone headed into the livery as Hank started telling Beaman a story about Fred the Mule and a railroad cart, as if they hadn't missed a day.

"Amelia," Boone called into the shadows. It always took his eyes a few moments to adjust to the dimmer light in the livery after being outside on a sunny day. Dust floated in the shafts of sunshine coming through the windows. The comforting smell of horseflesh and hay was a nice welcome after the icy, face-numbing ride back to town. He glanced at the forge, hoping for some warm coffee to heat up his insides.

"Over here, Mr. McCreery," Amelia called from his left.

"Your father and Hank are outside." He headed in her direction. "Hank is going to take you to dinner, and there are a couple of teams to unhitch if you don't mind."

"I don't mind at all. I've been stuck as a housemaid for quite a spell, and I miss working with horses."

Boone found her up on the stall rail stroking his horse's nose. He joined her at the rail. Nickel nickered and hung his head over the stall door. He nuzzled Boone's shoulder and then pushed his cheek against Boone's head.

"This one is mine." Boone bonked his forehead on Nickel's. "His name is Nickel. Might be I'm his, though. I'm not sure which is true. Maybe a little bit of both."

She giggled. "It's probably that last one. He's a beautiful horse. He's got that look to him, like he's measuring. He understands your meaning."

Dime sidled up against Nickel, snorted, and stuck his nose out at Amelia, blowing softly.

Boone nodded. "I do believe he does." He rubbed Nickel's face, and then pointed at Dime. "That one there is Dime. He's Rabbit's. Mr. Field's."

"He's a talker, I noticed." Amelia stroked Dime's forehead.

"Can be. Seems to be taking to you. He's a good judge of character."

Amelia smiled at the compliment. "Probably because I gave him a peppermint candy."

"Peppermint? Huh." That was a surprise. Boone didn't know that horses liked peppermints.

Amelia shrugged. "Some like the flavor. Not many, but some. And when they do like it, they can't get enough. Nickel doesn't," she added.

"Hmm." Boone looked back and forth between Nickel and Dime. They both watched Amelia like they were sweet on her. "Anyway, that's Fred the Mule in back there, eating as always. He's Hank's." Fred looked at Boone indifferently, chewing on a mouth full of grain.

Amelia laughed at Fred. The sound reminded him of her father's laugh, big for such a small girl and just as infectious. "I should have known Big H would have a mule. He needs a mount as stubborn as he is."

"Yeah, that sounds about right. So, are you happy with your rooms?"

"Yessir. Better than we hoped for."

A loud snort, followed by a long sigh, came from the loft overhead, interrupting their conversation.

Boone frowned at the ceiling. "Sounds like we got us a bear in the tree."

"Hibernating, I expect." She scratched Dime behind the ears. "I've got the feeding and grooming rounds worked out. Oh, we have four new boards this morning. Two paints, a spotted, and even a trotter with a buggy. I got the impression none of the owners were coming back."

Boone's frown lowered to her face. "Why's that?"

"None of them paid."

Damn. He shrugged off the news, focusing on the first part of what she'd said. "Already got the rounds figured? Good, good." Beaman's girl was on top. He liked her plenty already, and so did Nickel and Dime, judging from the way they kept nudging her for more attention. "There are two gentlemen who will take care of mucking and straw. Their names are Ling and Gart, so you don't need to worry about that. They're good fellas. Shouldn't give you any trouble." He'd dropped them off in front of the boarding house where they shared a room on the way into town.

"Okay."

"With four more horses, we must be full up again. All the stalls are double or tripled up." He let out a low whistle. "We'll need to sell those new ones and a few others in a couple days if the owners truly don't come back. Tell you what, you can pick out one of those for yourself, if you'd like."

She stared at him with wide eyes, her jaw slack. "What?"

"What is it?" Boone asked. Her frozen expression gave him pause. "What's wrong?"

"What?" she asked again.

"Ohhhh." Boone caught on to her confusion. "You'll need a horse, yes? To fetch supplies and such?"

She moved her head in a way Boone couldn't readily interpret.

"We have plenty to choose from." He swept his arm across the livery. "If it makes you feel better, we'll deduct a little of your pay for a stall and feed." Boone had no intention whatsoever of deducting any of her pay.

She continued to gape at him.

"That works for you?" He grinned. "Nod for 'yes' or shake your head for 'no,' " he teased.

She nodded slowly.

He clapped his hands together. "Well, your father and Hank are waiting for you, so ..."

"Yessir!" she said breathlessly. "Thank you, sir."

" 'Sir' isn't necessary. It's Boone. Or Mr. McCreery, if it suits you." Boone felt a tickle of satisfaction in his belly at the rosy glow on her face and sparkle in her eyes. Surprise mixed with what? Elation? Great. She could probably use a little of that after the things Hank had told him about her and her father while they were in Queen City.

As Amelia turned toward the door, Boone saw a grin beginning to spread across her face. She fluttered to the door, but then paused before heading outside. "Thank you, Mr. Boone! Thank you!" After a quick wave, she disappeared into the sunshine.

Boone reached out and stroked Nickel's cheek. "So, you aren't fond of peppermints, huh, boy? You sure were partial to those prickly pear candies Lupe used to make."

Another snort from the loft practically shook the building.

Boone grinned at the ceiling. "Now to you, curly wolf. Or is it *princess*?" He bounded up the stairs and found Rabbit on his bed, rolled up in blankets and snoring loud enough to rattle the rafters.

What the hell was Rabbit still doing in bed?

Boone tugged on the blankets, but Rabbit didn't budge. He pulled harder, unwrapping Rabbit down to his thermals, but Rabbit continued to call hogs.

"Snakes!" What had the numbskull been doing all night? Getting rowdy at one of the saloons with some dancing girls? He sure hoped there was no McCuddle's Magical Tonic involved.

"Snort-phhtsh." Rabbit tugged on the blankets, rolled over, and started snoring again.

"Damned lazy lizard." Boone took off his hat and flung it on the table. Then he shed his coat and yanked off his boots. He laid down beside Rabbit, wrapped a blanket over himself, and propped his head on his elbow, facing the sleeping bear.

Still, Rabbit didn't stir.

"Wake up, you knucklehead." Boone grabbed a piece of straw from the floor and began poking at Rabbit's nose.

"Hmph shtzz." Rabbit opened his eyes in slow motion, his eyelids apparently heavy as lead.

"Good mornin', precious!" Boone leaned down, almost nose to nose with Rabbit, and grinned.

"Wha? Is this …? Booney?" Rabbit blinked a few times and then jerked away, staring at Boone like he was a horse at a tea party. "Booney? Booney! What the hell are you doin'?" Rabbit sat up. "You're in my bed!"

"What I'd like a chance to appreciate is why a man of your prominence and earthly duty slept the morning away?"

"Huh?" Rabbit scratched at his head with both hands, which actually smoothed out the crop of rooster tails sprouting from his noggin.

"It's past noon and the chickens need fed."

He yawned wide. "Already? Shit. Wait! We don't have no chickens."

"That actually means we have some chickens." Boone rolled onto his back. "Was it McCuddle's?"

"Eat horse apples, Booney."

"Whiskey?"

Rabbit smirked and rubbed at the blanket lines on the side of his face.

"Ah. 'Course. Whiskey *and* skirts."

"Booney ..." Rabbit shook his head. "You gettin' out of my bed anytime soon?"

"Nope. I'm comfortable. I understand now why you're still in here. It's warm." He tucked his hands behind his head and stared at the ceiling. "Rub my tummy."

"You can rub my buttocks." Rabbit lay back down next to him and stared at the ceiling, too. "Glad you made it back from Queen City."

"Picked up a load of lumber and some grain."

"Good. We'll go through what we had in a couple days. We got too much horse and not enough livery. We'll need to put some outside pretty soon. Or sell 'em."

Rabbit and he were on the same track. "Mr. Beaman and Amelia moved in this morning. Seem happy about being here."

Rabbit peered over the side of the bed at the floor.

"Can't see them through the floor, knucklehead," Boone said. "Told Hank to take them to dinner, then they'll be back."

Rabbit relaxed and put his hands behind his head, too, bumping Boone's elbow with his own as he settled in again.

"So." Boone looked at Rabbit. "Why the late morning?"

"You got in my bed in trail clothes, didn't you? I smell horse on you, dammit."

Boone laughed. "Wouldn't that be funny, the two of us in bed in our flannels, like when we were kids? Quit changing the subject. Why the late morning?"

Rabbit turned to Boone, his eyes lit with excitement. "Booney, you ain't gonna believe what Miss Clementine and me did last night."

"I."

Rabbit paused. "You what?"

"Miss Clementine and I."

"Shut up, Booney."

"All right. Tell me."

Rabbit began spilling the beans. "We went to Ingleside. You know, the boneyard."

Boone pushed up on one elbow, frowning at Rabbit. "What the hell did you do that for? Without Hank? Without me?"

Rabbit pushed up onto an elbow, too. "She wouldn't stop, Booney. I swear. You know Miss Clementine just as good as I do. She'd have gone all on her lonesome. You know how she is."

"Sonofabitch. I know, I know. Was anybody hurt?"

Rabbit hesitated.

"Keep spilling."

"Tink got caught out."

A lump sank into Boone's gut. He stared at Rabbit, fearing the worst.

Rabbit put a hand up as if he were deflecting Boone's wrath. "No, no. She's okay. She got kicked. Maybe got a cracked rib. She's at The Pyre with Miss Clementine, probably sleepin'."

Boone laid flat and stared at the ceiling again. "Tell me what happened."

He listened as Rabbit spoke of Tink and gravediggers. He heard about guns and fighting sticks and throwing knives and swords. And he heard Rabbit's graphic depiction of Augustine's spectacular demise.

Boone had been around Rabbit long enough to know his tells. So, when Rabbit finished, it was Boone's assessment that his partner had left out a number of important details. It took him a moment to let everything sink in, and then the questions began to flood into his head.

"So the two of you carted all of the dead guys back to The Pyre," he stated. "Why would you do that?"

"Miss Clementine didn't want nobody finding the bodies. 'Stick to proper procedure,' she said. I think she wanted to look them over, too. See if there was anything to know. Took a good part of the night to move them all. Wish we'd had Fred and his wagon. As it was, we borrowed a two-wheel cart. That helped."

Boone glanced at Rabbit. "Nothing left of Augustine to worry about?"

"Nope. *Foom.*" Rabbit billowed his hands toward the ceiling. "I thought I was going plumb *loco*, Booney. Wasn't like them *Bahkauv* at all. All smoke. Even his clothes burned up. Miss Clementine got his sword."

"And one of the diggers is alive."

"Think so."

"At The Pyre?"

"Mm-hmm."

"With Clementine?"

"Yeah. Now, I see what you're aimed at. I worried a wee bit about that, too. But you know her, well as I do. You think that digger has a chance against her? *And* we tied him to the table, but good. Two ropes. You know I can tie. Besides, reaper might as well have been standin' in the corner with his scythe when I left."

Boone shifted, feeling something under his hip. He reached down and pulled out a dime novel. "*Peg Leg Willy and the Tiger of Gold,*" he read aloud and then held it up, both eyebrows raised.

Rabbit grinned. "That one is getting good. There's this tiger—"

"Made of gold?" Boone smirked. "If you need any help

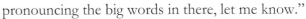

pronouncing the big words in there, let me know."

Rabbit knuckle-punched him in the thigh.

"Ow!" Boone laughed and pulled away. "I can read it to you at bedtime if you want. I'll even do the voices."

"You're a jackass." Rabbit elbowed him in the stomach.

"*Ooof!* Can I read it when you're done in case I ever have a peg leg?" Boone teased and dropped the book on the floor. Sobering, he asked, "You think he's dead by now? That gravedigger?"

"I expect he's good as gone."

"I don't know. Clementine has a way with her apothecary bag. She's probably got more skill than Doc Wahl." He looked at Rabbit. "She might have that gravedigger conscious by now."

Rabbit nodded slowly. "Maybe."

They frowned at each other for a few seconds, and then threw the blankets off and scrambled out of bed.

Nine

Boone closed the front door of The Pyre behind Rabbit, shutting out the commotion and din of Deadwood's main street. He found Clementine sitting at her desk in the parlor, writing in her notebook. When she met his eyes, he smiled, more than a little relieved to find her still in one piece. Uninjured. *And* looking a damned sight better than Rabbit did this morning, with his hair refusing to lie against his head until he'd pushed his hat down tight. The whiskers on Rabbit's face still looked as *loco* as the hair had on his head though, somehow.

Clementine faced them fully. "You two are breathing hard. Did you have a race?" she teased, watching as he and Rabbit shed their gloves and sheepskin coats.

"A little bunny told me you went on an adventure last night," Boone said, his gaze steady on her. With her hair braided, he could clearly see a cut across her left cheek. That was new.

She winked at Rabbit. "The bunny has fangs. And claws."

Rabbit nodded, patting the *fangs* and *claws* safely sheathed in his belt.

Boone frowned back and forth between the two of them, and then he knelt beside Tink. He stroked her head, searching for any injuries. She slept through his exam.

"Taking a vicious bunny with you on your ill-considered

adventures is one thing," he said to the two of them. "But an innocent, three-legged dog?" He clucked his tongue.

Clementine crossed her arms, apparently preparing to spar. At least verbally. "Tinker will be fine. She ate like a horse this morning. She's lucky to only have bruised ribs."

"She is lucky," Boone agreed. "Or unlucky, could be."

"Tink's fine, Booney. What I wanna know is, did the reaper take our buddy last night?" Rabbit sneaked a peek into the exam room. "Or did you bring him through?"

"Changing the subject?" Boone stood and meandered over to Clementine, wanting a closer look at the cut. "I see you picked up a scratch." So, this was one of the details missing from Rabbit's story. He aimed a hard glance at his *amigo*. "Left that part out?"

Clementine's brow furrowed. She touched her cheek. "Oh, this? I cut myself shaving this morning."

Rabbit burst out laughing. "Shaving! Ha! If I shaved with the blade that did that, I'd probably sneeze and cut my head clean off."

Boone pictured Rabbit scraping a razor along his jaw-line like he was finishing up a plate of beans. He always shaved that way. Boone had told him time and again, stroke up or down, not across. But Rabbit was stubborn and nicked himself darn near every time … *Wait!*

"What do you mean, 'the blade that did that'?" Boone pointed at Clementine's cut.

Rabbit grimaced toward Clementine. "Should I tell him?"

Ah-ha! Rabbit's earlier lack of details made sense. He was holding Clementine's confidence. Boone leaned back on his heels, not sure how he felt about that.

She nodded, rubbing her collarbone with her fingertips.

"You should've seen it, Booney. Augustine did it with his sword."

Boone figured it was something along those lines. Anger at

their carelessness for rambling off to the graveyard without him and Hank burned in his belly. He took a deep breath, trying to cool the heat building inside, and inspected the cut again. "Came close, huh?" His gaze lifted to her gray eyes. "Little bit closer, he might have gotten the job done. As it is, it looks like you got a shave from Rabbit."

"Booney, cut it out. She's okay." Rabbit sat in the leather chair next to the stove. He shook his head at Clementine. "Probably shouldn't tell him about the other thing, huh? He's already squawking like a mother hen."

Other thing? The fire in his belly climbed up into his chest. Damn Rabbit for making him ask. *Breathe through it*, Uncle Morton often said when Boone was a kid and Rabbit had lit his tail on fire.

"There's another thing?" Boone sat in the chair across from Rabbit, set his hat in his lap, and squeezed the brim tightly with both hands to keep from wringing Rabbit's neck. He focused on a deep breath. Repeat.

Rabbit glanced at Clementine again. She cringed, but nodded ever so slightly.

"Okay." Rabbit sat up and started talking with his hands as much as he was with his mouth. "I was into the marker stones, takin' care of the diggers rushin' us. Dropped them all, Booney!" He pointed his finger-gun at Boone. "Pow! Pow! Pow! They was shootin' back. Pow! Pow!" Then Rabbit threw an imaginary knife at him, too. "*Fwap!* Four of 'em down. One more to go."

That sounded true to Rabbit's usual skirmishes so far.

"Looked around to see if Miss Clementine was in the fight, and there she was." Rabbit sat up straight and poked his left collarbone and then moved his hand out in front of him about two feet. "Sword was sticking straight outta there, like that." He took hold of the imaginary handle of the sword in his shoulder.

"Wait, wait. Wait." Boone held up his hand to stop Rabbit. "You mean to tell me Augustine stuck Clementine with his sword?" At Rabbit's nod, Boone gaped at her, stunned by the idea that she had been not only cut last night, but also stabbed.

"It wasn't really that bad," she told Boone and swung her right arm around. "See, no pain."

What? How could …

"Pullin' legs, Miss Clementine. It was the other one." Rabbit pointed at her left shoulder. "I mean to tell you, Booney. I pulled on that sword, like I was draggin' a steer from the mud, but it was S-T-U-C-K. Stuck. In the bone I guess, right Miss Clementine?"

Clementine started to shrug, but stopped, wincing slightly. "In my scapula." She pointed at the hollow between her left shoulder and her collarbone.

"Hoo, Booney! Your eyes are big as silver dollars." Rabbit sat back into the chair. "You better believe it, mine were big as teacup saucers."

"And mine, too," added Clementine with a smirk.

"Rabbit, you're starting to sound like Hank," was all Boone could muster. His mind was still trying to wrap around the fact that if the blade had been stuck in a few inches down and left, Clementine might not be sitting here with them. Why in the hell couldn't they have waited for him to return from Queen City to go sneaking around the graveyard?

"So anyway, I pulled, and Miss Clementine pulled, and all at once it came loose, so fast I landed on my hind end."

Three or twenty things raced through Boone's mind. He couldn't decide which to focus on, so he stood, slamming his hat on the parlor desk as he walked over to where Clementine sat. He pointed at her shoulder. "Show me."

She glanced away. "I'm fine."

"Show me the wound, Clementine."

She looked at him, one eyebrow inching up. "Mr. McCreery, are you asking me to disrobe for you? You do realize there are plenty of women down the street who would be happy to show you their wares for a modest price."

Boone narrowed his eyes. "Clementine," he warned with a growl.

She sighed. "Fine."

He waited as she took off her vest and then unbuttoned her wool shirt enough to be able to slip it off her shoulder, leaving only her chemise. She slid the cream-colored, lacy cloth down her arm, far enough that he caught a glimpse of the side of her breast as well as the bandage over the wound. The glimpse turned into a stare.

"Is this what you wanted to see, Boone?" she asked, her voice huskier than usual.

He swallowed, his throat suddenly dry, his attention consumed by the vision of creamy skin for a moment. Maybe a little longer.

Rabbit cleared his throat extra-loud.

Boone rolled his eyes toward the ceiling, then he glanced at the wall, then he focused on Tink. A wave of heat rose under his collar and climbed up his face, firing clear to the top of his scalp.

"Uh, yeah," he finally answered. Boone glanced at Rabbit, who was grinning at him, his head tipped to the side.

Knucklehead is loving this, damn it.

Boone looked back at Clementine. She was smiling, too. Or was she teasing him? Yeah, that was definitely a smirk. Well, hell. Two could play this game.

He held her gaze. "I like what I see," he said, schooling his expression.

Rabbit let out a bark of laughter.

Both of Clementine's eyebrows arched up. "Oh, do you?"

"Yep. The dressing on that wound is first rate." He let his gaze travel over her bared shoulder, noticing several faded scars. Augustine's blade was not the first to pierce her skin. Boone wondered where and how many other battle wounds she had, and what she'd do if he ... *Stop!*

He took a step back and circled his hand in the general area of her shoulder. "I approve of all that."

Clementine tugged her chemise and shirt back over her shoulder, her cheeks pinker than usual. "I'm certainly gladdened I meet your approval, Mr. McCreery."

He could think of several other ways she could make him even happier. "Hurt much?" he asked as she buttoned her shirt.

"It aches a little in the winter," she joked, reaching for her vest.

Rabbit snorted.

Smartass. Boone offered to help her with the vest, but she shook her head. He could see she wasn't going to show much weakness. He couldn't blame her. He wouldn't either—if he could help it.

Maybe a change of subject would be best. He turned toward the hallway, remembering that there was probably a man on the table in the examination room. "So. The man on your table. He's dead?"

"Now who's changing the direction of the conversation, Booney?" Rabbit was still grinning.

"Not dead," Clementine told Boone. "But he's not doing well, either. I've done what I can, now it's up to him."

"Have you talked to him? Asked him anything?"

"He's in and out."

"You tryin' to save him, Miss Clementine?" Rabbit frowned.

"I think so."

"Why in tarnation would you do that?" Rabbit pursed his lips. "Good for coyote feed, you ask me. Tried to kill us, didn't he?"

Boone was with Rabbit. He didn't feel much mercy for anyone trying to put him or his *compadres* permanently horizontal.

"Maybe. But I found this." She held up a locket on a chain.

"What's that?" Boone asked. "Was he wearing the sign? *Capersus.* A ring or tattoo or scar?"

"He's been branded on his upper arm," she told him.

"So what if he had a locket?" Rabbit growled.

"Is there something special about an arm brand?" Boone asked her. "Do you think that shows rank? Or dedication?" He'd seen the *caper-sus* symbol—both the curled- and curved-horn variety—as chest brands, as tattoos in various places on bodies, on signs posted on buildings, and of course on the rings that seemed to be everywhere.

"I think there's more to it in general, given what I've heard so far from the gentleman on my table."

Boone and Rabbit frowned at each other and then at Clementine.

"You talked to him?" Boone shot a glance toward the exam room.

"He talked to you?" Rabbit stood up.

"Yes and yes. He's been delirious, mostly." She rose and straightened her vest. "I should check on him. He's fighting infection from the knife wound." She gave Rabbit a small smile. "And also from the dog bite on his forearm."

Rabbit beamed at the sleeping Tink. "Got that bastard, didn't ya, Tink. Big bad Tinkerdoo."

Boone could hear the pride in Rabbit's voice. Truth told, he felt a little of it, too. The tough-as-nails, never-back-down-from-a-fight Tink was still making her way back from near death and the loss of her leg.

"Did he tell you anything?" he asked Clementine.

"He muttered something about *Grande Armeé*."

Rabbit made a face. "Grond ardamay?"

"*Grande Armeé*," she repeated. "It's French. It means a large or great army. I'm not sure if he meant he had been or is part of a great army or …" She trailed off.

"Did he say anything else?"

"Yes. He spoke of chaos. 'The chaos is arrived,' or was it chaos will descend? Something like that. He's difficult to understand, he drifts in and out of consciousness, and he's mixing at least three languages—English, French, and a language I'm not familiar with."

"Three languages." Boone rubbed his fingertips back and forth over his thigh. "Three? And you don't recognize the third?"

Clementine shook her head. "It's nothing I'm familiar with." She started toward the exam room. "Let's go see if our guest feels like discussing his predicament."

Boone followed but paused, waiting for Rabbit to catch up. "Listen," he said in a quiet voice. "We need answers from this character. Don't swagger in there like you own the place. Keep your temper. Know what I mean? Don't get your dander in a tizzy. You got to—"

"Booney, how many different ways you think you gotta say a thing? Settle in on an idea, then stick to it. You're confusing the young'uns." Rabbit winked at him as he sauntered toward the exam room.

Damned cuss. Boone snorted, following Rabbit. "I'll pin your ears back is what I'll do," he said under his breath.

In the examination room, Clementine was bending over a figure wrapped in muslin with rope turned around and around his body and the table, chest to ankles. Rabbit had told him true, they had secured the hell out of this guy.

He heard the tied-up man mumble something and then groan.

"You think it's a good idea to get so close?" Rabbit stopped on the opposite side of the table from Boone and Clementine. He frowned at each of them and then the wrapped man.

Boone tugged on one of the ropes.

"You better believe that rope is correct, Booney."

"Jack made sure of that."

Sounded like Rabbit. "Was he talking just now?" Boone leaned in closer.

"Only mumbles." She examined the spot of blood on the muslin over his stomach and nodded. "Okay, I think," she said quietly. "Tink's bite on his forearm is clean and healing. That leaves the knife injury in his upper abdomen. Somehow Jack missed the important stuff—the spleen, stomach, liver, lung."

"Gettin' better all the time." Rabbit leaned against the second examination table, crossed his arms, and glared at the mummy.

"How do you know the knife missed all those parts?" Boone peered at the unconscious man's face.

"He'd most probably be dead by now if any of those organs had been punctured. He actually has some color back in his face and he's been waking more often as the day goes on."

The man on the table moaned and began moving his head back and forth.

"He's waking up." Clementine grabbed a bottle from her apothecary case, uncorked it, and dabbed a little of the clear liquid onto a rag. She waved it near the injured man's nose. He immediately shook his head and his eyes opened wide.

"You're safe," Clementine told him.

"I wouldn't say that," Rabbit mumbled.

Boone shot him a shut-the-hell-up look.

Rabbit leered back and muttered to himself.

"Who are you?" she asked.

The man stared down at his mummified body and then at Clementine, his eyes wide with fear. "*Le général?*" he croaked.

"General? What general?"

"*Général Augustine.*" His voice was so hoarse Boone could barely make out the name.

Clementine turned to Boone.

"General?" he whispered.

"Yes. Jack, will you fetch a tin of water?" Clementine lifted the man's head and pushed a folded piece of muslin under his neck.

Rabbit disappeared into the hallway.

"What's your name?" Clementine inquired again.

The man winced and groaned when he took a breath. "René."

"René," she said his name softly. "Why were you taking bodies from the graveyard?"

"*Une … gran … de … ar …meé.*" His voice hitched several times.

Clementine again looked at Boone, her brow furrowed this time. "That's what he said before."

"You suspected that, right?" Boone whispered, not wanting to spook the gravedigger. "They are building a grand army. But who is in charge of the 'they' part? Your boss?"

Rabbit returned carrying a pitcher and a tin cup. He poured the tin half full and handed it to Clementine. "The skunk talking?"

"Hush," Boone said, but nodded.

Clementine held René's head up and poured water into his mouth. Most of it went down the sides of his face and onto the table, but a trickle made it into his gullet. He blinked.

"Who is gathering an army?" she asked.

René watched her but said nothing.

"Who was Augustine's master?"

René shook his head slowly.

"He's afraid." Boone could see the fear in his eyes.

"You fear Augustine?" she asked the digger.

"Wouldn't you?" Boone asked her. "I mean not *you.* Obviously you're not scared. I mean if you were this guy."

"Should be scared right now." Rabbit snatched a knife from his belt sheath and began flipping it in the air.

René's eyes grew round again.

"Rabbit, would you shut up."

"René," Clementine said. "Augustine is dead."

Boone watched as the gravedigger seemed to deflate, his muscles relaxing.

"Who was Augustine's master?" she asked again.

René shook his head.

Clementine reached into her pocket and withdrew the locket

and chain she'd shown to Boone and Rabbit earlier. "I found this in your pocket." She pulled on the locket with her thumb and it opened with a click.

Boone went up on his toes to look at it over her shoulder, wanting to see the picture inside. A dark-haired woman gazed up at him.

"Is this someone in your family? Your wife? Daughter?" Clementine turned it toward René.

He stared at the locket for a moment and then looked away, his eyes becoming glassy.

"What would she think? Digging up the deceased in a graveyard." Clementine moved the locket so that it was directly in front of his eyes.

Boone shot a look at Rabbit, who was staring at René and looking as perplexed as Boone felt.

"Tell me. How would she feel about you doing these things?" Clementine closed the locket and put it back in her pocket. "Digging up bodies. Defiling a graveyard."

Still no answer from the injured man.

"Let me guess your story." She folded her arms and began slowly circling the table. "You came to Deadwood to make your fortune. You work hard. You're a good man and you take care of your family." She stopped in front of a pensive-looking Rabbit and stared down at him for a moment.

Boone realized that she was telling this story for Rabbit's and his benefit as well.

Clementine resumed circling.

"But you arrived here to find that the tales you heard in the saloons, or read about in news sheets, or wherever else you might have heard them were simply not true. The streets are not paved with gold. In fact, there was no gold to be had at all. Not by you. But you had hope. And you fed your need to be a decent and good husband and father with that hope."

Boone watched tears well in René's eyes and then run down

the creases of his worn face. It was the face of a man who had always made up for any absence of luck or providence with simple, hard work. He knew the look. He saw it in the mirror often.

"Your hope has been swallowed up, consumed," continued Clementine, "by those who arrived before you, or those who are greedier or nastier than you could ever be. You had no other choice. Your wife is counting on you, and you feel as if you've failed."

René turned away from Clementine as she continued circling the table.

"So you joined with Augustine. He offered you what recompense? Not power. That's not who you are. It was compensation in currency. Wages. Pure and simple."

René whimpered softly and focused on the window. "If I had known," he whispered in a broken voice.

"We understand." Clementine's tone was soothing, yet coaxing.

"I would never defile ..." He gulped.

"Of course you wouldn't." Clementine shot Boone a glance.

He nodded. She was on the trail. He had expected the questions to be more confrontational. So had Rabbit, he knew. However, Rabbit's folded arms and cocked head told Boone that he wasn't ready to let go of the idea that there was a potentially dangerous *hombre* strapped to the table.

She stopped beside the exam table again. "Where were you taking the bodies, René?"

He squeezed his eyes tight. "*Grande Armée.* I try ... but ..." He shook his head.

Clementine backed away and motioned Boone and Rabbit to her. "I think someone has reached into his mind. He's fighting for control."

"Tarnation, Miss Clementine." Rabbit gawked at René.

"So, this is what you meant when you said we might be

attacked not only physically, but here, too." Boone pointed at his temple.

"Exactly." She returned to René's side and clapped her hands once near his face. "You must fight! Control your thoughts! Push aside the others in your mind!"

René opened his eyes and focused on Clementine. "Slagton. To Slagton. There are tunnels there. Caves, they say. I have not been." He squeezed his eyes shut and began convulsing, his whole body quaking.

"Rabbit, there!" Boone pointed at the opposite side of the table. They held René tight, Rabbit on one side, Boone on the other.

"René! *Kaste ut det onde!*" Clementine commanded.

The injured man shuddered and then relaxed.

Clementine looked at Boone and Rabbit. "I told him to cast out the evil."

"Appears it worked." Rabbit loosened his hold on their captive and took a step back. "In his head." He cursed. "You believe that shit, Booney? Fuckers are in his head."

René opened his eyes again.

"Augustine's master?" Clementine pressed.

Staring straight at the ceiling, René spoke in a monotone. "All that is precious will be put asunder." He squeezed his eyes shut again and began moaning, long and low.

"That's unnerving," Boone said as he moved away. "Like someone else was saying it."

"Sheeat. Is somebody else in there?" Rabbit backed up until his legs hit the desk. "What the hell does that mean? 'Precious'?"

"It could be in the general sense," Clementine said. "Like everything that anyone holds dear will be shattered. Destroyed. But my guess is that it's essentially a threat directed at him and those in his predicament. If he doesn't do as he's commanded, they'll destroy everything he cares about." Clementine grimaced at Rabbit and then Boone. "They'll kill him and his family."

"Well then, this guy is roasted like the last chicken in the coop on Sunday." Rabbit ran his finger across his throat. "If we don't kill him, the other *caper-sus* assholes will probably think he's a traitor now and toss him in the pigsty over at Kee Luk."

Boone didn't disagree, and judging from Clementine's nod, she didn't either.

"I'm going to try again." Clementine leaned over "René. Augustine's master? Tell me."

He grunted. "Slagton." He began to convulse again, his whole body shaking. "S… S… Slagton." He grabbed her arm. "*Méfiez-vous du mangeur de peau.*"

His body relaxed and his head lolled to the side.

"That's all we get. He's fainted again. I think." Clementine put the back of her hand under his nose. "Still breathing. Good."

"Well, what the hell does that mean?" Rabbit asked. "Was it French? What did he say? The way he grabbed your arm … it's bad, right?" He took a hesitant step toward the table and then stopped.

"Take it easy, Rabbit." Boone frowned down at the gravedigger. What the hell had he said? "It is bad, isn't it?"

"He warned us to be careful if we go to Slagton." She squeezed her hands together, chewing on her bottom lip.

Boone watched her. There was something she wasn't telling them, but he thought it better not to press. At least not yet.

"Now what?" Boone didn't really need to ask. He knew what came next. And he understood Clementine well enough now to know she was thinking the same thing. Slagton was in their future, and it was clear that Clementine wasn't happy about it. That meant he wasn't happy about it either.

He looked at his *amigo*, wondering what Rabbit was thinking. It probably had something to do with food.

Rabbit rubbed his belly, as if he'd heard Boone's thought. "I'm going to go get some vittles. Then I'm going to Slagton. Who's comin' along?"

Ten

Over the last few weeks, Clementine had become adept at slinking unseen through the side door of The Dove and into Hildegard's private parlor whenever a clandestine meeting was necessary. Entering through the brothel's front door more than once every few days for a bath could garner unwanted attention. In particular, it was imperative that Masterson not learn of the liaison between the madam of The Dove and Clementine for the sake of Hildegard's health.

This afternoon, both Dmitry and Alexey were missing from the kitchen when she passed through. That meant the olfactory treat of freshly baked bread or sushki or pierogi—or whatever else the two Russian cooks stirred up as hearty sustenance for Hildegard's girls of the line—was also absent. Instead, a lone kettle of soup simmered on the hot stove. Clementine couldn't recall either of the Russians ever taking a day for themselves, but they had to, didn't they? At least once in a while? Odd, though, that Hildegard didn't have them stagger their days off.

Hildegard greeted her as graciously as always, sitting her down in one of the green velvet chairs next to her small woodstove and serving her impeccably good tea. Yet, she was distant. Or more like distracted. Her willowy frame seemed stiff under her dark violet gown. Her blond hair was curiously untidy, as if she'd been standing out in the cold wind for a time, and her pale skin looked flushed.

Clementine didn't bother with small talk. They were far beyond that now. "The twins' absence is more noticeable than I would have expected."

Hildegard nodded, a faint smile flitting across her face. "The wonderful aromas that usually emanate from the kitchen are greatly missed by all here. That alone secures their employment. Their other skills are welcome additions."

"Both men are taking the day off from The Dove?"

"You might say that." Hildegard shifted in her chair. "There are new stirrings this morning. I am unsure if it is my doing or yours."

It didn't escape Clementine that Hildegard shifted the conversation as well as her body position. What had the madam so distressed? She decided to move straight to her reason for coming today in order to leave Hildegard to whatever was troubling her. "You're familiar with the gravediggers in my employ? Ling and Gart?"

"*Ja, natürlich,*" Hildegard answered quickly in German. Then she gasped and covered her mouth. Lowering her hand, she repeated, "Yes, of course," in clear English.

Clementine sat back in the chair, frowning at Hildegard. She knew that Clementine spoke German as well as several other languages, so her reaction to using her native tongue seemed suspect. Something had the madam flustered.

In spite of Hildegard's apparent distress, Clementine continued. "These two have made it known to me that there are goings-on at the graveyard. They're afraid to venture anywhere near it after sunset."

"It is a natural development, given what we suspected."

"I suppose it's mostly confirmed now." Clementine watched Hildegard tap-tap-tap on the side of her teacup. "I decided to investigate the cemetery last night, and it was as you and I had thought. The dead are being claimed. I took Jack Fields with me. And Tinker, that darned dog, who led Augustine straight to us. In the ensuing fight, he was killed." She grimaced as she admitted, "Accidentally."

Hildegard arched one blond eyebrow.

"I know. I was careless. Negligent, even."

"It is …" Hildegard hesitated, apparently searching for the proper word, "Uncharacteristic of *ein Scharfrichter* to *accidentally* do … well … anything."

Clementine sighed. "That may be. But it's done. Unfortunately, we were unable to gather any information from him before his death, except the threat of genocide across this territory and a reference to some greater 'he.' " This time both of Hildegard's eyebrows lifted. "It sounded to me as if Augustine was implying a direct connection between himself and the architect of this insurrection. But logic leads me to doubt that he was anything more than an underling."

"*Ein Emporkömmling*," Hildegard said, returning to the name she had used in the past for the pompous, imperious horse's ass.

"Exactly. Yet again he displayed Napoleonic tendencies, including lengthy orations full of grandeur, so it would stand to reason that he was somewhat delusional concerning his position and rank."

"It is time to determine who is behind this," Hildegard said. "We must also find out how Masterson means to defend himself."

"Agreed." Clementine wanted to find out where exactly Masterson stood in the midst of all this. She was contracted to do a job, but he'd not been specific about her duties.

"As I said before." Hildegard frowned into her teacup. "I believe him to be untrustworthy. Even deceitful. Make no mistake, he will do what he deems necessary to protect his charge, including sacrificing you and your friends."

Clementine concurred with the madam's opinion of

Masterson. "The opportunity to learn any truths is lost with Augustine, but we did manage to keep one of his grave-digging minions alive. He is currently convalescing at The Pyre." René had been in a deep sleep when she'd left, which she believed would last for several hours thanks in part to the tincture she'd given him.

"Has this minion revealed anything useful to us?"

"Well, he couldn't manage to name Augustine's master, but he mentioned Slagton and verified the bodies were being taken there. At one point he also confirmed that the dead have been taken from other graveyards, as well. If he was telling the truth—and my gut says that he was—it's likely a significant number have been taken to Slagton."

Hildegard's teacup rattled in the saucer when she set it on the table between them. "Ludek has reported that there have been disturbances in that area."

Ludek acted as a spy for the madam, but his expertise was not in watching humans, but rather watching *others*—including *ein Scharfrichter* such as herself … and the Rogue. Clementine had not actually met Ludek, only seen glimpses of him out of the corner of her eye. At least she assumed it was him.

"Speaking of Ludek." Clementine set her cup down as well. "He hasn't relayed any of this to you already?" Clementine was accustomed to Ludek consistently being two steps ahead of her.

"He's been addressing some issues for Miss Hundt and me. I expect him to return very soon."

Clementine nodded. Maybe that was what had Hildegard so agitated. "Augustine's minion was also able to warn us about what he called '*Méfiez-vous du mangeur de peau*.' "

Hildegard's eyes grew round. "Oh my. *Beware the eaters of skin?* That is news, indeed."

"I haven't had much time to think about it, but I'm sure you recall that in our hunt for the *Höhlendrache*, we happened upon a cabin with four dead inhabitants."

"I most certainly recall. Miss Hundt and I have discussed it at length, although much of the conversation digressed to reminiscence." Hildegard smoothed her dress over her thighs. "As you know, many, *many* years ago, we resided in Germany, the Black Forest. We, and a few comrades along with us, were forced to deal with an insurgence much like the one happening here now."

Clementine wondered how many times Hildegard and Miss Hundt had been in this position. Had they worked with another *Scharfrichter* in the past? How many had they known in their time?

"Our vocation often exposes us to beings that don't have our best interest in mind." Hildegard's face lined. "Miss Hundt and I believe what you came across were the remains of a successful hunt."

Clementine shuddered. What kind of creature would skin its prey?

Hildegard stared at her lap. "So many similarities are appearing between the Black Forest and the Black Hills."

Judging by the sorrowful frown on Hildegard's face, it was clear that certain similarities with the Black Forest were bad news.

"I've not come across anything like that," Clementine said quietly.

"Miss Hundt and I have. A foul, vulgar business. It concerns me to think that it has found its way here."

"What has?"

Hildegard reached across the small table between them and clutched Clementine's forearm. "It's been known by different names depending on culture and time, but I know it as *Fhain-hai*. The tomes say it is descended from the joining of an *other* from the Black Forest region and a human suffering from madness. The offspring may inherit the traits of either or both, but most often acquire the baser qualities of the two. From the former, savagery, cruelty, rancor. From the human, cleverness, resilience, empathy. Occasionally, although it's said to be rarely, the *Fhain-hai* inherits the undesirable traits of both—such as the madness. I believe that is what we are facing in the forest near Slagton."

Clementine cursed. "Are you certain of this?"

"No, but I do know that the *Fhain-hai* that plagued our village in the Black Forest took many lives. In each case, it skinned the victim. It ate some of the skins, but left most, like those you happened upon at the cabin."

They had found four bodies at that cabin, but only three piles of skin. One skin had been missing. "Why? Why would it remove the skin but not eat it?"

Hildegard stood and walked over to the large china hutch filled with teacups, porcelain figures, and books. "It is believed that *Fhain-hai* find the taste of *others'* skin preferable to that of humans," she said, toying with a smoldering stick of incense that had her private room smelling of jasmine today. "I'm not sure, but what you found in the forest would seem to support that myth. If I were to guess, it—being a greedy creature—skinned them with the intent to eat them all, but found that human skin was palatable only to the extent that it could assuage its hunger."

"So, it ate one and left the rest," Clementine said.

"*Ja.* Like eating a green apple. If you're hungry enough, you eat it no matter how tart you find its flesh. Then again, it might be that the *Fhain-hai* is driven by cruelty and wanted them to suffer. You see, it skins them while they are still—"

"I get the idea." Clementine had witnessed the results of the carnage first-hand. "But how do you know this is the creature from Germany?"

"As I said, I don't. But its method is quite similar." Hildegard returned to her chair next to the stove, but didn't sit. "And there is another reason."

"Yes?"

"We attempted to kill the *Fhain-hai* that plagued our village, but it was quick and powerful. More than that, though, it was extremely clever. We tried to lure it, surround it, flush it out. Nothing worked. After weeks of planning, we set a trap, but it puzzled out our plan and escaped at the last minute. I suppose our efforts worked in a way, since the creature didn't return after that."

Clementine frowned up at her. "Neither of those details really explains why you think this is the same one."

"It's a feeling. When you are in a contest with an adversary, you become aware of its … what would you call it … style, perhaps. The way it thinks. The way it moves. It left me and Miss Hundt with the distinct notion that it wasn't done with us. The creature knew that the two of us were the ones responsible for trying to kill it." She kneaded her hands. "In any case, it doesn't really matter if it is the same one or not, except that it might possibly be hunting Miss Hundt and …" She trailed off, pointing her thumb at her chest.

"Well, now you have a *Scharfrichter* in your camp." Actually, they had two, counting the damned Rogue.

"As we did then," Hildegard said, the worry lines back between her brows.

A *Fhain-hai*. The hair on Clementine's neck was standing at attention at the mere thought of such a fiend, but it wasn't spurred by fear, rather by revulsion. She needed to rid the Hills of this abomination that would skin a human, *other*, or any …

"Tell me about the graveyard," Hildegard said, grabbing the teapot from its trivet on the top of the stove.

Clementine wrinkled her upper lip. "*Draug.*"

"More tea?" She poured when Clementine held her cup toward her. "It saddens me that some choose this path, but it does not surprise me."

"I'd sooner face a pack of *Drakona ragana* than a host of *Draug* again." Clementine lifted the cup to her mouth and blew on the steaming liquid. The blend had a sweet hint of orange today. She needed to find out which store in Chinatown Hildegard frequented.

Hildegard tilted her head slightly. "You've battled a sub-species of *chimera*?" At Clementine's nod, she said, "Perhaps one day we'll share a drink or two and you can tell me about that."

Clementine lifted her cup in a mock toast. "Make it wine from southern France and we have a date."

"So you didn't confirm the one responsible for Augustine's digging party." Hildegard replaced the kettle and settled back into her chair.

"No."

"Unfortunate."

"Yes." Clementine frowned down at her tea. "I don't know Masterson that well, but my sense is that *Draug* aren't his method."

Hildegard sighed. "We need to know what he is up to."

"Agreed. Masterson doesn't—or at least hasn't yet—confided in me. He was upset when we cleared out the Bloody Bones, so I suspect the *Bahkauv* were his doing. If so, *whoops*. Beyond that, I'm unsure."

They both sipped their teas in silence for a moment, until a soft knock at the door dragged them from their thoughts.

"Yes?" Hildegard turned her head toward the door.

"Ja, meine Dame." Clementine recognized the gravelly voice of The Dove's bouncer, Jurgen. *"Die Russen sind zurückgekehrt."*

"Danke, Jurgen. Schick ihn rein," Hildegard called back.

Clementine clapped. "The Russians are back. Let the baskets of bread be passed from table to table and all will rejoice, especially my stomach."

Hildegard chuckled. "It might be a while before that bread is ready. They'll most likely want to bathe first."

"There's no time for bathing. Bread first!" Clementine shook her finger in the air.

"Hear, hear!"

"So, where have Alexey and Dmitry been that they'd need to

bathe before baking?"

Hildegard's smile faded slightly. "Galena."

"You sent the Russians there?" Hildegard's nod prompted her to ask, "Why?"

She, Hank, and the Sidewinders had cleared out that saloon in Galena. Maybe it had to do with the flesh eater.

Another knock at the door interrupted them. This time, there was a certain pattern to the knocking—three fast bangs in a row and then one more after a pause.

Hildegard popped out of her chair and rushed to the door. "Come in," she said breathlessly, pulling it wide.

A long-legged, slim man dressed in black from head to toe strode into the room. His white hair hung down past his shoulders, his strong, angular face a mixture of crags and ridges. Clementine had seen a similar face before, deep in the Bloody Bones mine, only that "white devil" had tried to gut her.

In a blink, Clementine sprang from the chair. She grabbed the *other* and spun him around, lifting his chin toward the ceiling with one hand while squeezing his throat with the other.

"Stop!" The terror in Hildegard's voice startled Clementine. "Clementine! Please! This is Ludek!"

Ludek?

She released him, but kept her hands up, ready to strike. Her body was rigid with adrenaline, reacting on instinct to his kind.

"This is Ludek?" Clementine didn't wait for Hildegard's confirmation. "Why is he …? Where did …? But he's a …" *ein weißer Hund,* she finished in her head, which translated to "white dog" in English.

The madam's eyes were still wide with fear.

Clementine lowered her guard and stepped back. "My apologies," she told Ludek. "Your look is similar to that of the white devil who tried to slice me in half in the Bloody Bones."

Ludek bent over and coughed several times. When he stood upright again, he cleared his throat and extended his hand. "It is a pleasure to meet you finally, Miss Johanssen."

The back of Clementine's neck still bristled. Her afi's teachings flitted through her memory. His persistence had driven restraint, caution, and control into her very being: *Do not establish friendships on a notion. Trust is not a thing to be given out impulsively as one would to a lamb or dog.* But what about a "white dog"?

According to what Hildegard had told Clementine before, Ludek's kind were often used as a type of guard dog. They were well known in the Black Forest region for their loyalty and ferocity, which would explain the madam's choice in hiring him to be her eyes and ears around town. Although, judging by the way Hildegard had reacted to Clementine's response to the sight of Ludek, their relationship seemed to have more depth than merely master and hound.

"I'm sorry, Ludek," she said as she shook his hand. "My profession necessitates caution."

"As does mine. There is no need to apologize. I understand your position."

Per Hildegard's instructions, Clementine knew, Ludek had been keeping an eye on her since she'd arrived in Deadwood, along with many of the other players in this deadly game. Ludek knew more about what she was facing than perhaps anyone else. Well, anyone other than the Rogue.

"It's good to finally meet you face to face," she told him. "Although I imagine you might feel as if you know me after these months of observation."

"That is true."

"I could have used your help in the pigsty." She grimaced at the memory.

"I do apologize, but that was not my charge." He looked down at her hands. "I had every confidence that you would command the situation."

"Would you care to have a seat, Ludek?" Hildegard held her hand out toward one of the chairs by the stove. "I'm sure you haven't had the opportunity to rest for some time."

"Thank you, but no, Hildegard," he said, his gaze lingering on the madam.

Clementine watched the small smile Hildegard sent him. Even more interesting was his use of her first name. Not surprising, she supposed, even if there was nothing more between them than friendship. They'd probably been through some trials together over the years, especially if he was around when the skin eater was hunting her in the Black Forest region.

"Let me get you a cup of tea, then. I can do that much, at least." Hildegard headed to the china hutch and grabbed a cup and saucer.

"Thank you." He leaned against the door, so still he looked like a sentry made of white marble.

Clementine wondered where he'd come from today. When she'd had his throat in her hands, she'd smelled fresh snow and evergreens on his coat, as well as horseflesh and grain. He'd also smelled of things that were harder to discern. Blood, yes, along with many smells she associated with *others*. He'd remained calm in her grip, his pulse steady under her fingertips, his breath even, which led her to believe he had a strong sense of determination rather than fear.

"Interesting," she thought again, only aloud this time.

"What do you find interesting?" Hildegard handed a full cup of tea to Ludek before turning a raised brow in her direction.

Clementine decided to answer candidly. "I sensed no fear in you, Ludek. Even now, you know what I am and what I can do, yet you have a steady hand and calm demeanor. I'm not accustomed to that." Especially from someone she'd nearly slain moments before.

A bubble of laughter came from Hildegard.

"Thank you, Miss Johanssen." Ludek dipped his head and then sipped his tea, but said nothing further.

Hildegard returned to the chair by the stove, waiting for

Clementine to sit back down beside her before saying, "It's no surprise you are accustomed to sensing fear. Those familiar with the duties of *ein Scharfrichter* would normally display unease in your company, I'm sure."

"That doesn't explain Ludek's lack of trepidation."

"Miss Johanssen," he said, joining the discussion. "I know fully well that your kind are a threat to my existence. As for you personally, over the last few months I've witnessed your innate abilities and your tendency to shoot from the hip, if you will. I am also aware of the dangers inherent in associating with *ein Scharfrichter.*"

Clementine watched him over the rim of her teacup as she sipped the sweet, hot liquid.

At her silence, he continued. "While I am no Slayer, I have seen things that would make you tremble. I have done things that would make you cringe."

"Do not forget my role as Deadwood's undertaker through the heat of the smallpox summer."

He smirked. "Perhaps not cringe, then. But I have seen many things through the years, and I've become inured to the irrational, the outrageous, and the senseless behavior of both humans and *others,* and even hybrids such as yourself."

His dispassionate expression as he spoke told a tale of its own. He was a fellow killer, and Clementine decided right there and then that she liked him, white dog or not.

She crossed her arms. "Then I imagine the existence of a *Fhain-hai* in the Black Hills doesn't have any effect on your sensibilities."

Ludek shuddered. "You are wrong on that count. That is quite disturbing. It is unfortunate that one—or more—have arrived here." He looked at Hildegard, his gaze hooded.

"Tell us of your trip to Galena," Hildegard said. "I'm sure Clementine will be interested to hear."

"As you wish." His lips curled up at the corners. "But let me first verify that you believe those Russian twins to be stable. You have stated this much in the past. Is it still your opinion?"

Laugh lines crinkled the corners of Hildegard's eyes. "Of course."

Clementine had a feeling that they were continuing an ongoing debate.

"If you believe it, then I question your sanity as well." Ludek looked at Clementine with a gleam in his eye. "And you, Miss Johanssen?"

"Call me Clementine, please."

"Fine. Clementine, what is your opinion of Alexey and Dmitry?"

"I think they can fill a plate with food for which I'd kill. Literally." She avoided answering his true question, not wanting to ruin any future chances of eating in their kitchen.

Ludek nodded. "You would find little argument on that point. But those two men together can strum a nerve like no other pair I've met. Ever. The constant bickering." He sighed. "I'm sure this is nothing new to either of you."

Clementine couldn't argue. Sibling rivalry and a competition to secure the rights to maternal favoritism seemed to fuel their non-stop squabbling.

Ludek set his teacup down on a small side table and started to pace the room. "But I must add, I'd want no others by my side in a fight, present company excluded. The knifework displayed by those two—magnificent."

"There was a confrontation, then?" Hildegard asked.

"Yes. But a few laggards remained. Human zealots and two *Bahkauv* in the mine above the town. No *Höhlendrache*, fortunately. Those creatures are within the purview of *ein Scharfrichter*, not mine."

Clementine nodded. "They are deadly menaces."

"Your so-called Sidewinder crew was efficient. And the *capersus* tidied the drinking establishment, thoroughly."

Clementine and the Santa Fe duo had seen that for themselves. The following morning, there had been no trace of the exchange that had taken place the night prior. Was it fourteen? No, it was twelve. All traces of those twelve humans that Rabbit and Boone had dispatched in fairly short order were completely removed. Augustine had escaped that time, but only temporarily.

"The saloon was clean by the following morning," Clementine told him.

"I do not believe that was the work of humans," Ludek told them. "Humans always leave something behind. The Frenchman must have alerted the vassal."

Vassal? Was Ludek conjuring a medieval knight?

Clementine took another sip of tea. "The Rogue informed me that the vassal, whom she called a 'lieutenant,' had left minutes before my arrival at the saloon in Galena. I would gather that he's still alive." Unless the Rogue had hunted him down and taken care of him.

Ludek nodded.

"You killed all *caper-sus* in Galena then?" Hildegard asked him.

"We left one. He was badly burned from head to waist. We were unsure whether or not to slay him. In a moment of heightened empathy, I decided to let him live. Perhaps he will serve as warning to other humans who choose the *caper-sus* way."

Badly burnt? Could it be the bartender that Boone had … Wait a minute! "Did you say 'Sidewinder crew'?"

Dear Odin! How far had Jack spread that moniker?

Ludek smirked, holding still for a moment. "The Rogue approached me not long after the affair in Galena. That was the term she used for them."

Hildegard gaped at him. "The Rogue approached *you*?"

"Yes. She demanded that I stop interfering with what she called her *essential duties*. She was quite adamant."

"She was upset with the fact that you were observing her,"

Clementine presumed.

She wasn't surprised that the Rogue would make the demand. She had come close to doing the same thing. It was unnerving to have a living shadow. But it was also unnerving that the Rogue actually believed she had *essential duties* here in the Hills.

"Correct. My opinion would be that she takes some pleasure in dispatching human chattel, as well as *others*. I apologize for using that term," he said to both of them, "but that is how human *caper-sus* are viewed by *others*. Property." He resumed pacing. "I think the Rogue considers any *caper-sus* as a supplicant. Human, *other*, or creature, begging at the feet of the master. Whether they may be redeemable or not, I don't believe it makes any difference to your colleague."

Hildegard crossed her arms. "Have you stopped following her?"

"Of course. I value my life. I know my limitations and she did not mince words."

"Why didn't you tell me this before?" She glared at Ludek.

"I don't tell you everything." His chest visibly rose and fell. "And I have been particularly busy lately. Following Clementine. Following the Rogue. Cleaning up Galena. Gallivanting through the forest." He fluttered his hand into the air.

"Yes, yes. I understand." Hildegard's voice leveled out. "Did you find the cabin that Clementine mentioned?"

He nodded once. "All traces of humans and creatures were gone. No signs of ..." he grimaced, "... skin. There was no indication that anything was ever amiss in that location. It had snowed since Clementine was there, so that might cover bloodstains, but I believe the blood-stained snow was removed."

"That was to be expected." Hildegard scowled. "And the *Höhlendrache?*"

"There was no sign of it, either. Perhaps we were in the wrong location, but that is doubtful. Clementine's description was detailed." Ludek turned to her, hesitating before adding, "In the future, it would be wise for you, *ein Scharfrichter*, to make the kill if the victim is not human. If our adversaries are allowed to retrieve their dead, matters could be made worse."

Clementine's afi had warned her of that very thing. It was the Slayer's responsibility—even duty—to do the job properly. If *others* were allowed to retrieve the fallen, rituals could be performed that would result in dangerous, grotesque abominations.

"Did you find anything of interest in the mine behind Galena?" Clementine was sure that someone had been keeping the *Höhlendrache* there as a pet, or for some more sinister reason.

"The Russians and I investigated the tunnels to some depth and found evidence that multiple *Höhlendrache* were being held captive there in the past."

"Were the tunnels man-made?" Hildegard asked.

"I did not witness any natural cave formations leading …" He pointed at the floor.

"A cage, then," the madam said.

"That seems likely, although once we determined there had been and still could be multiple *Höhlendrache* roaming the tunnels, we retreated hastily." He looked at Clementine. "And I feel no shame in admitting it."

Clementine chuckled. "So, when you say 'to some depth'?"

"I had no desire to come upon or mount an attack on multiple *Höhlendrache*, so the venture was not as extensive as it could have been had you been present. The Russians concurred wholeheartedly with my decision to retreat."

Clementine sobered at the realization that there were potentially multiple *Höhlendrache* roaming the Hills, as well as an army of *caper-sus* and *Draug*. And if those weren't troubling enough menaces, add to them the possibility of more than one skin-eating *Fhain-hai*.

Verdammt! She squeezed the bridge of her nose. By the gates of Asgard, this was turning into a damned Viking saga!

Eleven

Clementine could hear Hank now. *A full belly does wonders for the disposition.* That was his assessment for most situations, and she tended to agree. A good soaking in warm water usually helped, too, which was why she had taken Hildegard up on her offer of a bath after Ludek had left her quarters.

While washing the smell of death from her hair and skin, Clementine had pondered Ludek's unsettling news and Hildegard's chilling story about the skin eater. She would have lingered in the hot bath water to warm her bones, but Alexey's and Dmitry's handiwork had the first floor of The Dove smelling of freshly baked biscuits and roasted meat. Clementine struggled not to drool as she toweled off and dressed.

The twins remained tight-lipped about their excursion into the forest, so she talked with them about their journey from Russia and how they came to the Black Hills. It appeared they had known Hildegard and Miss Hundt much longer than she had suspected, even as far back as their days in eastern Europe.

After leaving the warmth and safety of The Dove, Clementine strolled along the bustling boardwalk toward The Pyre in no particular hurry. The late afternoon sunshine was slipping down behind the dark hills, the clear sky foretelling of another cold, starry night to come.

She kept her eyes focused on the boards near her feet, glancing up only occasionally to watch the spectacle of a thriving gold town. Women in thick coats lifted their ruffled and pleated dresses to cross the slushy, muddy street. Men in vests, garret coats, and top hats sauntered to their destinations. Flea- and tick-infested mountain men with beards and hair so thick it was difficult to make out their faces through the scraggly, hairy mess trudged along with dreams and intentions known only to them. There were those, and everything in between.

The sheer number of people out and about was a sight to behold. The town was bursting at the seams with humanity, and it reeked like it, as well.

Occasionally, Clementine would look up to catch a glimpse of some oddity. Anything more than a quick look, though, and she'd incur a cutting remark concerning her profession as a death dealer, or choice in men's clothing, or her tall mannish stature, or even her potential to deliver a good poke. While her skin was plenty thick when it came to dealing with such rude comments, she wasn't in the mood to suffer nosy fools this afternoon. One well-aimed comment just might result in her fist slamming said nose into their pea-sized brain.

Her thoughts returned to Augustine and last night's events at Ingleside Cemetery. It would have been good to question the pompous blowhard, but Jack's enthusiasm had precluded that. At least René …

"Troll's blood!" She had completely forgotten about René. Her business with Hildegard, Ludek, the Russian twins, and hot water had kept her distracted through the afternoon.

Bentley, the owner of the tin shop next to The Pyre, leaned into the broom as he swept snow from the boardwalk in front of his window display of shovels and gold pans. He grimaced at her from under his bushy eyebrows. She hustled past him before he could comment, pulling out her key for the front door.

The air inside her parlor was chilly. She could smell the raw alcohol she'd used to clean her exam equipment earlier. The fires had died down and the cold dampness that went hand in hand with the deepening shadows had soaked through the building, extinguishing both heat and light.

"I'm here, René," she called out in case he was lying awake in the dark. "I'll stoke the …"

Clementine froze, the hairs on the back of her neck bristling. She darted to the side of the room, pressing her back against the wall. The heavy shadows dulled her sight, but her hearing was working overtime. The stove ticked as it cooled. The breeze whistled through the cracks in the doorframe. Across the street a player piano was plinking out a bouncy tune. Across the room a chair creaked.

"Greetings, Undertaker."

Clementine knew that voice. She sighed in relief. "Rogue."

The sound of wool sliding over leather followed. "I believe I've made it clear I find that term vulgar."

"It seems fitting to me."

"So be it. I would expect no better treatment from an undertaker."

"It appears as though the bad manners you exhibited in Galena are typical of your character. Why are you in my parlor?"

Clementine moved along the wall to her desk and lit the lantern sitting there. The yellow flame pushed the shadows to the corners of the room, illuminating her guest with an eerie glow.

To the inexperienced, the Rogue appeared as did many in Deadwood—leather boots, worn canvas trousers, woolen overcoat, and deformed knitted hat. She wore the same scarf she'd had in Galena, wrapped around and around, concealing everything from her collarbones to her bottom lip.

"No offer of hospitality, then?"

Clementine crossed to the stove and squatted to open it, mere inches away from the Rogue, who lounged in one of her leather chairs.

"My hospitality is limited in extent to the respect I am afforded by my guests. Again, what are you doing here?"

There was something about the Rogue that made Clementine's nerves poke through her skin. One of her afi's favorite warnings came to mind: *The bear may be sleeping, but it is always best to stay clear of the cave.*

"I would dearly love a *tasse de thé*," the Rogue said, asking for a cup of tea in French. "So long as it isn't tainted with the nettle leaves you uncultured Northerners are so fond of."

"You should have stoked the fire if you wanted tea. Now, you'll have to wait." Clementine knocked the ash from the remnants of coals in the stove with the poker, threw in a few wedges of wood, and slammed the iron door shut. She stood and wiped her hands off before planting them on her hips. "Why are you here, Rogue? And don't tell me it was to stop by for some *menthe* tea served alongside a silver tray filled with butter croissant sandwiches and lemon madeleines."

"I prefer the title of *tueuse*, or *Slayer* if that is easier for you."

Both rolled off the tongue more smoothly than *Scharfrichter*, but a killer was a killer, no matter the language. "Quit stalling," Clementine said.

The Rogue crossed her legs and clasped her hands together over her knee. "I presume you continue to neglect your duties." She stared pointedly at the half-finished knitted scarf Hank had left on Clementine's desk.

She was looking forward to wearing that scarf. Hank was using some of the softest yarn she'd ever had the pleasure to rub against her face. "That's …" she began, but then thought better. She owed the Rogue no explanation.

Then, she remembered the note this "Slayer" had left for her at The Dove. It ranked as one of the most condescending and contemptuous things to ever have been directed at her. And the author now sat in her parlor and presumed to take up the banner of disrespect again.

Clementine took a deep breath, pushing aside the urge to wrap her hands around the Rogue's scrawny neck. "Making presumptions is a bad habit."

"Not in this case, I believe. Many of my presumptions are based on observations, and my observations indicate that you are incapable of the task for which you've been contracted."

Not this dance again. "That's—"

"Nevertheless," the Rogue interrupted. "Unfortunate as the situation may be, I find myself in a position that requires your ..." The Rogue hesitated. "Attention."

Clementine raised an eyebrow and waited.

"I need ... you to ..." the Rogue stammered.

"Spit it out, Rogue."

She huffed. "You are familiar with the infestation currently plaguing Gayville, are you not?"

"I'm familiar."

Clementine knew that *Bahkauv* were roaming in the area and had slaughtered several of the citizens living there. She knew that she, the Sidewinders, and Hank had killed many of them inside the Bloody Bones and then sealed up the mine so any remaining *Bahkauv* would be trapped inside the oversized coffin. She also knew that miners had re-dug the tunnels and were working their way farther into the earth, far deeper than they had before.

"Are you aware they have spread to Blacktail?" The Rogue waited until Clementine shook her head. "Golden Gate? Anchor City?"

Clementine wasn't aware of that. She was aware that the number of deaths in the Bloody Bones had been escalating, but knew nothing about the problem spreading to nearby mining camps. How could the *Bahkauv* infestation advance so quickly? "What evidence is there to support that?"

The Rogue shook her head. "You think I come here on impulse? You insult me."

Good. Clementine owed her a wagonful before they were

even.

"I have labored endlessly to eradicate the *Bahkauv,* but I have not succeeded at holding in check the flood of creatures spilling from that mine." She stood, facing Clementine, who loomed over her. "With what foolish dalliance do you occupy your time while I toil in the field? Tutoring your cohorts? The menial labor of carpentry? Hobnobbing in houses of ill repute?" Her lips pursed as if she'd bitten into a sour fruit. "Bathing therein?"

Son of a … Was the Rogue watching her every move? "It's difficult to believe that you've been toiling in the field, yet you know all of these things about me."

"I am exceedingly more efficient than you."

Clementine couldn't help but smile. She was *exceedingly* insufferable, too. "Do you know anything of the *Draug* army being assembled in Slagton?"

The Rogue's furrowed brow was confirmation that she knew nothing about it.

"Or that graveyards are being plundered in the area?"

"Of course graveyards are being robbed. How else would one build an army of *Draug?*" The Rogue's reply dripped with smug self-assuredness.

Clementine clenched her fists. *Strength in serenity.* She shucked her coat and threw it at the coat tree by the door. The tree teetered, almost tipped over, and then settled with the coat hanging neatly from the top peg.

"Not that it is any of your business," she told the Rogue, "but I surprised and killed a group of grave robbers last night." There was no need to mention Jack's part in it. She could imagine what fodder that would be for the condescending bitch.

"A modicum of success. Good. You're making progress."

"And I killed Augustine, the 'lieutenant,' as you called him."

"*Bien.* It should have been done in Galena. But the other lieutenant charged with overseeing Galena still lives, does he not? The one you were too late to execute?"

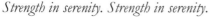

Strength in serenity. Strength in serenity.

Clementine didn't want to admit that she wasn't sure where this "other" lieutenant was at the moment.

"You don't know where he is, do you?" The Rogue appeared to be a mind reader, as well, damn it.

Clementine squinted. "Why are you—oh hell!" She'd forgotten about René again. "Excuse me." She rushed into the exam room and lit the lantern.

"No need to hurry," the Rogue called from the parlor. "Your captive is dead."

Clementine held the lantern near René's face. Blood still oozed from a fresh wound under his chin and dripped onto the table through the short whiskers covering the side of his jaw.

"He was *caper-sus*," the Rogue said, standing in the doorway of the exam room.

Clementine slammed her hand on the table next to René's head. "He was a man! And he was turning away from *caper-sus*."

"He was *caper-sus*," the Rogue repeated in a bored tone.

"He was providing me with information about the *Draug* in Slagton!" Clementine took a step toward the Rogue, her chest tight along with her fists.

"You have a temper, Slayer. You must learn to control it." The Rogue inspected her nails.

How many times had Clementine heard those words growing up? But still …

"You come to *my* territory and meddle in *my* business with no thought to the consequences." She spoke through gritted teeth. "You have no edict and no contract. Your actions threaten to upset the balance. I told you all of this in Galena, yet you continue to disrupt the order." She took a deep breath, preparing to continue her tirade.

"Your help is needed," the Rogue stated.

"Wha … what?" Clementine deflated slightly.

"Your help is needed in the Golden Echo mine. Or the

Bloody Bones, as you like to call it."

"No. Why? No." Her mind and tongue stumbled momentarily until she got her feet back under her. "No. I told you. Someone is assembling a *Draug* army in Slagton. I need to put a stop to that as soon as possible."

"Nonsense. There are *Bahkauv* massing around the Golden Echo. That is the primary threat."

Clementine scoffed. "*Bahkauv* are nothing more than trained dogs."

"*Draug* are walking dead. Brainless sacks of ambulatory flesh." The Rogue sauntered to the window, parted the curtains, and gazed out at the goings-on in the street. "Chattel," she added.

Ludek had said something similar. Currently, Clementine wasn't sure whether the Rogue was referring to the citizens of Deadwood or the *Draug* in Slagton.

If legend held, *Draug* weren't particularly dangerous, not to someone familiar with a weapon. She had thought back on that day—the day of decay—more than she'd liked of late. She had finally come to the realization that her afi had chosen the means of her initiation well. *Draug* were known to move slowly. The *Draug* in the village were no exception. They died easily and quickly. The danger they presented was plague. To a human settlement, for instance a mining camp full of unsuspecting and unarmed humans, *Draug* would be deadly. Some would be claimed simply because they didn't believe what was happening. Others would be rendered incapacitated by fear or shock. A horde of *Draug* would sweep over them like wind over green wheat. There would be little left, save rotting flesh and the *other* that commanded them. If any escaped, the disease and decay spread by the foul creatures would eventually catch up. It was a contemptible, abhorrent act, raising *Draug*, that much Clementine had learned very well. The compulsion for revenge on those who would do it was strong in her, overwhelmingly so.

The Rogue turned to her. "Have you finally reached the

correct conclusion?"

"Yes, I have. *Draug* in sufficient numbers would sweep across this settlement in less than a day. The citizens here would be slaughtered and disease would spread, unfettered. I've got to stop it before they are unleashed."

"Would that be such a terrible thing?"

"If you are attempting to persuade me to help your cause, you're doing a lousy job." Clementine scoffed. "But then, you actually haven't asked, have you?"

The Rogue continued undeterred, "I have been in the Golden Echo. I know why *Bahkauv* swarm the hills around there like ants."

"I am aware that the Golden Echo has been reopened."

"Are you aware that the miners have reached the caves?"

"Yes."

"I speak of the caves littered with hundreds of *Bahkites*."

Clementine frowned. Eggs? *Bahkauv* eggs? "You've seen them?"

The Rogue nodded. "In the hundreds. They are everywhere deep in those tunnels."

She shrugged. "So destroy them."

"I can crack them open until fatigue takes my legs from under me, but I will never break them all."

Clementine had fought *Bahkauv*. They didn't worry her particularly, so why was the Rogue so concerned? "I'll take care of them *after* I've investigated Slagton."

"Your lack of understanding does not surprise me."

"And here we are, once again. You extend one hand for help while you slap me with the other."

"If your resolve is weakened by your ignorance, please step aside for those more capable."

Enough! "Get out, *Rogue*. And mind your business in the future." She pointed toward the door.

"It would please me to do precisely that, but unfortunately, removing the threat in the Golden Echo will require your assistance."

"No." Clementine continued to point at the door.

The Rogue walked over to the desk and sat in the creaky wooden chair there, folding her hands in her lap. "Let me explain it to you with a question: Have you pondered the origin of *Bahkites* in the Golden Echo?"

"The *Osterhase*," Clementine shot back.

"The Easter Hare? Do you find our predicament humorous?"

Nothing about the Rogue's visit had been funny. She'd sooner endure an afternoon of acupuncture by those in Chinatown who found her "unclean."

As for the Rogue's question, Clementine hadn't thought about the origin of the eggs. She had experience with *Bahkauv,* but not their origins.

"I'll take your silence to mean you are ignorant of the process. The eggs are laid by a *reine*. A queen."

Clementine shrugged again. "I'll kill the queen."

The Rogue sighed with a good deal of drama. "You can't."

"Why not?"

"Let me ask you another question."

"No."

"This is the last. Your lesson is almost finished."

"Fine. Ask."

"Are you aware that Slayers often present as twins?"

"Of course. My great-aunts were twins."

"Have you wondered why?"

"I always thought it was in the water," Clementine joked.

"You wonder why my disapproval of you is often unbridled."

Clementine let out a harsh laugh. "And all the while I thought you were envious of my size."

The Rogue ignored her. "Do you have an account of your family history?"

"Of course." Clementine had read *Den Storslätte Boka Stil*

Johanssen as a child. It chronicled the lives of her ancestors, many of them, anyway. The stories about the slaughter of terrible, magnificent beasts, and the horrible deaths of her forebearers had frightened her into nightmares and dark thoughts that only her amma and afi could drive away. Later, when the stories no longer frightened her, her amma had used the book to teach Clementine about her ancestors. Her bloodline. Her afi had used it to teach her about the many deadly creatures she might face as a Slayer. His voice was still strong in her memory: *This will save your life, my little Liebling. Study this to know what they are and learn their weaknesses.*

Twins were mentioned occasionally in *The Grand Book of Johanssen*. It was her afi's belief, as well as hers after reading the book, that twin Slayers were occasionally needed to destroy particular creatures. Over the centuries, the bloodlines had been adapting to the need for twins, and as a result, Slayers were becoming more successful against those creatures.

Twins. It would have been nice to have a sibling. Someone to share her childhood with, like what Boone and Rabbit experienced. She'd often wondered over the years if she did have a sibling. One that her mother hadn't told her grandparents about for some reason.

"If you know so little of *Bahkauv*," the Rogue said, cutting into her thoughts, "then your family account must not have insights for you on their reproductive cycle." How could someone be condescending by merely tipping her head to the side?

The Rogue did spur a memory though. Clementine recalled the account of an ancestor, Hanne, who had slain a pack of *Bahkauv*. There were entries on strengths and weaknesses and how to disable them, but there was no mention of any baby *Bahkauv* in the pack. The only note on the subject indicated that they were of reptilian-type birth—meaning eggs.

"Perhaps you should take the time to read it," the Rogue

suggested.

"Why don't you save us some time and tell me."

"I would have dealt with the Golden Echo issue myself but in this instance two Slayers are needed."

The urge to give the Rogue a good dressing-down was strong. "You can't handle it by yourself?"

The Rogue groaned and covered her face with her hands.

"I don't see why it would be so difficult. I've wielded two blades on a number of occasions," Clementine teased.

"You haven't seen a queen, I gather," she said behind her hands. "She would not fit in the tunnels carved by men."

"So, it's big then." Clementine grinned when the Rogue dragged her hands down her face. "Larger than the *Bahkauv* I dispatched a few weeks ago in that mine? Those were as big as bears!" She struggled not to laugh.

The Rogue huffed. "Those were younglings. The queen is considerably larger than any other fully grown *Bahkauv*."

"Then how do I kill her?"

"As I said, it will take both of us."

Clementine circled around René and stopped near his head. "Did you take any of his teeth?"

Her question spurred a frown from René's killer. "Why on earth would I take teeth?"

"Never mind." Clementine continued her slow walk around the exam table. The *Bahkauv* could become a problem if left unchecked. How many men had been killed in Gayville? She should talk to the new undertaker about the numer of bodies coming into his establishment. Or maybe send Hank to ask?

"Well?" the Rogue prodded.

"Fine. I'll go to the Golden Echo with you and we'll slay the *Bahkauv* queen. But first, I am going to explore Slagton and find out who is creating *Draug*."

"No! We must destroy the queen as soon as possible!" The Rogue's voice was shrill, commanding.

"We will. But first—"

"She is laying scores of eggs daily. Her children tend her night and day. There are hundreds of eggs in those caves and antechambers. More hatch even as we speak. I regret taking the time to come here, but it was necessary to enlist the aid of another Slayer."

Clementine stared down at René. *Hel's fury!* The thought of the Sidewinders' uncle being torn to ribbons by a *Bahkauv* pulled on her emotions. How many innocents were being ripped apart in those towns? "We'll hunt down your queen." *After Slagton.*

"Excellent. I'll lead the—"

"First, though, business at hand." Clementine crossed her arms. "Don't ever—*ever*—enter my establishment again in my absence."

The Rogue lifted her chin.

"Second. I am leading the hunt in the Golden Echo."

"That isn't—"

"This is *my* territory. My charge. As far as I am concerned, you are a dilettante. A rogue Slayer." Clementine glanced down at René's lifeless form before continuing. "You do not belong here, and you will stay only as long as I allow it."

The Rogue harrumphed. "You think highly of yourself. Excellent. When plagued by inadequacy, swagger oft fills the void and carries the day." She stood. "You must not tarry, Slayer. The *Bahkauv* have a firm footing even now." Without another word, she turned away. Her footfalls thudded down the dark hallway toward the back door of The Pyre.

As the door creaked shut, Clementine stared into René's empty gaze. Sadness panged in her chest for him and the woman in his locket.

How many more like him would she find in Slagton? Lonely, starving, desperate to support family "back home"?

Worse, how many would she have to kill before her job here was done?

Twelve

I tell you what." Boone looked up from the hotel plans on the table and smiled. "Sometimes."

"What, Booney?" Rabbit resumed studying the drawings, keeping in mind some of Uncle Mort's many ideas for the place.

"*Sometimes* you have a good idea."

Of course, Rabbit knew Boone would be the first and last man standing next to him in a throwdown, regardless of the why or where of it. Hell, they both would take lead for the other. But Boone tended to be on the terse side when it came to doling out praise. Deliberate with thought and slow to wag his tongue—that was Boone. This tight-lipped silence was why the pit of Rabbit's stomach warmed a little when Boone had even a single word of praise for him. He'd be damned if he gave Boone the satisfaction of seeing it, though. The fact that he felt like a schoolboy who'd been given a piece of rock candy by the teacher for completing his maths chafed some. "I know."

"Oh, do ya? Which idea do I mean?"

"Who knows? I got so many."

"The livery. I wasn't sure at first, but I think you uncorked it."

"Seems right, don't it?" Rabbit grinned. "I mean, we got location, right across the street from the Drunken Rooster and smack-dab in the middle of town."

"Drunken Rooster? Who came up with that name, I wonder?"

"Don't know." Rabbit patted his belly. "But their fried chicken comes in right next to Lupe's."

Boone nodded.

Rabbit swept his arm wide. "Good, stout building."

"Yep. Now, if we can get this hotel built, we'll be bringing in as much as Morton and Sons *and* the ranch both. Thought on any names?"

Without hesitating Rabbit said, "Jack's Place."

Boone shook his head.

"Jack Rabbit's."

Boone pursed his lips. "Hank would like it."

"Hotel Fields."

"No."

"Shiver Me Timbers? Or, how about The Bosun's Booty?"

"Really?"

"McCreery's don't have a sweet sound like Fields's." Rabbit bobbled his head and said in a highfalutin tone, "Mac Reary's." He couldn't help but chuckle. "Sounds like something you'd name the hind end of a cow."

"An Irish cow," added Boone with a matching laugh. "We'll come back to that later. Right now, we need to decide if we have six rooms, or build a wall here." He poked the paper. "And make it eight."

"Eight. Upstairs. Two downstairs." Rabbit hovered over the table, squinting at the plans. "Where's Hank's room?"

"I don't know what his plans are. Is he staying in Deadwood? Have you talked to him about that?"

Rabbit shook his head. He'd held a little spark of hope that Hank would put down some roots here, but Hank had a history of roaming the range. Rabbit wasn't sure he wanted to hear the answer if he asked. "How much you pay for these hotel plans, anyway?"

"Wasn't much. The architect says this'll be the third one built on these plans. One in Carson City. Another in Denver."

"Ain't unique, then." Rabbit didn't really care. He felt like needling his *compadre* at the moment, but Boone wasn't on the same ride.

"Let's see. Kitchen. Chimneys there, there. Right here." Boone tapped the plans. "We'll need probably four, maybe five loads of brick just for those."

Rabbit watched him study the plans.

Boone glanced up at him. "Where's Uncle Morton?"

"Over there, trying to sit in that chair." Rabbit indicated the chair on the other side of the table from him. He knew Boone didn't believe him. Sooner or later he'd have to, but he didn't just yet. There would be proof. Somehow. That was Boone, though. Mr. Level Head. Gotta have the proof of a thing.

"Right."

"I didn't tell you before. When you sat down." Rabbit jutted his chin toward Boone. "You sat on him."

"Did I now?"

"Yep. He said your manners need brushin' up."

Boone smirked. "Tell him I apologize. I'll try not to sit on him again." He half stood, looked at the chair, sank back down, and then watched Rabbit, his head cocked.

"He thinks I'm still there?" Uncle Mort chuckled, floating out of the chair a little while continuing to study the hotel plans. "You just told him I'm over here."

Rabbit watched as his uncle tried to place his forearms on the table only to have them sink through it. "Why even try?" he asked.

He was becoming accustomed to his uncle inadvertently defying the solidness of a table or wall.

"Apology accepted," Uncle Mort said to Boone, as if he could hear him. He winked in Rabbit's direction. "Sounded gratuitous, though. Tell him next time I'll pinch his ass. Nobody likes getting sat on." Uncle Mort gave up and let his arms float aimlessly.

Rabbit laughed. "He can hear you, Booney."

"You boys should put toilets in your hotel," Uncle Mort said, back to the business of building a hotel. "Lot of the posh hotels back east have internals now."

"Since when have you been back east? Lately."

"Since ... hmm." Uncle Mort shrugged. "I don't know." He leaned over the plans and pointed. "Right here. And here. Tell Boone."

"He says we need indoor privies. There and there." Rabbit stuck his finger through Uncle Mort's hand and tapped on the paper.

Boone grimaced at Rabbit.

"That's what Uncle Mort says," he repeated. "Back east they're doin' it, he says."

"Tell him he's *loco*. That'd cost a fortune. Besides, there's no plumbing in Deadwood. Tell him that."

Rabbit was getting damned tired of everyone ordering him what to *tell*. "I told you, he can hear you."

"Okay, Uncle Morton." Boone talked to the ceiling. "Baths, but no toilets. That's the deal."

"He's right there." Rabbit waved his hand toward his uncle across the table.

Boone growled in his throat. "Dammit, Rabbit."

"Tell the skinflint to let go of the money purse," Uncle Mort shot back. "You boys need feather beds, too. They'll line up to sleep in your feather beds. And gas lights for—"

Rabbit put his palms up. "Okay, okay, Uncle Mort."

Uncle Mort looked down at the plans again. "I think those beams aren't big enough for the second floor. It's a floor *and* a ceiling. Got to account for that. Might collapse on you, you make those beams too light."

"Uncle Mort, it ain't gonna collapse." Rabbit regarded the

plans. Maybe they were too small. His uncle knew how to build, after all. He'd built the main house and several of the barns at the old ranch down in Santa Fe.

"What'd he say?" Boone frowned at the plans.

"Feather beds and gas lights. Beams are too small." Rabbit chuckled when Boone scrubbed his forehead with his palm.

"The beams are fine. These plans were drawn up by one of the best architects in Denver." Boone began a rhythmic tapping on the table with his knuckles.

"Uncle Mort. You'd better quit. He's about cracked." Rabbit scooted closer to the table. "So, you think we'll get started layin' floor tomorrow?"

Boone squinted at him. "If Uncle Morton is done throwing in his two bits, then yeah, I think we get started on the floors. Got the planks stacked and ready."

Dime nickered deep in his throat from down below.

Nickel answered.

"Boys are tellin' stories down there." Rabbit listened to the two horses nicker softly back and forth. "Spooky stories, I reckon."

Boone chuckled. "Probably give each other bad dreams. And poor ol' Fred, too." He rolled up the plans and tied them with a strip of leather.

"Getting late. I'll go check the edges." Uncle Mort sank down through the chair.

Rabbit watched as he disappeared through the floorboards. "Can't use stairs like normal folk?" he hollered.

His uncle had made a habit of checking the grounds around the ranch in Santa Fe every evening. "Tuck in the chickens and kiss the cows night-night," Rabbit called, just as he had from the porch of the ranch house.

"Uncle Morton." Boone cracked a smile. "He'd come up to our bedroom window in the dark of night and howl like a wolf."

"Then run around to his bedroom and yell, 'You boys hear

that? Wolf pack got us surrounded!' " Rabbit slapped his knee. "It's a wonder he didn't scare a year of life outta both of us."

"Didn't help his cause, us being able to hear him run back to his bedroom." Boone's grin turned into another chuckle.

"Too many animals in this building!" Uncle Mort shouted from below.

Rabbit opened his mouth to tell Boone, but didn't want to remove the grin from Boone's face. Naw, he'd let it ride this time. "Beaman works like a steam donkey. You notice that?"

Boone nodded. "Doesn't take much of a break, either. Quality work as well. That's a man I don't mind paying. Amelia does a fine job with the animals, too. Seems right-minded that way. Simpatico."

Rabbit shook his head, squishing his lips together to hold in his two cents. He wasn't so sure about the girl. Some of the things he'd seen had him wondering about her fitness for the job.

"You just shake your head? You don't agree?"

"I don't know, Booney." He rested his elbows on the table and aimed his hands at Boone. "Now I ain't saying she's not takin' care of the animals, feeding them and such. She is. Stalls are cleaner than Keller kept. Smells a damned sight better around here, too. But she's clumsy or something, you know? Always runnin' into things. Droppin' tack. You ever see her tie a rope bridle? Takes her three times longer than it should. Almost stuck me with a pitchfork right here." He pointed at his side. "She just moves wrong."

Boone looked at him as if he'd sprouted a horn. "That's not my experience at all."

Rabbit threw his hands up. "Eh, maybe I'm wrong. She's nice enough and all. Got some aspects I don't mind looking at."

"Careful now."

"You asked." Rabbit sat back. "Getting the animals cared for, that's what counts." He couldn't understand the disparity in observations between the two of them, but it didn't really matter. And besides, she really was easy on the eyes. "Expect Hank and Miss Clementine along shortly."

"Yep." Boone shook the empty coffee pot. "Time for supper. Uncle Morton still here?"

"Doin' his edges." Rabbit knew Boone wanted to believe their uncle was still hanging around. Hell, Rabbit couldn't remember the last time he'd lied to Boone, or Boone to him. Neither ever felt compelled to. The confounded look on Boone's face every time they talked about their uncle now told the story of the dilemma with which he was grappling.

Boone normally had a good handle on the natural order of things, but Rabbit knew the circumstances of their putting down roots in Deadwood was weakening his grasp. And the idea that his uncle was back from the grave wasn't helping.

Boone rubbed his jaw. After a moment he broke out into laughter and shook his finger at Rabbit and scrunched up his face. " 'You two put crickets in my bed one more time, and I'll tan your hides so hard we'll be able to make boots outta your rumps!' "

Rabbit laughed along with Boone until his eyes watered. "That sounded just like Uncle Mort."

"I sure miss him, Rabbit."

That stopped the laughter.

Sadness squeezed at Rabbit's heart. "I wish you could see what I see, Booney." He would do anything to help his *compadre* see and talk to the crusty old shade. And the fact that Boone half-believed that Rabbit had gone *loco* made the whole raw deal hurt even more.

Boone nodded slowly. "Maybe some of that McCuddle's would ..." His voice faded, his gaze drifted to the table.

"Hank's here!" Uncle Mort called from below. "Got himself a head of steam up, too."

"Hank's here," Rabbit repeated quickly to get it said before

Hank opened the door.

Boone looked past Rabbit at the stairs. "I don't—"

The front door of the livery creaked open and banged against the wall.

"Evenin' to the Sidewinders from Santa Fe!" The door thudded shut.

"Hiyo, Hank!" Rabbit strode to the top of the stairs. "Ready for supper? Might eat a whole steer between us."

"You boys comin' down then?"

"On our way. Miss Clementine outside?"

"She ain't comin'. Had other business to attend. Told us to eat a spud for her."

Rabbit turned to his *compadre*, noticing the frown lining Boone's forehead. When he realized Rabbit was watching, he looked away and reached for his hat. "Let's go."

Hank was busy rubbing Fred the Mule's nose when Rabbit descended the steps.

"Ol' Fred likes Amelia," Hank said.

"How do you know?" Rabbit asked, pulling on his sheepskin coat. Everybody seemed to like Amelia. He still didn't see it.

"His disposition has improved somewhat considerable."

Rabbit looked Fred over. "Oh?" He didn't see that either.

"He doesn't nip at my buttocks when I'm hitchin' his britchen. Amelia says I was tyin' it too low. Causes sores, she says. Guess I was lucky it didn't take his legs from under him down a hill. That's what she said."

Rabbit chuckled. "I reckon she knows something, then." He looked up the stairs. "Get the molasses out your pants, Boone. Thought you were hungry!"

"That hole in your head is puffin' hot air again. Stuff some straw in it, loudmouth." Boone bounded down the steps two at a time. "Mr. Beaman and Amelia already turned in for the night."

"They ain't sleeping yet." Rabbit headed for the door. "Don't call me 'loudmouth,' mush head."

"Okay, petticoat," Boone shot back. He patted Hank on the shoulder and followed Rabbit. "Who's serving the grub tonight? Café?"

"Whoa there, fellas," Hank said.

Rabbit stopped at the door and looked back at Hank.

"Miss Clem has somethin' she wants us to do."

"Bash a *Bahkauv*?" Rabbit guessed.

"Hoo hoo! No, that ain't it."

"Harpoon a *Höhlendrache*?"

"Ha! What's a harpoon?"

"It's a spear on a rope. Sailors use it to hunt big fish or whales." Boone smirked. "Rabbit should have been born a sailor."

Rabbit shook his finger at Boone. "Or sea serpents. Or giant squid. And I should've been born a pirate, not a sailor. Leastways I'd have a treasure hidden in a grotto, guarded by mermaids."

"Right, Captain Rabbit." Boone grinned.

"Captain Jack Rabbit," Hank hooted back.

"Captain Jack," Rabbit corrected. "The Terrible."

"Well, I'm hungry, Mr. Terrible. Let's go eat." Boone rubbed his belly.

"Hold on there." Hank caught up to them. "Miss Clem. Remember?"

"What about her?"

"She told me, 'Go get the Sidewinders and look for Buck. Find out what happened to him in Gayville. What he knows about Gayville.' "

Buck was a little wire of a man who'd ridden with Hank throughout the Nevada Territory. Had a good dose of *loco* to him, too, in Rabbit's opinion.

Hank motioned Rabbit and Boone in close and put his hand beside his mouth, whispering, "The Rogue was to The Pyre earlier."

Rabbit stared at Boone, who stared right back. "The Rogue

went to The Pyre? Today?"

"Yessir. Left not more'n half an hour ago. Just before I got there to fetch Miss Clem for dinner. You boys were still bustin' your humps on the hotel."

"Hot damn. We missed the Rogue again, Booney."

"Rogue says packs of them *Bahkauv* are roamin' the hills near the Bloody Bones again. Gayville. All them little towns poppin' up around there. Blackville. Down to South Bend. Up to Oro. That's why Miss Clem wants to know what ol' Buck knows. Like I said a'fore, it's my opinion he got his nut cracked back in those woods. The Bloody Bones woods."

The three of them thought on that for a moment.

Rabbit wasn't particularly worried at the idea of coming up against the sharp-fanged creatures again. But in big numbers? They might get the drop. Damned big teeth on those beasties. Shouldn't forget those fuckin' claws, neither. How many was it they were talking about? "A passel of them, she's thinking?"

Hank nodded. "Rogue said so."

"She's thinking Buck's cracked nut is related to the *Bahkauv* somehow?" Boone rocked on his heels, a move Rabbit knew meant he was working a problem.

"I'm supposin' so. Ain't we all been thinkin' that way? What with all the doin's up there?"

Boone sighed. "Yep."

"Agreed then. Find Buck. Work some facts outta his noggin. Up one side of the street, down the other. Drink our dinner until we find him." Rabbit didn't mind the idea at all. Might be he could spark a little with some of the pretty doves he'd noticed here and there.

"Rabbit." Boone looked him in the eye. "We need to keep our heads. There's no need for drinking with Buck in absentia. Have a look around. He's not there, move on."

"*Inibsencha.*" Rabbit bobbled his head. "Fine. No drinking." He headed for the door. He'd be damned if Boone was going to tell him when to drink. "Hank and me will commence to drinking *when* we find him."

Behind him, Rabbit could hear Boone mumble to Hank.

He stopped and looked back. "You two comin'?"

"I'm with you, Jack Rabbit." Hank trotted up to Rabbit. "Let's find us a cracked nut."

Outside the livery, Boone veered off, up the left side of the street. "I'll see you boys directly." With a wave, he waded into the shadowy crowd of drinkers and gamblers heading toward a night of debauchery and excessiveness—and for most of them, a good fleecing.

Rabbit and Hank weaved through the throng of humanity toward the Drunken Rooster saloon across the street.

He led the way through the door and smiled wide when his eyes landed on Blossom, a five-foot, eleven-inch redhead dressed in a blue striped corset with buckles over a ruffled undergarment and frilly bloomers. *Ay yi yi*, that girl radiated enough confidence and sexuality to engulf everyone in the large saloon. And if those two qualities didn't do the trick, she had other mesmerizing attributes that would do the job.

She turned her perky nose toward Rabbit as if she sensed he'd entered. He started toward her, but the sawdust-covered floor of the Drunken Rooster couldn't hold another ten pair of boots without one pair skirting the threshold. The twinkle in her eye and the shiny smile on her face compelled him to part the sea to reach her shore. Or maybe it was the extra ripe and ample fruit about to burst out the top of her ruffles.

"Fields!" the bartender called. He held up a mug of beer in one hand and motioned him over with the other.

Rabbit grabbed Hank by his vest and maneuvered him through the whooping and bellowing patrons filling the coffers of the place with gold dust and coin. Rabbit didn't mind the owner, Longshanks, making a business of it. He was a good man, Rabbit felt. He liked him, and for that matter, the bartenders and the girls, too.

"Heyo, Foster!" Rabbit called to the barkeep. "It's a goldmine, eh?"

Foster looked out over the crowd, nodded and grinned. He pushed the beer toward Rabbit. "On the house."

"Thank you kindly. One for my *amigo*, Hank?" He patted Hank on the back.

Foster slid a full mug to Hank. "Friend of Jack's, friend of mine." He extended his hand for a shake.

"Right neighborly." Hank took Foster's hand and shook it hard.

Rabbit leaned toward Foster. "We're looking for a little wire of a man, goes by the name of Buck. Talks nonsense mostly. Good at wheedlin' beer and whiskey from those not paying attention. I haven't seen him here, maybe you have."

Foster squinted, and then shook his head. "Nope. Ain't seen that."

Rabbit nodded once, and then held up his mug toward Hank. "Ready?"

Hank furrowed his brow, and then his eyes got wide. He

grinned. "Ready!"

Rabbit tipped his mug and poured the golden liquid until there was only a trickle of foam streaming into his mouth. He slammed the mug down on the bar and looked up to see Hank had already finished and was watching him, a smile spread a mile wide across his face.

"Hank! I never!" Rabbit punched Hank on the shoulder. He pulled a five-dollar coin from his vest pocket and tossed it to Foster. "For my friend's drink. Thanks, Fossy." It was twice what the beer cost, but Rabbit liked Foster.

Outside the Drunken Rooster, Rabbit stopped Hank. "What did Booney say to you over in the livery before we left?"

"Huh? Oh, nothin'. Let's head on down."

"Hank." Rabbit dropped his chin. There was a reason Boone vamoosed and didn't tell Rabbit what he was doing.

"He's, uh, goin' up the other side. Could cover more ground thatta way, he said."

Rabbit was sure there was more to it, but he let it stand for now. No need getting Hank flustered. Besides, another beer and that secret would spill right out of him.

Thirteen

Three saloons and two beers later, Rabbit spotted Buck in the Crusty Goblin saloon, boot to the bar rail and cozied up closer than what would be considered normal to a short pudgy man topped with a stained and tattered plains hat.

The place was grimier than any of the others they'd been in, the dirt floor peppered with broken glass, chunks of tobacco and spit, and cigar butts. The lanterns, hung too far apart to offer good light, swirled veils of black smoke into the air.

Rabbit turned back toward Hank. "Miser must own this place. No spittoons, burnin' cheap oil. Make everybody sick is what he'll do." He rubbed his nose with the back of his hand, recoiling at the stench of rotten tobacco, lamp smoke, and week-old sweat.

"Word has, he's from St. Louis," Hank said. "Baldwin, I think it was. Ain't got no concern but fillin' his pockets. Guess most folks here feel thatta way, though." Hank spotted Buck. "There's the *little wire*. Up to the bar there."

"I saw. Go secure us a table, huh? I'll fetch him."

"Yessir."

Rabbit watched Hank wade into the crowd of hats and coats toward the back of the saloon.

It took one mug and half a minute to coax Buck to the table

Hank had procured near a wall in the smoky saloon. A boozer sat hunched forward on the table, his face buried in his crossed arms. Rabbit sat and handed Hank one of the mugs of brew.

"Ho there, Buck. Sit a spell with us." Hank pulled a chair away from the table.

Buck didn't move, but instead watched the man with his head on the table. "Don't know 'im. Don't."

"He's sleepin'. No worry. He don't mind sharin'." Hank patted the chair. "Sit."

Buck slowly shook his head. "Hank Varney. Good rights by Hank." He looked sideways at Rabbit. "Scaly boy. Buck knows. Scaly boy don't share." He glanced at the mug full of beer in Rabbit's hand. "Maybe he do. Maybe." Then he returned to the sleeping man. "Don't know 'im."

Rabbit set the beer on the table. He grabbed the collar of the sleeping stranger's coat and dragged him to his feet. "You got a bed, sleepy bear? Git yourself along." He gave the staggering drunk a push into the mass of saloon patrons.

Hank stared up at Rabbit with surprise and a little amusement in his eyes.

Rabbit grinned. "Don't worry. So crowded in here he'll be on his feet for half an hour. Should be sobered up by then." He sat and pushed the mug of beer toward the edge of the table where Buck still stood.

After one more squint at Rabbit, Buck sank into the chair next to Hank and grabbed the mug.

"How's the claim, Buck?" Hank started.

"Whole caboodle's a wash." It didn't really seem like Buck was listening to his own words.

Rabbit frowned at Hank. If he knew what a caboodle was, well then …

"Ain't plucked a nugget?" Hank asked. "No dust panned out?"

"Flippin' eggs in a cold skillet." Buck downed half his beer, clunked the mug on the table, and gazed at it.

Rabbit continued to frown at Hank, not entirely understanding the conversation yet.

"Means his claim's about the same shape as mine. Hollow."

Oh. Of course. "No use tryin' to flip an egg in a cold skillet. I'm with you." Rabbit shook his head. He might need Boone to help interpret these two prospectors. "Hank, what say you go get Boone? I'll keep Buck company."

"Ohoo! Right. Boone. I'll be back in a shake." He sprang to his feet. "Don't let Buck come away from the table. Might lose him in this mess."

"I got him." Rabbit watched Hank wind his way through the crowd to the door and then disappear into the night.

Elbows on the table, Rabbit waited while Buck gulped the rest of his beer. "Looks like you need another." He pushed Hank's full mug toward Buck, then wiped his eyes. "Smoke in here is makin' my eyes water."

"Scaly boy's noggin is all caterwampus. Cryin' don't help it none."

What the hell did that mean? Rabbit grunted. "I gave you a couple drinks now. Name's Rabbit. Or Jack. Or if you think it's better, Mr. Fields. No need to keep on with that 'scaly boy' nonsense. I ain't scaly."

What did he mean by *scaly*, anyway?

"Scaly boy got some sand to him. Gonna need it. Grit is what'll do."

Rabbit leaned back and growled at the ceiling. Goddammit. He needed Hank and Boone. He couldn't see which way was up with this little man. Before tonight, Hank had also called him "One Horn Buck" on account of a big horn sheep they'd hunted a few years back.

"Where's your horn?" Rabbit didn't expect a coherent answer but figured he needed to change tack.

Buck turned his head deliberately and stared at Rabbit.

Rabbit stared back. After a few moments, he began skimming the saloon for something interesting to watch. Looking into Buck's eyes unsettled him. He couldn't really make out why. A darkness maybe, hiding there. Or they were eyes that had seen things that would chill a man's soul. Either way, he wished Hank and Boone would return, pronto.

He glanced back. "Claim is a bust, huh? Where is it?"

Buck continued to stare at him.

Rabbit had the distinct feeling he was being studied. The sudden heat in the saloon had him thinking about taking off his coat. He pulled at his collar. Normally, Buck's attention was focused on anything but the conversation at hand. Right now, Rabbit seemed to have his full attention.

He was about to repeat the question when Buck spoke. "No color in the mud. Only mud."

"Where's that? Only mud. On your claim? Where's your claim? That in Gayville, is it?"

Buck began to tap on the table with his fingertips.

"Your claim near Gayville, Buck? You know that area?"

Buck tapped harder and quicker on the table. His gaze darted around the saloon.

"You seen things there?" Rabbit pressed. "Been up to the Bloody Bo—the, what was it? The Golden something?" He tried to spur Buck into finishing the name for him.

"Golden Echo it was. Wicked things. Devil's deeds. Stirrin' men's guts to soup. Down there. Stealin' teeth and stirrin' guts. Pack a demons'll save ya first, then eat the soup." Buck was rocking now. He stared at the table like it was covered with bugs.

"Okay. Okay. Simmer down, now. Drink your beer. Hank'll be back directly and then we can get you another."

Stealing teeth? Rabbit could understand that. He'd seen men steal the gold teeth from the dead. He used to think that was unsettling, but after the things he'd witnessed lately, well, stealing gold teeth had dropped a fair way down his list of disturbing things.

But mix a man's guts to soup? If Buck was saying anything worthwhile, Rabbit couldn't puzzle it out.

Buck was rocking faster, tapping the table harder. "Corruption!"

Hold on. Rabbit recognized that word. That was the same thing Hank mentioned when they tried before to figure what had happened to Buck.

"Ruin! Ruin's here!" Buck was rocking so far forward he was almost hitting his head on the table.

"Easy, Buck!" Rabbit glanced around to see if the *hombres* at nearby tables had taken notice.

They had.

He grimaced and shook his head. "Lost it all on a bad claim," he said loud enough for everyone near to hear. "Ain't got a dollar to his name now."

His ruse was met with a chorus of *Me too* and *Poor bastard*, along with grunts of understanding and toasts to anti-prosperity.

Buck continued to rock and rap his knuckles on the table. "Ruin … Ruin … Ruin …"

What the hell had Rabbit done? Fretting his hands together, he watched Buck. Shit! Had he broken the man for good?

Someone tapped on his back. Rabbit turned to see Boone with a shot of whiskey in one hand and another mug of beer in the other. Hank peered over Boone's shoulder. He sighed in relief at the sight of them.

Boone cocked his head at Buck. "What happened to him?"

Rabbit shrugged. "Bad whiskey."

"What?"

Rabbit fessed up. "I think I broke him."

"I'll help him through." Hank squeezed past Boone, grabbing the mug of beer on his way to Buck. He sat and pushed the mug in front of Buck. "One Horn. You seen Tennessee Pete around?" Hank patted Buck on the shoulder. "Huh? You seen him? Or Colonel Jessers? You seen either one of 'em? I ain't see neither of 'em."

Buck's rocking slowed.

"Pete. You seen him?" Hank repeated.

Buck stopped rocking and knocking. "He got et." He turned to Hank. "Got hisself et, didn't he?"

Rabbit looked up at Boone, his brow creased, and mouthed, *Et?*

"I think he means 'ate,'" Boone said quietly.

"He got et and we didn't help him."

"Buck, you know there weren't nothin' could be done to save him. Took his own trail."

Boone set his mug on the table and leaned in close to Rabbit's ear. "What the hell did these boys go through?"

Rabbit had waning doubt Hank had a history that would curl the toes of a dead man. "Everything all right, Hank?"

Hank glanced over at Rabbit. He held up his palm and shook it a little, and then he gave a quick nod.

"We got beer here. And Boone. 'Member Boone? Dan'l Boone, back in town."

Buck scanned the saloon. "Dan'l Boone? Come to see me?"

"In the flesh. Standin' right here. Sit yourself, Mr. Boone."

Boone shrugged at Rabbit and took the last empty chair, between Rabbit and Buck.

"How-do, Mr. One Horn?"

"Dan'l Boone, dead too soon."

Boone grimaced at Rabbit. "Still says that. Wish he wouldn't."

Rabbit couldn't help but grin. "Don't feel so special. He's still callin' me 'Scaly.'"

"Rather be standing with the name 'Scaly' than horizontal buzzard food like Daniel Boone."

"Hoo! Boonedog. Dan'l Boone, dead too soon. That ain't you he's speakin' to. He's aimed at the real Dan'l Boone." Hank paused and scratched the back of his hand. "I think."

Buck grabbed the mug of beer and began to gulp it down.

Rabbit leaned across the table toward Hank. "You think you can get him talking? I tried it, and I think I heard his noggin crack like steppin' on a dry branch."

"Sometimes you gotta come in sideways, Jack Rabbit." Hank scooted up close to Buck.

Rabbit winced slightly. He wasn't cut from a cloth one could call subtle. Anything but straight at the pickle was too much bother and took too much time. Boone would agree. So would the Pinkertons, damn them anyway.

Boone sat back and took a sip of his whiskey, lowering his glass with a scowl. "This ain't whiskey, consarn it."

Rabbit scooted his chair closer to Boone and sat back, too. "You said 'ain't,' Booney. Hey, they got tequila here? Forgot to check."

Boone shook his head. "Nope. And apparently no whiskey to speak of either. Too much to ask for a decent glass of whiskey in this town?"

Rabbit smacked Boone's shoulder with the back of his hand. "Drunken Rooster. Across from the livery. Tell 'em I sent you, and they'll pour you the good stuff."

Boone smirked. "Tell 'em I sent you," he repeated, imitating Rabbit's head bobble.

"You're even pompous doin' that." Rabbit chuckled.

"Your lips are *doin'* this." Boone flapped his fingers and thumb together, same as Rabbit often did to him.

Rabbit grinned wide. "Just stop. You can't be me, much as you try. It makes me sad."

They both chuckled and turned their attention to Hank, who had been talking quietly to Buck the whole time. Buck seemed to be back to his old self, tapping his knuckles on the table and watching the patrons milling about in the Crusty Goblin.

"Hank?" Boone sat forward and rested his forearms on the table.

Hank glanced at him. "Buck's minin' claim was this side of Gayville, in Black Tail Gulch. Got that name on account of the blacktail deer up there." Hank sipped his beer. "Prospectin', were ya, Buck?"

"Diggin' the mud. No color to the mud. Diggin', diggin', diggin'. Mud's jus' mud. Rocks jus' rocks."

Hank leaned toward Rabbit and Boone. "Didn't find no gold on his claim," he translated for them.

"We all was bad, all bad," Buck said. "Bones an' skin is all."

Hank leaned back toward Buck. "Guts growlin' for vittles was they, Buck? Ever'body needs vittles. Coin."

"Lotsa work for them that do. Gotta work for the man, though." Buck turned his bony leathery hands this way and that, looking at them as if they were new to him. "Work enough fer ever'body. Work the hands raw."

Buck picked up his empty mug and began clunking it on the table.

Hank turned to Rabbit. "Jack Rabbit, 'nother beer or two for Buck?"

"I'll get it." Boone stood and waded to the bar.

"Where was that you was workin', Buck?" Hank winced and shook his head. He glanced at Rabbit. "I should know better. Can't go through the mountain. Gotta take the trail goes 'round the side with Buck."

Buck began rocking forward and back again, still banging his mug on the table.

"Give me a minute. I'll get him back," Hank said and bumped shoulders with Buck. "Tell me about Tennessee Pete."

Rabbit couldn't hear anything after that. Hank mumbled near Buck's ear, saying something that sounded rhythmic, as if he were trying to send Buck into a trance. Shit. It sort of reminded Rabbit of tiptoeing through a passel of sleeping snakes, trying not to disturb their peaceful slumber.

"I don't like that bartender," Boone said when he returned.

"He's got a barrel full of attitude." He sat and clunked two more full mugs on the table. "Told him his whiskey was water with a little road dust added in for color."

Rabbit barked out a laugh. "Now I wonder why he didn't like that." Sarcasm dripped from his tongue.

"Somebody has to tell him. If you don't register a voice, then nothing will change."

"Ha! Good ol' Booney. Gonna change the world. Hey, you want I should go rough up that mean ol' barkeep for ya?"

"Shut up, knucklehead. You're on your way to soused."

To be truthful, Rabbit did feel kind of warm and buzzy around his nose and lips. And eyes. And fingers.

"Tell me something, Booney." Rabbit got in close. "What'd you tell Hank in the livery? Why'd you go off on your own? And don't call me 'knucklehead.'"

"We could cover more ground that way."

"No." Rabbit knew better than that. There was more to it.

"Okay. You want to know? I told Hank to watch out for you. Keep you out of trouble. Might be we could have split three ways and been even quicker, but I always gotta worry about you starting something, don't I? And if you say 'I don't start something, I finish it,' I'll box your ears."

Rabbit smirked. "Aw. You worried about me?"

Boone rolled his eyes.

"Buck worked in the Golden Echo, like we figured," Hank said. "At one time, lotsa men worked that mine. You boys maybe don't remember, but I did, too."

"You don't flap too much about it," Rabbit said.

"It wasn't what I'd call an agreeable experience. Short-timer, they called me, on accounta my quittin' them to come work for Miss Clem." Hank shook his head. "They worked us hard. Buck says his hands were raw." He held his hands up. "These, too."

Rabbit teetered toward Boone. "I don't want to be a miner."

"Nope," Boone concurred.

"Weren't the worst of it though, hard work," Hank said. "Worst was, ever'time we went in, didn't know if we'd come out again. Men got disappeared ever'day. Bossman said 'Dig!' We dug. Man's gotta eat." He huffed out a wry chuckle. "Or, workin' that mine, might be he got 'et,' like One Horn here says."

"You reckon it was *Bahkauv* eat—I mean takin' those men?" Rabbit shuddered at the thought.

"I do. Now anyhow. Back then, we didn't catch sight of a hair or wisp of them devil dogs. My guess is, the men that got took probably got nose-to-nose with 'em, though."

Boone rubbed his chin. "Like fish in a trough. Those boys didn't have a chance. Even if they got an opportunity to stick those fuckers with a pickaxe, it wouldn't have mattered."

"Take the head." Rabbit emphasized his point by running a finger across his neck.

Hank pointed at Rabbit. "That's the tonic."

"You think it was planned?" Rabbit asked. "Somebody sending those beasties out? Or was it like a nest of rattlesnakes? Festerin' all on its own?" He watched Buck as the geezer scanned the saloon yet again, wondering who he was looking for.

"That's some fodder to ruminate, Jack Rabbit."

"Or ..." Boone crossed his arms. "They were food."

"Sheeat, Booney. You gotta say a thing like that?"

"Never did see no bones," Hank said. "Or blood." He turned to Buck. "Ho, Buck. Bossman treat you fair? Got good coin for your hard work?"

"Bossman, bossman, bossman. The sailor shade."

Hank shrugged at Rabbit and Boone. He looked back at Buck. "The sailor shade, was he?"

"Shady white as snow, head to toe. Snake eyes he had. Blade o' coal."

Boone's and Hank's eyes rounded like saucers as they looked from one to the other to Rabbit, whose eyes probably matched theirs.

"White devil," all three of them said, almost in unison.

"Sonofabitch," Boone said. "You never saw the white devil when you were there, Hank?"

"Not a whip. Things got a lot worse after I left, so they say. Must be he showed up at the Bloody Bones after I started in at The Pyre."

"Remember Weeks?" Rabbit tapped Boone's forearm. "What'd he say? Helped carry that miner out rolled up in a patch of canvas?"

Boone squinted. "Brody Brewster, I think. Ripped open, top to bottom."

"Terrible." Hank shook his head. "Same kinda thing I was hearin' about outta that mine." He watched Buck for a few seconds, then patted him on the shoulder. "So, there it is. That devil Miss Clem dispatched. Got to be."

Boone nodded. "But that can't be what sent Buck over, can it? Unless he's sensitive to such things." He glanced at Rabbit and then Hank. "We heard you mention something about Tennessee Pete getting ... eaten?"

Hank's mouth drooped in the corners. "Nothin' to do with this. Tell you about it another time, maybe."

Boone took the hint and changed course. "I mean, the white devil and the *Bahkauv* didn't send Rabbit's feeble mind over the edge. Although he is seeing Uncle Morton's ghost, now. So, why Buck? Unless something else is down there."

"Oh, now isn't that a fine window shine from an old-timer with rocks rattlin' around up there." Rabbit pointed at Boone's head.

"Ho!" Hank said with a grin. "Now don't you two get me to chuffin' like a steam engine."

Buck half stood and then sat again. "Clementine, mighty fine. Clem, Clem, Clemytine. Mighty fi ..." He trailed off.

"How in *thee* hell does he know Miss Clementine?" Rabbit had been curious about that since he first met Buck when they came into town looking for Uncle Mort.

"Golden Echo's all opened up now, Buck," Hank said. "Lots of color comin' out again."

Hank knew how to phrase the question so that it wasn't really a question. Was that the key? Rabbit was intent on figuring out how to talk to Buck. It bothered him that he had disquieted the little man so quickly.

"Color's there," Buck said. "Streams shimmerin' in the walls."

"Down deep, in them tunnels," Hank continued with his method of not-questioning.

Buck seemed to look through Hank, his gaze focusing on nothing, his pupils widening to black bottomless pits. His face paled before Rabbit's eyes.

"Saw it," Buck whispered. "Saw it down there."

"It was down there," Hank said, nodding. "With the color."

"Waitin', waitin', wait … got in me … got in me …" Buck recoiled and started running his fingers down the sides of his head, as if he were trying to peel his skin away from his skull.

"Gettin' in deep water here," Hank said to Rabbit and Boone.

Rabbit gaped at Boone. If his expression was anything like Boone's, he needed to close his mouth.

"Bossman's down there," Hank pressed. "Down in the dark."

"No! Nonononono." Buck's gaze dipped to the table. He sat dead still, his eyes dark, sunken. It was as if he were looking his tormentor in the face.

Rabbit tried to blink his eyes into focus and shake the dizziness from his head. Shouldn't have had so much malted barley and hops, goldurn it.

"Bossman says dig, dig, dig," Hank prompted. "Dig down in the deep dark." His voice was steady and rhythmic, but Rabbit could see him wringing his hands together off to the side of the table.

"Fire in its eyes. Orange fire. Fire in its eyes." Buck touched his face with his fingers. "Black as coal. Bumpy like a horny toad."

"He's describing what he saw down there," Rabbit realized out loud. He leaned closer, engrossed by the description of Buck's brush with ... what? What the hell had he seen down there?

Buck touched his mouth. "Knives. Yellow and white. Drippy, drippy pointy sharp knives."

"Teeth," Boone said in a low voice.

Buck tried to grab something on each side of his head. "Twisty li'l horns. Crazy goat growlin' at the walls."

"I'd say somebody's crazy," Rabbit whispered.

"Shh!" Boone held his hand up at Rabbit.

Buck coughed out a maniacal chortle.

"Oh, he's gone," Rabbit said.

"Rabbit!" Boone growled at him.

"Piglet. Pink little piglet." Buck pushed his nose up with a finger and chortled again. Suddenly, he sat up straight and his eyes went round. "Pack'a dogs! Hide! Listen! A pack's a-comin'!"

Buck was getting pretty loud. Rabbit glanced at the tables around them. Thankfully, no one was taking any notice. They all looked too drunk to care.

All except one round little man whose face was almost obscured by his long oily hair. He seemed to be paying particular attention to Buck.

"Ho there! Pilgrim!" Rabbit stood. "What's your business?"

The round little man hopped up and scampered into the crowd, rushing toward the front door.

Rabbit began to give chase, but Boone snagged his arm. "Don't worry about him. Sit. Let's finish this."

Rabbit sat, looking from the door to Hank to Boone, and then back to the door.

"Forget him," Boone said. He bobbed his head toward Hank, who was murmuring something in Buck's ear.

"Got him, Hank?" Rabbit sat forward, trying to hear what

Hank was saying.

Nodding, Hank sat back, but didn't take his eyes off Buck. "Got Sourpan Saul," he said to Buck. "The pack got him."

Buck's forehead puckered. "Pack got him. Chased the demon. Chased him away. Got Sourpan." His eyes went glassy, and a tear followed a crease down the side of his face. "Tore his belly. Ate his guts." Buck began to sob silently, his shoulders quaking. "Screamin'. It et Sourpan. Screamin'."

Hank glanced at Rabbit and Boone. His eyes were glassy, too. Rabbit could tell this was taking a toll on him. Back to Buck, he said, "Left the mine, then. Up and out the bloody mine."

Buck wiped his nose with his sleeve. "Up and up. Out to the sun. Never back. Never back to the Bloody Bones."

"Demon's gone." Hank squeezed Buck's wiry shoulder. "Back down he gone? Down and down?"

Buck shook his head slowly. "Demon's here. Always here. Never gone." Then he began to pull at the skin on his face again.

Fourteen

Boone stared up at the night sky. The stars looked like ice crystals, making him shiver even harder. Clementine's parlor would be warm and cozy compared to the loft in the livery. "We're going to The Pyre," he told Rabbit and Hank.

"It's gettin' late. Maybe we should head over to Miss Clementine's in the mornin'." Rabbit pulled his sheepskin tight around his chest. The fuddled fool had been dragging his drunk ass since he teetered out of the Crusty Goblin into the street not thirty minutes earlier.

"You're jingled is all," Boone told him, holding him steady when he started to teeter again. "I warned you not to drink. Besides, it's not even midnight yet. Little bunny rabbit can sleep later."

"Might be I've been workin' like a mule last couple days."

"Mm. Could be. You think that's what it is, Hank?"

"Hmm? Oh, sure it could, Boonedog."

Boone had noticed Hank hadn't been bending too many ears since they left the Crusty Goblin. He looked tired, droopy. The talk with Buck seemed to wear him out, too. If anybody needed rest, it was Hank.

"Why don't you head on back to the livery, Hank? Bundle up in your blankets and take a rest."

Hank stood up a little taller and smiled at Boone. "I'm fit to ride, Boonedog. Don't you worry none about me."

Hank was a headstrong man in a soft-handed way. There was no telling him what to do since he usually had a direction. It was best to let him be. Boone knew someone else like that. He looked at Rabbit and chuckled to himself.

"Let's head on, then." Boone led the way toward The Pyre. The crowds of miners and gamblers in the streets had thinned by half, but there were still a fair number of men staggering here and there.

The icy gusts of the earlier evening had given way to a heavy, still, cold that penetrated every crease and crevice of clothing and froze the moisture in Boone's nose to a crackly coating that whistled every time he breathed in.

Hank had made the call when it came to Buck. He'd told Rabbit and Boone that if he'd continued to prod and push, Buck's head might not have come back at all. So, they'd shepherded Buck to his shack at the edge of town and tucked him under a pile of blankets to sleep the memories away, if he could.

On the way back, Rabbit had peppered Hank with the same questions burning in Boone's mind, but Hank was slow to respond and his answers were clipped. It was apparent that he wasn't in a mood to explain himself, and Boone would be damned if he'd push the man. Rabbit, on the other hand, wanted answers. It took a fair amount of clandestine cajoling to get him to ease off Hank.

Still, Boone couldn't keep the questions from bouncing around in his head. To start with, how the hell did Hank get Buck to spill like that? It reminded him of the neuro-hypnotist he'd watched at the Piccadilly Traveling Carnival in Albuquerque a couple years back. The thought still made him chuckle. Twenty people prancing like horses, and then later scratching at the ground with their feet, clucking like chickens. The way Buck acted, he was under that same kind of spell. Hank had him spouting tales about things Boone doubted few others had seen. Except maybe Sourpan Saul.

And about Sourpan … What the hell happened to him? What was it exactly that the pack of *dogs* chased away?

He glanced into a saloon window as they passed, noticing a couple of men with their heads down on the bar. Maybe Rabbit was right, it was a little late to be dropping in on Clementine. Boone kept walking toward The Pyre, though. He had questions, and the best person to talk to about them was Clementine. She would have insight about Buck's experiences, he was sure of it.

Luckily for tuckered-out Rabbit—and Hank, too—they were standing in front of The Pyre in only a few minutes. Boone's light rap on the door had Tink barking from inside.

"Clementine," he spoke loud enough to hear through the door. "It's us."

If she'd been asleep, Tink's yips and barks made sure she wasn't anymore.

A short time later, they were sitting in the front parlor with cups of hot coffee. He'd been right, the scene was downright cozy, and the air smelled like warm pine needles, making him want to settle in for a long spell.

Tink was up and around, but she was moving slowly, favoring her bruised ribs. Rabbit sat cross-legged next to her blanket on the floor by the stove while she alternated between snuggling into his lap and staring up at him.

Clementine's hair hung loose down over a long gray wool shirt, looking shiny in the lamp's light. She wore a pair of what looked like silk pants—the sort he'd seen some of the men wear down in Chinatown. The design and stitching of her slippers indicated that they were definitely from that part of Deadwood as well. When she caught him looking at them, she smiled. "A recent gift from a friend. Why don't you shed your hat and coat and stay awhile?"

That was right. Christmas was right around the corner. He wasn't sure if she usually celebrated the day, but he had something to give her anyway.

Boone grabbed his hat from his head and hung it on the coat tree near the door. He ran his fingers through his hair. "I was hopeful you hadn't retired for the evening." He took a sip of the coffee she'd handed him to wash the cobwebs from his brain.

"There are always notes to be taken, those of an undertaker, and my other profession, too." She aimed a soft smile at Hank as he slumped down into one of the plush leather chairs by the stove. "Long day, Hank?"

He opened his eyes and raised one side of his mouth.

"He had Buck spillin' beans all over the floor. It was a sight, Miss Clementine. Told us about things in the Bloody Bones." Rabbit patted Hank on the knee. "Hard work, though, I think. Took the sand out of ol' Hank."

"I'm chipper," Hank said without moving. It was obvious to Boone he was the opposite of that.

"It was almost like neuro-hypnosis or something." Boone stood beside Hank. "Worked on me some, too. Everything went away. All the noises in the bar faded for a little bit." Boone turned to face Rabbit. "Did you feel that? Like you were falling or something. Everything quiet except Hank's voice?"

Rabbit shook his head. "I think you're the one needs some rest there, Booney."

Across the room, Clementine was still watching Hank, her head now cocked to the side. "Excuse me. I'll be right back." She glanced at Rabbit before walking away. "You two can sit in chairs if you'd prefer." She pointed at her desk chair and the other soft leather chair next to the stove.

"Thanks, Miss Clementine, but I'm comfortable as a tick on a hound dog." Rabbit stroked Tink's head.

"I'm happy to stand right now," Boone told her, afraid if he sat down he might fall asleep like Hank seemed to be doing.

His and Rabbit's days were overflowing with work. Running the livery was a job on its own, not including time spent training for hours some days with Clementine. It seemed like building a hotel right now was the worst possible timing. He wondered how Rabbit had gulled him into that. It didn't matter, really. It was under way now. It had to be seen through.

"All right, give me a minute." She disappeared into the dark hallway.

Rabbit held his palms toward the popping and crackling stove and then rubbed them together. "You knocked Booney's one last good nut out of his tree, Hank. Next thing we know, he'll be talkin' like Buck."

"Rabbit, did I ever tell you Uncle Morton never liked you?"

"Ho, you two," Hank mumbled. "Like you was hitched."

"He liked me all right," Rabbit said. "He wanted to drop you off in a wolf den, but I talked him out of it."

Clementine strode back into the room carrying a tin cup. She handed it to Hank. "Drink that down, silver tongue." She winked at him.

He looked at it, and then the coffee tin in his other hand, and then shrugged. He took a sip and scrunched his face up like a raisin. "Miss Clem. That's awful."

She laughed and stood in front of him, hands on hips. "Drink it."

He downed the rest of the contents and gagged. "Bah! Miss Clem, if I didn't know better, I'd be inclined to think that was coal oil and peppermint."

She grinned. "As a matter of fact—"

"Don't say it!" Hank wiped his mouth and handed the cup back to her. "I promised myself I'd never drink coal oil again."

"Sounds like McCuddle's." Boone smirked at Rabbit.

"You sayin' that don't surprise me. Takes a man to handle McCuddle's." Rabbit chuckled. "It's okay, Booney. Don't feel poorly about it. Sooner or later you're bound to grow into a fine man … or maybe not."

"You go on ahead and fondle McCuddle's all you want. I want no part of it." Deciding to compromise between sitting and standing, Boone leaned against Clementine's desk.

"I didn't say 'fondle,' ya old plug. I said handle—"

Boone held his hand up, "Clementine, how's our *caper-sus* cemetery friend on the table in there? Improving at all?"

Clementine pursed her lips, looking at each of them in turn. Then she sighed and said, "He's dead."

What? Boone was pretty sure René had been on the mend when they left earlier. "Took a turn, did he?"

Hank sat up. "How's that?" There was noticeably more color in his face.

Rabbit spared Clementine a look, but then returned his attention to Tink. Boone couldn't be sure of Rabbit's reaction, but it seemed he wasn't exactly happy at the news.

Clementine set the cup on her desk next to Boone and then dropped in the other leather chair. She crossed one leg over the other, letting her slipper dangle. "The Rogue was here earlier."

"Hank told me that," Boone said. "What does that have to do with René?"

"She killed him." Clementine didn't seem any happier than Boone was. How could she let that happen?

"Seemed like the digger was decidin' to make a turn for the good, didn't it, Boonedog?" Hank looked up at Boone for affirmation.

"Hard to tell, Hank, but I think there was good in him." Boone pondered the news for a moment, and then looked at Clementine. "How did she get the chance?"

"I enjoy taking baths from time to time, especially after spending an evening in a graveyard." She shrugged, meeting his gaze. "Apparently, I dallied too long at The Dove."

She'd bathed this afternoon? That explained her loose, shiny hair and the fresh smell of lavender he'd noticed when she set the tin cup down next to him. He shoved aside memories of her in a tub and focused on the troubled expression lining her face.

"Good idea for you too, Booney." Rabbit grinned up at him. "The bath part, I mean." Tink wiggled in his lap and whined, but didn't open her eyes. His grin slipped. "She *is* okay, right, Miss Clementine?"

Clementine nodded. "Bruised ribs. She'll be sore for a few days." She watched Tink shift in Rabbit's lap until the dog got comfortable before continuing. "I came back from The Dove to find the Rogue sitting in that chair." She pointed at Hank.

He looked down at the chair and frowned. "This'n?"

"Yes. She has a penchant for entering establishments uninvited, apparently."

Boone was starting to catch on. "She broke in and killed him while you were away, and then waited."

"Damn," Rabbit said, shaking his head.

Boone refilled his coffee cup and returned to leaning on her desk. "Had some things to discuss, did she?"

Arms now crossed and foot bobbing, Clementine was a picture of frustration. "He *was* on the mend. I was planning on checking up on him and then meeting you three at the livery to discuss releasing him into the care of Hildegard. She and her friends might've been able to get him talking more than I could. She probably could've helped him make better decisions, too. But now I have another body to bury instead."

"That Rogue is good for bustin' a plan, no doubt about that." Hank was sitting upright now. "Didn't come to a scruff, Miss Clem? Wouldn't blame you if it did."

"No, Hank. No dustups, but as sure as Thor can wield his hammer, I wanted to …" She squeezed something imaginary with both hands.

Boone grinned. "Is that a neck in there?"

"As thin as she is, it could be her waist, too." She sighed. "The Rogue killed René simply because he wore the sign of *caper-*

sus. Her morals have gone the way of the mighty mammoth."

Rabbit chewed on his lower lip as he stared down at the sleeping dog in his lap.

"Still thinking he needed to die, Rabbit?" Boone asked.

"Aw, shit. I don't know, Booney. I thought so. But …"

"Yeah. Me too." Boone focused back on Clementine. "So, the Rogue."

"There's no ambiguity of thought in her," she continued with her rant about the Rogue. "No indecision or empathy. She is a killer in the purest sense, and she's very good at it. She …" Clementine frowned at the ticking and crackling stove.

Boone continued for her. "And she isn't going to leave."

Clementine leveled her gray-eyed gaze on him. "Nope."

"What was it she was all afire about tellin' you, Miss Clem?" Hank rose to refill his coffee tin, and then stood beside Boone.

"As you all know, the Bloody Bones is opened up again."

Boone nodded, along with Hank and Rabbit.

"If we are to believe the Rogue, then the *Bahkauv* are back, and in greater numbers. They have spread farther into the Hills, and culling them has become a task that she can't handle alone."

Rabbit shrugged. "We can handle a few *Bahkauv*."

Boone glanced Rabbit's way. He could see the apprehension in Rabbit's rigid shoulders. He felt more than a little of it himself.

"Agreed, and with little doubt." Clementine studied her fingernails. "*But* there is more."

After a few seconds passed, Hank broke the silence. "Miss Clem, are you gonna finish that troublin' start?"

She lowered her hand. "The Rogue has found *Bahkites* in the caves below the Bloody Bones."

Boone exchanged a bewildered look with Rabbit and Hank.

"Eggs," she explained. "There are *Bahkauv* eggs everywhere in the caves. That is, if we are to believe the Rogue."

"Sheeat," Rabbit said, his jaw hanging loose.

"Eggs," Boone repeated. "Those things came from eggs?"

"Tarnation. Like chicken eggs, Miss Clem?" Hank's eyes were wide now.

"Bigger."

"Ostrich eggs then?" Boone asked.

"Even bigger than that."

"Sheeat."

"Rabbit, is that the extent of your remarks this evening?" Boone asked.

"I'll take two with a side of bacon." Rabbit cracked a smile.

"Right."

"What's an ostrich?" Hank pulled on his ear.

Rabbit flung his hand in the air. "So we smash 'em, along with the *Bahkauv*."

"If only it were that easy," she said.

Boone groaned under his breath. Of course it wasn't going to be that simple. Where there were eggs, there was something laying eggs. "What lays *Bahkauv* eggs, Clementine?"

"Sheeat!" Rabbit scoffed. "Giant chicken?"

Clementine laughed before answering Boone. "A queen *Bahkauv*, which supposedly takes two Slayers to kill. Meanwhile, she keeps laying eggs deep in the Bloody Bones."

"Fuuuck."

"Great, Rabbit. You're improving." Boone sloshed the dark liquid in his tin cup. "I don't suppose the Rogue is agreeable to the idea of having three *hombres* along for the ride, either, right?"

"I can't imagine she would be anything but displeased," Clementine said, a small smile playing at her lips as she looked down at her bobbing foot.

"Ain't gonna make no difference if'n she likes it or not, Miss Clem," Hank stated. "Ain't no way you're not thinkin' that we ain't goin'."

Rabbit huffed out a laugh. "Come again?" He grinned at Clementine. "That concoction you gave him must be powerful strong."

Clementine cocked her head. "Hank, you want to try that again."

"All's I'm sayin' is, you ain't goin' with me." He nodded once.

"Without, Hank," Rabbit corrected, still chuckling. "And you ain't goin' without any of us is what I think Hank means to say." Rabbit gently set Tink on her blankets and flopped into the desk chair. He clunked the heels of his boots on Clementine's desk next to Boone's hip and clasped his hands over his belly. "But we got us a little problem with disappearing bodies. *Draug*-ies, remember?"

"Trust me, I remember the *Draug*." Clementine's brow creased deep. "I've thought on it but haven't come up with a solution yet. I need to get to Slagton. I need to know how many are there, and find out who is creating them."

"Dead guys ambulatin'," Rabbit said flatly as if he'd come to terms with the idea. He grabbed his Bowie knife from his boot sheath and began flipping it in the air. "Booney. That sound anything like what Buck was talkin' about? The beasty Hank got him to tell us about?"

Clementine's puzzled expression landed on Boone.

Boone pointed at Hank "He's got a way about him. Spurred Buck to describe some things down in the Bloody Bones. It sounded like they were working the natural tunnels deeper down, below the mine." Boone lifted himself up to fully sit on the desk. "He described something with black skin covered in bumps. Teeth like knives."

Rabbit nudged Boone's butt with his boot. "Sounds like nearly everybody we meet now, thanks to Miss Clementine. Hey, fire in its eyes, don't forget."

"That's right."

"Twisty horns," Hank chimed in.

Boone nodded. "He said whatever it was got into his head, then he started pulling at the skin on his noggin."

Rabbit mimicked Buck raking his skull with his fingertips.

"Like it was manipulating him," Clementine said with a nod.

"Then a pack of dogs—that's what he called them—came and chased it away," Boone continued. "Saved Buck, maybe, but killed his *amigo*, Sourpan Saul."

"That sound like a *Bahkauv* egg layer, Miss Clementine?" Rabbit flipped the Bowie knife in the air again.

"No."

" 'Course not. Ain't got enough beasties to cause concern. Might as well add a couple more. Sheeat." He knife-flipped again.

Boone watched the knife arc up and fall. Rabbit was going to catch that thing by the blade if he wasn't careful. Or stick it into his leg. "Rabbit …" Boone stopped himself. If he said anything about the knife, Rabbit would probably start flipping it higher. Or faster.

"What?"

"Nothing." Boone scooted a few inches away from Rabbit.

"It sounds like a pack of *Bahkauv* chased something away, though." Clementine sat forward. "Was that all he said?"

"No," Rabbit said, glancing at Hank and Boone. "Remember how I said I broke him? Before you two sat down, Buck was talkin' about somethin' else. Or maybe it was the same orange-eyed devil, I don't know. He said something about a pack of beasties. Said they were lappin' up some kinda soup." Rabbit cringed.

Boone cringed, too. So did Hank.

But not Clementine. Her attention had wandered out the window. "Soup? Was there anything else?"

"Something about somebody taking teeth."

Boone smirked. "Rabbit, you still swirling from the not-whiskey?"

"Shut up, Booney."

"You sure got Buck talkin', sounds like," Hank said.

"Didn't make no sense, though. After that, he started in on the …" Rabbit started rocking forward and backward, mimicking

Buck's actions. "That's when you two got there."

"Teeth," Clementine repeated, looking down at her hands.

Boone watched her. There was definitely something grinding its way through her thoughts. "That strike a note with you, Clementine?"

"What?" She frowned, her gaze lifting to his for a moment before darting away. "Oh. Possibly. I'm not sure yet."

He decided not to lean on it since she wasn't offering anything more. "What did Hildegard have to say?"

"Hildegard? That's right. Oh, I met Ludek."

Boone wondered what it was about gut soup and teeth, other than the obvious disgustingness of it, that would distract her so thoroughly, but still he didn't push for more on that subject. "Was Ludek what you expected?"

"Not at all." She clasped her hands together in her lap and smiled. "I almost killed him."

"What?" he asked in unison with Hank and Rabbit.

"You boys might have, too. He looks very much like the white devil we killed in the Bloody Bones."

We killed? She was being generous about the white devil's demise. Besides a little help from Hank, she'd skewered him on her own.

"He's a white devil, too? Well, I never." Hank seemed disgusted by the idea.

"Actually, in case you three meet Ludek face to face, his kind are called *der weißer Hund* in German, or 'white dog' in English. But 'devil' seems more fitting for the way they fight."

"White doggie," Rabbit said. "Got it."

"Apparently there are good white devils, and bad white devils. Now I've met one of each."

"So, this is the Ludek that has followed you for the last few months for Hildegard?" Boone felt more than a little doubtful about Ludek's kind being "good."

"The very same. He and the Russian twins cleaned up around

Galena and checked the cabin where we saw the skins."

"I knew there was something about those two Russians." Rabbit filled his coffee tin and dropped back into the desk chair.

"They didn't find anything at that cabin, did they?" Boone figured he already knew the answer.

"No, but Ludek believes he saw signs that the area had been 'cleaned.'"

These *caper-sus* characters were thorough. Hell, all of the *others* seemed to be, whether it came to killing or cleaning or whatever else they might be up to. Since the bodies had been removed from the saloon in Galena, it could probably be expected elsewhere. "I wonder what they did with the bodies. And the piles of skin. Fed something?" Boone pushed the images of the skinless bodies from his mind.

"Aw, Booney. Now you got that in my head."

"At least something is in there."

Rabbit ignored him. "Is that some kind of *other* rule or something, Miss Clementine? Cleanin' up your own messes and whatnot?"

"Not a rule." She hesitated, her mouth twisting. "Well, perhaps it is. In a way, it's a method of doing business." Clementine stood and walked to the window, her satin trousers as shiny as her hair in the light of the oil lamp. She stared out into the night. "Why did they leave those two trees in the street?" she asked so quietly Boone almost couldn't hear her.

"What's that, Miss Clem?" Hank asked.

She shook her head. "You see everyone out there?" She indicated out the window. "Each is doing business of one sort or another. Each agrees, more or less, on certain rules to maintain order. In Deadwood, there are few laws and fewer to enforce them. All we really have is a social agreement." She turned and faced them. "For instance, take the profession of undertaker. What do you think would happen if we all decided to stop burying the dead? If we chose to leave bodies in the streets?"

"Summer comes around, I'm headin' out of town." Rabbit nodded once to Hank.

"An odiferous condition, no doubt," Hank added.

"Can you imagine? Not to mention the sight of bodies decaying in the street. Disease would be rampant. We can all agree, for many reasons, that burial is the best thing to do."

"Miss Clem. The swig you gave me is gonna make its way back up if you don't quit," Hank protested.

"Or," she continued, "what if a citizen of this town happened to go berserk and began killing everyone wearing a hat. He would be put down in a matter of minutes, if not seconds, and rightly so. He was an infection. The infection would be eradicated. Otherwise the organism—the town—might not survive."

"I got an infection of my own." Rabbit grinned and stuck his thumb toward Boone. "Can't seem to shake it."

The corners of Clementine's mouth curled up a little. "Of course, the social contract in Deadwood is tenuous compared to more developed cities, but it still exists." To Rabbit, she added, "We, *others*," she paused to swirl her hands in the air. "We have agreed to such social contracts, too."

"Bet the *Bahkauv* were the rowdy ones at that sit-down." Rabbit chuckled.

"They weren't invited. They, and countless more like them, must be controlled." Clementine settled into the leather reading chair again, folding her legs partially under her. "And that's why my kind are here in this realm."

Boone rubbed his jaw. So, if there were rules, did that mean there was a governing body of some sort? It occurred to him that there was an order, a way of doing business in Clementine's world. Of course! Otherwise, it would be anarchy. Just like she had described for Deadwood.

"Controlled anarchy," he said softly. "You can't allow every *Bahkauv* or *Höhlendrache* or whatever else happens along to run loose. There would be chaos. Even in your world, there must be balance."

"Yes, Boone." Her eyes glassed over as she stared at him. "Even in *my* world." Her voice sounded hollow, melancholy. Something in her tone tugged at him.

Rabbit grinned at Hank. "Booney has been flippin' pages in his big books again." He bobbled his head. "I think I am, therefore," he quoted in a deep voice.

"Donkey." Boone rolled his eyes. "It's *Cogito, ergo sum.*" When Rabbit just looked up at him, he translated, "I think, therefore I am."

"You speak Latin," Clementine stated. She seemed pleased.

"Just that. Maybe a few other things." Boone smirked at Rabbit. "Read it in a book."

"*Touch me loot, feel me boot.* That's what I read in a book."

"That's what you read, huh?" Boone crossed his arms.

"*Avast and pull me mast.*"

"Hoo hoo! That's a good'n." Hank slapped his knee.

"Rabbit," Boone warned while trying not to grin, sensing that the conversation was beginning to take a turn.

"*Pirates do it harrrder.*"

Clementine pretended to cough, hiding a smile behind her fist.

"*Don't walk the plank, wench, ride i—*"

"Rabbit!" Boone jabbed his thumb toward Clementine, whose shoulders were shaking while she tried to keep a full-on laugh from erupting.

Rabbit grinned, lopsided. "Sorry, Miss Clementine."

Hank broke into a flurry of hoots and sniggers.

To Clementine, Boone said, "I guess the question is, which is the more immediate threat—decaying dead miners walking around; or a yet unseen but probably terrible monstrosity laying gigantic eggs that hatch into foul cantankerous beasts?"

"That sums it, I guess." A small smile still played on her lips. "I'll need to think on it for a time. At the moment, I'm not sure which is the bigger problem."

"I don't suppose you would be happy with the idea of letting Rabbit and me go to Slagton first without you to look things over?"

"You dirty *Draug*!" Rabbit made a gun with his finger and thumb, shut one eye, and aimed his finger at Hank. "Bang!"

She tilted her head to the side. "Do I really need to answer that?"

"Worth a shot. I don't like the idea of you going to Gayville without us, either." Boone's guts churned at the idea. In any case, he probably wouldn't have been able to follow through with a plan that split them up.

Hank grunted. "No sense in drivin' without swings and flankers."

Rabbit gawked. "You a drover too, Hank? What *ain't* you done?"

Clementine turned to Boone with vertical lines between her brows. "Swings? Flankers?"

Boone was familiar with cattle drives. He'd been on three so far and didn't mind the idea of *never* going on another in his lifetime. "Swings and flankers are drovers on the sides of a cattle drive. They keep the herd tight and pop brush for strays." Boone understood the reference, but he was curious how Hank would fill out the drive. "Where does that put you, Hank?"

"Miss Clem is the pointer, and me—well, I'm ridin' drag."

"I'm a drover now, Hank?" Clementine shrugged. "Fine." Apparently, she was up for playing along. "What are my duties? As long as I'm not at the south end of a north-facing cow."

Hank snorted. "Miss Clem, you blaze. You show the bell cow where to go. Ever'body else follows along after."

She nodded, taking on her task solemnly. "Will do."

"Then who's trail boss, Hank?" Boone dipped his head at Rabbit. "Not that cowboy. He'll lead us into a box canyon."

"I'll lead you behind the woodshed for a tanned hide,

buckaroo."

"I reckon it's that Masterson fella. Tho', I'm thinkin' Miss Clem could handle him well enough."

"You figure you're drag, huh, Hank?" Boone always figured it took more man to ride drag than almost any other position. It was grueling what with the constant work to keep the herd moving with cattle always bogged in thick mud or dust. Or stuck chasing strays.

"Yep. Keep all y'all movin' forward."

"Drag." Rabbit made a face. "Eatin' dust at the tail end. Always hated drag." He grinned at Hank. "You do keep us on the straight and narrow, Hank."

Hank nodded once.

"We got a problem, though." Boone fixed his stare on Clementine. "The pointer's not sure where to point us."

She flicked something off her silk pant leg. "I need to talk to the trail boss."

Boone caught the hint of contempt in her voice. "Walk up and knock on his door? Invite him out for tea?"

"We'll go with ya, Miss Clementine. Sounds like this Masterson character is a poison-drinkin' scorpion."

"I appreciate that, Jack, but I'll go alone. You're right, though. He doesn't seem like the tea-drinking type."

"He was mad as a hornet last time we went to Gayville. Can't imagine it'll be any different this time." Boone couldn't square Masterson's reaction to the news that Clementine had ghosted the white devil, along with a score of *Bahkauv*, in the Bloody Bones. Did the devil betray Masterson, or was he fit to be tied just because Clementine had killed his man? Or white dog. Or whatever he was.

"That's why I need to talk to him first," she told them. "There's no sense in upsetting Masterson if it can be helped. I've had too little interaction with him to gauge any threat he may pose, but I do not trust him. Nor does Hildegard."

Boone didn't trust him either, and they hadn't even met. Maybe it was because everything he'd been told about Clementine's boss had sounded nefarious. Maybe it was something in his gut.

He looked sideways at Rabbit and found him staring back. "If a meeting has to take place …"

"I'll meet Masterson alone," Clementine said, her tone leaving no room for debate. "That's the way it works."

Rabbit shook his head.

Boone could have argued the point, but he knew as well as Rabbit that it was useless with the headstrong Northwoman. "What's your opinion, Hank?"

But Hank had slouched against the wing of the chair and was quietly snoring.

"What did you give him?" Rabbit asked.

"Believe it or not, something to help him up his pluck." She smiled warmly at Hank. "Not sure what I'd do without him." Her smile spread to Boone. "Probably easiest if we let him spend the night in that chair. I don't think we could wake him, anyway. I'll grab a blanket for him."

"First," Rabbit said, holding up his hand to stop her. "Your thoughts on our dilemma. Slagton or Gayville? I'm sure you're thinkin' a way."

"Slagton."

"Sheeat. *Draugies*." Rabbit stood and brushed the dog hair from his trousers. "Ain't lookin' forward to shakin' hands with walkin' buzzard food."

"Slagton," Boone repeated and shuddered.

"I'm concerned that the problem has already grown out of control. A legion of *Draug* is more dangerous than a pack of *Bahkauv*. And, if I'm correct, Masterson is controlling the *Bahkauv*. Although, I'm still not sure who I killed in the Bloody Bones—his betrayer or loyalist. In any case, he'll be fit to be tied if we slaughter the *Bahkauv* again."

Boone smiled.

She did a double-take. "You smile?"

"I was wondering almost that same thing not long ago. Betrayer or loyal lackey?"

"Were you now?" She stared at him with slightly lowered lashes.

Something about the way she was watching him made his mouth dry. He cleared his throat and asked, "What about the Rogue? Does she agree with you about Slagton over Gayville?"

She scoffed. "The Rogue believes that the *Bahkauv* are the greater threat."

"I just wanna know if we gotta take the *Draugies'* heads, same as the *Bahkauv*. That's gonna take some grit. I mean, I can do it, but …" Rabbit frowned down at his knife. "Turn a doorknob, can they? Or chase us up a set of stairs?"

Clementine stooped by the woodstove and opened the door. Firelight lit her face with a warm glow, but couldn't reach the shadows haunting her eyes. "If you're asking about their mental abilities, they all seem to differ slightly. But still, taking the head always works best." She tossed a couple of hunks of wood into the stove, and then clanked the door shut, pushing to her feet. "Otherwise, they tend to keep wiggling."

Rabbit cringed.

"What if Masterson doesn't have answers?" Boone asked.

She stepped in front of him, her squint full of ice and steel. "Then we'll come up with some solutions ourselves."

Fifteen

Chinatown, at the northern end of Deadwood, wasn't what Clementine considered a desirable place to visit. She had two cultural prejudices working against her in this part of town: She was an undertaker, a job that was typically spurned by the Chinese due to an age-old fear and stigma connected to touching the dead; and to make matters worse, she was a woman.

After enduring endless shunning for being a dealer-in-death over the last few months, she was inclined to agree with many of the citizens of Deadwood that Chinatown was deserving of its other name: the Badlands.

If she heard the word "unclean" in Chinese one more time, heads were going to roll. It was a simple, phobia-driven insult that shouldn't have needled her more than any of the other rude remarks, but Clementine couldn't tolerate it. She was accustomed to having insults flung at her, but there was something about being called unclean that made her grind her teeth.

Shaking off her frustrations about her ill treatment in this part of town, she focused on the uneven boardwalk under her boots and the task at hand—a meeting with Masterson. Why would he choose the Badlands as a place to rendezvous? Was it to keep her off balance by forcing her to enter into hostile territory? Or did he keep a residence at this end of town? She had no idea where he lived. He had instigated all of their previous meetings with express instructions to contact him only through the madam at The Cricket and only if the circumstances were extremely urgent.

Today was that day. Today, she would secure answers and advice, or she'd proceed on her own no matter his damned rules.

It had been a fitful night, knowing that first thing in the morning she would need to send word to Masterson requesting a meeting. She already knew his feelings about her killing the *Bahkauv* in Gayville, so she had little doubt that telling him she planned to pursue them once again would result in another round of scolds and threats. And then, there was the Rogue.

Clementine clenched her fists several times, trying to ease the frustration that came with being caught between the two. This was by far the most convoluted post she'd taken since striking out on her own so long ago.

She looked up as she neared the Wing Sai Emporium and Restaurant where she was supposed to meet Masterson. The Emporium sat at the northern edge of Deadwood's Chinatown, next to a crookedly constructed clapboard building with no external indication of the happenings within its walls.

On the other side of the Emporium, the Kam Fu Singh Chinese Curios building with its canvas roof seemed to heave with life. Breathing deep at the door or seams between the canvas tent panels would probably produce an opium high if she were so inclined.

"Curios my rump," she muttered.

A line of people waited to enter the Curios building, blocking the front door of the Emporium. Across the street, Clementine slowed to a stop beside a barrel full of brooms in front of a mercantile to decide exactly how to enter the building without being ridiculed or shamed, or without causing some sort of commotion. *Or* without being denied entrance, plain and simple. If the latter happened, then there would definitely be a commotion, because she was going in the Emporium one way or another.

She gazed at Kee Luk Laundry a little farther up the street. It suited her fine if she never entered that establishment, or rather the hog sty behind it, again. She still hadn't figured out why there'd been a hand with a *caper-sus* ring in that hog pen, but it was a reasonable bet that the hand's owner had crossed the wrong *hombre* or *other*.

"*Hombre*," she repeated quietly and snorted. The Sidewinders were rubbing off on her. The thought of Boone and Jack building their hotel or shoveling muck in their livery warmed her in spite of the cold gusts of air whipping through the gulch this morning—and the even colder glares directed her way from passersby.

She pulled her hat lower and tucked her chin to her chest so as not to make accidental eye contact with anyone. She watched the door out of the corner of her eye, waiting for a break in the line to sneak through to the Emporium.

Two Chinese men, both tall and thin, flanked the Emporium's door. They were doing their best to look like disinterested street denizens, but Clementine knew, thanks to one of Hank's many tales, that their vibrantly colored and ornately embroidered *changshan* robes with Mandarin rank squares indicated they were an elite guard—and that there was probably someone inside worth guarding.

Their robes billowed and fluttered in the icy wind as they scrutinized the nearby crowd. Apparently, they were immune to the cold of a Black Hills winter. Clementine squeezed her wool coat tightly around her waist. If Hank was right, these two were capable fighters. A quick dispatch would be difficult.

"*Potzblitz!*" she growled, using one of her amma's favorite curses. Impatience goaded her to go at them, head on, and be done. But the voice of reason stepped in, warning: *Don't be ridiculous. There must be two hundred people who would see you.*

For the next half hour, she watched and waited. The guards

were diligent, but the many distractions and commotions in the street competed for their attention. When a scuffle started a few paces down the boardwalk and the guards rushed to intervene, she slipped through the crowd and into the Emporium at last.

Inside, she stood for a moment, allowing her eyes to adjust from the cloudless sky outside to the shadows draped throughout the place. Hazy blue wisps of smoke fed by incense smudges swirled randomly toward the ceiling, filling the room with an exotic, spicy scent she couldn't place.

The room was more or less the same size as many of the bigger saloons in Deadwood. But that was the extent of the similarities. Brightly colored tapestries of blue birds, red flowers, and intricate scenes too complex to decipher without closer inspection hung from all the walls. Even after her eyes adjusted to the dim light, Clementine continued to gawk at the innards of the Emporium. Jars and urns and lanterns and porcelain finery of all types and colors imaginable covered every available table, chest, and counter, excepting the six or so tables toward the back of the room that were obviously reserved for dining. Bright green, yellow, and pink parasols hung upside down from the ceiling in numbers enough to obscure the patterned tin nailed there. A row of jars with tin lids lined the counter like the candy jars in a mercantile; though, she couldn't even guess at the contents of these. Spices, maybe? Or seeds?

It seemed everything in the building was made of something colored with dyes or paint. Even the patrons wore brilliant red, green, and blue silks, excepting the few who wore black or gray straight-cut frocks or shirts with knot buttons over their straight-legged silk pants.

Her gaze lifted to find a narrowed pair of dark eyes watching her. She looked away quickly, noticing several other heads were turned in her direction. Another search of the room found sideways glances and stares filled with loathing and contempt. She was unwelcome, just as she had expected.

Best not to linger.

She slinked through stacks of porcelain and linens toward the restaurant in the back, keeping her gaze cast downward, and sunk into a chair at one of the empty tables.

She pulled a bronze Roman coin from her coat pocket and set it on the edge of the table where it would be easily seen by anyone who cared to look.

Then she waited.

She waited while men passed by her, hustling to or stumbling from a door hidden behind a grand red tapestry with golden dragons swimming through it.

She waited as women with feet too tiny shuffled back and forth to the other tables with pots of soup and tea.

She waited and listened to the conversations around her in a language she didn't understand.

She glanced at the coin. Placing her fingertip on it, she pushed it in a circle on the table. Had the madam at The Cricket saloon given her the wrong coin this morning?

She sat back and took a deep breath. The heavy smells that mingled in the air around her enticed her appetite and nauseated her at the same time. For the better part of an hour now, she'd suffered through the pungent odor of urine … and the floral scent of what she knew to be burning opium along with three or four different types of incense … and some type of medicinal herbal teas … and a hint of baked buns and slightly rancid fried pork.

Even if she had wanted something to eat, it was now plain to see she wouldn't get it. If the patrons and workers at Wing Sai Emporium weren't leering at her, then they were ignoring her altogether. She should have eaten breakfast before coming. It would have saved her stomach the trouble and confusion of feeling ill and hungry at the same time.

At least she hadn't been called *unclean* yet. Not that she'd heard or understood, anyway.

She continued to eye the front door, the door to the kitchen, and the hidden door behind the tapestry—the latter of which she was now sure was the entrance to the opium den.

What was it like in there? Undoubtedly wall to wall with abused brains and lungs. She thought of Ling and his past addiction, and then of his continued affliction thanks to that hit to the head. Was there more to his mental malady than brain damage? Had the injury opened up a window to his senses that had been closed off previously? She'd heard stories of such metaphysical changes when the brain was compromised.

A prickling sensation ran down her spine, causing her breath to catch. She searched the room.

In a corner of the Emporium, a group of bowing and smiling patrons were gathering and swarming a dark-haired, dark-eyed, familiar face. He stood a head taller than those around him, and his black, towering top hat emphasized his stature. He smiled gregariously as if he were running for town mayor, bowing in return to a few, even shaking hands with some. Yet through it all, his gaze seldom strayed from Clementine.

"Masterson," she said under her breath. That explained the tingling now spreading throughout her limbs.

He waded through the small crowd toward her. His smile had settled into a thin-lipped curve frozen on his face. The closer he came, the more the crowd dissipated, until he stood over her, alone. A wave of nausea extinguished any signs of the hunger that had gnawed at her previously.

"Miss Johanssen." His voice was smooth and even, emotionless.

"Mr. Masterson," she mimicked his tone.

He shrugged off his long coat. "May I sit?"

"I suppose." As he hung his coat on a peg stuck in the wall next to them, she toyed with the Roman coin, rubbing the smooth surface with her thumb. "You certainly kept me waiting long enough. I was beginning to wonder if this coin was a ruse."

She held it out to him.

"I thought I arrived rather quickly." He waved her off and took a seat opposite her. "Keep it. You may need it again."

She palmed it and studied the portrait. "Flavius Constantinus." She frowned up at him. "Is there some significance, using this particular coin as a summoning token?"

Masterson sat back, clasping his hands across his tweed waistcoat, and stared at her with a small frown. "Why are we here?"

"Straight to busi—" Clementine paused as a young Chinese girl in a snug, floral silk dress set a tea tray with a small pot, a lone cup, and a handful of tiny white cakes on the table in front of Masterson. She bowed to him, her profile to Clementine, and then poured tea into the cup.

Clementine glared at the girl. *"Nǐ hǎo,"* she spoke loudly and clearly to the waitress. The greeting was the only thing Clementine knew of the Chinese language, and that was thanks to Hank, who had many acquaintances here in Chinatown.

The waitress set the full, steaming cup directly in front of Masterson and bowed again.

"Xièxiè, Meu Hua," he said. His smile had returned, wide and dripping with charm.

The girl's face bloomed bright pink. She covered her mouth with her hand like it was a fan and lowered her chin. Clementine recognized the submissive feminine pose, along with the fake shyness as the waitress fluttered her eyelashes. *"Bù kèqì, tóu rén."*

Masterson ignored the girl's attempt to flirt with him and aimed his smile at Clementine. "Now, where were we?"

Clementine battled another wave of queasiness. "Drop the smile," she told him. "Your charms are wasted on me."

The waitress shot Clementine a hateful sneer before flittering away toward the kitchen. Her tight, ankle-length dress kept her steps short and quick.

"That's a beautiful dress," she called to the girl's back. "Too tight, though. Hard to land a good kick to the ribs in that. Oh, and no tea for me, thank you."

Masterson's face betrayed his contempt for the other patrons. "Simpletons."

"You mean the wait staff?" He couldn't mean the Chinese, not with their cultural depth and wisdom. They were rude to her in particular, but their ingenuity was admirable, and Hank had nothing but positive words for those he'd worked with on the railroad.

Masterson chortled. "I mean humans."

Why the disdain? Clementine pocketed the coin. What made him think he was so superior? Were longevity and acquired wisdom always accompanied by a notion of eminence? She didn't sense that from Hildegarde.

"How pretentious of you," she said, needling him.

He plucked a bite-sized cake from the tray and popped it in his mouth. If her affront found purchase, he hid it well. "To the contrary. You'll find I comport myself in a manner commensurate with my station." He popped another cake into his mouth and then brushed his hands together.

Station. Her jaw clenched. Arrogant bastard.

"Now, Miss Johanssen, since you seem somewhat reluctant to announce your explanation for this meeting, let *me* begin." He sat forward, his focus intense. "You have sought outside counsel to perform your tasks," he stated, rather than asked.

Her stomach fluttered, and not due to his proximity this time. She held a straight face. Did he know of Hildegard? Miss Hundt? Ludek? Or was he simply casting nets into unknown waters?

"You must introduce us," he continued, studying her. "Perhaps we can all help each other."

Ahhh, so he must not know for sure exactly who her so-called "outside counsel" was. She thought of Hank, Boone, and Jack. There was no point in attempting to hide them from Masterson, especially with the way Jack was brandishing his identity in the news sheets and every other saloon in town. And now, with the purchase of the livery and soon-to-be-built hotel, Jack *and* Boone were somewhat more prominent than most of the citizens in Deadwood, if not the surrounding hills as well.

"They are tools that I use at my discretion," she bluffed.

"No, Clementine." His use of her first name suddenly didn't pass by her unnoticed. "I'm aware of these so-called *Sidewinders*. How could one not be? And Mr. Varney, as well." His jaw tightened visibly. "The Sidewinders are not attendants, in any case. That much is certain."

Dritt! She still kept her poker face in place, waiting to see where he was heading with this particular topic.

"I have no objection to you acquainting yourself with the denizens of Deadwood." He raised a finger. "You would be well advised, however, to refrain from soliciting their aid while tending your duties. It may cause unnecessary complications." His dark gaze narrowed. "Lethal distractions, shall we say, for everyone involved."

Clementine took a long slow breath. *Sonofabitch.*

At her silence, he continued. "A Slayer shall work alone," he stated, as if reading from a tome or writ. "At least that much is being done correctly on your part."

So, he didn't know of the Rogue either. Interesting.

"I commend you on your efforts at Ingleside Cemetery." He laced his fingers together and rested his hands on the table. "There is much more to be done there. We must not allow our adversary to establish a grouping of *Draug* too numerous for you to slay when the time comes."

On that point, they agreed. "I'm concerned we may be too late already," she said.

His charming smile returned.

Another bout of nausea rolled through her stomach. She reached across the table and stole the steaming cup of tea out from under him in a blink. She raised the tea to him in a mock toast before taking a drink. The hot, bland liquid burned its way down her throat and into her belly, loosening the knots that had formed there.

Masterson raised one eyebrow. "I was aware that Slayers possess unrivaled quickness, but … bravo."

She set the cup down. "There is another issue." Actually, there were many issues, but first things first.

"Before you begin, let me commend you on a most impressive performance in Galena. Your work there was exemplary. There is little concern the region poses an urgent threat to us now."

Clementine acknowledged his compliment with a nod, wary of his purpose in handing it out. She didn't trust the forked-tongue of a snake, especially when such a snake also came with fangs as deadly as Masterson's.

"But the Sidewinders and your attendant foul the task. It is risky."

She squeezed her hands into fists. Clementine disagreed. All three men were certainly capable. Take Jack at the cemetery—his knife skills were improving by the day. He certainly was capable of *kicking ass*, as Jack would say.

"Not to mention you allowed a ranking *caper-sus* to escape."

"I caught up with him at the cemetery," she told him. Good Valhalla! How many times would she be reminded of that misstep?

"The point is, he escaped. That was careless. Carelessness leads to chaos. Chaos results in defeat."

"It was unavoidable." Clementine thought back on that night in Galena, replaying the moment when Jack almost took a knife to the ribs.

"Unavoidable." Masterson watched her with a smirk on his lips. "Your acquaintances interfered, I assume."

She shrugged. "The details are not your concern." At least Jack had gained a well-crafted knife from the encounter.

She finished the tea in the cup and poured another. The concoction continued to ease the tightness and nausea in her stomach. What herbs were in this tea? She'd have to ask Hank to find out and buy her some.

"Be careful it doesn't become my concern, Slayer." Masterson sat back and took a deep breath. "Now, to your issue."

Clementine hesitated. She had many issues. Egg-bearing *Bahkauv*, *Höhlendrache*, and skin-eating beasts roaming the forest, to name a few. Then there were the "white grizzlies," as Boone and Jack called them, which were also out there hiding in the trees. She hadn't even come across one of those yet.

The *Bahkauv* was the issue she wanted to address. But it was also the trickiest. If Masterson had his hand in the goings-on in Gayville, as she suspected, she would need to tread softly. Their last meeting on the subject of the Bloody Bones had ended with terse threats about bodily harm—first to her, and then to him.

Masterson regarded her expectantly.

"I need to know …" She pretended to hesitate, figuring it was best to let him think she was seeking his guidance.

"Yes?"

"I need to know how you would like me to proceed with Gayville."

He stiffened and then leaned over the table, his finger jutting toward her face. So, he was back to threatening already.

"We have discussed this in full. You are to refrain from any task that takes you near there, including any mining activity in the area."

By "mining activity," he undoubtedly meant the Bloody Bones.

She plunked her elbows on the table, crossing her forearms. "*Bahkauv* are running loose in those hills."

"And?"

Ah, so he knew about them. That wasn't really surprising. She was beginning to wonder if Masterson not only knew about them, but was responsible in some way.

"I'm told that there is little to no shepherding of the beasts."

"And?" he said again, sounding bored.

"They are beginning to kill humans."

He snorted. "I fail to recognize the issue."

"Is this your machination?"

He watched her in silence.

She waited for several beats and then smirked. "Now you go silent? You were singing like a mockingbird a few minutes ago."

"Gayville is not your concern."

She disagreed, in spite of the underlying menace in his reply. "But it might be if the infestation spreads to Deadwood."

"Everything is under control."

Clementine doubted that. "So you say, but if the threat is sufficient, I will feel justified in rectifying the problem." She hit him with a hard glare of her own. "*That* is my duty as a Slayer."

"Noted." He brushed nonexistent lint from his sleeve. "Your immediate concern is *Draug*."

She bristled at being told what her priorities should be. She may have agreed to his contract, but she did not agree to heel to his every command. As he'd said before, Slayers worked alone.

"Who was the notable I killed in the Golden Echo?" she asked.

Masterson huffed, eyeing her with a slight tilt to his head. She had the feeling he was deciding on what level of trust he was willing to place in her, if any.

"Who?" she pressed.

"From time to time, you will find yourself faced with situations in which things are not always as they appear." He stood up from the table and reached for his coat. "I will supply the information you require to complete your tasks. I'll leave it there."

Clementine sat back, shaking her head. And so ended another mentoring moment for the resident Slayer given by the resident untrustworthy jackass who considered himself her boss. Why had she even wasted her time coming here today?

"Leave Gayville to me," Masterson said as he slid his arms through his sleeves. "If you interfere again ..." He shook his head slowly. "Let's just say there are casualties in our professions, Miss Johanssen. Don't be one of them."

Sixteen

The next morning …

Boone woke to Hank gone and Rabbit snorting and snoring at the ceiling. He grabbed his saddlebags, which were stuffed to bulging, and headed down from the loft to find Nickel already in the grooming stall. He patted the horse's shoulder and looked him in the eye. "Amelia wake you up already, *Jefe Grande*? You ready? We have a job to do today."

Boone had given Nickel his new nickname, which meant *Big Boss*, after watching the piebald double back-kick a *Höhlendrache* so hard that the reverberations practically shook the snow from the trees around them. Well, maybe not *that* hard, but Nickel had clobbered the beast in the head with both hooves and knocked it on its scaly tail. That kick had taken the momentum away from the bastard at just the right moment. That was the way Boone chose to see it.

Nickel sidled closer to Boone. He stroked the horse's neck and smoothed down his mane.

"Saved Dime's life, didn't you?"

The horse nickered and craned his neck to press his cheek against Boone's.

"All right, ya big softy." He scratched the horse's shoulder, his cheek still pressed against Nickel's.

He was in awe of the quiet power horses held in calm reserve until the moment it was needed. Behind him, Dime snorted and stomped at the ground. Boone smirked. Then there was Dime …

"Hello, Mr. McCreery."

He jerked and pulled away from Nickel. "Good morning, Amelia. You startled me. You're up early. Not even dawn yet."

"It's the rhythm of the livery." She looked all around her. "It breathes. Do you feel it?"

Boone paused, listening, trying to feel the livery *breathe*. "Can't say I do. But that's why you're here, right?"

She nodded. "It's good. The way you talk to Nickel. You know Mr. Fields does, too? To Dime, I mean."

Boone knew. "Horses talk, if you care to listen. This one here, he'll talk your ear off. So will that one." He dipped his head toward Dime, who pricked his ears and watched his *amigo* Nickel from their shared stall across the way.

She tilted her head. "If I didn't know better, I'd think Hank actually has conversations with Fred the Mule."

Boone grinned. "I know what you mean. If Fred wiggles his ears, Hank scratches at his own."

Amelia giggled and nodded.

"It's time we saddled up. You brushed and hoof-picked this fella, right?"

"Yep. All done." Amelia threw a saddle blanket over Nickel's back. "You know, Hank's been that way since I've known him. He's … what did my pop call him? *Empathic*, I think it was."

Boone thought about that for a moment. Yep. He'd have to agree. Hank had a way of understanding what people were feeling, same as animals.

"Is Hank still sleeping?" She pointed at the ceiling.

"Nope. Up early taking care of some business or other that nobody else knew needed taking care of." That was Hank's way, too.

"Hmm. That explains why I didn't hear Fred when I got

Nickel out. He usually starts up his morning commotion as soon as you open the livery door, huffing and snorting and complaining like a steam locomotive."

"Did you say Fred or Hank?" he asked, chuckling.

She laughed along with him.

"Then that's Mr. Fields snoring up there."

Boone shot a frown toward the loft. "I'll probably have to rouse him."

Amelia moved closer and dipped her head. "I don't think he's warming to me, Mr. McCreery," she whispered.

Now that Boone remembered it, Rabbit had mentioned some notions about Amelia not doing the best job. Unfair sentiments, in Boone's opinion. "Oh now. That's not true. Just the other day he was saying how much cleaner the livery is since you arrived."

"He did?" She glanced at him, then back at the ground, kicking straw into a little pile. "My thoughts get all tied in knots when he's around, like I took a snort of hooch or something." She grimaced up at him with pink cheeks. "I don't snort hooch, I mean, Mr. McCreery. I just hear some folks talk about it sometimes."

He patted her on the shoulder. "I don't think you have anything to worry about, Amelia. You do right fine by us and this livery. Keep on and let me handle Mr. Fields."

Boone turned back to Nickel and smoothed out the saddle blanket before heaving his saddle onto ol' *Jefe Grande's* back.

"We could use some lanolin for the livery," Amelia told him as she helped him. "And Pop said he could use a new hoof rasp. He was going to ask you today, but he's sleeping yet."

Boone nodded. "It might need to wait, though, since we're headed out for a day or two."

Her dark ponytail fell over her shoulder as she reached under Nickel to grab the cinch. "I can collect supplies."

Boone watched her grasp the latigo and in one fluid motion loop it through the cinch and tie it off. Her technique was new to

CAN'T RIDE AROUND IT

him, and he was sure he couldn't repeat it without some practice.

She looked up at him expectantly. "Pop has had me collecting supplies since I was this high." She held her hand out at chest level.

He had considered putting Beaman in charge of supplies for the livery, but he was thinking of the older, hairier Beaman, not the pretty young one who might find herself in dire straits if she happened into the wrong circumstance while walking the unpredictable streets of Deadwood.

"This town tends to chew on lasses, especially those on the fairer side." Boone threw his saddlebags over Nickel's rump and began lacing them tight to the back of the saddle.

"I could take Ling and Gart with me." Amelia wiggled the saddle and then pushed her hand in between the blanket and the crest of Nickel's neck.

Boone watched her with a smile. *She knows how to tack.*

"If you push the blanket up into the gullet a little," she told him, "it'll keep him comfortable around the withers on a long ride."

Nickel blasted hay and dust from his nose and then nickered. Dime huffed back from the stall where he was still confined.

"Guess they agree." Boone knew how to set a saddle blanket, but he was impressed that a girl as young as Amelia did, too.

"Ling and Gart, or your pa," he nodded, agreeing to her suggestion. "Having any of them along would make me more comfortable. We have an account at Nussbaum's Mercantile down the street a way. They'll have whatever you or your pa need. Put it on the Sidewinders' account."

She giggled. "Sidewinders?"

Boone stuck his thumb toward the loft. "Rabbit, uh, Jack set that up. He's partial to the sound of it. Kind of growing on me, too. Sidewinder Hotel and Livery." He spread his hands out along the imaginary sign they'd paint on the fronts of the two buildings.

"I like it." She grabbed the bridle from a peg.

"So do I," Rabbit called from the top of the loft stairs. "Some smart *hombre* come up with that? Oh yeah, I did." He finished buttoning his shirt as he clomped down the steps. "I'd be inclined to think you're useful, Booney, if you handed me a plateful of breakfast right about now."

From the corner of his eye, Boone saw the bridle slip from Amelia's hands. Her hand shot out, but she began juggling it in the air in an attempt to snag it. Boone lunged forward to steady her as she stumbled over her own feet trying to catch the elusive bundle of leather, but she was just out of reach. She staggered forward, caught the noseband of the bridle and stepped on the pole strap. Her legs tangled in the strips of leather and down she went.

A bark of laughter filled the room. Boone glared at Rabbit, who was heaving with laughter, his hand over his mouth.

Amelia shot up with bridle in hand. She faced Boone, her cheeks scarlet in the lantern light, her eyes as big as wagon wheels. "See? I told you," she whispered.

Boone worked to keep his expression subdued to a smile. He held out his hand for the bridle. "I'll do that. Nickel's particular about that throatlatch."

After Rabbit stopped laughing, he sauntered over. He pulled on his sheepskin coat and rubbed his hands together. "Who'd a thunk? Breakfast and a show! But I still ain't got no breakfast." He looked pointedly at Boone.

"Shut up, Rabbit." Boone strung the bridle over Nickel's head. "Go get Dime."

"I'll get him." Amelia scurried off across the livery.

Nickel snorted and eyed Boone.

"Nickel says he's got a question." Rabbit leaned in closer and whispered, "He says he wants to know if he should dance along with her next time."

"Dunderhead. You make her nervous," Boone whispered

back.

Rabbit shrugged. "That was funny though, right? Bridle straps every which a way."

As Amelia pulled Dime into the grooming stall beside Nickel, Rabbit stood up straight and closed his mouth. "Does Dime run bitless, too?" she asked as she grabbed the currycomb and began working Dime's sides. "Looks like it." Dime nickered and huffed and pushed lightly against her.

"He's quite a bit less horse than Nickel." Boone grinned and winked at Amelia, then patted Nickel's shoulder. "But we still like him anyway, right, *Jefe Grande?*"

"What's that, Nickel?" Rabbit held his ear close to Nickel's mouth. "Okay. Okay. I'll tell him." Rabbit smirked at Boone. "He says to quit callin' him fat."

"I'll get your saddle, Mr. Fields." Amelia hung up the brush and reached for a blanket.

Rabbit looked her up and down. "Hmm. You're not much bigger than the saddle but alrighty then. Booney, go get my pack and rifle."

"Look in my eye," Boone told him. The first time he'd ever said that to Rabbit, they were still little shavers. At the time it meant: *I'm serious.* Now it simply meant: *fuck off.* More or less.

Rabbit laughed and punched Boone on the shoulder before heading for his pack and rifle.

Dime continued to nicker softly as Amelia worked the blanket and saddle onto his back. By the time Rabbit returned with his Sharps, bandoleros, bedroll, and saddle bags, Amelia had Dime saddled and neat.

"Can you handle Fenrir?" Boone asked her. "Or should we wait for Clementine or Hank?"

As far as Boone knew, they were the only two people Fenrir would allow the honors of grooming and tacking.

"I can get her." Amelia headed toward the towering, black Morgan.

Boone shot Rabbit a skeptical smile. "Are you sure?"

Amelia turned and nodded back at Boone, and then trotted on to Fenrir's stall.

Boone pulled his rifle from the scabbard strapped to his saddle, dribbled a few drops of armor oil onto the lock of the Winchester, and worked the action. "Smooth. Not like that Sharps of yours. That thing is like trying to shoot with a rusty pump handle." He slid the rifle back into its scabbard.

"It's okay, Booney. Don't feel bad. Maybe you can ping us a squirrel for dinner with that little pea-shooter. Might be you'll get lucky and bag us a hare. Or you could throw rocks. Better chance that way."

"I'll bag a *Rabbit*, all right." Boone backed Nickel out of the grooming stall. "Mr. Fields, someday you'll learn. The gun doesn't make the man. But don't you fret. You're young. You'll learn how to be a man someday."

"I'm only six months younger than you." Rabbit smirked. "And, if you remember—"

The livery door banged open and Clementine stepped inside. She paused after closing the door behind her, looking around the place as she stretched her neck to one side and then the other. She had her hair braided down her back today under her fur trapper's hat and a scarf hanging loosely over her thick wool coat.

"Clementine, over here." Boone waved once, smiling at the sight of her. She looked even better this morning than she had last night in his thoughts, although not as soft as the night before last since she'd traded her silk pants for heavy canvas ones. Realizing Rabbit was watching him with narrowed eyes, he dropped his gaze and began to check his horse and gear, pulling on straps and testing knots.

Rabbit moved in closer, a big grin spread from cheek to cheek. "What're you doin', Booney?"

Boone patted Nickel. "Good smooth job. What Amelia did."

Rabbit held onto the fat grin and shoulder-bumped him. "Is it now?"

"Morning, *banditos*." Clementine carried saddlebags and a pack that were all as overstuffed as Boone's.

"*Buenos dias, gringa*." Rabbit gave her a two-finger salute.

"We should have helped you with all that." Boone nodded at her baggage.

"Thanks, but I managed. I'm strong, remember?" She added with a wink. "Good morning, Amelia." She watched the younger woman lead Fenrir to the grooming stall, and then shot Boone a raised brow look.

He nodded and shrugged. In less than a week, Amelia had done what both he and Rabbit had given up on—making friends with Fenrir.

"Morning, Clementine." Amelia ran her hand down Fenrir's leg and then headed for the brush hanging on the wall. With the help of a stool, she brushed and saddled the statuesque horse almost as effortlessly as she had Nickel and Dime, asking for help from Boone only to heave the saddle onto Fenrir's high back.

"Are you boys ready for a hoedown in Slagton?" Clementine set her packs on the ground, her back to them as she opened one of the flaps and sifted through the bag.

Rabbit tapped the sawed-off hanging down his left leg, his single action on his right hip, and his belt bristling with knives. Then he grabbed his crotch. He nodded at Boone. "Let's ride."

"Rabbit." Boone jutted his thumb toward Amelia, who was on the other side of Fenrir, reaching up to strap on her bridle. Luckily for the fool, Beaman's daughter hadn't been looking.

Rabbit grinned and held his palms up toward Boone.

He was acting like he was raring to go, but Boone knew better. In fact, Rabbit had mentioned *Draug* in one way or another a number of times the previous evening as they settled into their bunks. He seemed particularly concerned that they would follow him around and eat him alive, piece by piece. *You think they'll try to chew on us?* he'd asked after they'd put out the lamp. Boone had tried to allay Rabbit's fears, but truth be told he wasn't entirely sure the notion was out of the realm of possibilities.

They had to trust in Clementine and her decision that dealing with the *Draug* in Slagton was the looming issue. Boone wasn't looking forward to saying hello to a walking corpse any more than than he was facing off with a pack of *Bahkauv*. Both gave him pause along with plenty of chills.

Clementine hadn't been exactly forthcoming about her meeting with Masterson yesterday, but she'd said enough for Boone to know that the *Bahkauv* in Gayville were Masterson's doing. She also made it clear that there would be hell to pay if she disobeyed him and pursued the trouble in the Bloody Bones.

So, was Boone ready to go to Slagton? Hell no! But when Clementine looked his way, he said, "I'm ready to ride." He wasn't going to let her face the *Draug* without him.

Amelia opened the main livery door for them a short time later. Boone led Nickel out into the chilly, still mostly dark morning, following behind Clementine and Fenrir. Rabbit and Dime brought up the rear. All three mounts had lumpy packs on their backs, since this trip would require sleeping out in the cold for at least a couple of nights.

Crusty snow and ice crunched under the assemblage of horse and human feet, adding emphasis to the brisk, bitter breezes churning along the almost deserted street. A shiver worked its way from one horse to the next.

Dime snorted and sidled toward Amelia, who stood with her arms wrapped around her waist inside the open livery door.

"Goddamn winter." Rabbit closed up the lapels of his sheepskin coat over his mouth and nose.

Where was Hank? They were supposed to be hitting the trail early. Boone pulled his hat down tighter over his head. "I'm with you, Rabbit. Damned Black Hills winter. Can't get a day of respite from ol' Jack Frost."

"Hey, winter's close to over though, and it ain't snowin'. Spring must be just down the road a piece." The tone in Rabbit's voice held a healthy advantage of sarcasm over humor.

Winter was just getting started and Rabbit darn well knew it. "Let's buy that livery, he says." Boone's voice held no mirth, either.

"Throw that at me, why not? On a morning like this," Rabbit grumbled.

Clementine took a deep breath. Then another. "Ah! It's bracing. You Sidewinders need a hot rock to sun yourselves on."

Fenrir pawed at the ice and snow, breaking it into hunks.

All three horses suddenly looked up the street with ears perked, and then began to blow and stomp.

In the gloomy but gaining light of morning, Boone made out a figure tramping toward the livery hunkered low against the cold while leading a mount. There was no urgency to his pace.

Up and down the street, a few hardy souls braved the cold while hunched, shuffling with quick purpose toward their destinations or the nearest doorway that divided wonderful warmth from icy discomfort. Boone wished he were headed for one of those doors instead of the frigid indifference of the winter wonderland between them and Slagton.

The figure stood up from his hunker and waved. *At them?*

"Hank!" Clementine waved back.

"Hiyo, Hank!" Rabbit called out. His disposition seemed instantly improved.

"Mornin' ever'body!" Hank hauled up to a stop and slapped Rabbit and then Boone on the back. Without Boone's thick sheepskin coat, it would have stung.

"Promise kept?" Clementine collected Fenrir's reins.

"Yes, ma'am. I keep my promises, Miss Clem."

Promise? What promise? Boone knew there was a depth to

Hank most people overlooked. His unassuming appearance concealed a complexity that Boone had yet to understand.

"Who you keepin' promises to, Hank?" Rabbit bounced and whipped his leg up and over Dime's saddle.

Clementine sprang onto Fenrir's back with the nimbleness of a cat. It was something Boone and Rabbit were accustomed to doing on their horses as well, but Fenrir was almost a foot taller than Nickel or Dime.

Boone sent her a half smile as she looked down at him. "You could at least make that look like it took a little effort. Make an old man feel better about it."

"Aw, Booney. You need a stool? Say the word, I'll get down and push your bee-hind into that saddle." Rabbit tightened his coat around his chin again.

"You need some McCuddle's, Boone?" Clementine winked at him. "Put some energy in your old blood?"

"Well, mornings like this," he said, huffing a cloud of steam into the dry, frigid air, "I'm feeling pretty old." He rubbed at the crick in the small of his back and then took hold of the saddle horn and launched himself up onto Nickel's back.

"There ya go, ol' man. You made it!" Rabbit clapped his gloved hands together.

Hank hooted and began the slow crawl up Fred the Mule's side and toward the saddle. "Hoo, Boonedog the ol' man." He raised his leg to swing it over and kicked Fred in the hip. The mule grunted and shuffled sideways.

Rabbit erupted in laughter. Boone joined him.

"Simmer down now, Fred." Hank raised his leg again just enough to slide it up and over the cantle and down the other side.

"Looks like you need a shorter mule, Hank." Rabbit chuckled as he steered Dime up next to Nickel.

"Or longer legs," Boone chimed in.

Hank's eyes twinkled above his short beard. "Maybe take a

little off Fred's legs. Step right over thatta way."

Fred whinny-hawed his disapproval of the idea and shuffled closer to Fenrir, who was pawing at the snow again.

"She says it's time to go." Clementine patted Fenrir's shoulder.

Hank leaned forward against Fred's neck and rubbed the mule's cheek. "Don't hold nothin' against me."

"Give him a beer and he'll forgive ya." Rabbit kicked Boone's boot in the stirrup. "Scoot. You're in my way." He reined Dime past Nickel and up next to Fred. "Say, Hank, who you doin' favors for so early in the mornin'?"

"Dutch Oven Sal. She's got herself a fried elk steak concoction as—"

"Hold it." Clementine nudged Fenrir up next to Hank and Fred. "Before you get started on Dutch Oven Sal, how about you strike out for Slagton since you know the way."

"Oh. Surely, Miss Clem." He clicked his tongue at Fred, who trudged down the street.

Rabbit rode along beside him. Clementine fell in behind them with Boone bringing up the rear.

"Anyway, Sal rubs this lichen she gets from the caves around these here hills into the elk steaks and …"

Boone lost Hank's voice in the growing din of a waking gold rush town. "*Draug*," he muttered to himself. "Who'd have figured?"

If anyone had told Boone a year ago he'd be contending with corpses risen from the grave, he would have choked on his whiskey. Because surely he would've been in a saloon, and that "anyone" would have been telling a tale the likes of which Rabbit would read in his dime novels.

Clementine slowed up so he could ride next to her. "Yes. *Draug*." She'd apparently overheard him talking to himself. "Some call them *Draugar* if there are many."

"Shit. Many? And you think they pose a bigger threat than the

Bahkauv around Gayville?" Who was he to question her? He'd had the displeasure of meeting *Bahkauv* a short time ago and hadn't yet seen a *Draug*. Clementine had first-hand experience with *Draug*, and at the very least, knowledge of the *Bahkauv* queen.

"I believe so." She frowned at the road in front of them. Boone got the impression she was seeing something other than the muddy snow and frozen wagon wheel tracks.

"You're thinking of your grandfather—your afi? The slaughter that day? Because that's what I'm thinking of. What was the name of that town in Germany?"

She nodded, her brow still lined. "Kremplestadt. The Day of Decay."

Boone remembered her story. She had fought and killed a host of *Draug*, she and her afi. He struggled to imagine what it would be like to slaughter an entire village of people turned to monsters. "The corruption," he repeated what she'd called it.

"Yes."

"We should know what to look out for. Their strengths. Weaknesses. How to kill …" There was a troubled shadow in her gaze when she looked his way that made his chest tighten. "What aren't you telling us?"

"I'm worried we're too late. If what Ling and Gart have told me is true, it's possible someone has been raising them for some time." She rubbed the saddle horn with her glove. "I should have dealt with this before now. I've waited too long." Her tone was heavy with guilt.

Boone shifted in his saddle. "We are going to Slagton to kill *Draug*, or *Draugar*, I guess, right?"

"If we can. If there are not too many. I'll make that determination when we get there."

"And if there are too many?" The fluttering butterflies in Boone's stomach were growing into fire-breathing dragons.

How many was too many?

"Then I'll need to meet with Masterson again. But the longer I take to dispose of the *Draug*, the farther they wander, spreading disease and death."

"What about the Rogue? Whose side is she on?" If the Rogue was as capable as Clementine, the two of them should be close to unstoppable together.

"The Rogue is unreliable. She heeds no call, nor does she answer to a benefactor."

"Shit."

"Exactly. What we need to do now is determine the extent of the ..." She turned to Boone, her lips pursed. "What would you call it?"

"Well, it sounds something like the snake den we had to contend with back at the ranch in Santa Fe." He shuddered at the memory. "It kept getting bigger and bigger until Uncle Morton finally decided we needed to eradicate the snakes or they would eradicate us."

She made a face. "I'm not fond of snakes."

"Neither am I." He chuckled. "Rabbit wanted to use dynamite. In the end, we ate a lot of rattler meat for a while."

Clementine wrinkled her nose. "Rattler meat?"

"It's not bad, actually, if it's cooked right."

"Someday you'll have to cook it 'right' to convince me."

Boone laughed. "The den of snakes on our ranch was an infestation. Sounds like that's what we're dealing with now. An infestation of *Draug*."

"I've not heard it described any better."

They veered left as the road split into a crooked Y.

"So, what's the best way to kill a *Draug*? No wait. Let me guess." He ran his finger across his throat.

Clementine nodded. "When you wonder, rend it asunder."

Boone let out a bark of laughter. "That was really bad."

Rabbit craned his neck to look back at them. "Keep it down back there. Too much laughin' and Uncle Mort is gonna give you some chores."

Boone patted the hilt of the black-bladed scimitar hanging from his saddle. "Well, I don't know about you, but I got exactly what I need to finish *my* chores. Where is Uncle Morton, anyway?"

He hadn't thought about his uncle this morning, nor heard a peep about the ghost from his *amigo*. According to Rabbit, Uncle Morton seemed to have some set habits, just as he had when he was alive.

"Probably still sleeping, the ol' coot. Or whatever he does when he's not botherin' me. Usually doesn't show up until breakfast, or until he's good and ready."

"Yer uncle is takin' things leisurely, is he?" Hank asked. "Sounds like Fred lately. Sometimes he don't want to come outta his stall all day."

"You talkin' about Boone?" Rabbit aimed a smartass grin in Boone's direction and snickered.

"Nope, just ol' Fred. Cantankerous as Boonedog in the mornin', though."

"Hey, now. I just need my coffee." Boone glanced at Clementine, enjoying the sight of her smile.

"Hoo! Just funnin' ya, Boonedog. Ol' Fred, he wants to chew his hay an' oats while watchin' the goin's-on sometimes."

Up ahead in the road, a lone figure stepped from the shadows between the buildings, standing in the middle of the road with one hand raised. Rabbit and Hank slowed to a stop. Clementine and Boone pulled up next to them.

Boone leaned forward, trying to see who blocked their path. The early morning gloom made it hard to see. A long, dark hooded cape effectively concealed the figure's identity.

He thumbed the hammer of his peacemaker. Out of the corner of his eye, he saw Rabbit's hand move slowly to the butt of his Colt. A glance at Clementine found her watching the figure intently, but not making any move toward her weapons.

The cloaked being seemed to glide toward them.

The horses and mule snorted and shifted, but appeared untroubled overall. Boone was pretty sure if this figure were an *other*, the horses would be pitching a fit. But what did he really know about *others*?

Clementine turned to him. "It's Ludek," she said, loud enough for only the group to hear. "Hildegard's spy."

Boone wasn't sure if he should feel threatened or not. Clementine's world had muddied the waters the day he met her.

"Ludek? The skulker that's been watchin' you?" Rabbit squinted into the morning gloom, too.

"Yes, that Ludek." She glanced down at Boone's hand on his gun. "We can trust him." Her attention returned to the cloaked figure. "But why is he here now?"

"Looks like he's going to tell us," Boone said.

"Good morning, *Scharfrichter*." Ludek spoke in a deep voice. "Mr. McCreery. Mr. Fields. Hank." He faced each in turn and bowed slightly. Ludek's focus returned to Clementine. "There is something you must know before you set out for Slagton."

How did he know they were heading for Slagton? Had Clementine confided in Hildegard yesterday after her talk with Masterson? She hadn't mentioned anything about sharing their plans.

Clementine stared down at Ludek for a moment, her eyes narrowed. Then she huffed and swung a leg over Fenrir's rump, landing lightly on the ground.

Again, she reminded Boone of a cat.

"What is it, Ludek?"

He motioned Clementine closer and then spoke so quietly to her that Boone couldn't follow. It was English, he was sure. He heard the words "Rogue" and "Gayville," but that was it. He turned to Rabbit, who was watching him with a what-the-hell grimace on his face.

Boone shrugged.

After a few moments, she looked to the sky and shook her fist. "*Hva i helvete!*"

Boone didn't know what those words meant, but it was obvious Clementine was ready to spit nails and break bones.

After a few more words were exchanged, Ludek bowed to Clementine and then to Hank, Rabbit, and Boone. He stepped aside and quickly receded into the heavy shadows between the buildings.

Clementine faced them. "Change of plans," she said and stalked back to Fenrir.

"What sorta change?" Hank asked, his face a mess of lines and furrows.

She vaulted into the saddle. "We're going to Gayville."

Seventeen

Several hours and miles later ...

Rabbit stood and stretched. His behind hurt. He'd been sitting on the same cold, jagged, lumpy hunk of rock for too damned long. The rock was sucking the heat out of his bottomside, but at least the sun, unobstructed by clouds, was warming his topside.

Hank didn't complain, he just kept sitting and waiting.

They had come to the Bloody Bones by way of Gayville, as they had before, but this time the town had been almost as frenetic with gold seekers as Deadwood. The hills around them on the way into the small, bustling camp were crawling with prospectors of every type, but Rabbit had seen none since leaving out of Gayville toward the mine.

There were tracks left by men, though. And *other* things. Everywhere.

"Hard to follow if we need," Hank had said as they'd continued on toward the mine.

A short time after that, they'd come across two patches of disrupted snow, stained with blood and strewn with torn pieces of woolen clothing and leather boots. They knew what they were looking at—*Bahkauv* had claimed their prey.

When Boone and Hank had asked about the diggings at the

Bloody Bones, the citizens of Gayville had either refused to take part in the conversation, or warned them to stay away from the "Devil's Hole." It was abandoned and should stay that way, according to several locals. Rabbit had heard stories of cat-like creatures inhabiting the mine more than once.

Devil's Hole. Rabbit liked the sound of it more than Bloody Bones. That was something, at least.

"Does she even know if the Rogue is in there?" Rabbit dipped his head toward the adit leading into the Bloody Bones.

Hank shrugged. "No telling. Rare occasion to see Miss Clem that angered."

"Wet hen." Rabbit nodded. "You got your bow ready?"

"What's a wet hen got to do with my bow?"

"Mad as a wet hen." He was used to partnering with Boone, who usually finished his sentences.

Hank shook his head. "What?"

"Doesn't matter." Rabbit scanned the valley below them and up the other side of the gulch to the ridgeline. "Too many places for the buggers to hide."

Hank pulled two whacks of jerky from a muslin sack and handed one to Rabbit. "It's gonna get busy, that much we can count on. Miss Clem thinks them *Bahkauv* will come runnin' home once they figure out their queenie's in for it." He ripped a bite of jerky with his teeth and began sucking on it like it was hard candy.

Rabbit thought back to Clementine's eruption earlier that morning when Ludek had delivered the news about the Rogue's plans in Gayville. "Who-ee! She was spittin' hornets, wasn't she?"

"Saw the lightnin' then heard the thunder." Hank's eyebrows steepled in the middle.

"She really gonna kill the egg-laying *Bahkauv* mamma, you think? Or the Rogue? She didn't say nothin' about killing the Rogue, but ..." Rabbit pushed the jerky into his mouth and started working the salty, leathery strip with his tongue and teeth.

"Don't rightly know. Prob'ly the first one, but riled like she was …" Hank shook his head once. "There's no tellin'. Both are in her sights, might be."

"That Ludek," Rabbit said. "Like he fell in a barrel of cream and it didn't wash off, ain't he?"

"Ain't many on this earth with skin so pale, 'ceptin' that white devil got himself killed in there." He jabbed his thumb over his shoulder toward the Bloody Bones.

"We trust him?" Rabbit wasn't sure if he did or not, but if Clementine did …

"Miss Clem does. And Miss Hildegard, too. I reckon I don't got a reason to or not."

Rabbit was pretty sure Hank was saying he *did* trust Ludek. "Strange times. Sometimes I get to thinkin' I'd just as soon head back to Santa Fe." He slurred around the jerky. "But what good would that do us? Me and Boone? You and Miss Clementine?"

"Be a sorry thing, seein' the backend of Nickel and Dime headin' outta town for good." Hank chuckled. "Wouldn't be so good to see your backend neither! Hoo!"

Rabbit grinned. "Shut up, you ol' donkey." Rabbit couldn't really tolerate the thought either. He'd grown close to his Deadwood *compadres*. "We've been saddled with this thing, it feels like. Ain't nobody else gonna ride against the beasties we seen. No going back. There's no going around it." The more he thought about it, the more the idea didn't sit well. At all. "Never been one to go around a thing. Ain't gonna start now."

"Ain't never seen you ride around a thing yet." Hank pointed his finger out in front of him. "Straight as an arrow." He stood and arched his back, scowling down at the rock. "You are an unfriendly sort." He rubbed his backside.

Rabbit scanned the gulch again. Nothing. No miners. No animals. No beasties. He strolled to the hitching rope Hank had looped around two trees and gave Fred, Nickel, Fenrir, and Dime each a pat and rub on the hip. The hitching rope was for show more than anything. "Make the boys and girl think they got a reason to stand around," Hank had said. None were really tied to it anyway. Their reins were looped once around the rope. One pull and they would be loose to make a quick getaway.

Dime looked back at Rabbit and nickered softly. Rabbit read uneasiness in his eyes. He skimmed his hand across the wounds the *Höhlendrache* had ripped into the horse's haunch. "Just scabs and scars now, *amigo*. I'll be right over there with Hank. You got Nickel beside you. I ain't gonna let nothing happen to any of you. You hear that, Nickel?"

Rabbit patted Nickel's haunch again. "You keep your hoofs to yourself. Be a gentleman. No pawin' at the lady."

Fenrir snorted.

He drew his Sharps from the scabbard strapped to Dime's saddle and rejoined Hank.

Hank studied the bandolero slung over Rabbit's shoulder. He usually had two, but he'd given Boone the one full of shotgun shells, along with his sawed-off. It was more likely Boone would have the chance to use it in the mine than Rabbit would outside in the forest. Besides, he had Boone's Winchester and for short-range scuffles, his Colt revolver and knives.

"Gotta have three usually, don't ya. Two bandoleros and a belt. Course, Boonedog has one."

Rabbit nodded. In a minute or two he would need to explain why he didn't carry guns that used the same ammo as everyone else.

"Scattergun shells." Hank said. "45s and babies' arms."

What did he just say? Rabbit looked down at his chest. "Babies' arms?"

Hank tapped one of the cartridges for the Sharps. "Those things are big as my tent pole."

Rabbit snorted, coughing out a belly laugh. "Hank! I can't believe ..." Another belly laugh rolled out.

"What? Maybe not that big. But I'd be just as careful holdin' on to one of them things."

"Me too." Rabbit choked out. "Tent pole." He wiped the tears from the corners of his eyes.

"I get the scattergun and the pistol. Why that Sharps buffalo killer? Single shot. Slow in a fight."

"Never killed a buffalo, never will." Rabbit respected the big beasts too much. "And if *that* thing ever did, it never will again."

"Not me neither."

"That was Ebby Garret's cannon," Uncle Mort said, who was suddenly standing next to Rabbit, admiring the rifle.

"Shit!" Rabbit's heart pounded in his chest. "Uncle Mort! Goddammit! Every time! You scared the starch outta my pants." He squeezed the rifle barrel. "I almost dropped it."

Uncle Mort began turning in a circle, stopping as his eyes landed on Hank. "Hello, Mr. Providence."

"Uncle Mort says 'Hello.' He called you Mr. Providence."

Hank nodded. "Haven't been called that for some time."

"What are we doing in a forest?"

"Uncle Mort. Can't you give me just a little warnin' when you show up? Maybe come at me this way?" Rabbit pointed in front of him.

"I don't know. Say, you remember Ebby? Not much taller than the rifle. He tried to hunt gophers with that horse leg. Boom! Disappeared. Couldn't even tell he hit a critter excepting one little smoking foot on the ground." He meandered off toward the Bloody Bones. "There's a mine here." He stopped and looked back at Rabbit, his eyes sad. "I know this place." He turned back toward the adit. "We going in there? Not overly concerned about the places I go these days, but this? *Muy malo.*"

"Uncle Mort."

He turned to face Rabbit. "Where's Boone? And that handsome Amazon?"

"He wants to know where Boone and Miss Clementine are."

Hank pointed at the adit. "They went—"

"Shh!" Rabbit slapped Hank on the shoulder.

"Ooh. Uh." Hank jutted his chin out and used his hand to block the sun, making a point of craning his neck back and forth and looking off into the distance.

"What's that now, Mr. Providence?" Uncle Mort returned to Rabbit's side.

"He's lookin' for *Bahkauv*, Uncle Mort."

Hank leaned forward and squinted, making an even bigger show of it.

"*Bahkauv*. That his horse?"

"No." Rabbit hesitated, wondering if he should tell his uncle, then decided he'd need to know, sooner or later. "We think it was a *Bahkauv* that killed you."

Uncle Mort grimaced and nodded slowly. "So, you're gonna kill it back? Avenge me?"

"Now you're on the plot."

"You got me outta there, right?"

"Yep. Buried you proper. Right in the Deadwood cemetery, remember?"

Uncle Mort float-walked along the edge of the tailings. "That's right. Memory fails me sometimes. Sometimes I forget my predicament. It's different now." He frowned at Rabbit. "Don't suppose it was feasible to take me all the way back home to the ranch."

Rabbit's stomach turned. His uncle didn't know that he and Boone had sold the ranch in Santa Fe, and he hesitated at the thought of telling him. In any case, now was not the time.

"Uncle Mort. Can you do me a favor?"

He returned to Rabbit. "I'm here to help you."

Rabbit wasn't so sure. "Can you check on the livery? Make sure Mr. Beaman and his daughter are runnin' it proper?"

"Mr. Beaman. Yes. His daughter. Hmm." Uncle Mort twisted his arms behind his back and floated in a circle. He stopped. "Oh. The blacksmith and his boy?"

"That's his daughter."

Uncle Mort floated through Hank. "That boy is good with horses."

Rabbit looked up and shook his fists toward the sky. Talking to his uncle these days was more frustrating than saddling an unbroken mustang. He gave half a thought to yanking the pendant from his neck and throwing it into the woods. "Right. That *boy*. Can you look in on them?"

"Your mama would be proud of you, son. Not quite a man yet, but you cut a figure she'd be proud of, I'm sure of it."

"Now that's a fine thing to say," Rabbit grumbled.

"What'd he say?" Hank had been listening intently to Rabbit, but apparently that wasn't enough to keep him apprised of the conversation.

"Says I'm not a man." Rabbit grunted. "I'm a man. Suppose you think Boone is."

"Boone. I'm sure proud of him."

"Goldurnit, Uncle Mort. You are gettin' me riled."

"This is what I mean. Always the temper with you." Uncle Mort patted the air near Rabbit's shoulder. Rabbit jerked away.

"You need a hug." Uncle Mort reached out, his arms wide.

"No."

"You're a good boy." He poked his finger through Rabbit's chest. "In here. In your heart."

"Quit callin' me a *boy*." Rabbit rolled his eyes at Hank, who shrugged back. Boone would be loving this.

"Boone," Uncle Mort continued. "He's a boy grown to man the way a boy should. I had some small part in that and it makes me proud. You follow Boone's lead, you're bound to end up proper, too."

Rabbit gritted his teeth. "That's it." He slipped the bear pendant from around his neck, tromped over to Dime, and shoved the pendant deep into the haversack tied to the saddle.

"If you think that pendant controls me, boy," Uncle Mort said from behind him, "you're mistaken. I choose the 'where' and 'when' these days."

Sheeat. Rabbit turned to his uncle. "Show yourself to Boone, then. Listen, Uncle Mort. I am carryin' a fair amount of concern for that livery. You wanna be helpful, go check on it for me."

"Fine. I'll go check on your livery. Because that's what *I* choose to do." Uncle Mort faded into the trees with a wave.

"What's that about? He's gone?" Hank sat back down on the rock and plucked at the string of his bow.

"Say I ain't a man. Call me a boy." Rabbit was talking to himself more than he was Hank. "Show you what a man is capable of, that's what I'll do."

"He's gone?" Hank asked again.

"Yep." Rabbit dropped down next to Hank and laid the Sharps across his lap. He pulled his Colt and began clicking the cylinder slowly. He watched the forest, wishing he were in the mine with Boone and Miss Clementine. This sitting and waiting was for lizards and snakes.

Eighteen

The Bloody Bones was just as dark this time as the last time Boone had dared to step inside. Maybe darker. A few steps ahead, the drift tunnel in which they'd found Uncle Morton's body veered off. It felt like only days ago, but in fact had been weeks.

"The citizens down in Gayville were right," he said quietly. "Doesn't look like anyone is working this mine."

He paused at the junction to the drift, switching his sword and lantern to opposite hands. Holding a lantern high for more than a few minutes made his shoulder muscles burn, especially on the side that had smashed into the rocks on his first trip into Deadwood thanks to the white grizzly. That long-clawed bastard was still out there, too, along with *Bahkauv*, *Höhlendrache*, *Draug*, skin-eating abnormals, and who knew how many *others* they hadn't even met yet.

What were all these creatures? Rabbit was right. *Beasties.* That described the whole lot of them. He took a step toward the drift, peering into the deep shadows.

"Boone."

He looked over to see Clementine staring at him, holding her lantern high. "What?"

"Keep your head. Let's go." She adjusted her weapon-filled

pack and strode off, deeper into the adit.

He gazed into the darkness where his uncle's crumpled body had laid. A crypt—at least that was the way he thought of it now.

"Right." Shaking off the past, he followed Clementine. It took long strides to catch up and match her pace. "Damned sawed-off is heavy in my belt," he whispered.

Clementine focused straight ahead and said nothing. She bristled with weapons, most of which Boone recognized from the cabinet that she kept under lock and key.

"I'm not accustomed to wearing a bandolero, either," he said quietly, continuing the conversation in his head out loud. He rotated his sore shoulder underneath the shotgun shell–studded belt of leather. "Should've left it with Rabbit. But he's gotta be all protective."

Rabbit always felt a sense of responsibility for him. And Boone did for Rabbit, too. Since they were shavers it had been so. There were five different times Boone could recollect that Rabbit had probably saved his life, or at least a lot of hurt. The reverse was true, as well. " 'Your aim ain't so good,' he says," Boone told her, doing his impression of Rabbit's voice. " 'This'll fix that.' "

Rabbit, always a smartass. "I'll aim my foot right at his—"

Clementine looked over at him pointedly. "Shh."

"Isn't even here and he gets me feeling surly," he growled.

She stopped, frowning up at him.

He raised his hand and pressed his lips together.

Outside of the sound of their breathing, the mine was unnaturally quiet except for the *ploinks* of water dripping into puddles here and there ahead of them and behind. The air hung heavy. Worse, it seemed to be getting thicker the deeper they went, with the spores of who knew what kinds of fungus and lichen, and stale humidity, and … what?

Death and decay, a voice whispered in his head.

Shut up, he told that voice.

But what if there were hundreds of *Bahkauv* this time?

Dammit. Keep your head.

Struggling to contain his imagination, he asked Clementine, "You sure the Rogue is in here?"

She nodded.

"The tracks?"

She nodded again.

"And that's all? Just tracks and you know?"

Clementine stepped closer to him, going up on her toes to speak near his ear. "I know because she is *ein Scharfrichter*, like me." Her breath was warm on his neck. "I know because this is what *we* do. I know how she thinks. That what she does is who she is. Slaying is everything to her. There is no ambiguity. There is no middle ground. No compassion. No empathy. There is the task to kill, nothing more."

"Shit." Boone leaned back to get a look at her face. There was no emotion there, only a steely calm.

He contemplated the absoluteness of what she'd said. *No empathy, no compassion.* And this was how Clementine chose to describe herself, too? Was she capable of cold-blooded murder like the Rogue? "Is that how you see yourself, Clementine?"

Her brow furrowed. "No. I see middle ground where the Rogue sees none. I see possibilities of redemption. She sees none."

Boone rubbed the back of his neck, frowning down at her. What was his and Rabbit's stake in this fight? "Why are we here? You haven't been exactly clear on that point. Are we here to kill beasts that don't belong? Or are we here to stop the Rogue?" He very much hoped it was the former.

She stretched her neck from side to side. "I intend to stop the Rogue from killing the *Bahkauv* queen."

Damn. "I see. Well, your pleasant demeanor on the ride here certainly proved that you are in complete control of your temper," Boone said sarcastically. Her expression remained stony. He cleared his throat and changed his approach. "But do you think it's a good idea to stand against the Rogue? You said yourself, the *Bahkauv* presented a problem that required correction. Maybe the Rogue is right. Maybe they need to be destroyed for good."

Boone thought he saw her eye twitch.

He had run the plot in his head a number of ways, and it always ended in a clash between the two Slayers. He knew—and Clementine had just reaffirmed—that the Rogue was unbending. She was set in her self-assigned task of killing *Bahkauv*. He also knew Clementine had been instructed to avoid Gayville, and more specifically the *Bahkauv* here, at all costs. For what reason, he could only guess since she was frustratingly tight-lipped about anything to do with Masterson.

She aimed a hard squint up at him. "What are you doing?"

And then there was her anger at the fact that she was being forced to reckon with a Slayer who didn't belong here and had no charter, or whatever Clementine called it. That anger made what was otherwise a steadfast, reasonable woman completely unpredictable.

He shrugged. "I'm talking to you. We talk, don't we?"

Her lips thinned. "You know what I mean."

"I'm wondering if this is a fight we need to start. With the Rogue, I mean. It seems to me, as long as we're here and we have the help of another Slayer, we should get the job done. When a thing has started down a path, maybe instead of trying to stop it, we nudge it along."

Clementine huffed. "I'm going. Come along if you want, but don't try to stop me." She started to turn away.

"Dammit, Clementine." He caught her elbow, holding her fast. "You're like Rabbit. All steam and get up, but no 'Whoa!'"

She lifted her chin. "I like that about Jack."

Of course she would. "Clementine, I deserve a little more consideration. This *Are-you-with-me-or-against-me* deal of yours isn't going to ride. You have partners now. Like it or not, you need to include me—us—in the decisions that may get us killed."

She stared at him, her eyes narrowed. He could almost hear her brain working on his petition. Then she blew out a breath. "You're right. You should leave." She turned away.

"What?" Boone frowned.

Before he could get another word out, she turned back, a teasing half-smile in place. "I'm pulling your leg, Boone." She took a step closer, shadows softening her expression as she said quietly, "You and Jack and Hank deserve consideration. But you need to realize that I'm not accustomed to having partners. It's going to take me some time to think like I'm part of a team. I've been riding solo for years and years. It feels unnatural to …"

He waited for her to finish. When she didn't, he tried, "Rely on anyone?"

"Yes."

"I'm here for you, Clementine," he said, his focus drifting to her mouth.

The smile on her lips flattened. "You say that now, Boone, but for how long? My world isn't exactly full of rays of sunshine and fields of flowers. How long until you've had enough?"

Good question. "That depends," he answered honestly.

"On what?"

His gaze lifted to hers, holding steady there. "You."

Her eyes darkened, widening slightly. She sucked in a small breath. Then she grabbed him by the lapel of his sheepskin coat. Before he realized what was happening, she pulled him down and kissed him. By the time he'd gotten over the shock and registered the taste of her on his lips, she was easing back.

An awkward silence swirled between them for a few beats as they stared at each other in the semi-darkness.

"What was that for?" His blood was pounding in his ears.

She licked her lips and glanced farther into the mine's throat. "Good luck, of course." She looked back, not meeting his gaze.

"You ready, then?"

Without waiting for his reply, she started forward again, this time with a measured step while peering into the darkness beyond the lantern light.

Boone stared after her. That was a first kiss. It wasn't how he'd imagined their first kiss. At all. For one thing, it was supposed to last longer. For another, the setting was all wrong. Deep in the dark, damp bowels of the earth inside a mine infested with *Bahkauv* was hardly the place for courting.

But still, Clementine had kissed him.

He smiled and hustled after her.

When he caught up to her, she said, "If I cross Masterson again due to my actions here today, there's no telling what he might do. He may challenge me. If that happens, it could end in death, and I'm not sure whose."

"So you're thinking it might be better to avoid all of that, at least for now." Boone nodded, beginning to understand her dilemma.

She scowled. "That *forbannet* Rogue! This region has already become complicated by the incursion of a usurper. She compounds the problems we face."

"She's jamming sticks into the spokes of the wagon wheels."

"Yes, and I need to stop her before she crashes the wagon."

"Or we abandon the wagon altogether."

The adit opened up into the cave Boone had hoped he'd never see again. Memories of *Bahkauv* scampering along the walls and on top of rocks flooded his mind as he surveyed the room. It had been picked at by countless fortune seekers since he'd been here last, most of the glittery beauty destroyed. If only the miners knew what lurked below.

"Look here." Clementine stepped closer to one of the larger boulders in the cavern. She stooped and held her lantern close to the rock.

Boone stood over her and focused on a pile of brown, broken

shards. "I don't remember any pottery in … wait."

He squatted next to her and examined the shards. A slimy swirly red and green ooze coated the shards and pooled on the floor. The stench of sulfur and rancid flesh hit him. He grimaced, covering his nose. He looked around. Broken shards lay strewn around the base of the boulder, and other boulders, too. They were everywhere.

Still shielding his nose and mouth, he stood and pointed at the slimy debris. "Eggs?"

Her brow pinched, she nodded back at him. "Fresh kills."

Nineteen

W hat time is it, you think?" Rabbit squinted at the bright sun not far above the tree line on the opposite side of the gulch.

"Ten o'clock, maybe." Hank poked a string of leather through his quiver, into what looked to Rabbit like the beginning of a tulip decoration.

They'd changed rocks to follow the sun, and Hank was of the notion that this one might be a little more forgiving on their saddle pads.

"Not been too long, then." He flicked a knife into a nearby fallen tree and plucked another from his belt. "This one. The one that rascal from Galena almost skewered me with. It's better than the ones Miss Clementine gave me. Can't tell why really."

He balanced the black blade on his finger.

"Answered your own quandary." Hank pointed his stitching needle at the knife.

"What?"

"Balanced, isn't it?" He poked the needle into the quiver again.

"Ah. 'Course! You know knives, Hank?"

"Some. Never been what you might call a knife man."

"Me neither. Not 'til Miss Clementine gave me these. Guess I got a knack of some sort. Feels natural to hold a throwin' knife. Quick. Smooth. What I can't figure is how did Miss Clementine know?"

Hank chuckled. "She's what I call an enigma."

"A curiosity? Surely."

"Now you take Rails. He's got him a knack, too." Hank paused and regarded Rabbit. "That lock he made for the livery. You think anybody could make that?"

Rabbit shook his head. "Never seen nothin' like it. We lose the key and Mr. Beaman's not around? We're not gettin' in that livery less we break a window."

"Right. That's a knack, followed by a lot of practice. Same as you and those knives." Hank continued stitching his tulip.

"Can't say the same for his daughter." Rabbit stared down at the knife without really seeing it. "Seems all right in the livery, but she's fumblin' around all the time." His mind wandered to Amelia, lingering on her finer points. "Ain't hard on the eyes, though."

Hank quaked with a chuckle. "You give her the twitters."

"Boone said the same thing."

"Yep. Smart man, Boone."

"How do you know?"

" 'Cause of the way he talks. Reasons things through."

"No, you donkey. How do you know I make Amelia twittery?"

"All you gotta do is pay attention."

"I do." Rabbit thought he did, anyway.

"It's the way she looks at ya. You add that to the way she acts, sure as Fred there likes his beer."

Rabbit grunted. "Ain't my intention to make nobody a-twitter."

"All the same."

"Then I'll try and put her at ease."

Hank nodded. "Ain't only that. She's been through a hurt

that'd make your heart ache."

"That little filly? Like what?"

"Ever wonder about her mother?"

"Oh, I suppose. Passed right back outta my mind though. What, she leave Mr. Beaman?"

"Nooo." Hank drew out the o's with a deeper voice. "She was a good woman, hear Rails tell it. Amelia, too."

"Tell me then."

"Happened before I met him workin' on the railroad. Rails was the man you go to when you needed somethin' smithed just right. Ever'body knew. Drove spikes same as any three or four other men put together. Woulda been near undoable, finishin' that railroad quick as we did without men like Rails."

"And you, probably." Rabbit sheathed his knife. "But what about his wife?"

"They moved into a little house outside Chicago. Nice little place, to hear Rails describe it. He was startin' up his smithy business, but it was slow with them bein' from the South and all. Nobody givin' business to the separatist. That kinda blather."

"Was he? A separatist."

" 'Course not. Anyway, bank started makin' noise about takin' the house back, so Mrs. Beaman—Adele was her name—picked up work where she could. Laundry. Cleanin' houses, that kinda thing. Worked hard. Enough to keep their house."

"Salt of the earth type." Rabbit had no doubt his mother had been the same kind of woman.

"Surely." Hank tied off the leather strip and began on another tulip next to the first one. "Weren't the best part of town, their little house, but it was a home."

"You can make any house a home, work at it enough."

"Yep. Adele had picked up some work for a well-to-do family a ways away. She'd make them kids breakfast, clean and whatnot all day, put 'em to bed, then walk home to say good night to Rails and her little Amelia. Rails said they'd wait up 'til she got home, no matter how late she was. Otherwise, she'd wake 'em up and put 'em to bed again." Hank chuckled, but it was edged with sadness.

"Dammit, Hank, what happened?" Rabbit was pretty sure he wouldn't like where this story was heading.

Hank shook his head. "One night, she didn't come home. Rails and Amelia waited up, but she didn't show. They went out into the night lookin' for her. Went to the house where she worked, but they said she'd left for home."

Rabbit grimaced.

Hank stared out at the trees, his eyes glassy. "A week of lookin' the two of 'em. Hardly ate. Hardly slept. A week. Then the constable shows up at the door one day. They found Adele … what was left of her anyway, when they was loadin' wagons from the offal piles at the slaughterhouse she passed by ever' night on the way home."

"How'd they know it was her?"

"She carried papers to work in those big houses."

"Sheeat."

"They made John take a look at her. Make sure it was her. I don't know, maybe he wanted to make sure himself. Me? I couldn't do it, I don't think. He said he couldn't say for sure it was her anyway."

Rabbit's heart ached for the two of them. He'd come across Uncle Mort's body in the Bloody Bones a while after he'd died. He knew how the sight could knock a man's knees out from under him. "Nobody deserves that kind of grief."

"Wasn't too long after that three butchers from that slaughterhouse turned up in the same pile of cow innards. Same things done to 'em as what got done to Adele."

Rabbit scratched his bristly jaw. "They figure it was the same guy doin' it?"

"Now this is where it gets interestin' instead of sad. Rails won't say much about it, but Amelia was goin' out ever' night for a while there after her ma had been found. He didn't know where to, but she was gone, and sometimes for hours. She said she needed time alone, but Rails ain't sure. Almost scattered his brain after what happened to Adele, but Amelia would wait until he fell asleep and then sneak out. Tied her to a chair once, but she got free." Hank paused, pursing his lips. "Maybe he was sure," he said more to himself than Rabbit. After a slight nod, he continued. "She kept goin' out ever' night, but then stopped all of the sudden."

"What? Just stopped sneakin' out? All sudden like?"

"Yep. And it was right after that they found those dead fellas at the slaughterhouse."

Rabbit's mouth gaped. "Hank, you don't think …"

"I don't know, Jack Rabbit. But it bears some thinkin' on. And if ever a person deserved it …"

Rabbit nodded. "So was that the end of it, then?"

"Oh, the constables stopped in a few times, Rails said. Questions. Always the same questions. But whoever did it, they were sly, ya know? Smart enough to not get strung up for it."

"Mr. Beaman thinkin' a certain way? About Amelia?"

Hank shrugged. "He won't say. He wanted some distance from it. From where it happened. That's when they moved west to get out of Chicago, and he found work on the railroad. Blames himself. Says he shoulda been walkin' Adele home ever' night."

"What makes—"

Fenrir snorted. Then Nickel and Dime, too.

Rabbit threw off his gloves, bouncing to his feet. He grabbed his Sharps with one hand and skinned his pistol with the other.

Hank was on his feet a blink later.

Rabbit scanned the surrounding trees, expanding his search to the opposite side of the gulch.

"They's troubled, but not scared," Hank said, pointing at the horses as they shuffled and snorted and bobbed their heads. Fred the Mule whinny-hawed lightly and stood tall, staring across the gulch, ears pricked.

Rabbit's first thought was a cougar, but that was quickly replaced given the circumstances. He searched the opposite side of the gulch again, following the ground as best he could through the dappled shadows under the trees there.

"Damned wind has everything movin'," he growled. But then he saw something in the dusky shadows. "Hank, look here."

Hank joined him, shielding his eyes from the sun with his hand. "Whatcha see, Jack Rabbit?"

"The outcrop there that looks like Boone's hat. See it?"

"Even looks like it's got the hole in it. Got it."

"Now, bear left. Under that extra big pine. That ain't no normal …"

The shadow flitted between trees and stopped, appearing to dig at the snow.

"See that?" Rabbit whispered.

"Damned if that ain't a *Bahkauv*, right there," Hank whispered back. "Want I should sneak around, down the draw there?"

But Rabbit wasn't listening. He kneeled, left foot forward, and rested his elbow near his knee.

"You gonna shoot at it?" Hank asked.

"That's the idea."

"Yeah. But is it a good'n? If there's more out there, might get 'em riled."

"That's the idea, too." He drew up his Sharps, flipped the sight up, and cradled the fore stock in his left hand.

"That's a little ways beyond a fair distance, Jack Rabbit. You sure?" Hank's voice had plenty of worry in it.

Rabbit looked up at him and grinned. "Don't worry, Hank. This ain't nothin'." He adjusted the sight. "Seven hundred yards. Plus fifty. Little bit more." He watched the trees sway and waver. "Steady wind, little stronger through the middle." He spoke softly, mostly to comfort Hank more than anything else. "Keep an eye. Don't want any of them beasties sneakin' up on us."

Hank snapped up straight and scoured the hillside behind them.

"Ain't doin' nothing except pawin' at the ground over there." What the hell was it digging for? "Doesn't matter," Rabbit muttered. "Losin' his head in a few seconds."

He adjusted the butt against his shoulder. The mule-kick the Sharps would deliver could break bones with an ill fit to the shoulder.

He squeezed hard on the back set trigger, *click*, and moved his finger to the front trigger. A light squeeze now, and the Sharps would explode, unleashing a steam locomotive of lead.

"Ready," he said for Hank.

Hank dropped his quiver and stuck his fingers in his ears.

Rabbit blinked and beaded the creature, which was sitting motionless, as if it was watching him back.

He drew in a deep breath and let his lungs empty slowly. At the bottom of the exhale, he squeezed.

Click

BOOM!

The rifle slammed against his shoulder, shoving the right side of his body back several inches. A ball of fire erupted from the muzzle. Black smoke billowed, roiling in the air, and immediately began floating away with the wind.

"One … two … thr …" The *Bahkauv's* head disappeared into a carnation of dark bits of flesh and bone and brain.

"Dead shot." Hank slapped his thigh.

Rabbit stood and faced Hank, whose grin reached from one ear to the other. He smiled a mile wide, too. "Miss Clementine always says, take the head."

Twenty

Boone kicked at a pile of broken egg shards. "Is it normal for *Bahkauv* eggs to stink this much?" Rabbit and Hank were lucky to be playing watchdog at the mine's mouth. Blue sky and fresh, clean air sounded like paradise.

"I don't know," Clementine said. "This is the first time I've seen them."

"What?" He frowned her way. She was holding her lantern high, turning slowly around inside the cavern. The heavy shadows on her face gave her a haunted look, especially with the grimace she had in place.

"I've only heard about them," she said, lowering her light.

"You're not serious."

She shrugged. "Well, I read a little about them, too, if that makes you feel better."

He guffawed. "That makes all the difference," he said, his words dripping with sarcasm.

Chuckling, she returned to his side.

He pulled his glove off and squatted near a cluster of smashed eggs. After swirling his finger in a puddle of green sludge, he held it in front of the lantern to examine it. "Not like the yolk of a chicken egg, is it?"

"You had to touch it to figure that out?" She kneeled next to him.

"I was curious."

"I believe the reason they look and smell like this is because the Rogue came through and destroyed them. When a Slayer kills an *other*, including the young, the *other* tends to return to the earth quickly in one form or another. In this case, the babies dissolved into this disgusting slime, which will quickly decompose." She wrinkled her nose at his finger. "Now your skin is going to smell like rancid egg. There's nothing to wash that off with."

"Hmm. Yeah." He wiped off his finger in the gravelly dirt as best he could and stood, hauling her up by the arm along with him. "Shall we go, Slayer?" He pulled on his glove.

At her nod, they continued across the floor of the cavern, lanterns held high. All signs of the *Bahkauv* they'd slain and broken into dust and rubble weeks ago were gone, replaced by gravel and stone picked free from the walls and broken into pieces by industrious hard-rock miners on the hunt for gold.

At the far end was a slightly descending tunnel, roughly the size of the one leading to the cavern.

"This is where Rabbit chased the critters last time," Boone said.

They ventured in, side by side, both nearly brushing the walls. Broken *Bahkites* covered the floor of every niche and bulge in the tunnel they passed, some piles of broken shells reaching shin-high. Slimy egg sludge mixed with dirt and pebbles to form a muck that in some places covered the entire width of the tunnel.

Boone's boots soon became heavy with the *Bahkite* goo and dirt slurry that stuck like wet clay. He kicked the walls of the tunnel to clear the muck. "The deeper we go, the more broken eggs I see."

Clementine nodded.

"At least the queen can't be too big, right? To fit in this tunnel, I mean." He didn't have to reach much above his head to touch the rock that formed the ceiling.

Clementine scraped her boots on the wall. "I have a feeling these eggs were carried here."

Boone frowned as her words sunk in. "Shit."

She nodded, her lips thin. "In Norwegian, you'd say *dritt.*"

"*Dritt.* Got it. How about German?"

"*Scheisse.*"

"Shy-sa," he repeated, pronouncing it as it sounded. She stared at his mouth as he repeated it a couple more times. "I like that one. *Scheisse.*"

She lifted her eyes to his, a small smile playing on her lips. "You almost sound like a German."

"*Ja, danke,*" he said, trying to sound like the big German who manned the front door of The Dove. With a bow, he swept his arm toward the narrow path in front of them. "After you, *Fräulein.*"

They eased deeper into the darkness. After a couple of bends, he said quietly, "So, that means two things to me."

"I'm all ears."

"First, you think the queen is too big to fit in this tunnel."

"You're one for two." Clementine nudged a rock from her path and stepped deliberately, avoiding puddles of sludgy slime.

Boone followed in her tracks as best he could. "Second, her ill-tempered offspring delivered those eggs here."

"Right again."

He covered his nose with his forearm, breathing through the sheepskin for a brief respite. "I just thought of a third thing."

"What's that?"

"The reason why they'd carry them here." At her raised brows, he said, "Too many in *there.*" He indicated toward the dark tunnel ahead of them.

She nodded solemnly. "Things will only get worse now."

They continued onward, down, down, down into the earth. *Bahkite* pieces still littered the ground, but now Boone noticed the odor of decaying flesh periodically overwhelming the sulfuric stench of the rancid eggs.

The tunnel jogged left and began to descend more rapidly. Boone's chest tightened along with the walls around them. How deep did it go? Halfway to hell?

"The smell reminds me of The Pyre before winter set in," Clementine said at one point when she paused to clean the muck off her boots again.

Boone lifted the collar of his coat and breathed in the scent of his own clothes and skin. "I probably won't visit much come summer," he said in a muffled voice. Although, with the way things were going, they might be lucky to stay alive long enough for the snow to melt.

She cleaned off the heel of her other boot. "Move the bodies through quickly. That's the key."

He glanced around. "Did you notice that this isn't a tunnel anymore? It's natural." He held his lantern out, turning this way and that. The rock walls had been worked some, but they were mostly caves now, not deliberately cut from rock by a miner's pickaxe. The same went for the pockets and fissures. "The ground has been leveled enough to walk on, and there are places … there." He pointed at a small stope carved into the side of the cave. "And there, where veins have been worked, but otherwise these are all natural formations."

She nodded, checking the soles of her boots in the lantern light. "We're on the same trail."

She started off again, catching his coat sleeve and pulling him along with her, not letting go when she could have. A short way ahead, the cave veered sharply to the right and narrowed, forcing them to stoop and go single file. Boone shuddered at the notion of a cave-in this deep into the hillside.

Clementine stopped suddenly in front of him, and then took a step back, almost coming down on his toe. She sniffed the air. "*Scheisse*," she cursed. "I believe we've found the source of the smell."

Twenty One

Hank squatted down next to Rabbit and pointed across the gulch. "Things a-movin' all over that hillside, Jack Rabbit." "May be. Might be the wind in the branches, too." Rabbit's satisfaction with his bull's-eye shot had been quickly tempered by a string of howling shrieks that worked its way across the side of the gulch like the fuse on a bundle of dynamite. There were things out there. Probably *Bahkauv*, but Rabbit hadn't heard them scream like injured pumas when he fought them in the mine.

"Ain't wind curdled my blood," Hank said. "It was screams. Like they was feelin' the pain of that one you splattered."

"Now calm down, Hank. This ain't unexpected. We just got it started is all."

"*We?*" Hank snickered. "It just occurred to me that makin' your acquaintance mighta put the spurs to my demise."

Rabbit laughed. "You just figure that out, did ya?"

"We should maybe cut the horses loose, then vamoose into that mine?"

"What if they come spillin' out of that hole?" Rabbit glanced at the adit. "We'll have beasties on both sides. No. We hunker next to the mine between that pile of rocks and the edge of the tailings. Make them line up in front of us. We can see them come up over the top of the tailings, and they won't be in our laps."

Hank rubbed the side of his face with the back of his hand. "You sound like Wyatt the Wise. Got it considered and reckoned already."

"We'll see. Make sure the horses are loose. They got a better chance of runnin' than fightin' if this gets outta hand."

Twenty Two

Clementine held her lantern high, surveying the grisly scene spread before her. She couldn't shake the feeling she'd been here before. She had been in the Bloody Bones before, of course, but they hadn't descended this far into the mountain during that visit. However, she was relatively certain her déjà vu was stirred not by what she saw, but rather by the stench of decay that was seeping into her sinuses and clinging there, waking memories she preferred remain dormant.

She shuddered. This was almost as bad as when she had to lie in wait for several hours in the lair of those carnivorous mountain trolls, surrounded by the putrid remains of their previous kills. But not quite.

She covered her mouth with her arm, breathing into the crook of her elbow. Sweet Valhalla, why was her profession so often accompanied by such horrible smells?

"That's part of a ..." Boone gagged. "A leg."

Clementine glanced his way. The stench of decaying flesh, as well as other fetid offenders, had almost overwhelmed him once already as drafts from this macabre dining room wafted through the cave's throat. Now, having come upon the source of the stench, Clementine feared the breakfast of biscuits and bacon Boone had eaten on the way to Gayville would soon be discharged on the floor of the cave.

"I don't know how you keep your stomach in times like this," Boone said between guttural coughs and wheezes. "I can feel the foulness coating my skin."

"Well, I don't find the bouquet agreeable, if that's what you're thinking."

He tiptoed around a pile of bones and wet, rotting flesh. "Can't they finish a meal? Is that a … oh, Jedediah!" Boone threatened to liquidate his breakfast again.

Clementine turned away from him and yanked up her coat collar, burying her nose in it. She would have plugged her ears, too, but for the lantern she carried in one hand and the baton she now brandished in the other. She couldn't blame Boone. Between the rancid egg slime and decaying human body parts, Clementine doubted that many could hold their ground. Years of exposure to death in many forms and stages had given her an edge.

The gravel and dirt ground inside the small cavern had transformed some way back to rock and debris. Previously, the way had been blocked by glittering stalagmites and stalactites. But those had been either smashed into rubble or completely removed, most probably by miners with pickaxes or sledgehammers seeking the glittery gold locked inside.

His gag reflex subdued again, Boone picked up a particularly sparkly piece of broken rock and examined it in the lantern light. "I'd wager this was a sight before the miners and *Bahkauv* arrived and busted up the place." The gray piece was peppered with faceted, milky blue and white crystals. "Calcite. Beautiful. I don't see gold though."

"Miners probably took the pieces with gold." Clementine moved closer to see the rock he held. "I think the calcite crystals are prettier anyway."

She glanced at a pile of slime and smashed eggshell just ahead of the debris. *Busted up the place …*

Boone's words spurred a notion. Someone had cleared this path. "If this is a gateway, it hadn't been used for a long period of time." She frowned up at the ceiling and then down at the floor. "Long enough for stalactites and stalagmites to grow four or five feet."

He dropped the rock and held the lantern out toward the darkness awaiting them up ahead. "Is that normal? Unused gateways?"

"I'm not sure. I'm not even sure this is a gateway. Miners may have opened it in their zeal for all that glitters."

"From the looks of that cavern back there," Boone thumbed over his shoulder, "seems to me there's a good chance of that. These tunnels didn't reach the surface until they cleared these crevices." He stepped closer to her, lowering his voice further. "Unless Masterson did it. He wouldn't have opened it up, would he?"

Clementine grimaced and shrugged.

Had mining the Bloody Bones facilitated the confrontation between Masterson and the usurper for control of the Black Hills? Probably not. Territories were the manifestations of supremacy, influence, and power. It was inevitable there would occasionally be contests for control of this territory, or any other for that matter. Territories were like pieces to be collected in a deadly game. Her amma had told her of such skirmishes happening innumerable times over the centuries.

Masterson had indicated no designs on furthering his control, but she couldn't be sure what his motivations were. She was reasonably sure, however, that those in Masterson's position universally suffered from overly developed egos and craved ever more sovereignty.

As for the usurper, why else would he—or she—vie for jurisdiction of the Black Hills?

She shook the question from her thoughts.

"Couldn't solve it?" Boone asked, watching her closely.

She sighed. "I feel like a pawn."

"Of course you are. We all are. Rabbit would tell you it's the natural order. Then I'd say, don't like it? Then take the queen. Rabbit might say that, too, but he doesn't play chess."

Take the queen. She nodded, liking the sound of that. "Let's go find us a queen then."

As she led the way, she glanced back once more at the ghastly scene. Where in the hell was the Rogue?

Twenty Three

Rabbit watched Hank free the reins of each horse and Fred from the hitching rope. "Run if the notion strikes ya."

The horses began snorting and shuffling and bumping into each other. Nickel squealed and reared. Then all three of them and Fred backed away from the rope hitch, heads high, ears pricked toward the trees up the slope behind the mine.

"Shit," Rabbit growled. "Buggers got behind while we was tongue whittlin'." Knife in his hand, he searched the trees, his breathing shallow and quick. Adrenaline shot bursts of energy from head to toe.

A dark shape flitted across the snow from one tree trunk to the next. The deep shadows from the thick evergreens blocked most of the sunlight that was ample everywhere except beneath the trees.

Hank joined Rabbit, fidgeting as much as the horses. "You think there's more up there?" He pointed his bow, ready with an arrow, up the hillside.

Rabbit leaned his rifle against the boulder he'd been sitting on and skinned two more knives. He'd been in a scuffle or two now alongside Hank, but to have harmony, as Boone called it, took adversity and habit. If it were Boone standing beside him, Rabbit probably wouldn't need to say anything. He knew how Boone moved, what decisions he'd make, and what he expected from Rabbit in return. It was the same in reverse. Hell, a little part of him wished it were Boone standing next to him now.

"Take a breath, Hank. Settle in. You need to watch that edge." He pointed at the rim of the tailings. "They might come up over the top and bushwhack us from there." Rabbit scanned the gloom under the trees up the slope.

Hank turned and watched the edge of the tailings, bow and arrow at the ready.

Out of the side of his vision, Rabbit saw a shadow hurling toward the horses in great, long loping strides. There was no way in hell a horse could outrun that. For sure not in shin-deep snow.

"Son of a bitch!" Rabbit raced toward the horses as the *Bahkauv* closed in on Fenrir, the closest prey.

Twenty Four

Clementine paused to listen for any indication that they were nearing either the *Bahkauv* or anything else that might want to make a meal of a Slayer and a Sidewinder. The cave was quiet, save for the steady drip of water here and there. Unnervingly quiet.

The silence was so deep that on occasion, she could hear the blood rushing through her ears in steady, thrumming pulses. The heavy hush filled the narrow cave, broken only by the sound of their footfalls, or the clinks of pack buckles, or the rustle of leather scraping against fabric.

Hell, she would prefer to hear a covey of banshees charging toward them rather than all of this silence.

Fortunately, the stench had lessened as they descended into the mountain. Now that they had moved beyond where miners had ventured with pickaxe and hammer, the decaying flesh of men was no longer mingled with the odor of sulfur and rancid *Bahkite* slime.

"It's like a maze down here now," Boone said through the kerchief he had tied over his nose and mouth. "When did that happen?"

Clementine didn't answer. She knew he was simply breaking the silence with rhetorical questions. Rather than distracting her from the task at hand, she found the deep timbre of his voice something of a comfort, especially given the disagreeable atmosphere of their location. Boone's presence at her side on this hunt soothed her, dulling the sharp edges of her anger at the Rogue for putting her in a perilous position with both Masterson *and* the *Bahkauv*.

And then she went and kissed him. *Hel's* kingdom! What had she been thinking?

She shook off all thoughts of that misstep and focused on the task at hand.

He was right. What had begun as a singular tunnel, unconnected to a natural cave, had turned into a labyrinth. The sides at times squeezed them into single file or widened so that two or three could walk abreast without touching shoulders. Side passageways broke away into the darkness in chaotic fashion, like the branches of a twisted old oak. Choosing the correct route had become more difficult, but following the trail of greatest size and with the most broken eggs seemed to be effective. At least that was what her intuition told her as it guided her, pointing the way.

Boone caught her sleeve and stopped abruptly. He looked at the floor, standing completely still.

He'd done this thrice previously and Clementine was beginning to think she should disregard his false alarms. But she waited for his sign to continue.

How many destroyed eggs had they seen? She had given up counting after cresting one hundred. They occupied every pocket and crevice she had seen since leaving the cavern. So many eggs. All destroyed by the Rogue, presumably.

What was Masterson going to think? What was he capable of? He would be a dangerous adversary should he choose to blame her for the destruction of his … what? Pets?

And where was the Rogue? Had she already confronted the *Bahkauv* queen? If so, she was likely already dead. Was Boone capable of taking her place? Would he know how to move against such an adversary? Where to place his blade and when? Did he possess the natural instincts of a Slayer?

A screeching howl echoed along the main tunnel.

Clementine froze.

Boone startled, rattling the lantern in his hand.

Her fingers began to tingle. Her senses heightened, smells and sounds magnified. Huffing growls commenced from three directions at once: one from the tunnel ahead, one from behind, and another from the narrow tunnel that branched to the right.

"It's an ambush!" Clementine hissed.

Boone set his lantern down near the wall and drew his scimitar.

Clementine held her lantern tight and raised the baton, ready to strike.

Boone glanced at her dubiously. "Mr. Pistol surely would like to announce his presence."

"Mr. Pistol may bring down the ceiling. And if there are more beasts near, gunfire will bring them to us all at once." She turned slightly, her back to the wall so she could keep an eye on all three of the approaching *Bahkauv.*

He gripped his scimitar with both hands and swiveled his head to look up, then down, the tunnel. "Rabbit would say, 'Bring 'em on.' I say, where's a damned Rogue when you need one?"

Clementine chuckled in spite of the apprehension she could hear in his voice. "This is what you practiced for, Boone. Feel the weight of the sword in your hand. They're not cunning fighters, so use deception. Keep your hips square. Remember your blade is also your shield. The tunnel is small, so keep your movements tight or you'll catch your blade on the rocks."

He nodded once, his stance showing confidence. She had prepared him well over the last couple of weeks.

"I'll take care of the one behind us and the one coming from that branch." She pointed toward the *Bahkauv* she could hear scrambling up the tunnel. "The fella coming right there is yours."

Boone turned to look behind him. "What do you mean, behind us?"

Another rhetorical question. Clementine gave him a brief nod and then focused inward, beginning to plan her strategy.

The *Bahkauv* were advancing in the darkness. She could hear their labored breathing now. All three would be upon them at the same time. Not cunning creatures, but damned good at timing their attacks.

She breathed deep, taking up a defensive position. A calmness flowed through her yet her skin tingled as her senses began registering everything around her. The steady drip of water to the left. The rustle of clothing. Boone's quick breathing. The chuffing of the approaching *Bahkauv*. Their guttural growls. Claws scraping against rock. The swirls of air against her skin. The bloodlust pulsing through her veins.

She was ready.

All three *Bahkauv* emerged from the shadows at the same moment, their heads low, their movements deliberate and purposeful. Sturdy fore- and hind legs, massive paws with claws to match. Sinewy, thick muscles bulged below short, dark fur. The long snouts didn't seem big enough to hold so many dagger-like fangs.

She glanced at each beast and planned her attack in a blink. Upper windmill to the jaw of that one. Side-kick to the chest of the other. Use momentum. Long arc, backward swing to the top of the head. She'd need to turn her head quickly to aim the second blow. Too slow and she might get bit. But that wasn't the worry. The worry was Boone. Could he take the third *Bahkauv* by himself without his pistol?

The last time he'd helped her fight *Bahkauv*, he'd used his gun. Now, the area was more confined, limiting his options. She took a moment to assess his position. His attack was set. Swing, parry, displace, and counter-cut. If he executed properly he would remove the beast's foreleg, or if he was accurate enough, the head.

The huffing beasts closed the distance quickly, but for Clementine time slowed to a crawl. The steady beat of her heart sounded in her ears as she watched their claws scrape at the rocky ground beneath them. Nostrils flared and spittle flew from their teeth and maws. She had only to wait for the moment to swing.

Boone took a deep breath and blew it out. "Here we go."

Clementine gripped the baton as all three snarling, gnashing beasts leapt into the air, claws extended. She glanced at Boone then thrust the baton up into a great backward arc over her head. He had raised the sword over his shoulder and begun his slashing swing.

"Aahhhh!" Boone's war cry echoed through the tunnel.

She cringed. "Shh!"

As her baton neared the bottom of the arc, she tightened her grip, pulled hard on the handle and swung it into a powerful upward thrust. She focused on the head of the beast now hurtling at her, jaws spread wide.

Boone grunted, then a gurgling, hysterical squeal rose and instantly stopped.

As the first *Bahkauv* leapt at her, she gauged the distance and speed of the second. Instinctively, she raised her leg, cocking it like a giant spring, and kicked out. Her foot slammed into the thick chest of the *Bahkauv*. The baton smashed into the underjaw of the beast in front of her. *CRUNCH!* Its head jerked backward with a loud crack and then flopped over on a rubbery neck. It froze into a pale gray statue of hardened ash.

She turned to the second as it rolled back upright and opened its mouth wide. It howled, its jaws pointed at the roof of the cave.

Damn it, it was calling for help. She raised her baton.

A shiny black streak sliced through her vision and the howl instantly ceased. Boone.

"Well done, McCreery. A clean cut." She held up the lantern to inspect his other kill. "I heard you dispatch this first one." Its head lay a few feet away, one black eye aimed at Boone. "He doesn't look happy with you."

Boone stood over its body and drew each side of his bloodied sword across its spine, leaving small pools of blood to soak into its fur. "He wasn't playing nice." He grimaced. "At least these guys don't smell as bad as the eggs."

She kicked the *Bahkauv* she'd killed, breaking the statue into a pile of rubble and dust. "But they look so cuddly with all that fur."

"Cuddly, she says." He looked her up and down. "No injuries, of course." He pointed at her hand. "Still holding the lantern, I see."

She shrugged. "We still need it."

"I wouldn't imagine we need to hide these things at this point. Not down here, anyway."

She shook her head. "You didn't hack. You sliced, right?"

Boone pointed the tip of his scimitar at the *Bahkauv* head. "Ask him."

Clementine couldn't help but chuckle. A strong urge to kiss him again made her look away. That earlier kiss could be written off as a foolish whim. A second would be a serious mistake with potential long-range consequences, because she'd liked that first kiss too much to stop at just two.

"Was that last one calling for h—" He paused, holding his hand up.

"What?" she whispered.

"Do you hear that?"

Twenty Five

Rabbit drew back and aimed the knife at the *Bahkauv* bolting at Fenrir. He hadn't practiced with anything moving so fast, or at this distance.

"Hank!"

Hank turned and brought up his bow, but before he could aim and shoot, the *Bahkauv* closed the distance and leapt for Fenrir.

Fenrir screamed, quickly hopped forward and let loose with a side-kick as the *Bahkauv* descended on her. Her hoof connected with its paw, bounced off, and then slammed into the side of its face.

The *Bahkauv* dropped into the snow, convulsing.

"Fenrir! Like to broke that beastie's neck!" Hank lowered his bow.

"That's one." Rabbit trotted to the horses and mule. All four were rearing and snorting now, but they hadn't bolted. Rabbit was sure they figured to be part of the fight. He couldn't help but smile.

His tickled smile dropped into an open-mouth gawk as Fred the Mule whinny-hawed and trotted to the edge of the tailings.

Fenrir, Dime, and Nickel whinnied and nickered and craned their necks to watch Fred as he aimed a double back-kick in

Hank's direction and disappeared over the edge of the tailings.

Hank seemed to shrink a little, his shoulders slumping as if Fred's departure had pulled a plug and let the air out of him. He stared at the spot where Fred wasn't anymore and turned to Rabbit, his face one big frown. He looked back at the tailings. Then back at Rabbit. "No, he didn't."

Rabbit tried not to laugh. He nodded. "Yes, he did."

A whinny-haw from far away echoed through the trees.

"I think he aimed that kick at me." Hank stood stone-still, totally deflated, the disappointment written all over his face.

"Get past it, Hank. There's gonna be more. Take up a spot by that boulder. I got the hill behind us and the adit." Rabbit jogged to the *Bahkauv* and looked it in the eyes. Its legs twitched and claws repeatedly retracted and extended. It watched Rabbit, hissing.

Fenrir had broken its neck and probably torn its spine apart. Rabbit brandished his fancy knife from Galena and with three quick movements, removed its head per the instructions Clementine had given him the last time they were here—always remove the head, one way or another.

He scanned the hillside for signs of more *Bahkauv*. When he saw none, he approached each horse in turn. Taking as much time as he dared, he let them smell him and tell him about the dangers around them with their snorts and blows. To his surprise, even Fenrir let him in close. As he strode back to Hank, the horses huddled together, face to face. He could swear they were planning the battle with their nickers and snorts.

"Well, I didn't figure the horses would be a help out here." Rabbit stood with his back to Hank, watching the hillside above the mine.

Hank didn't answer.

"Makes our job easier, them helpin' us. Got better ears than we do. Better snorters, too. Fred smelled them from across the gulch. Maybe we should be watching horses, not the damned trees."

Hank was silent.

Rabbit looked back at him. "Hank?"

Hank stared at the edge of the tailings, slowly shaking his head.

"Aw sheeat, Hank. He was scared is all."

"He left me." Hank looked up at the sky.

Rabbit patted his shoulder. "Lost his head, that's it. Can't say I blame him. He's probably the smartest out of all of us."

Hank pursed his lips and nodded. "May be at that, Jack Rabbit."

A scream like the one they'd heard before sounded off on the hillside above them.

"Damn," Rabbit whispered. "Got one more up there."

Another screaming howl followed.

Then another.

And another.

"Maybe not just one," he added. He counted shrieks and howls in eight different locations. Soon, the beasties were all howling at once. Rabbit shuddered. The piercing screeches hurt his ears.

"Are we in hell?" Hank winced against the cacophony of wails and shrieks.

"Hillside is covered with them!" Rabbit yelled over the din. He wished he had his sawed-off, but he knew that Boone was somewhere down in the mine probably fighting for his life. His stomach turned at the thought. The fact that Miss Clementine was there, well, that helped, but his gut still clenched for his *amigo*.

He tensed as he watched the hillside come alive. More shadows than he could count darted from tree to tree.

"They're fuckin' everywhere!" Rabbit grabbed the Winchester and patted the fully loaded bandolero strung over his shoulder.

"We're in it now, Jack Rabbit!"

"Lay in with the sticks and string." Since Hank didn't carry a rifle, his Sioux bow and arrow would have to do. "Then your pistol. When you're empty, drop it and grab your knife. You need help, holler. I'll do the same!"

He couldn't keep track of all the shadowy flits of movement that were converging on them. "You got anything there, Hank?"

"Not a one. You?"

"The whole hillside is moving!"

Hank turned. "I'll back you."

"No. You watch that edge."

A commotion welled up near the horses, but Rabbit couldn't see from his position behind the boulder. The screaming and roaring of horses mingled with the growls and screeches of the *Bahkauv*.

"I'm gonna help them horses!" Hank declared and started out from behind the rock.

Rabbit grabbed his coat and hauled him back. "You do, you're dead. You stay right here. Those horses are on their own." Even as he said it, his heart ached for Dime, who was neighing frantically. *You fight like it's the devil, big Dime.*

He had little time to fret over the thought of Dime getting ripped to pieces. The swarm of *Bahkauv* crested the small rise between their position near the adit and the tree line along the uphill side of the tailings, where the horses continued the cacophony of whinnies and snorts and screams. It chilled him as much as the shrieks of the *Bahkauv*.

A front of what Rabbit guessed was five or six *Bahkauv* crested the sloped tailings and sped toward the adit.

"This is why we're here," he whispered. "Hank. They're going for the adit."

Hank spun around and drew back his bow in one fluid motion. Rabbit raised the Winchester and drew a bead on the lead beast. "I got the one in front."

Arrow and lead flew.

Thwip!

Boom!

The *Bahkauv* out front stumbled and then tumbled, pushing up a pile of snow as it slid to a stop. The next froze mid-stride, an arrow sticking out of its ear. It crumpled beside the first.

"Helluva shot!" Rabbit shouted as he worked the lever of the Winchester and took a bead on another.

Thwip!

"Down he goes!" Hank laughed.

Rabbit glanced at him. Hank was reaching into his quiver for a third arrow. *Goddamn, that twig shooter is fast.* He focused back on the herd heading for the adit.

Thwip!

Another tumbled into the snow as an arrow sunk into its eye socket.

"Got 'im!" Hank shouted.

Rabbit beaded the next. "Lead it," he whispered and squeezed the trigger. *Boom!*

Another *Bahkauv* crashed into the snow with half of its head missing. The Winchester didn't do nearly as impressive a job as the Sharps, but it surely did shoot true.

A howling scream erupted from over the edge of the tailings and the pack scattered.

Rabbit managed two more shots before the fleeing *Bahkauv* disappeared into the shadows under the trees, both hitting hindquarters but doing no real damage.

"Who-ee! Jack Rabbit. I do believe we make a team!"

"Damned fast with that bent stick, Hank."

"Yessir, Jack Rabbit." Hank reached back and felt the sticks in his quiver. "Fifteen more. You think that's enough?"

Rabbit shook his head. "No telling. Hillside is crawlin' with those bastards."

"Maybe we scared 'em off?" Hank's question was tentative, as if he knew otherwise but hoped just the same.

"Somethin' called them back, just like when we fought them in the mine." Rabbit wasn't at all happy how this was shaping up. It was too much like their encounter before. Was there a white devil leading this pack, too? Or were they alerted to a danger in the mine?

Boone. Clementine. Were they even still alive? Did they find the Rogue? The *Bahkauv* queen? Was that why the beasts were swarming? Or was it because he dropped one on the other side of the gulch?

Rabbit decided it didn't much matter. His job—and Hank's— was to make sure no *Bahkauv* entered that mine and flanked Boone and Clementine.

"Probably didn't expect nobody guarding the front door." Hank elbowed Rabbit's arm.

Rabbit grinned at Hank's double negative. "Reverse that." He began reloading the Winchester with the cartridges from his belt. "You know you laughed at the first one? The one with an arrow in his ear?"

Hank snorted. "I get excited sometimes."

A series of howls and shrieks welled up all around them.

They looked at each other and then Hank wilted a little. "That there's a lot of *Bahkauv*."

Twenty Six

Boone could swear his hearing was better in this cave than anywhere else. The distant *scritch-scritch-scritch* of claws on rocks had him stopping time and again to listen. From the sound of it, there were hundreds of claws coming their way.

But his mind was also often given to exaggeration when compromised by fear. Or alcohol. Or women. At the moment, he was running on two out of three in here.

Clementine had been anxious to move on. Him, not so much. But they had, and the farther they progressed, the louder the disconcerting sounds became. Shuffling snorts. Shrieking howls. Hair-raising screams. Boone began to hope that it was only *Bahkauv* he was hearing. The lanterns seemed pitifully lacking now, not even capable of lighting the inevitable next downturn or dogleg in the passageway.

Each glance he darted at Clementine reassured him just a little that they were doing the right thing. Her steadfast determination to proceed bolstered his resolve as well.

"There's another." Clementine raised her baton and brought it down on an unbroken egg. *Crack!* A spark burst from the inside, temporarily blinding him if he watched, before quickly fizzling out. Just like the previous handful of eggs she'd destroyed, the green, red, and black slimy contents oozed out onto the cave floor.

Boone grimaced. The slime reminded him of bloody snot.

They'd been finding more and more unbroken eggs as they continued, most obscured by other eggs or inadequate light. Some were hidden behind stalagmites along the tunnel walls.

The cave had grown increasingly warmer and more humid. He contemplated removing his jacket, but he didn't want to take the time to unfasten the bandoleer and strip down, or risk dropping it on the slime-covered floor.

"We must be close," Clementine whispered, pausing to listen. Then she shook her head slightly. "*Jævla!* I can't determine how many, but it doesn't seem like there are great numbers."

What was her definition of "great"? Ten? Twenty? Fifty?

"There's something I can't make out, though." She tilted her head slightly. "You hear that slapping noise. It sounds … wet. Like shoveling slushy snow."

Boone stilled, listening. He couldn't hear anything. What did it matter? He was committed now to facing whatever three-headed Cerberus or dagger-toothed, scaly, mutated cat that wanted to coat him in gooey, rancid saliva and devour him piece by piece. He groaned at his damned imagination.

Clementine squinted at him in the shadows. "You ready?"

"No." And he wasn't. He unholstered and holstered his peacemaker a few times. Then he switched the sword to his other hand and did the same with the scattergun. He patted the bandoleer and wiggled it back and forth on his shoulder. "This thing is uncomfortable," he muttered. He wouldn't have time to reload it. All this for two damned shots. Darn Rabbit anyway.

There had been no sign of *Bahkauv* from behind. That meant Rabbit and Hank were doing their job. Or all the damned atrocities were in front of them, along with that mutated cat.

He shifted the bandoleer again. "Shit."

"Struggling to cope with our strategy?" Clementine wiped the slime from her baton with her ungloved hand and then flung the slime against the wall of the cave.

He stretched his neck one way and then the other as he watched her. "*Your* strategy. You know you're the one who said there's nothing to wash your hands with down here."

"I know it's a shitty deal." Clementine chuckled and wiped her palm off on the rock wall.

"It's your hand that smells shitty now."

"All the better to caress your cheek with," she joked, holding it out as she stepped closer.

He wrinkled his nose and lightly batted her arm away.

She picked up a handful of dirt and pebbles, scrubbing her hands with it and then used her canvas pants as a towel. "Whew, it's too warm in here for this coat." She leaned her baton against the rock wall, set her lantern on the ground, and shed her pack. She slipped out of her coat and laid it on a boulder, working her arms in big circles. "Better. Now I can swing."

"How's the left shoulder?" he asked, thinking of the results of her last battle in Ingleside Cemetery.

"I've been hurt worse." She adjusted the second baton she had secured to her belt and then picked up her pack. "Remember, sword in front. If you get tired, fall back. Keep in mind the defensive positions you've learned. Use them to rest." She picked up the slime-covered baton and lantern from the ground. "All right. Let's keep moving."

Boone fell in beside her as she approached the next curve in the tunnel. He rested the scimitar on his shoulder and held the lantern in front of him. "We'd better hurry. I know you don't want to miss teatime with the dastardly Rogue and her Royal Highness, Queen *Bahkauv*."

A smile worked its way up her face. "You're funny, Boone." She shoulder-bumped him. "And I'm not just talking about your looks."

He chuckled. "You've been spending too much time with Rabbit."

Twenty Seven

Rabbit hunkered behind the waist-high boulder near the adit and waited for two—or fifty—*Bahkauv* to spill down from the hillside.

A flurry of snorting and huffing caught his attention. He swung the rifle toward the tailings that sloped down and out of sight and along to where the horses had been hitched near the tree line. That didn't sound like *Bahkauv*.

Shit, the horses!

He'd lost track of their mounts when the shooting started, but he was pretty sure he hadn't heard them for some few minutes.

They must have bolted.

He hoped so, anyway.

A whinny-roar pierced through the *Bahkauv's* shrieks and howls. Suddenly, Nickel's head appeared, coming up the slope.

Rabbit rose up for a better view and caught sight of Dime, behind and off to the side of Nickel, trailed by three *Bahkauv* close to striking distance.

Both horses' ears were flattened back, their mouths open and teeth bared. Nickel roared again and began leaping over the snow in great bounds instead of plowing through it. But the three *Bahkauv* behind them were gaining on the panicked horses with each bounding stride. Dime squealed and snorted as he kept pace with Nickel. They crested the slope and shot across the tailings within a few yards of Rabbit and Hank.

Rabbit nestled the rifle butt against his shoulder and leaned forward. He took a bead on the lead *Bahkauv* as it swiped a massive set of claws at Dime's haunch.

Boom!

The *Bahkauv* shrieked and rolled, but recovered almost instantly and continued the chase.

Thwip.

An arrow sunk into its neck and it tumbled again, this time writhing in the snow before regaining its footing.

The next *Bahkauv* in line swiped at Dime as the horse

approached the edge of the tailings.

Nickel leapt and disappeared over the edge.

The wounded *Bahkauv* slapped at the arrow in its neck, snapping the shaft off. It lurched upright and took off in pursuit again, moving faster than before but in jerky, frenzied leaps.

"Like it got mixed up in a swarm of bees," Rabbit said, dumbfounded. He caught himself watching the show. "Dammit!" He raised the rifle to his shoulder again.

Thwip. Another arrow sank into the beast's neck as it writhed and lurched and gyrated, leaving swirly loops and chaotic tracks through the snow as it headed toward the edge of the tailings.

"Damned beast is movin' too fast," Hank said. "Can't pin its head."

The *Bahkauv* nearest Dime swatted at Dime's rump. Dime grunted and kicked out at the beast. His hoof smashed into the *Bahkauv's* snout, snapping its head back, leaving it at a twisted, grotesque angle.

Dime disappeared over the edge of the tailings, not far behind Nickel.

The *Bahkauv* with the twisted neck collapsed into the snow, convulsing. The remaining healthy *Bahkauv* let out an ear-piercing howl and then bounded over the edge and out of sight, still trailing the horses. The lurching, shuddering beast with two arrows in its neck tumbled out of sight over the edge of the tailings, following Dime.

Rabbit's jaw went slack. "Fuuuuck."

"I got him." Hank dropped his bow and took off at a sprint, skinning his Bowie knife on the way to the quivering *Bahkauv* Dime had kicked in the head.

"Hank! Get back here!" Rabbit turned a circle, rifle raised, looking for anything heading for Hank.

Hank sawed at the creature's neck but stopped and looked away. His shoulders heaved.

"Hurry up, you donkey!" Rabbit hollered. The shrieks and

howls on the hillside above them escalated.

Hank turned back but looked up at the sky and grimaced. He resumed sawing, glancing down occasionally to observe his progress.

The head fell away. Hank back-pedaled from the dead creature, stooping long enough to wipe his knife in the snow.

Thump! Thump! THUMP!

A shriek rang out behind him.

Rabbit pivoted and brought the muzzle of the rifle up. The *Bahkauv* was already in the air, its jaws and fangs and huge spiked paws were all he could see. He flicked the muzzle toward the bastard and pulled the trigger.

Nothing.

FUCK! Dead trigger. He hadn't levered a cartridge into the chamber.

Massive claws clamped onto his chest but didn't penetrate the sheepskin coat. The creature's momentum slammed him against the boulder. Rabbit opened his mouth to scream but the blow had knocked the air from his lungs. He slid to the ground, covering his face as the *Bahkauv* landed on him, snarling and gnashing. His lungs seared with pain with each gasp. A bolt of lightning shot up his arm as the *Bahkauv* latched on and began shaking him, like an empty burlap sack, in its huge jaws. He reached down to his belt and grabbed hold of the first knife hilt he found. He skinned it and thrust it at the beast, sinking the blade into its chest. It shrieked and swiped wildly at him. The meat of its paw slammed against his temple. Pain shot through his head.

So dizzy … Everything went black.

Twenty Eight

Boone wiped at the sweat on his brow with his forearm. He'd struggled out of his thick coat and left it on a boulder a little ways farther on from Clementine's, yet still cursed the uncomfortable climate in this tomb. Near as he could tell, it wasn't even that hot. It was just the damned humidity. He was accustomed to the sun-dried heat of New Mexico, not a musty, sweltering cave. Then again, maybe it wasn't the humidity that was so objectionable. Maybe it was the variety of revolting smells that had him gagging every few steps.

There had been what felt like hundreds of turns since they'd entered the adit what seemed like ages ago. First this way, then that. The passageway had steadily descended for some time, so much so that Boone thought they must be close to China by now.

"Boone. Look at the ground." Clementine stopped and lowered her lantern, pointing her baton at an oddly shaped pile of rocks near a two-foot tall, glittery, white and silver stalagmite that appeared to be pushing its way up through the floor.

Boone leaned in. "What? Silver?"

"Yes. But ... look closer."

Boone held his lantern near the pile of rocks. "Oh, shit!" He reeled back, catching his heels on the rough cave floor.

Clementine grabbed him before he landed on his backside.

"That looks like a ..." He couldn't finish.

"A baby *Bahkauv*."

"It's dead?" It looked paler than the adults.

Clementine nodded. "It's turned to hardened dust, same as when I slay the adults."

Boone gripped the hilt of the sword. "The Rogue."

Clementine nodded again. "If you had any doubt about her being here before, you shouldn't now. Only Slayers have this effect on a *Bahkauv*."

"She's killing everything she sees." He looked at the lump of petrified flesh, no bigger than a housecat.

"That's about the extent of it."

Boone wasn't sure how he felt about the dead young'un. Queasy, certainly. But the *Bahkauv* needed to be put down. He recalled Uncle Morton dispatching a litter of mice pups they'd found in the barn. Boone was primer school age at the time, and he hadn't known how to feel about that then, either. Mostly queasy, too, if memory served him right.

"But babies?" he frowned.

Clementine shrugged. "Kill them now, or kill them later." She gave the baby a tap with her baton, turning it into a small pile of pebbles and dust. "Let's keep moving."

Boone stared after her. When it came to deadly foes, he had a feeling Clementine and the Rogue were cut from the same cloth.

Scritch-scritch-scritch.

Hell. He hurried after Clementine.

A few turns later, she stopped again, silencing him with a finger to her lips. Quietly setting her lantern on the ground, she tugged the second baton from her belt. With both batons held in what Boone knew to be a strike-ready stance, she cocked her head to the side, listening.

He listened, too, his scimitar raised.

A cloaked figure stepped from the darkness of a side tunnel in front of them, a long thin blade in hand.

Was that the …

"Rogue," Clementine said in an annoyed tone. She lowered her batons. "You've had a productive morning, I see."

So this was the Rogue. Boone sized her up. She was smaller than Clementine, not only in height, but in all proportions. In fact, Boone might have confused her for Amelia if the conditions were right. She was nothing more than a slender waif.

Her garments were unlike any he had seen. Dark, loose-fitting pants and shirt. A black cape hung to her knees. A hood covered her head and obscured most of her face. One petite hand protruded from the cape holding a slender, long knife. Dark, viscous liquid dripped slowly from the length of the blade.

"Your arrival is belated, Undertaker, but that much I expected." The Rogue stepped closer, eyeing Boone. "You brought a mule. How amusing. Yet *you* carry the pack."

Mule? Boone gritted his teeth at her condescending tone. He stood a generous head taller than this pint-sized killer, and would have an easy time of picking her up with one arm. The weight of a sack of flour over his shoulder would give him more pause than this haughty …

"He's a killer, not a mule, and far less reckless than you," Clementine snapped. "You've really stepped into a mire this time, *Rogue*."

She whirled on Clementine, slimy blade raised. "You are not to call me that."

Clementine knocked the blade aside with a baton. "You've given me no other name to call you, so you are *Rogue*." Her voice was steady, but Boone noticed the rigidness in Clementine's posture.

"You would struggle to pronounce my name. Your brutish tongue would twist like a bow on a package in the attempt."

"Then I will continue calling you *Rogue*." Clementine's muscles flexed as she squeezed the handles of the batons. "You upset the balance by being here."

"You and I are here for the same reason. No pretense will mask your true nature, Slayer." The Rogue lowered her weapon. "Now, if we're done with trivialities, the *frayer* are eliminated to here. *La reine mère*, the queen mother, is there." She pointed down the tunnel, in the direction they'd been heading.

"My orders are unambiguous," Clementine bit out. "Stay clear of this place. Your selfish, reckless actions have not only forced me to jeopardize my contract by coming here to stop you, but also risked the lives of my friends."

"Yes, yes, I can see you're upset." The Rogue sounded bored.

"I'm not 'upset.' I'm extremely aggravated."

It was Boone's assessment that Clementine was quite a lot more than aggravated. He'd known her long enough to see that she was near exploding. What would that mean between these two? He wasn't sure, but backing Clementine's play was his only concern at the moment. He palmed his pistol grip.

The Rogue smirked at him, looking deliberately at his pistol, and then returned her focus to Clementine.

"You know as well as I do, Undertaker, these creatures must be slaughtered. This gate must be cleansed." The Rogue turned toward the tunnel they'd come down.

"You possess a confidence in your actions I don't share. As I said, you may well be upsetting the balance."

The Rogue scoffed. "Point in fact, our being here together is a manifestation of nature seeking harmony. The power of two is required to kill the queen. Our presence here is not a coincidence." She continued to watch the tunnel.

Clementine crossed her arms, the batons sticking straight up. "You can't be sure."

"But I can." The Rogue spared her a glance. "You can acknowledge who you are, be true to your nature. Or you can bow dutifully and take orders from a power-hungry *médiocre* with aspirations of grandeur."

Boone assumed she meant Masterson. But what did he really know of Clementine's world?

Clementine sighed. "There must be order. We are meant to maintain it. You disrupt it." She faced the tunnel as well.

"On the contrary, I bring a stronger and longer-lasting order more swiftly than you could possibly manage on your own." The Rogue slipped into the side tunnel in which she'd been hiding.

Boone heard the huffing and the *scritch-scritch-scritch* he knew all too well.

"Boone. Behind me." Clementine raised her batons, holding one horizontal, one vertical.

Boone obeyed, but struck up a defensive position with his scimitar.

A *Bahkauv* appeared from around the turn, then another, and another. The first raced toward Clementine, mouth wide, fangs bared.

Clementine raised one baton and spun the other into a blur. The *Bahkauv*, distracted by the spinning baton, hesitated. Clementine lunged forward and brought the other baton down on its head with a *crunch!* It crumpled to the ground, its body paling as it morphed into hardened dust.

Boone turned as the second *Bahkauv* slumped to the ground, also turning into a dust statue. What the ... ?

The Rogue flitted across his field of vision and closed in on the third. She weaved and ducked as the *Bahkauv* swiped at her with its massive paw. Boone was stunned motionless by her speed. It was almost as if the *Bahkauv* wasn't moving at all. She crouched and shot up between the beast's front legs, driving her blade up through its lower jaw into its brain. Then she dropped and rolled to the side as it crashed to the ground. She kicked it as soon as it stilled, sending a cloud of dust and pebbles into the air.

At least that was what Boone thought he saw. She'd moved so quickly, though. In the feeble lantern light, he wasn't exactly sure.

As soon as he recovered from his stupor, he joined

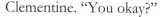

Clementine. "You okay?"

She focused on Boone and nodded but didn't answer. Her eyes were dark, shining with a ferocity that hadn't been there moments before. And she seemed taller. Boone took a step back.

"Now, to the queen mother," the Rogue said, strolling over to the *Bahkauv* Clementine had killed. "I assume you brought a blade, yes, not just a pair of sticks?" The Rogue kicked the dead beast into rubble.

Clementine tucked her batons into her belt. She frowned down at her hands for a moment.

"Sticks will not suffice when it comes to the next task," the Rogue said, as she passed Clementine.

Boone watched, waiting to see what Clementine would do. Would she fight the queen now that they were here, or walk away from the Rogue and follow Masterson's orders?

A loud sigh filled the tunnel, followed by a whispered curse. Clementine reached behind her and drew a sword from the sheath strapped to her back.

Boone knew that sword. It was the *Ulfberht*, Clementine's favored blade.

It appeared that the queen was in for a battle.

Twenty Nine

Something was shaking Rabbit.

Someone was bashing his head with a rock.

"...abbit! Jack Rabbit!"

Rabbit opened his eyes. The searing light of the blue sky sent more lightning bolts of pain ricocheting through his head. He squeezed his eyes shut again.

"Jack Rabbit! You're livin'! Are you livin'? You're movin' at least. Get up! Beasties are extra double dandered-up now. So riled they'll like to bring the trees down on us."

Rabbit groaned. His temple throbbed. "Help me up." He reached out, eyes still closed, to where he thought Hank's helping hand would be. It was. His world spun as Hank yanked him to his feet. He opened his eyes.

"Whoa!" Rabbit swooned. Everything swirled and twirled. Hank's face filled his vision. He tried to focus, but couldn't get all the blur out of Hank's features.

"We gotta move, Jack Rabbit! They got us beaded and they're comin'. Don't know how many. We gotta head for the adit. Make our stand there."

"Where's the rifle? Boone will kill me if I lose that rifle."

"I got it." Hank slid his arm under Rabbit's armpits and nearly lifted him off the ground, half-carrying, half dragging him toward the adit.

A pain shot through Rabbit's ribs, but not enough to mean they were broken. Wait! He'd left *his* rifle leaning against the boulder. "The Sharps!"

Hank kept moving. "Sure. And I'll fix up some vittles and grab a deck for a game of faro while I'm at it. The Sharps has gotta stay put for now. I don't expect none of them mongrels is gonna figure on that double-trigger contraption no-how."

Rabbit laughed and the pain in his ribs stabbed him like a knife. He grimaced and groaned. Maybe he had one broken rib after all, but his head was clearing.

Hank had him in the adit, leaning against the side of the tunnel in nothing more than a moment.

Rabbit peered out at the horizontal layers of white snow, dark green trees, and blue sky. *Bahkauv* bodies lay strewn about the tailings like so many fallen soldiers on the battlefield. He guessed they had incapacitated or killed fifteen, maybe a couple more. Those they'd only maimed continued to shriek and howl and slash at the ground, or attempt to crawl toward the adit.

He contemplated finishing them with his Bowie knife, but that would mean breaking cover. He swept his gaze across the tailings as he plucked cartridges and reloaded Boone's Winchester as quickly as he could with numb fingers. He hadn't figured on there being so many of the damned bastards.

Three reloads in the Winchester and the beasts were still coming. He had about fifteen more .45 cartridges for the Winchester or his pistol, but then he was out.

A deep, roaring whinny sounded below, out of sight over the edge of the rock tailings. It sounded like Nickel, but he couldn't be sure. It might have been one of the other horses for all he knew, but one thing was certain—those sons-a-bitches were still after the horses.

Dammit! But Dime was young and strong. And he'd stick with Nickel, if he could.

You fight those fuckers, amigos.

Three *Bahkauv* had managed to slip past them and disappeared into the adit while they set up for their last stand. From the scores of howls and shrieks on the hillside around them, there were plenty more on the way. Unfortunately, they were running low on ammo.

Down in the trees, the horses were probably being swarmed, too. Shit! It wouldn't be long before all the *Bahkauv* rushed the adit and he and Hank would be overrun.

Rabbit tried to shake the sinking feeling in his gut. "Hope there ain't too many more, Hank. I'm runnin' out of things to shoot. We'll be down to harsh words before long." He thought about his Sharps again. "Bah. Sharps takes too long to load anyway." Not to mention he'd need to go get it.

He rubbed his hands together and almost blew warm air on them but stopped. Dang Boone anyway. Always gotta know everything. Knew about blowing on hands. About the unpractical-ness of this rifle and the practical-ness of that one. About Pinkertons. About women.

Rabbit fretted about those three *Bahkauv* and the problems they might cause Boone and Clementine, but given the number of shrieks and howls he was still hearing from the woods, he daren't leave the adit unguarded.

Nor could he leave Hank.

"Here they come again!" Hank aimed an arrow and let it fly.

Thwip.

Rabbit raised the Winchester. Ignoring the stabbing pain in his ribs and head, he lit into the wall of *Bahkauv* that crested the edge of the tailings. By the time the last one crumpled to the ground near their feet, Rabbit had emptied the rifle again and Hank had dropped his bow and started in with his pistol. They both ended the volley with *clicks* and immediately started reloading.

"How many you got left, Jack Rabbit? I got one more load

after this." Hank slammed the cylinder shut and gave it a spin.

"Last full load. Fourteen, I think. Full load in the Colt yet, then I'm done. You grab my Colt if you go empty."

They looked at each other for a moment. Rabbit knew Hank was thinking the same thing he was.

"There's nothing for it, Mr. Varney."

"We'll make 'em work for it, Mr. Fields," Hank agreed.

They couldn't let any more of these beasts through. Every one of the bastards that slipped past was a threat to Clementine and Boone, and Rabbit wouldn't have it.

They nodded at each other without saying another word, turned back toward the entrance, and waited.

Outside, a wounded *Bahkauv* writhed and crawled across the tailings, disappearing over the edge. Another with an arrow sticking out of its spine crawled toward them, dragging its motionless hindquarters. Rabbit resisted the urge to shoot it. He needed to save the bullet.

"We'll go to knives after the guns," Rabbit said.

Knives against so many claws and teeth? He didn't like the odds and didn't hold much hope in it.

Hank nodded. "Knives'll do, in the thick of it."

The shrieks and howls began to escalate again.

Thirty

Boone hustled to stay abreast of Clementine, who had no trouble matching pace with the petite but nimble Rogue. After witnessing the smaller Slayer take down a couple of *Bahkauv*, it was obvious that her strength was not in her size like Clementine's, but in her speed.

He followed the two killers through the snaking tunnel, descending even deeper into the earth.

Sweat ran trickled his back.

The Rogue slowed only to stab and kick the eggs that lay along the edges of the tunnel. She seemed not to care that her boots were covered with slime, nor the stench that came with the goo. Her ability to skewer scores of the newly hatched wriggling baby *Bahkauv* while showing nothing even remotely resembling emotion gave Boone pause. He'd just not been in the company of a cold-blooded killer before. Well, there was Clementine after all, but he was beginning to understand some of the differences between the two.

While he averted his eyes from the freshly dispatched young as he passed, he did notice that the Rogue was extremely quick and effective at her task, which he attributed to efficiency rather than empathy. He also noticed that Clementine left the task to the Rogue.

As they rounded yet another bend, a glow shining bright filled the tunnel from an opening further on.

"*La reine mère* is there. Prepare yourself," she told Clementine specifically. Other than using the term *mule* occasionally, the Rogue still refused to acknowledge Boone's presence.

"I'm ready," he goaded.

Clementine sent him a sideways smirk.

After a glare in Boone's direction, the Rogue continued. "You will need to exercise extreme prudence during your approach. She is a queen for a reason."

Clementine scoffed. "*Prudence*? Do you even know the meaning of that word, Rogue?"

The smaller Slayer moved like the wind, pressing her blade to Clementine's chin. "*Rogue* is not my name."

"Do not threaten me." Clementine knocked aside the tip of the knife, her gaze narrowed, her jaw taut.

Boone pulled Clementine back a step, trying to diffuse the tension. They were down here to kill a queen, dammit, not each other. "What's your name?" he asked the Rogue.

Still glaring up at Clementine, the Rogue rattled off something long and tongue-twisty in French.

Boone exchanged frowns with Clementine. "She's right," he said. "I don't think I can pronounce that."

Clementine rested the *Ulfberht* on her shoulder, looking at the Rogue with a small smile. "Let's call her 'Prudence' for short. Maybe that will teach her to start being more *prudent* when it comes to reckless killing in *my* territory."

The Rogue huffed. "My name is not …" She cursed and threw up her hands. "Since your excess in brawn has resulted in a weakness of mind you most assuredly are not capable of pronouncing my proper name. I'll allow you to call me 'Prudence' for the time being."

Clementine nodded. "Well, *Prudence*, are you going to lead the way into this fight, or do I need to use my 'brawn' to show you how to slay a queen?"

Boone chuckled.

After hitting Clementine with another glare, Prudence the Rogue turned and rushed into the darkness ahead.

As they neared the opening, Boone was able to see farther in the darkness. The cavern before him was immense and magnificent, bathed in a green glow that seemed to be coming from the newly laid eggs.

Hundreds of stalactites hung halfway to the ground from a ceiling he estimated to be forty or more feet high. Stalagmites, some short and slender, some very tall and thick, thrust up from the floor and reached for their hanging counterparts. In some places, they actually connected to form hourglass-shaped columns. Calcite draped from the ceiling like undulating curtains in a queen's bedchamber. All glittered and glowed, seemingly studded with gems and jewels of orange and green and yellow and white.

The walls appeared to be painted with rivers of color that branched out and divided into ever-smaller streams before joining into larger rivers again. Each swirled with vivid reds and golds and browns.

His eyes wandered to the far side of the cavern, a distance of at least a hundred feet, maybe more. Brown and white rocks rippled along the walls. He'd never seen rock that looked like it was flowing. Adding to the effect was the sound of water roiling, bubbling, and splashing. He caught a glimpse of a stream here and there, shimmering and glowing green and blue, churning its way along the wall before disappearing under the rocks halfway across the cavern.

And Rabbit thought the cavern they'd fought the *Bahkauv* in was a sight. His eyes would pop out of his skull if he saw this.

"Boone!" Clementine whisper-yelled.

He felt a tug on his sleeve and looked over his shoulder. Clementine was there, unease lining her face. She hauled him back into the tunnel and out of sight against the wall.

"You plan to take on the queen all on your lonesome, Sidewinder?" she asked, still holding onto him.

"That's spectacular," he whispered and peeked around the corner.

"Boone." She yanked him back again.

"All right. But did you look in there?"

"I did. Did you happen to see the queen?"

"No. Too many distractions and obstacles."

"I did. Look again—carefully."

Movement at the far end of the chamber caught his eye. He squinted. Dark, glossy fur reflected the glitter of the rocks in the cavern. "She blends in. It's almost like a disguise," he whispered over his shoulder to Clementine.

He looked again, trying to see the beast in its entirety. His jaw slackened. She was enormous! At least five times the size of the smaller *Bahkauv*. She stood at least twenty feet tall, and her tail.

"Holy shit!" he murmured.

The queen shifted so that her, lumpy, bulging belly was fully in view. Oh, hell. She was near bursting with glowing eggs.

He pulled back and stared at Clementine, who was stretching her shoulders. "We can do this," he said, more to himself than her. He glanced around the shadows, looking for the third Musketeer. "Where's the Rogue?"

"She's already in there scouting the cavern."

"She is?" He hadn't seen her slip by.

Clementine frowned at him. "You need to pay better attention if you're going in there with us."

He nodded slowly. She was right. He'd let himself become enraptured by the beauty of the cave, and then the bizarre sight of a *Bahkauv* queen, but now it was time to focus.

"Are we waiting for her to come back?" he asked, wiping sweat from his forehead with his sleeve.

"Probably best."

Prudence slipped back into the tunnel. She glared at Boone for several seconds before turning her attention to Clementine. "You need to hobble your mule before he gives us away."

"Stop calling me a mule, *niñita.*" He'd had enough of Prudence's slights.

"I'm no *little girl*," she said, pointing her narrow blade at him. "You might be bigger and stronger, but you are bovine. I could gut you before you'd even take a single swing at me."

"Enough, you two!" Clementine hissed. "What did you see in there?" she asked Prudence.

"There are *Bahkauv* guarding *la reine mère.*" She pointed into the cavern. "There. There. They wait and protect. When we attack, so will they."

Clementine leaned out and scanned the cavern. Back to Prudence and Boone, she said, "We will need to deal with that nuisance." She glanced at Boone.

Shit. "By *we* you mean me."

She squeezed his arm. "You have the skill and strength for this task."

Prudence didn't look convinced, but she continued to Clementine, "When I have control of the tail, you will *prends la tête*."

"English, Prudence," Clementine snapped.

She sighed. "Take the head, Slayer."

Clementine crossed her arms. "No."

"Eh?" Prudence did a double-take.

"No. When *I* have control of the tail, *you* will take the head."

Boone watched their back and forth with a frown. What the hell did they mean? Take the tail? He peeked around the corner at the queen. Its long tail was coiled, piled up on itself like a giant snake. If he were to guess, it must have been twenty-five feet long and as big around as his waist at the base. How did one "take" such a tail?

"Have you ever fought against a *Bahkauv* queen mother?" Prudence sneered, poking her finger at Clementine. "Have you been charged with this task before? A queen mother's tail? Or even fought a beast so large?"

"Yes, I've fought beasts this size before."

Prudence scoffed.

"Mountain trolls," Clementine threw out.

"They are nothing more than oversized, lumbering cattle."

Clementine huffed. "Listen, I've got a big sword. You've got a little knife. What do you plan to do with that? Clean the queen's teeth?"

"She does have big fucking teeth," Boone said, earning a frown from both Slayers.

"Your club is barbaric." Prudence waved her long, slender knife in front of Clementine's sword.

Clementine flicked the sword, knocking the knife from her hand.

Before it could hit the ground, Prudence snatched it from the air. "Enough! You'll know when I need you." She shrugged off her cape and dashed into the cavern.

Clementine cursed under her breath. "She'll get us killed."

Boone didn't doubt it, not with the claws, teeth, and tails of the creatures they were about to face.

"Not if I can help it." Scimitar raised and ready, he rushed into the cavern, plastering himself against the wall as he surveyed his surroundings. The *Bahkauv* were supposed to be waiting to slice him into ribbons, but he saw no movement, no foes. He couldn't see Prudence either. Darting from one stalagmite to the next, hiding where he could, he made his way closer to the queen. Glowing eggs lay everywhere, a fact he'd missed when he was busy ogling the glittering walls.

He was crouching behind a stalagmite when Clementine sidled up and leaned into him.

"What do you think you're doing?" She peered around the stalagmite at the queen.

"I'm going to kill some *Bahkauv*. You go poke that big sword into their queen." He peeked around the other side of the stalagmite. "You see any of the sharp-clawed buggers?"

"Yes. They're nestled into the alcoves and niches in the cavern walls."

Goose bumps peppered Boone's skin. He searched the walls. Sure enough, there they were. He swallowed what felt like a large rock in his throat and looked back at her. "How many can you see?" He'd counted four.

Clementine puffed out her cheeks and shook her head.

Ah shit. His gut twisted. He wished his *amigo* was next to him. Rabbit had a way of bolstering Boone's resolve.

"Son of a three-headed dog!" Clementine whispered.

"What?"

Clementine nodded toward the queen.

Boone poked his head out to see. "Hellfire." He watched as Prudence flitted behind stalagmite to boulder, boulder to column, column to stalagmite, until she was within a few feet of the gigantic beast.

Clementine pulled him back behind the stalagmite. She caught his hand and gripped it tight. Her eyes were dark, her expression fierce. "Be careful, Boone. Keep your back to the queen, but watch that tail. Use your pistol if you need to. I'll try and keep an eye on you, but I might be busy."

Boone looked down at their entwined hands. Along with heat from her touch, adrenaline and confidence surged through his body. He wasn't sure if Clementine was bestowing some special power upon him, or if it was the thrill of the moment before battle, but he felt he could take on a herd of *Bahkauv* right then. Hell, and a *Höhlendrache*, too, just to keep it interesting.

"The Rogue will go for the tail," Clementine continued. "But I don't think she'll be successful. My hope is she will only be injured." Clementine glanced toward the queen and back, her brow lined. "If she is killed, it's up to the two of us. You'll need to use that," she pointed at Boone's scimitar, "along the queen's neck." At his nod, she let go of his hand and added, "In case you're wondering, the queen will resist your advances."

Boone reached up and brushed his thumb over her cheek below the cut she'd gotten from Augustine. "Be careful. That tail looks like it's going to be a handful."

She winked. "Wait until she raises the spikes."

"Spikes? I didn't see spikes."

After another quick peek around the stalagmite, she told him, "Wait until the *Bahkauv* attack, then light into any getting close to the Rogue or—"

A piercing screech echoed through the cave. It was the sound Boone would expect to hear if he were standing at the gates of hell. He winced, his ears ringing after it ended.

Without another word, Clementine slipped around the side of the stalagmite and zigzagged her way toward the queen.

Boone watched as she closed in on the huge beast.

Meanwhile, Prudence darted from one side of the queen to the other, stabbing and slashing at the tail. The queen screeched with each strike of the blade. Boone cringed time and again.

The tail, now covered from base to tip with a line of six-inch cone-shaped spikes, seemed to have a life of its own, pursuing Prudence in flurries of thrashes and lashes. Clementine was right about the spikes. She must extend them when she's attacked.

The tail rose high above the ground and smashed down in a thundering boom, crushing and exploding anything it touched, but always missing Prudence by a hairbreadth. It even pursued her around obstacles, and then snapped at her with a cobra-like strike.

The queen lumbered in slow circles, encumbered by her bulging belly of eggs. Slow, swooping swipes with her massive arms seemed almost comical to Boone, until she smashed a stalagmite into a pile of rubble. If she found purchase, it would be the end of Clementine or Prudence.

Boone glanced around the cavern. "Goddammit!" While he'd been distracted by the queen, the walls had come alive with *Bahkauv*.

He pushed to his feet and raced toward the melee. *Bahkauv* crawled down the walls, howling and shrieking. Six, eight, nine of them Boone counted before he glanced back to the queen.

Clementine dashed, thrust her sword, and dashed again. She deflected and dodged long curved claws and dagger-like fangs. The air resounded intermittently with the clang of the sword or the thundering clap of the tail as the queen whipped at Prudence.

Boone moved in closer, keeping his back mostly to the queen. Out of the corner of his eye, he saw Clementine duck as a massive paw swiped the air over her head.

The queen screeched at the ceiling of the cave. Boone craned his neck to find Prudence. He felt the wind as the mighty tail swooshed over, clipping Prudence as she sank her knife into the haunch of the queen. She flew through the air and then tumbled, head over heels, across the cavern until she crashed into a stalagmite.

The tail whipped up into the air and snapped back at Boone. He dove to the ground and covered his head with his arms as it brushed along his backside. He rolled over, looking up at the tail as it looped and swung back over him. He scrambled up and dove at a pile of rubble just as the tail snapped down, smashing into the pile, exploding rocks and dust into the air.

Clementine flew over Boone's head, her sword leading the way. He sat up and watched as she swung *Ulfberht* in a wide, long arc. It slammed into the tail and ricocheted off the spikes with a clang. The queen screeched.

While Boone had been dodging the tail, Prudence had managed to recover and work her way around to the queen's chest. She attacked with thrusting jabs.

Boone sprang to his feet and held his scimitar up in front of his chest with both hands. A *Bahkauv* rushed him from the shadows, mouth wide and fangs glistening.

He crouched, ready to dodge and slice. The *Bahkauv* lunged. Boone leapt right and cut up through its neck as it writhed in the air to swipe at him. It crashed into the ground in a heap. The head rolled to a stop some feet away.

Clementine was right. They were dimwitted fighters. "Once you jump, I got ya. Can't change directions in mid-air, ya big ass."

"Boone!" The urgency in Clementine's voice had him on the move before he realized where he was going. As he rounded a stalagmite, he saw Clementine surrounded by three *Bahkauv* and the queen's tail undulating back and forth over her head.

She cleaved the arm from one *Bahkauv*, deflected the gnashing teeth of another with a baton, and kicked the third in the chest.

The tail whipped into a spiral above Clementine's head. She dodged and parried as it stabbed at her.

Too far away for the sword and the pistol won't penetrate the armor on that bitch. He dropped the sword and yanked sawed-off. *I hate this fucking gun.*

The tail rose up, preparing to smash Clementine into the rubble strewn about the ground.

The queen shrieked again. At least Prudence was doing her job.

Boone aimed at the tail and bent his knees and braced the shortened butt of the sawed-off against his hip. He gritted his teeth and pulled both triggers.

BA-BOOM!

The shotgun jammed up against his hip, sending a flash of pain down his leg and knocking him back a step. His ears rang, muffling the sounds around him. "Ow ow ow! Sonofabitchin' gun!"

A rumble started up somewhere in the distance. Dust and pebbles fell from the ceiling.

The queen screeched so loudly that Boone nearly dropped the shotgun to cover his ears in spite of them still being muffled. He couldn't help but scream back. "Arghh!"

The *Bahkauv* that had been closing in on them howled in unison and scurried back into hiding. The roar of the gun must have sent them running.

While Boone checked the queen for any damage he'd done, he cracked the barrels and racked two more shells. The earth-shaking sawed-off had taken a sizable hunk of meat out of the base of the tail. It flopped about but still looked lethal.

He spared a glance at Clementine, who was finishing severing the head of the last of the three *Bahkauv* attacking her. A cloud of dust rose into the air around them.

The distracted queen began lumbering in a circle, turning in Boone's direction. Prudence took that moment to climb the beast's neck like a tree. She began jabbing her knife into the neck of the beast repeatedly.

Clementine let out a sharp whistle.

Prudence paused to look at Clementine.

"You need a real weapon!" Clementine flipped *Ulfberht* into the air. Prudence sheathed her knife and watched the sword spin through the air toward her.

Boone was mesmerized, watching Clementine, then Prudence, then the sword.

Prudence, who still clung to the neck of the thrashing queen, coiled and sprang to catch the sword. She grabbed the hilt as it neared and accelerated its spin directly into the queen's neck as she flew over the beast's head. She folded in half with effort and drove the sword through flesh and bone.

The queen began a shriek but didn't finish. Her head dropped to the ground with a squishy, sickening thud.

At once, a cacophony of mournful howls rang out all around them.

Now we're in for it.

Boone picked up his scimitar and strode to Clementine, who was bent over, catching her breath.

"Step one, huh?" he said. "Now the kids are mad and want revenge."

"No." Clementine shook her head. "Listen."

The howls were fading into the distance.

Prudence walked back and forth along the body of the dead queen, and then she stopped near the middle. She sank the *Ulfberht* into the beast's chest, sawing and hacking down through the belly to a point between the hind legs. Dark sticky blood and slimy entrails spilled and spread out over the ground into a squishy mess. Eggs, too, poured out into viscous, slowly flowing pools of glowing green slime.

Boone pulled his handkerchief up over his mouth and turned to Clementine. "That's unpleasant."

Prudence began stomping on the eggs, apparently taking some satisfaction in squishing them and splattering more goo over her boots and legs.

Boone backed away. So did Clementine.

"No, *that's* unpleasant." Clementine pointed at Prudence.

The howls were quiet now, fading into silence. Distant rumbles crescendoed and then subsided.

"You think the shotgun started something?" Boone asked Clementine.

She shrugged. "No telling. Does it make you nervous?"

Boone frowned at the ceiling. "A little, and I don't mind saying it. We might want to head back."

Prudence smashed the last egg and approached Boone. "If ever I am again forced to endure the displeasure of your company, I insist you refrain from utilizing that monstrous, barbaric thing." She glared at the shotgun.

Before Boone could reply, she turned to Clementine. "This could have been accomplished much more efficiently, if only you would abstain from employing brutish techniques." She tossed *Ulfberht* at Clementine.

Clementine caught it without taking her eyes off of Prudence. "You should have cleaned it."

"It reminds me of the club I used to hunt frogs when I was a girl." Prudence smirked. "While you two were watching me kill the queen, you failed to notice several *Bahkauv* escaping with eggs."

"The queen is dead," Clementine said.

"This one is." Prudence strode to her cape and scooped it up. "The natural light from these eggs will fade. I advise you to retreat to the surface before you become lost."

He watched her disappear into the shadows. "Huh. She left, just like that."

"You're welcome, *Rogue!*" Clementine shouted. She turned to Boone with a grin. "I may have to kill her someday."

Thirty One

"Cocksuckers!" Rabbit pointed the barrel of the Winchester at the crest of the hill, waiting to bead the next *Bahkauv* head to appear.

"I second that," yelled Hank. "Pour on the lead, Jack Rabbit!"

Three *Bahkauv* appeared, sprinting toward the mine.

"I got left and middle." Hank drew up his pistol in both hands.

Rabbit chuckled and aimed at the one on the right. "I got right and middle."

The game was on. If they were going to die, why not have a little fun.

Boom! Boom!

They fired within a split second of each other.

Both *Bahkauv* dropped. Two more appeared from the side, closer. Rabbit shoulder-cocked and fired.

Boom!

The third one crashed into the snow alongside the first two.

They swung their guns to the new threat from the side, but both paused when a figure rushed up behind the two *Bahkauv*.

A man. No. Shaped like a man but not moving quite like a ma ... Ludek!

Ludek shot forward with a blurring burst of speed and caught up to the galloping beasts. He leapt in front and between them, brandishing a short sword in each hand. He dug his heels in and skidded to a stop with the blades pointed behind him, toward the beasts. He waited, chin down, looking straight at Rabbit and Hank. The *Bahkauv* writhed and twisted and plowed snow with their paws in an attempt to stop, but it was too late. Ludek had timed it perfectly. Momentum carried them, and they shrieked as Ludek's swords sank into their wide chests.

Ludek yanked the swords free, lifted the blades high, and swung them down on the beasts' necks. The heads fell into the snow simultaneously in one muffled thump.

After cleaning the dark blood from his blades in their fur, he held up one hand and waved, and then he started toward them. "Hank! Mr. Fields! I trust you are both uninjured."

"Hooweee, Ludek." Hank clapped Ludek's shoulder. "Sure am happy to see you."

Rabbit realized his mouth was still open and closed it.

"I apologize for my lateness. I was otherwise engaged." He pointed to the hillside below them.

"So, that's why most of them came from the hillside above us and hardly a one from down there," Rabbit realized out loud.

Ludek nodded.

"Thank you, partner." Rabbit shook his hand. "We were startin' to compose our tombstones."

Ludek scanned the gulch. "There may be a stray here or there, but we've eradicated the bulk of them. Your mounts did a fair job as well. Your horse—Dime, I believe you named him." He looked at Rabbit. "He was brave. As was the one named Nickel."

Rabbit's stomach knotted. "*Was?*"

Ludek smiled. "A poor choice of phrase. *Is.* Is brave. He is a warrior. He was struck on the neck but recovered and rejoined the battle."

Rabbit blew out a long slow breath. "Nickel?" He worried for Boone.

"Uninjured."

"Fenrir?"

"I resisted counting the dead and dying beasts surrounding her in the interest of saving time and assisting the two of you."

"Fred?" Hank asked with a cringe, as if he knew he wouldn't like the answer.

Ludek shook his head. "I last saw him heading north into the forest. I am sorry, Hank, I could not follow. My instructions were to aid your party in any way I could, and *Bahkauv* were gathering. A shot from a large-caliber rifle alerted them to your presence." Ludek looked over at the Sharps still leaning against the boulder.

Rabbit cringed. "Yeah. Probably should have held off on that." He felt like an idiot, but it was one helluva shot.

"Hoo hoo! Hell of a shot, Jack Rabbit." Hank punched Rabbit's arm, apparently reading his thoughts.

"No matter. They would have answered the queen's call."

Rabbit and Hank looked at each other.

Boone! Clementine!

"Shit! We gotta get in there, Hank."

Hank nodded.

"I suspect the job is done," Ludek said. "But go if you must. There might be stray younglings in there as well, so be mindful. Their bite is highly venomous until they reach adulthood. I'll finish these." He indicated those on the flat top of the tailings. "And search the hillside for strays when I finish."

"You're a good man, Ludek." Rabbit patted his shoulder. He wasn't sure whether or not Ludek took being called a "man" as a compliment. "Hank, let's go."

"I'll grab the lantern and be with you directly, Jack Rabbit."

Hank caught up with Rabbit just past the side tunnel that led to where he'd found Uncle Mort's body. They traveled in silence until they reached the cavern where they'd first faced the *Bahkauv* some weeks back. The tunnel had been widened since their last visit, so they had no problem walking abreast the entire way. They didn't run across any *Bahkauv* or even hear any troubling sounds until they entered the shadow-filled cavern.

The *clicks* and *taps* and *shwoosh* of pebbles and sand falling against rock in a cave or tunnel could be disconcerting, and Rabbit was definitely disconcerted. He heard those sounds, followed by a scurry of footfalls, tracking back toward the entrance of the mine.

"You hear that, Hank?"

Hank nodded, hunkering down behind a boulder. Rabbit joined him. After listening and watching for a few quiet minutes, Rabbit decided they were wasting time and decided to push on. Boone and Clementine might need help, and he was anxious to see they had whatever help he and Hank had to offer.

They continued on the path deeper into the mine. "This is the tunnel I chased the *Bahkauv* into last time," Rabbit said.

Hank chuckled. "Nearly brought the roof down on us with that scattergun."

"Yeah. That boomer is an earth-shaker, ain't it?"

Footfalls echoed from farther on.

"Shh. You hear that?" Rabbit whispered.

Hank nodded. He held the lantern higher and pointed his pistol into the darkness.

Rabbit aimed Boone's Winchester at the silhouettes that began to take shape in the darkness.

Hank cocked the hammer.

"You see any irony in a man being shot with his own gun?" Boone's voice was just about the sweetest thing Rabbit could have heard right about then.

"Booney!" Rabbit let the barrel of the rifle drop and hustled over. He wrapped his arms around his friend and squeezed Boone. His ribs stabbed him with pain, but he didn't care.

"Hank, did you take care of Jack?" Clementine put her hand on Hank's shoulder.

"We took care of each other." Hank grinned at Rabbit, then he picked up Clementine with a grunt and shook her a little. "Surely glad to see you two livin', Miss Clem." He set her down and slapped Boone on the back. "How come yer carryin' your coats?"

Rabbit noticed an odd glow coming from Boone's and Clementine's feet. He bent over for a closer look. "What the hell is all that green shit on your boots?"

Clementine smiled at Boone. "It's messy work when you take the queen."

Thirty Two

The sun had slipped below the ridge as the horses trudged toward the outskirts of Deadwood. Clementine shivered in the cold still air, daydreaming about a hot bath at The Dove.

Fenrir snorted and snuffled beside her, but kept plodding forward at a steady pace. After leaving the mine, Clementine had found Fenrir not far away, surrounded by an impressively large number of dead *Bahkauv*. Nickel and Dime were nearby, too, standing belly-to-belly, nose-to-nose, nickering and nodding to each other. Boone told her they were probably discussing the battle, which drew a laugh from Clementine.

None of the horses were seriously injured, at least not so anyone could tell. Judging by what Jack had said, all three of them had taken the *Bahkauv* to task.

Jack mentioned that Ludek had turned up to help, which explained the fact that some of the *Bahkauv* she saw surrounding the mine had not been shot, but brought to the block, cleanly beheaded by sharp steel.

Since the horses were exhausted, Clementine and the men had decided to walk most of the way back to Deadwood. They also walked because Fred the Mule was missing, and Hank's concern had the poor man rattled from hat to boots.

Hank was sure that his faithful companion had been run

down and done in by the "bastard *Bahkauvs*," as he called them. However, upon arriving back at the livery, they found Fred safe in his stall with his nose stuffed into a bucket of grain. Laughter had filled the livery, drawing Amelia to them. She'd explained that several hours before, she heard someone trying to lift the latch on the big front doors. It turned out that someone was Fred the Mule.

Clementine hadn't ever seen Hank's disposition improve so quickly. It was the happiest she'd seen him in some time. But after a few neck hugs and ear tugs with Fred, Hank had started in on a lengthy lecture about shirking duties and abandoning friends. Time would tell whether or not Fred took heed. She'd left the livery then, with Hank currying Fred while Boone and Jack bantered back and forth about who was responsible for cleaning which gun.

After stopping by The Pyre for some clean clothes and to drop off her pack and weapons, she'd headed to her favorite bathtub at The Dove and the hot meal that she hoped would follow.

Later, after a good soaking in hot water and bubbles, she feasted on roasted beef, potatoes, and fresh warm sourdough bread. Hildegard sat across from her and listened to Clementine's recount of the day's events, hanging on every detail. As Clementine had thought, the madam was responsible for sending Ludek to back their play at the mine. There was evidence enough now, between Hildegard, Ludek's actions, and Clementine's gut, to trust Ludek. There was little doubt whether or not he could handle himself in a row.

With a full belly and a tired body, Clementine wanted only to fall into bed and sleep away the memories of *Bahkauv* and *Draug* and skin eaters and countless other beasts that occupied her mind.

It was fully dark when she returned to The Pyre. She closed the front door, turned around, and smiled. A hot fire crackled and popped in the stove and the lanterns were lit. She could kiss Hank for his thoughtfulness.

Dousing the lamps, she wanted nothing more than to sink into her bed and burrow under the layers of thick blankets. She grabbed her weapons, wrinkling her nose at the smell of sulfur. They still reeked of dead *Bahkauv*. As she headed down the hall to her bedroom, her afi's deep voice echoed from her past: *An uncleanly weapon serves not well those who depend upon it.*

She stopped and growled at the ceiling. "*Oh faen, afi.*"

One's choice of poor phrase often illustrates weakness of mind, Liebling. His voice continued in her thoughts. *You must take care of your weapons if you expect them to take care of you.*

She rolled her eyes. "Apparently you weren't done." She spoke to the ceiling, and then looked at the weapons in her hands. Green and red slime clung to the *Ulfberht* and both batons.

"Fine, I'll clean my weapons." She trudged toward her bedroom. "Sometimes you can be … frustrating, afi."

The egg gunk had become sticky. Only with muslin rags and grain alcohol did it loosen from the weapons. She finished cleaning the *Ulfberht* and set it in its case in her weapons cabinet. As she finished polishing the two batons, a feeling of foreboding swept over her, sending chills down her arms.

She sniffed, smelling the grain alcohol, the sulfur from the slime, the lavender soap she'd washed with in her bath, and the jasmine from the incense sitting on her trunk that she'd lit before she'd started cleaning her weapons.

The fire crackled out front and a few muffled shouts from one of the saloons came through her bedroom window.

A board creaked.

Footfalls.

Someone was out front in the parlor.

She grabbed a dagger from the cabinet.

Closer now. The trespasser was coming down the hall. Too

stealthy to be human.

That smell. Her gut clenched. Nausea rose in her throat.

Masterson!

She flipped the dagger around in her hand so that the blade was obscured by her wrist and forearm, closed the doors to her weapon cabinet, and waited, keeping her gaze lowered. He stopped at her doorway. She could feel his presence without looking up. She could feel his fury, too.

He must know already about the Bloody Bones. She shouldn't have been surprised. News traveled fast in Deadwood, especially when it came to *others*.

Masterson wouldn't use firearms. That would give her the chance to parry. She would dodge his attack and should have a scant second to lower, whirl, lunge, and stick the dagger in his side. He would anticipate her movements, of course. She would take a blow to her side as well, but if she spun as she drove the dagger home, his blade might miss her vitals, if she were lucky. Then she'd roll out and face him with another parry.

She could not see beyond that.

"Clementine." The coolness of his voice surprised her. He was back to using her first name again. She expected a tantrum or outright hostility, considering his reaction to her last visit to Gayville.

She slowly looked at him, ready to spring or duck.

She'd been right about the fury. His eyes burned with it. But he didn't attack outright. Instead, like a hungry wolf, he stalked into the room.

"Good evening, Mr. Masterson. To what do I owe the pleasure of your company?" She played dumb.

"No games, Clementine." His voice was hard, edged with tension.

"Fine."

"I need your advice." He began pacing the room.

This wasn't going to end well, she could feel it in her bones.

"I'm happy to help."

"My course has become unclear." He stopped by the end of her bed and stared at her again. His anger had turned his eyes completely black. "I have described my requirements with no ambiguity. I have made clear what must be done." He pointed in one direction with one hand. "And what must not." He pointed in another direction with his other hand.

"Listen, Masterson. If you'd—"

He held his palm up to silence her.

"What is it I'm describing? The word escapes me."

"Free will?" she suggested. That was two words, but ...

"DISOBEDIENCE!" he bellowed.

She stiffened in surprise. "I don't know if I'd go so far as that. Noncompliance, perha—"

"No!" Masterson rushed her, slamming her back against the weapons cabinet, his hand on her throat. She felt the sting of a knife tip on the underside of her jaw.

She glared at him, unblinking. Adrenaline and rage fired through her, blasting aside any nausea brought on by his nearness, tightening her whole body until she was ready to spring.

"How would you punish such a rebel, *Scharfrichter*?" His breath was hot on her cheek.

She could smell cigar smoke on his collar. "Offer them tea and biscuits?"

Masterson wiggled the blade at her jaw. By the bite of it, she knew he'd drawn blood. She'd make the bastard pay for that.

Strength in serenity.

Taking a calming breath, she said, "I might strike out in anger."

She held his stare for a few more seconds, and then glanced down pointedly. His gaze followed hers. She watched as his eyes grew round at the sight of her dagger pressed against his ribcage.

"I might even slip a dagger between his ribs and slice his heart to ribbons." She placed her hand on his chest and shoved him away.

He lowered his stiletto blade, his focus vacillating between her dagger and her face.

"That knife looks familiar," she told him. "I know someone who carries one just like it."

Masterson's blade looked very much like the one Prudence carried.

"Who?" he asked, holding up the slender knife.

Clementine wasn't sure how much he knew about Prudence, but it was time he learned. "A rogue *Scharfrichter*." She watched him for a reaction. Nothing. "Here, in the Black Hills." He was either a good actor, or he already knew about Prudence. "She's the reason I found it necessary to visit Gayville again. She destroyed the *Bahkauv*."

Masterson frowned and sheathed his knife inside his black frock coat. "How could that possibly be?"

"She would have perished if I hadn't intervened."

He waved that notion aside. "Senseless. What does it matter, her failure? I would have preferred it. Then I would have a full stable. I am not concerned with charlatans and actors."

"You should be." Clementine did her best to conceal her surprise at the fact that Masterson was perfectly willing to let a Slayer die.

"You've destroyed my stable. You slaughtered my pets."

"*Pets*? Your so-called pets were running loose and killing humans. I cleansed that gate."

"Humans? Gate?" He scoffed. "Your naïveté astounds me. That was a stableyard. There was no gate. Your concern for humans is a weakness, especially for your three associates." His face pinched, and he muttered something in a language Clementine didn't recognize. Was that Latin?

He clenched his fists. "There is a veritable horde of *Draug* out there!" he roared. "How do you propose we remedy that now?"

It wasn't a gate. Clementine's mind raced. If it wasn't a … Did Prudence know that already? *Jävla gris!* She may need to doubly kill that Rogue. The damned fool was creating one problem after another.

"Answer me!" Masterson continued to roar, chopping the air with his hands for emphasis. "How will you repair the damage you've done?"

Clementine knew she needed to tread softly. She may have subdued him momentarily, but her intuition was screaming *DANGER!* She was holding a lit matchstick near a keg of gunpowder.

But her blood raged, too. She was not Masterson's attack dog nor common subordinate. "I am prepared to fulfill my commitments, but I need something from you."

His nostrils flared, his hands flailing about. "What? Do you need instruction on the duties of *ein Scharfrichter*? Do you need me to write out your tasks and include detailed instructions on how to accomplish them?"

The angrier Masterson became, the more he used his hands for emphasis. The whole scene reminded her of someone shooing away flies. She snorted. Twice.

"This is amusing to you?" He threw his hands in the air.

Yes. Very much so. "Not at all." She swallowed the last of her laughter. "From you, Masterson, I need communication. Until now, I've had to assume much concerning the accomplishments you require of me."

"*Ein Scharfrichter* is—"

"Let me finish!" She stood her ground, her fists clenched. "Our charter is vague, critically so, but I assumed you would be forthcoming about your expectations. You haven't been. That must end."

Masterson's forehead smoothed, but his jaw remained tense. "I believe I was clear about Gayville."

"You weren't."

"I said, in fair terms, stay clear of Gayville. That is explicit."

"Fine. But from my perspective, I am charged with maintaining the balance, as are you. I would like to believe that you are upholding your duties, but in my position, I won't assume."

He watched her, his face unreadable.

"If there is imbalance, I will address it no matter what is causing it. Or whom." She stared at him. "That is what I consider explicit."

"By decimating the *Bahkauv*, you have thrown this region into chaos." He folded his arms. "Perhaps this Rogue would be a better choice after all."

Damned Prudence. She had to go after that queen.

"You think I'm difficult to govern? The Rogue would make your head explode."

"I find it hard to believe this Rogue would be more troublesome than you."

"She isn't concerned with harmony, and she is far less predictable than I am. Trust me, you cannot handle her." Nor could he handle Clementine if she didn't allow it.

He scowled, rubbing the back of his neck. "And still we have no answer on the subject of *Draug*."

"Who is raising them?" she asked.

He shook his head.

She wasn't sure if that meant he didn't know or that he wasn't going to tell her. "I mean to address the *Draug* soon, but it would be helpful to know who is behind it."

"In time."

"Damn it, Masterson!"

He sighed. "If you must know, I myself am unsure."

"Then let me help. Is someone attempting a *coup d'état*?"

"As I said, in time. At present, your task is to rid this region of *Draug*." He walked out into the hall, but then paused to look back in at her. "Or am I being too equivocal?"

He left her. She listened as the front door opened and closed behind him, and then went to lock it once more.

She leaned back against the door. "What an exasperating bastard!" Masterson had left her with more questions than she'd had before he came.

An hour later, she lay awake in the dark replaying the events at the Bloody Bones. She could see the benefits of fighting alongside another Slayer even though Prudence was disagreeable in the extreme.

And then there was Hank and Rabbit.

And Boone.

She closed her eyes, thinking about that damned kiss as she fell asleep.

Thirty Three

Rabbit woke to the sound of Hank's hooting laughter from below in the livery. He sat up and groaned at the pain in his ribs. They weren't broken, Clementine had said, but may as well be the way he felt. The thumping in his head had almost subsided at least. He scratched his ear and tugged on a lock of hair, noticing how long it was. He needed a haircut. And a shave. Later.

Right now? Coffee.

The loft was vacant except for him. He heard Boone's muffled, deep voice and then laughter again. By the sounds of it, Amelia and Mr. Beaman must be down there, too.

He'd need to make a point of cutting Amelia a little extra rope after hearing Hank's tale of her ordeal in Chicago. She was pretty good with animals, if he was telling truths. And Dime wouldn't shut up around her. It seemed apparent that his horse had a head full of pony stories, and for some reason Amelia was the one he wanted to tell them to.

The smoky, savory aroma of frying bacon drifted by his nose, and his stomach rumbled like a demon at the bottom of an empty pit.

Less than three minutes later, he was downstairs. He detoured to Dime and Nickel's shared stall to check on the boys. That blow Dime had taken from the *Bahkauv* had given him a slight limp by the time they'd reached Deadwood yesterday, but there were no open wounds, thankfully.

The sight of Tink kicking oats around up in the horses' feedbox made Rabbit pause and then cough out a laugh. He watched as the crazy dog pushed her tiny weight against Dime's head, wrestling for position in the box, and then paw some oats toward Nickel. Dime must have been hogging the feed again.

"Tink, did Nickel lift you up there?" Some things never changed, no matter if they were in Santa Fe or Deadwood. Tink had always tag-teamed with Nickel when it came to eating, since Dime had the bigger appetite and ate faster.

He left the three animals to their antics and headed for the forge. After saying his "hellos" and "good mornings" to Boone and Hank, he warmed his hand on a tin of hot Arbuckles'. Each time Hank turned his back to chat with Boone, Rabbit picked at the bacon in one of the cast-iron skillets nestled into the coals of the forge. It tasted like smoky heaven.

"I thought I heard Mr. Beaman and Amelia." Rabbit glanced

toward the door leading to their place out back.

"Left for the mercantile just 'fore you came down." Hank frowned at the pan of bacon. "Bacon's disappearin' right before my failin' eyes."

Rabbit opened his eyes wide, covered his mouth with his hand, and stared at Boone.

Boone grinned. "So, the intrepid hunters bagged a few beasties yesterday."

"Yessir, Booney." Rabbit slapped Hank on the shoulder. "Plugged a beasty at over eight hundred yards. Put down probably forty or fifty of the buggers."

"Seven hunerd fifty yards," Hank corrected him.

Rabbit grinned "Closer to eight, maybe eight fifty. Might as well round to nine."

Boone smirked. "Remind me. Was that the shot that had a herd of *Bahkauv* crawling up your asses?" He snapped his fingers and pointed at Rabbit. "It was, wasn't it?"

"Nope. That was you. You lit into that egg-layin' bitch and then they were all over us. We handled them smooth, though."

"Right. How many got by was it? Five or six?"

Rabbit waved his hand in the air. "Only three. Now, if I'd had a better than moderate rifle to bead those beasties, well, things would've gone even smoother."

"With Ludek's help. And that rifle of mine is smoother than cream from a happy cow."

"Pulls right. And Ludek just cleaned up, really." Rabbit knew full well the Winchester shot truer than any other gun he'd ever used excepting his Sharps.

"*You* pull right. A little practice should fix that up. I'll give you some points. You'll have to try hard to keep up, though." Boone turned to Hank. "Where'd you get that bacon?"

"Points on the top of your head," Rabbit muttered and snitched a bite of bacon.

"Kee Luk," Hank said over his shoulder as he cracked eggs

into one of the pans.

"No," he said to Rabbit. "The point is that Winchester is a One in One Thousand." Boone moved over to watch Hank with the eggs.

The livery door creaked open. "Hello, boys!" Clementine closed the door behind her and joined them. "What a fine bunch of dandies we have here," she said with a smile that landed on Boone last and seemed to get stuck there.

"Ain't no dandy," Hank said, still turned toward the forge.

"No such thing," added Rabbit, noticing the way Boone looked sort of lost in Clementine's smile. "Booney's too ugly to be a dandy."

Boone dragged his gaze away from Clementine, focusing on Rabbit. "I'm more of a dandy than you, Mr. Rooster Tail." He stuck his thumbs under his armpits, stood up tall, and smiled ear to ear. "See?"

Clementine laughed as Rabbit tried to pat down his hair.

Rabbit gave up and focused on the linen-wrapped bundle Clementine held by her side. "What's that there? Biscuits, I hope." He dearly loved Aunt Lou's biscuits.

"Nope. Better. These are blini from The Dove. Alexey and Dmitry send greetings. They also sent this." Clementine untied the bundle and pulled out a jar filled with something orange. "This is apricot preserves to put on the blini. Alexey made it himself last summer."

Hank turned around and squinted at the jar. "I haven't had apercot since ... I ain't never had apercot. What is it?"

"Fruit. It'll be your new favorite. I guarantee it." Clementine set the jar on the blacksmith table and began clearing spots for the tin plates.

"Miss Clementine. Here's to you and Boone killin' that egg layer." Rabbit raised his coffee tin.

"Well, we didn't actually do the honors. Prudence did."

"With *your* sword," Boone said, holding the jar of preserves up to the light from the window for inspection.

"Who's Prudence?" Rabbit asked.

"That's the Rogue's name," Clementine said. "Or the name we gave her anyway. She took the queen's head."

"Couldn't have done it without you two, no how," Hank added.

"Have you made up with Fred the Mule?" Rabbit asked.

"Bah. Don't know if'n I'll be able to trust the deserter no more." He waved his spatula toward Fred, who was standing down the way at the front of his stall, ears perked, watching Hank. He let out a quiet whinny-haw.

Rabbit thought it was best not to let Hank stew on his deserter mule too long. Let some time pass and Hank would forgive him. Hank's nature was kindness and generosity. If Rabbit knew anything, he knew that much.

Clementine glanced at Rabbit and then Boone. "Masterson surprised me with a visit last night."

"Sonofabitch," Boone said through gritted teeth. "I knew I should've checked on you after we all ate." He eyed her up and down. "Did he hurt you?"

Clementine smiled, but her eyes weren't in on it. "Of course not. He was upset, though. We killed his so-called pets."

"Pets?" Boone scoffed. "They were killing people."

"They surely was." Hank tapped his chest. "Pert near this one and that one, too." He pointed at Rabbit.

"He planned on pitting those pets up against the *Draug*." Clementine sniffed over the pan of cooked eggs and began spooning them onto the plate Hank handed her, followed by a healthy serving of bacon. She handed it to Boone.

"Thanks," he said, taking the plate of eggs and bacon and plopping a blini on top of it all. "That'd never work. Those *Bahkauv* are *loco*. Nobody can control them, can they?" He leaned against the table, watching Clementine dish up more eggs.

"*Ein Jäger* could." She paused and looked at Boone,

explaining, "That means *hunter*." Then she continued, "But the *Bahkauv* are beasts. I don't think they can be trained beyond simple commands. And they're unpredictable." She stopped spooning eggs onto a second plate for a moment. "Or maybe they can be trained," she said quietly, and then grabbed more bacon and handed another full plate to Rabbit.

His stomach growling at the smells alone, Rabbit scooted one of the wooden chairs closer to the worktable for Clementine, then grabbed Beaman's stool for himself.

"Masterson said that wasn't a gate at all," Clementine continued, grabbing a third plate. "He called it a stableyard."

"Just a place to keep animals? Sheeat. You know, it's funny. I thought we were done with Gayville before yesterday." Rabbit took a blini and scooped a spoonful of apricot preserves in the middle, rolling it up. "Turns out some things you just can't ride around."

"Even if it means riding straight into hell," Uncle Mort said from beside him.

Rabbit jolted, knocking a piece of bacon off his plate. "Goldurnit, Uncle Mort," Rabbit muttered. "Made me spill my bacon."

"Feed it to Tinker," Uncle Mort said as he turned his back to Rabbit and walked toward the door.

"Where you goin'?" Rabbit asked.

"I'm going to take my morning constitutional. Maybe do some haunting at Yellow Strike. That barkeep, Porter, deserves a good pestering."

So, was he going haunting every time he disappeared? Rabbit turned back to his plate of food and Boone's stare.

"Are you finished?" Boone asked. Without waiting for an answer, he looked at Clementine. "What's a real gate look like?" He picked up a piece of bacon, then paused, staring down at it. "Hank, where did you say you got this bacon from?"

"Kee Luk."

Boone frowned at Clementine.

She raised an eyebrow at Hank. "Kee Luk?"

"Yes, ma'am. Only place in town lately that's got any hogs."

Boone sniffed the bacon and then grimaced, setting his plate on the blacksmith table. "This gate business makes you wonder. Maybe we're not done with Gayville yet."

"We are for now," Clementine said, spooning preserves onto a plate. "We still need to reconnoiter Slagton, but that will have to wait for a few days, until after Christmas anyway." She licked a bit of apricot preserves from her finger. "I have a few things to take care of first."

Rabbit looked at Boone's plate, and then Boone. "What? You ain't hungry?" He stuffed a hunk of bacon in his mouth.

Boone sniggered. "You don't remember?" When Rabbit stared at him, Boone shrugged. "Maybe you don't."

Clementine handed the loaded plate to Hank and then started to pile eggs on her own.

"What?" Rabbit slurred through the mouthful of bacon. There was some sort of seasoning that made it taste a little different from normal, but still good. Probably something in the way they smoked the meat down in the Badlands.

"Kee Luk is where Clementine had the fight at the hog sty."

Rabbit swallowed part of his mouthful. "So?"

Boone grinned. "The same sty where she found all those human body parts."

Rabbit stopped chewing. His stomach turned over.

"Hogs didn't seem to mind," Boone said, chuckling now. "Good as any steak dinner to those oinkers. Bones and all, right, Clementine?"

"We can leave the details out." Clementine grabbed a blini and took a bite. "That'd be fine with me."

Rabbit turned away and spit out the rest of his partially chewed bacon. "Plah!" He scraped at his tongue with his spoon, but little bits of bacon were stuck between his teeth and in the nooks and crannies of his cheeks. "Dammit, Hank!"

"What?" Hank sat on a stool next to the table with his plate in hand. He scooped up a big gob of eggs with a hunk of bacon and stuffed it all in his mouth. "Good smoke on it. Chung Lu knows how to smoke a pork belly," he said around the mouthful of meat.

Clementine gnawed off a sizable chunk of bacon, too, and began chewing. "Delicious breakfast, Hank," she said after swallowing. "Hits the spot. Thanks."

"Miss Clementine! Not you too." Rabbit held his stomach to ease the flipping and flopping. Images filled his mind of hogs chewing on hands and feet and … He swallowed hard to keep from gagging.

"What?" Clementine held up a strip of the meat. "It's really good."

Rabbit shook his head, holding out his hand for her to stop.

Boone picked up his plate and looked at it, and then at Clementine. He grabbed a hunk of bacon and sniffed it.

"Don't you do it, Booney!" Rabbit warned.

His gaze on Rabbit, he opened his mouth and brought the meat to his lips. Then he laughed at the face Rabbit made and dropped the bacon back on his plate, reaching for the blini instead.

"How can you stomach that pork after what you saw in that sty up close and personal like?" Rabbit asked Clementine.

She shrugged. "I'm a Northwoman, remember? You might be surprised at some of the things I've eaten, Jack. It gets pretty cold in the middle of winter. Hard to find much food with all of that ice and snow." She wrapped a blini around another hunk of smoked meat. "You haven't truly enjoyed some of the finer foods until you've had roasted caribou stones."

"Stones?" Rabbit asked.

Hank snorted. "Miss Clem, surely you didn't."

Boone tipped his head to the side. "When you say 'stones,'

you don't mean …" He grimaced.

"What?" Rabbit looked from Boone to Hank to Clementine.

"Testicles," she said with a big grin and pushed the bacon-wrapped blini into her mouth.

Rabbit cringed, turning to Hank. "She's kiddin', right?"

Hank laughed and scooped up another bite of eggs with his bacon. "Miss Clem, I do believe ya hornswoggled ol' Jack Rabbit."

"Good." She held out her plate toward him, her eyes sparkling. "Now how about you two dandies hand over that bacon before it gets cold."

The End … for now

Book 4 in the Deadwood Undertaker Series will be coming your way in 2021!

*Read on for the first chapter of Book 4
(The Backside of Hades).*

The Deadwood Undertaker Series

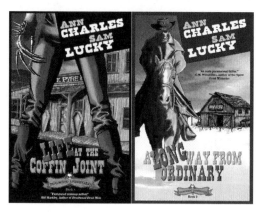

Deadwood (late 1876) … A rowdy and reckless undertaker's delight. What better place for a killer to blend in?

Enter undertaker Clementine Johanssen, tall and deadly with a hot temper and short fuse, hired to clean up Deadwood's dead … and the "other" problem. She's hell-bent on poking, sticking, or stabbing anyone that steps out of line.

But when a couple Santa Fe sidewinders ride into town searching for their missing uncle, they land neck deep in lethal gunplay, nasty cutthroats, and endless stinkin' snow. Their search leads them to throw in with Clementine to hunt for a common enemy.

What they find chills them all to the bone and sends them on an adventure they'll never forget.

More Books by Ann

Books in the Deadwood Mystery Series

Welcome to Deadwood—the Ann Charles version. The world I have created is a blend of present day and past, of fiction and non-fiction. What's real and what isn't is for you to determine as the series develops, the characters evolve, and I write the stories line by line. I will tell you one thing about the series—it's going to run on for quite a while, and Violet Parker will have to hang on and persevere through the crazy adventures I have planned for her. Poor, poor Violet. It's a good thing she has a lot of gumption to keep her going!

Books in the Deadwood Shorts Series

The Deadwood Shorts collection includes short stories featuring the characters of the Deadwood Mystery series. Each tale not only explains more of Violet's history, but also gives a little history of the other characters you know and love from the series. Rather than filling the main novels in the series with these short side stories, I've put them into a growing Deadwood Shorts collection for more reading fun.

About the Authors

Ann Charles is a *USA Today* bestselling author who writes award-winning mysteries that are splashed with humor, adventure, paranormal, romance, and whatever else she feels like throwing into the mix. When she is not dabbling in fiction, arm-wrestling with her children, attempting to seduce her husband, or arguing with her sassy cat, she is daydreaming of lounging poolside at a fancy resort with a blended margarita in one hand and a great book in the other.

Facebook (Personal Page):
http://www.facebook.com/ann.charles.author

Facebook (Author Page):
http://www.facebook.com/pages/Ann-Charles/37302789804?ref=share

Twitter (as Ann W. Charles):
http://twitter.com/AnnWCharles

Ann Charles Website:
http://www.anncharles.com

Sam Lucky likes to build things—from Jeep engines to Old West buildings to fun stories. When he is not writing, feeding his kids, attempting to seduce his wife, or attending the goldurn cats, he is planning food-based booksigning/road trips with his wife and working on one of his many home-improvement projects.

Sam Lucky's Website:
http://www.samlucky.com

DEADWOOD UNDERTAKER

The Backside of Hades

Ann Charles
Sam Lucky

Sneak Peek

The Backside of Hades

Chapter One – Sneak Peek

Really, Really Late 1876
Deadwood, Dakota Territory

Boone McCreery pushed aside a scrubby branch shielding him and his companions to peek at the rickety log cabin in the valley below half-buried by drifting snow. He squinted in the early morning light. There was no smoke coming from the chimney, but … "Definitely somebody in there. Can't see who or what, though."

"It's *Draug*." Clementine Johanssen stood tall next to Boone, almost his height short a couple of inches, with her arms crossed over her thick wool coat. Her expression was as cold and stony as the craggy outcrop behind them. "And there isn't just one, there's a small herd. Eight or ten, I'd guess."

"Of course. We're not even in Slagton yet." Anxiety dropped a pile of rocks in his belly at the notion of riding into the small mining town that was supposedly overrun with … "*Draug*." Boone repeated, sniffling in the cold dry air. "The diseased, abnormally strong, rotting carcasses of the dearly departed being used as an army by a malevolent usurper who means to take the Black Hills as a prize, killing anything that gets in his way?" He shivered against a frigid gust. "You mean that kind of *Draug*?"

She turned to Boone, lines fanning out from her gray eyes. "Don't forget shapeshifting."

Boone did a double-take. "What?" He'd heard her. He just didn't believe *what* he heard.

"Shapeshifting." Clementine shrugged. "Of course, I don't believe that, or that *Draug* can grow to colossal size. Those are myths." She bit her lower lip. "I think."

"What?" Boone said again. He was listening more intently now, but still having some difficulty comprehending.

"Need help makin' sentences there, Booney?" Jack "Rabbit" Fields piped in, joining them. After a glance through the branches, he grinned big and fluttered his eyelashes at Boone while skinning his pistol and spinning the cylinder. Quick as chain lightning, his expression sobered and his brow furrowed. "I'm good for four, maybe six. You stand behind me, Booney. Don't want you gettin' hurt."

"Shut up, Rabbit." Boone shook his head. After spending the better part of his life with Mr. Quickdraw, who'd become as close to him as a brother before they were even knee-high to a grasshopper, Boone knew Rabbit was just as nervous as he was. He reached for his pistol, too, but changed his mind and veered to the hilt of his black-bladed scimitar.

They were holster-deep in an icy cold winter in the Black Hills. Boone and his companions, along with their mounts, had opted to spend the night at the edge of Slagton, since none of them had any intention of approaching the sinister little camp in the dark—not even Clementine, who'd faced off with *Draug* in her bloodstained past. Boone measured last night in the woods as one of the coldest, most fitful, and frigid he'd ever had the displeasure of spending under the stars, and Rabbit's complaints had helped keep the campsite warm until almost midnight. And his list of expletives was far more colorful than Boone's in spite of the presence of a female. So far, things weren't looking any better in the morning light.

Clementine had been quiet since they'd left Deadwood. Too quiet. Boone could see she was uneasy, apprehensive even. Her normally stoic demeanor was absent, replaced by repeated shifting—twitching almost—both in and out of her saddle, undoubtedly due to her past experiences dealing with *Draug*. He didn't blame her. The description alone of the abominations nearly curdled his blood.

"Somebody just tell me what I'm shootin' at." Hank Varney spoke up from behind them. Boone turned to see the well-weathered man jerk his Lemat pistol from the holster. Ice crystals in his short-cropped beard added a sparkle to Hank's appearance, matching those in his eyes. Hank was ready to ride into the backside of Hades, if that's where Clementine led them.

Rabbit put his gloved hand to the side of his face. "You're so strong and brave, Hank," he said in a high-pitched voice, pretending to swoon.

"Now cut that out, Jack Rabbit. Likely to make me blush." Hank lowered his pistol and smacked Rabbit on the shoulder.

Clementine peered around the branch, staring at the cabin. "You can't use that pistol, Hank. You'll bring every creature in a half-mile radius down on us. Besides, it's best—"

"Let me guess," Boone cut in.

"Take the heads," Rabbit said before Boone had the chance.

Clementine nodded, stepping away from the branch. "Leave the horses and Fred here." Without a backward glance, she made for the cabin in long strides.

"There she goes." Boone sprang after her, followed by Rabbit and Hank.

"Dammit, Miss Clementine!" Rabbit said in a loud whisper as he fell into a jogging step next to Boone.

"No guns," Clementine said over her shoulder.

"Goldurnit, Booney. No guns?" Rabbit holstered his pistol and skinned one of the five throwing knives from his belt sheath.

"You know, well as I do." Boone rushed to keep up with Clementine.

Rabbit sheathed his throwing knife. "This is close-in fighting and I ain't none too fond of it, so's you know. Gonna need my Bowie." He grabbed his Bowie knife from his boot without missing a step.

Hank sounded like a locomotive chuffing along behind. "Rather stick an arrow …" He puffed and sucked a breath, then continued, "in 'em myself, Jack Rabbit."

"Wanna trade?" Rabbit pointed his Bowie at Boone's sword.

Boone scoffed. "Not today. But I'll keep an eye on ya, in case you get yourself into a pickle." He rested his scimitar on his shoulder as they approached the cabin. "Clementine," he whispered when he caught up with her. "You have a plan?"

"Sure. Kill everything in that cabin." She stopped behind a stand of yearling pines that offered cover and faced the three of them. "You've prepared for this. Remember the cattle driver terms you used a while back?" When they each nodded, she continued, "Well, I have *point*. You two are *flanks*," she said to Boone and Rabbit. "And Hank is *drag*." She started to turn away, but then looked back again. "Oh, and don't let them bite you."

"Yes, ma'am!" Hank said, his bow and several arrows in hand. He had secured the Lemat in the holster Rabbit had tooled for him. For Hank, arrows flew swifter and more true than words or bullets with a far deadlier effect.

"Yep. We're with ya, Miss Clementine," Rabbit joined in, pulling a second knife from its sheath.

"No biting." Boone paused mid-nod. "Wait, you didn't say anything about … They bite?" He tried not to allow his fear to taint his voice, or let on that his heart was thumping hard in his chest. This was happening too damned fast. His mind was still wrestling with the idea of colossal, shapeshifting corpses.

But Clementine was already heading for the cabin. When Boone and the others caught up with her at the pine pole door, she pulled two short, thin-bladed swords from within her coat and aimed an intense glare at Boone.

He knew that look. She was bent on destruction, and they were in the thick of it with her.

She cocked her leg and kicked out with a grunt. Her foot smashed into the door, breaking it clean away from the hinges. It flew into the cabin, slamming into two *Draug*, knocking them to the floor.

Stunned, Boone watched as she barreled inside, her swords spinning so fast they looked like wagon wheels on a runaway stagecoach.

He leapt through the doorway to join her. Rabbit pushed in behind him and split left, his Bowie raised and ready to strike.

A wave of foul, fetid air washed over Boone, stinging his eyes and coating his tongue and throat. He doubled over, gagging. His knees wobbled under his weight, and the biscuits he'd had for breakfast worked their way up into his throat.

Rabbit reeled backward, crashing into Boone's side. "It's like somebody stuffed a week-dead rat in my mouth." He spit and gagged, wiping at his tongue with his coat sleeve.

Hank pushed into the cabin, his knife drawn. "Boonedog! What—" He retched, grabbed Boone's shoulder and straightened him back up, but then bent forward next to Boone, convulsing. "Tar... *agph*...nation!"

"Like swimmin' in the guts of a dead cow in the summer!" Rabbit bent over and spit again, coughing in between.

Hank grasped Rabbit's sheepskin collar and stood him up too.

"To *Hel's* kingdom with you devils!" Clementine's voice rang out above the din of moaning *Draug*, not to mention Boone's gags, Rabbit's retches, and Hank's curses.

Clementine! Boone wiped the tears from his eyes, raised his sword, and swung around to help her just as the head of the last

Draug sailed in a graceful arc up and away from its body. It landed with a squishy thump on the chest of one of the many headless *Draug* bodies piled around her feet.

He turned back to Clementine. The dark, cold fury in her eyes and hardened expression on her face chilled him more than a night sleeping under the freezing winter sky.

That's the look of a Scharfrichter. A true killer.

"Clementine?" He spoke quietly, not sure what to expect.

She took a deep breath and then shoved her hair away from her face with the back of her hand. After surveying the carnage around her for a moment, she looked at Boone and grinned. "Did I forget to mention they stink?" She scrunched her nose. "I don't remember their odor being this disagreeable last time. Must be because they're penned up in here."

"Sheaat." Rabbit sheathed his knife and evaluated the mess she'd left behind, his expression a mix of disgust and awe. "Miss Clementine, you didn't give us a chance!"

"You'll get your chance." She pulled a scrap of muslin from her coat pocket and wiped the dark, sticky blood and pieces of rotten flesh from her blades, then tossed the rag to the side.

Boone flicked a chunk of rotten *Draug* flesh from Rabbit's coat with his blade and gave Clementine a once-over. "You don't have any, uh, *Draug* guts on you. How could you not have …" he trailed off.

"None at all, even," Hank agreed, inspecting her up and down.

She glanced down. "I think I got a little on my boots." She lifted her booted feet, one at a time, shaking loose the hunks of flesh that clung to them.

Boone looked sideways at Rabbit, who held the same *You're shittin' me* expression that Boone was probably wearing, too.

"Miss Clem," Hank said. "We ought to mosey. You shook the tree. No tellin' what might fall out. Vapor in here is like to burn my eyeballs out, anyhows." He backed out the doorway, pinching his nose with his finger and thumb. In a nasally voice he added, "The Pyre ain't never stank so much as this."

Rabbit was quick to follow. "I'm with you, Hank. Spurs the mind to bad recollections, like Boone's bedroom when we was growin' up." He disappeared out the doorway.

"Bangtail!" Boone hollered at Rabbit's back.

Clementine chuckled, sidling up next to him. "Not one to spend time on cleaning your room, huh?" She slid one of her short swords back inside her coat.

Boone felt a pang in his gut. "He's full of shit." He shot Clementine a quick frown, not liking the idea of her getting the wrong idea about his cleanliness. Or thinking ill of him at all, for that matter. "We didn't see the floor of his bedroom for five years after he turned twelve. He's just a windbag."

"I heard that, fiddlehead," Rabbit called from outside.

"I know. I said it for you, Bunny Rabbit."

"Don't call me 'bunny,' dammit," came back from outside.

"We should go." Clementine patted his chest, her hand lingering for a moment along with her gaze, and then she headed out into the morning sun.

Boone fell in behind her, happy to breathe the cold, fresh air again. A glance back at the cabin sparked a realization. "They didn't turn into dirt, or dust, or fire, or whatever it is they turn into when a Slayer put the squabash on that walking buzzard food in there." Usually, death by Clementine's blade or hand yielded much different results.

She frowned his way. "They were human once."

"Of course." Boone had forgotten to draw the distinction between humans and *others*, as in those non–homo sapiens that Clementine had been contracted to eliminate when necessary. "Why were the *Draug* crammed into the cabin, do you think?"

"I'm not sure. But did you see the pile of mangled deer in the corner?" She wrinkled her nose.

"No."

"It looked to me like someone was keeping them fed." She stopped alongside Hank, scanning the trees and hills around them. "Maybe they were corralling those that escaped. Or they could have been readying them for an attack on a nearby camp or mine."

"You see that, Miss Clem? Jack Rabbit?" Hank pointed, his voice low. "Over there, through them trees."

Rabbit used his hat to shield his eyes from a slice of sunlight. "I see it."

"You see, Miss Clem? Thought it was a deer first thing, but it ain't. It's one of your *Draug*-ies."

Rabbit squinted at it. "Walkin' along with a purpose."

Boone saw it, too. The *Draug* lurched along through the snow in a tattered and dirty shirt, suspenders, and torn trousers, as if out on a leisurely morning stroll. Its shock of black hair was mussed, sticking up on one side, as if it had just rolled out of the grave.

Clementine aimed her short sword at it. "Who wants it?"

"I got it." Hank pulled his bow and plucked an arrow from his quiver. "Just gotta get a wee closer." He tiptoed toward the meandering corpse, slinking tree to tree to remain unnoticed.

Clementine drew her other sword, spinning both blades in her palms. "That Sioux bow won't do him any good."

"Are you going to tell him that?" Boone asked, glancing from her to Hank and back.

"No. He can manage one *Draug*. Let's see how he does it." Boone noticed a twinkle in her eyes to match her grin.

Rabbit smiled, too, only his was tinged with a dab of concern. Probably the same concern knotting up Boone's gut.

Hank worked his way to a tree within thirty yards of the lone *Draug*. He strung his arrow, drew back, aimed, and the arrow disappeared. *Fwhip.*

Boone watched as the *Draug*'s head pitched to the side, coming back upright with an arrow jutting from its cheek. *Good aim!*

"Nice shot, Hank," Rabbit whispered.

The *Draug* swatted at the arrow, staggered, turned, and began shuffling toward Hank, its legs plowing through the shin-deep snow.

Clementine shook her head. "He needs to—"

"Right." Boone interrupted her.

"Hank!" Rabbit whisper-yelled.

Hank looked back at them and shrugged.

"The head!" Rabbit grabbed his own head and pretended to remove it and throw it on the ground.

Hank stuck his finger in the air and nodded. He drew his Bowie and swung around behind the arrow-stuck *Draug*.

Meanwhile, the staggering *Draug* wandered too close to a tree, and the shaft of the arrow tangled up in a low branch. It pulled clumsily against the snag, attempting to free itself. Boone would have laughed if the smell of rotting flesh wasn't still clinging to the inside of his nose … and except for the fact that what he was looking at was real and not just the effect of imbibing bad whiskey.

Rabbit did laugh. "Ha! Too beef-headed to free itself."

Hank swung around behind the struggling *Draug* and raised his knife. He paused for a few breaths, then backed up and looked at Clementine, Boone, and Rabbit, and shook his head.

Boone watched as Hank's shoulders sagged and his head hung low. "He can't do it."

"His heart's too big for his own good." Clementine sprang forward and trotted to Hank's side. She patted his shoulder and in a flash the *Draug* head was sitting half buried in snow, propped upright by the arrow sticking out of its cheek.

"There's another one." Rabbit pointed into the trees to their left.

Boone squinted through the shadowed tree trunks streaked with sunlight. This particular *Draug* had been one hell of a brute at one time, judging from the breadth of his shoulders and thick legs. Even more unfortunate, the undead bull of a man appeared to have spotted them and was headed in their direction, pushing through the snow more quickly than the first, but still at no more than a leisurely saunter.

Boone was utterly repulsed by the sight, especially taking into account the smell of these plodding creatures, but they seemed too slow to be very dangerous. Why had Clementine considered them such a threat?

He jabbed Rabbit with his elbow. "You or me?"

Rabbit bowed and twirled his hand toward the *Draug*. "Be my guest."

"Watch and learn, whippersnapper." Boone took off at a trot and covered the distance quickly. He drew his black-bladed scimitar and sliced cleanly through the thick, rubbery neck skin of the *Draug*. He'd already cleaned his blade in the snow before Clementine and Hank had returned to Rabbit.

Half an hour and four headless, no-longer wandering *Draug* later, they stood on a rocky bluff overlooking the small mining camp of Slagton. Their mounts huddled together a short distance behind them, nickering back and forth, while Hank's buddy, Fred the Mule, rubbed his haunch on the rough bark of a pine tree.

Down below, a scattering of shacks formed loose lines along what looked a little to Boone like the deserted main street of Gayville, a small mining camp outside of Deadwood they'd passed through on their way to deal with a previous menace—*Bahkauv.* Unlike Gayville, however, this thoroughfare was writhing with movement, overrun with what looked like masses of *Draug.*

"Look at all 'em." Hank's voice was whispery with disbelief. "This what you wanted to know about Slagton, Miss Clem?"

"Most are *Draug,* near as I can tell," Rabbit whispered, confirming Boone's thought. "Something else mixed in."

"Too many and they're moving around—can't get a count." Boone cocked his head toward Clementine, who stood silent beside him. "Can you make out what else is down there besides *Draug*?"

Clementine's gaze narrowed. "Humans. Probably wearing the *caper-sus* brand in one form or another. I'm not sure what else."

The *caper-sus* represented a cult, led by others with ranks composed of humans aspiring to reap the rewards of faithful service: food and money. Black Hills gold drew in all sorts of folks, the adventure seekers and the desperate, and everyone in between. But there were only so many claims in the hills carrying any color, and for those that didn't hit it rich, clothes and skin were soon hanging off their bones. Eating didn't come cheap, and the *caper-sus* brand offered a meal ticket few could refuse.

"Look how they're beatin' them *Draug*-ies with sticks," Hank said, scowling.

"Herding them like they're cows," Rabbit added.

"Looka that one. Fightin' back." Hank chuckled deep in his chest.

"They don't like getting hit by sticks, looks like." Rabbit scratched at one of his sideburns. "Can't say whose side I'd take, the *Draug*-ies, or the *capers-sus* sonsabitches."

"They seem to have a mind, but they're slow." Boone smirked. "Like Rabbit."

Rabbit reached out and flicked his hat.

"They have a border set up around the town." Clementine used her sword to show them where. "See? There. And there. Those men with the sticks have got to be *caper-sus*. They're blocking all the routes out of town, including the road and between buildings."

Boone nodded. "So, one must get out from time to time. The escapees are what we kept finding in the forest."

"Probably." Clementine rubbed her shoulder, the one that had been stuck with the tip of a *caper-sus* bastard's sword not too many days back.

He nodded once toward her shoulder. "Still sore?"

"A little. The cold makes it ache. Usually wounds like this heal more quickly. This one seems to be taking longer."

A piercing shriek echoed through the forest around them.

The hair on the back of Boone's neck prickled. The shrieking continued for a couple of seconds, growing louder, seeming to slice through his brain. He winced and ducked low, along with the others.

"Lord-a-mighty," Rabbit said when it stopped, his fingers still jammed in his ears. "What the fuck was that? Sounded like a wounded puma cat."

"Sounded like hawk right in my ear." Boone's ears were still ringing.

"More like a woman, mad as a hornet." Hank shook his head. "Got my head to spinnin'."

"Wait until you're right next to one when it does that." Clementine was still staring down at Slagton, apparently unaffected by the screech. "Look," she said to them, pointing.

Boone followed her line of sight down to the street.

Chaos abounded. But it was an oddly symmetrical chaos, as all of the *Draug* were moving toward one building near the center of Slagton, lurching and scrambling and stumbling. It reminded him of feeding time on the ranch back in Santa Fe.

A collective moan muffled by distance rose and fell as the *Draug* began packing together between two of the buildings. Then they began to tear at each other. Wails and growls and snarls rose above the din before sinking again.

"Jehoshaphat," Hank murmured, his jaw hanging low.

"Booney." Rabbit grabbed Boone's shoulder, holding tight.

Boone glanced his way. "You all right, Rabbit?"

Rabbit slowly shook his head, his brow furrowed in disbelief. "I don't think so. That ain't right."

Boone's focus returned to the macabre scene below them. He

watched as the *Draug* pushed and tore and ripped at each other. Screams rang out—human, this time. Before his eyes, one of the guards was torn to pieces by the advancing horde.

More guards pursued, swinging their sticks impotently at the throngs of stampeding *Draug,* only to disappear in the masses. Screams continued as more of the guards were swallowed up and ripped to bits by the frenzied creatures.

Boone leaned toward Clementine, shoulder bumping her while still keeping his wide eyes on the scene below. "One wail set all of this off?"

"The scream of a *Draug* is like a war cry." She spoke low, the disgust in her voice unmistakable. "It drives the other *Draug* into a frenzy. They'll attack anything that moves, including each other."

"Wait just a goddamned minute." Rabbit shook his finger at Clementine. "When you told us about the time you and your afi slaughtered that village full of *Draug,* you never said nothin' about a war cry." He huffed. "Nothin' about them going plumb *loco,* either."

Clementine made a slight grimace. "I forgot about that part."

"You forgot." Boone pushed the brim of his hat up his forehead. "I don't know if you noticed, but—"

A low reverberating hum rose up, seeming to come from the far end of Slagton. Boone felt it as much as heard it.

It kept building, growing louder.

"What now?" The thrumming drone began to resonate through his body.

"My noggin's shakin'!" Hank covered his ears.

The deep, bone-quaking hum grew louder.

Boone gaped at Rabbit, who had one eye squeezed shut tight while holding his head. "It's rattling my brains out, Booney!"

The hum faded into silence.

Rabbit and Hank turned to Clementine, open-mouthed. Boone followed suit.

She shrugged. "I don't know what it was, but I do know it came from an *other*. I suspect it's the one who is responsible for creating these *Draug*."

The deep hum began to build again.

"Open your mouths, and cover your ears with your hands!" Clementine instructed.

Boone obeyed, along with Hank and Rabbit.

She was right. It helped with the rattling as the hum grew, same as before.

Below them, the *Draug* had settled, now as gentle as a herd of cattle bedding down for the night. The frenzy had ended, and the entire group seemed to be shuffling toward the biggest building at the far end of the street—a barn, from the looks of it. As Boone watched, the creatures began to file calmly through the open doors.

"Somebody called for them critters," Hank said.

"Suppertime?" Rabbit suggested.

"Hoo! Jack Rabbit, stop that. This ain't funny." Hank chuckled nonetheless.

Clementine's brow lined. "You may be right, Jack."

Boone watched as the *Draug* paraded into the building.

"Sheeat, Hank," Rabbit said from behind him. "Your nose is bleeding." Boone turned to see for himself as Rabbit pulled a kerchief from the pocket of his trousers and handed it to Hank.

" 'Magine that." Hank wiped at his nose with the cloth. "Does that on the occasion, when the air's dry."

Clementine's gaze narrowed as she watched Hank. "You okay, Hank?"

"Fit as can be, Miss Clem."

Doubt lined her face, but she looked back down at the scene below.

"That seem odd to you?" Boone asked all of them, waving toward Slagton.

Rabbit snorted. "What about this fuckin' whole kerfuffle

doesn't seem odd to you, Booney?"

"What I mean is, how are they all fitting in that barn? I know it's big, but that's a lot of *Draug*."

"*Odin's beard*." Clementine turned away and dropped onto a downed tree. "It's a gate."

"What?!" Rabbit blurted out, beating Boone to the punch.

"Probably," Clementine clarified, looking up at each of them in turn. "They're not coming out the other end of the barn, so there must be enough room in there ..." She scowled. "For *all* of them."

Boone watched the last few *Draug* disappear into the barn. He moved over next to her. "Could be just the entrance of a cave. Or a mine." He didn't believe it even as he said it, though. Who builds a barn over a mine?

"Things just got more complicated." Clementine sighed and then pushed to her feet again.

"I'd say." It was Boone's estimation that things were *likely* to get more complicated whenever Clementine was around, in more ways than one. "What made it scream in the first place?"

"I don't know." She returned to his side, studying the barn below.

"Them things the same as that German town you was in, Miss Clem?" Hank asked, moving up next to Clementine.

"The Day of Decay," Boone remembered out loud. His thoughts flitted through the story about the battle Clementine and her grandfather had fought against a town full of *Draug*. "If I recollect," Boone said, "those *Draug* were made from freshly dead people." He looked around to see all three of them staring at him.

"Booney, c'mon now." Rabbit grimaced. "They ain't beef hangin' on the hook."

Clementine nodded at Boone. "Most of those in Kremplestadt were newly dead, whereas these *Draug* here were people *already* dead."

"Does that make a difference?" Rabbit asked.

"I don't know." She wrinkled her nose. "They certainly smell worse."

"*Blah*. Think if it was a summer day. Flesh and guts rotting in the hot sun." Rabbit stifled a gag.

"Jack Rabbit! That's a revoltin' thought." Hank shuddered.

"How many were in that German village?" Boone waved an arm at the barn. "That many?"

"A few less, maybe, if I had to guess."

Boone frowned at her. "That's too many for just the four of us, right?"

She didn't answer, but instead stared over his shoulder, her brow furrowed.

"Seems like too many," Rabbit answered for her.

"Maybe get us somebody to back our play, Miss Clem?" Hank suggested.

Clementine still didn't answer.

Why was she hesitating? "Let me sum everything up to now," Boone said, leaning over into her line of sight until she made eye contact with him. "We're facing dead-but-walking, half-witted, pestilence-spreading, rotting corpses that may or may not be able to change their appearance at will, *and*—I can't believe I'm saying this—may or may not be able to make themselves bigger. Oh, and they might or might not be unusually strong."

Clementine pursed her lips. "That's about right."

"And not just one or a couple, but hundreds," Boone added.

"Don't forget the smell." Rabbit buck-snorted one nostril and then the other into the snow.

"Or that dad-blasted, ear-splittin' screech the buggers do," Hank tacked on.

"Not to mention," Boone continued, still not finished making his case. "we have no idea what to expect in that barn."

"We can expect a lot of *Draug*," Clementine replied with a shrug.

Boone threw his hands in the air. "Lordy, woman! I'm talking about whatever it was that called the *Draug* in there." He felt his eye twitch a few times.

"Easy now, Booney." Rabbit patted Boone's shoulder. "We don't know that they can grow. Or change the way they look. We don't know they're strong as an ox, either."

"Yes, but …" Clementine scratched under the side of her fur trapper's hat, her face partly scrunched. "They are powerful. I once saw one—"

"Miss Clementine," Rabbit interrupted. "You ain't helpin'!"

She pinched her lips together and turned to Boone.

"Right." Boone held her stare, wishing they could just climb on their horses and ride out of here—back to hot coffee and a warm dinner. But he knew Clementine too well. "Is there anything else we don't know about *Draug*? Anything else that you might have 'forgotten' to mention?"

"Well, there's one other thing." She picked up her pack. The cold, fierce look was back in her eyes when she met his gaze again.

Boone grimaced. "What now?"

She leaned closer to him. "They like to eat fresh brains."

Hank coughed into his fist, looking away.

Rabbit gaped at her. "They what?"

Boone frowned. "Are you serious?"

"No, I made that up." She strung her pack over her shoulder. "Now, are you boys ready to go kill some *Draug*?"

Look for the next book in the Deadwood Undertaker Series in 2021.

NOTES

NOTES

Made in the USA
Middletown, DE
14 September 2023